Jennifer,

Thanks for sub [...]

Hope yo [...] joy the book !!! :)

A DREAM OF STEWARDS

KEYS OF TIME, BOOK ONE

YOHANN MARTIN

Ebook ISBN: 979-8-9857028-0-4

Print ISBN: 979-8-9857028-1-1

First edition

Cover Artwork & Design by Jeff Brown Graphics

To my wife, Erica.

Without you, this would still be "a, like, totally cool time travel book I'm thinking about writing someday."

I love you always.

1

THE CHRONOS PROJECT 2022

From beginning to end, I watch it all
Through the perils of venture since the Fall
Yesterday, I explored the night
For tomorrow's protection, I bring my fight.

He recites the creed over and over. Though the words are monotonous, their truth continues to pierce his heart.

Ten minutes. My world ends in ten minutes, but I must wait ten years for it.

It's a paradox, Nolan knows. *Always true but rarely right.*

He walks them and knows them, the mundane halls housing an extraordinary power. His watch, clinging tight to his wrist, strays from his stride and nicks the cinderblock wall beside him, robbing him of routine. He glances down at the watch's grimy analog display. Its wear nearly matches his own being, and not for the first time he wonders where the years have gone.

Nolan Greyson is a physicist to his core, precise in his work while obscure in all else. He's adrift but not aimless. Never aimless. His thoughts are trapped in time while his burdens feel infinite. Decade long memories haunt his every step as the facility's cold walls and empty halls welcome him to the familiar path, to order and chaos. But more, they welcome him to yesterday and tomorrow and eternity beyond.

A dullness grips his stomach, pulling. His heartbeat quickens with each step closer to the lab, pumping mounds of sweat through the pores of his paling face. He lets out a sigh, but the unease stays with him as he turns the final corner and continues forward. Forward to the end and back to the beginning.

It's today, Nolan thinks as he strides toward the security checkpoint. Florescent lights dangle in an equidistant series lining the hall, like soldiers in formation. Its constant buzzing lingers, radiating its stale presence throughout the windowless space as though the drab concrete walls whisper their haunted tale.

It's foreign to him.

The layout and décor may be the same, but its essence has become but a ghost of its former self. The purpose that once filled these hallowed halls has gone, left with the people who formerly served them—his friends.

The two security guards take a step toward him, interrupting his stride.

"Good morning," the weathered-faced guard says, his voice hoarse with age.

"You know the drill," the other guard growls, his hand extended. Nolan inspects the aged lines of the guard's trembling appendage before fumbling for his identification card.

"Of course." Nolan forces a half-smile. The guard snatches his ID, inspecting the weight, surface, and flexibility before raising it between him and the invasive light above. He then levels it in front of Nolan's face, alternating his gaze between the photo and the man. Nolan's hand strays to his watch once more, his fingers trailing across the familiar dials. The guard notices, but Nolan plays off the nervous gesture with an itch. It wouldn't do to draw attention now.

"One would think that you'd memorize my twenty-three-digit ID number by now." Nolan wipes off the accumulated sweat from his forehead. He feels the disk shift in his coat pocket as if it were trying to burn a hole into his chest. It's the key to everything and, if they find it, it's all over.

The years of preparation.

The sacrifices he's made.

Everything.

The world rests in his pocket, and yet, at this moment, it couldn't be further from his grasp.

"Dr. Greyson." The guard scowls. "You know we have to be thorough. Especially with what's been goin' on around here. It's our ass if another one of you scientists croaks." He hands the badge back to Nolan.

Nolan's heart slows for a moment, only to drop into his stomach. "You're livelier than the electronic badge scanners we previously employed. Though not by much."

He had forgotten. Or did he?

Are there other items I've missed?

It doesn't matter now. There is nothing that Nolan or anyone else can do now except let time march forward.

"Age don't stop me from pulling this trigger," the guard laughs, his hand coming to rest on the gun at his side. "Less easy to fool, too. You know how it is these days."

"These days. Days past. And days to come. The methods vary, but time elapses all the same." Nolan's false smile has all but eroded. Breaking eye contact, he glares at his watch. The hands rest in the same position since the last glance. He taps

3

the broken watch out of habit, knowing the gentle force will fall short of reviving it.

"It happens to all of us," he says, just barely a whisper.

"What?" the other guard asks.

"Keep watch, and maybe—ehm—you'll be spared." Nolan clips his badge to his lab coat and proceeds past the guards. Before he reaches the entrance, their muffled voices carry to his ears.

"That has to be the weirdest dude I've ever met," one of the guards says. Nolan closes his eyes, exhales, and adjusts his glasses before walking through the set of double doors.

The lab's hangar-like space embraces him as he enters. Like much of the facility, the walls are cold and concrete, yet at the room's center lies a terrifying warmth, the unknowable soul at the heart of the entire operation. The ceiling towers well above, tailoring itself to house the thirty-foot high masterpiece.

A circular platform hovers only a few feet above the ground as a single staircase runs to it from the lab floor. Two angled columns hug the entrance, reaching the top of the machine at a thirty-five-degree angle, like a set of pondering hands uniting at the fingertips. Seven other vertical columns border the platform, supporting a metallic ring that encircles the entire circumference.

Nolan edges down the pathway between the entrance and the foot of the platform. As he maneuvers toward it, his head moves up and down, taking in the entirety of the machine. Each step extends his neck further until, finally, Nolan must bend backward to see the top. He shudders as what little ease he has left escapes him.

"Dr. Greyson," a voice calls from behind him.

Nolan turns just as his assistant settles alongside him. "Hello, Nea," he says before looking back toward the machine.

"Hey, so I just finished running those tests like you asked me." She pulls out a tablet and swivels it in his direction.

Nolan's eyes meet the screen for a brief second, but he sees nothing other than the ground beyond.

"Are you okay?" she asks, her usually cheerful pitch low with concern.

"I'm..." Nolan pauses, clenching his jaws. How can he even begin to answer that?

Okay.

The word seems so empty to him.

Resolved, Nolan thinks.

That would be more appropriate. He's resolved, and everything is going along as planned.

But *okay*?

No, he's not okay.

Nothing is okay.

He tears his eyes away from the machine. The naïve innocence in her young brown eyes strikes him. "Thank you for running those. You've been an excellent asset to us, Nea. I understand the strenuous workload in the absence of our other colleagues."

"Absence?" She lowers the tablet and scratches the top of her head. Nolan watches as a single thin blonde hair glides to the ground. "I mean, it's more than that, right?"

"It certainly isn't less." Nolan peels off his glasses and runs a hand up and down his face. He feels every wrinkle and smile line, a story of his life in brail beneath his palm. "How long have you worked here?"

"With the Agency, three years. I've only been at the Center here for a little less than a year, though."

"And what's been your impression?"

"Of what?"

"Everything."

"Uh, I don't know, Dr. Greyson." She takes a step backward. "I just don't really know. I want to say it's fine."

"I've been here many years and have worked on it even longer than that. Very few places that can happen."

"It's special. I'll say that." Nea gives an awkward smile before returning to her work.

Nolan stares at the machine for another few seconds before forcing himself into a nearby desk. His stomach clenches as he stares at the blank computer screen. His flesh prickles at the click of the keyboard. As the screen illuminates, Nolan reaches into an inner pocket within his lab coat. He pulls out a small photograph and smiles. It's not on a screen like what other aging adults have surrendered to using.

No.

This is something tangible and true, ancient but enduring.

A real picture. A photograph.

His thumb brushes the picture's gloss. There, in its center, his graduated son smiles back at him, boastfully donning his cap and gown in a sign and seal of things past. Moisture creeps into his eyes, pooling and nearly overflowing onto his cheeks.

The reason, he reminds himself.

The reason.

Nolan holds back the tears and tucks the photo back into his coat. The weight remains. Its purpose, justified.

He slips the glasses back onto his face, rolls his shoulders, and focuses. He removes a thumb drive from the opposite breast pocket and inserts it into the workstation. After a few clicks, he runs the code and watches as his screen turns black. Less than ten seconds later, the surrounding computers follow like a chain of dominoes. Nolan watches as the entire lab is infected with blank screens of nothingness.

Nea jumps up from her workstation, her tiny frame just barely visible over her computer. "I think our servers just went down," she says with a higher pitch than usual. "I'll call HQ to see what's going on. I know it's the weekend, but I don't remember any notice about maintenance."

"No need." Nolan stands, moving toward her. "Our servers are fine. It's our entire data warehouse and its backup archives that have been deleted."

She tilts her head in confusion. "How can you tell?"

"Because..." he says, stopping only a foot from her, "I deleted it."

"What? Why would—" she stutters, taking a step back with wide eyes.

He grabs her by the upper arms. "Nea, listen to me very carefully."

She looks up, her eyes quivering as they fix on his. His stomach lurches, but he has to continue.

His plan is in motion, and time waits for no one.

"In approximately forty-seven seconds, the building's power will go out. Shortly after, Adam Drazen will take out the guards before coming for me."

Nea's eyes widen. "But if you know this, then—"

Nolan holds up a hand. "My future is written, Nea. Please, do not make this difficult. I need you to take this." He holds up the orange octagonal disk. "But you must be quick. If he crosses that threshold and you're still here, then you'll be dead."

"But why would—"

"Nea!" he says, his eyes narrowing even as he tries to steady his tone. "Time is running to an end in every way imaginable and without our consent. Find Aperio. He's the only one of us left you can trust with this." He shoves the disk into her hands, his own lingering. "Until then, disappear. Drazen won't stop until he finds you. Now go!" The light overhead vanishes, and Nea gasps. Nolan can feel her hand tremble as she tightens her grip on the disk.

She says nothing, only nodding, eyes steady with determination before sprinting toward the rear exit.

Nolan stands at the center of the lab in the dark, waiting. Seconds pass before the sound of a single gunshot echoes

7

throughout the open space. His shoulders flinch as the bullet's shockwaves pummel into the room from beyond its walls. Emergency lighting flickers on just as the double doors swing open. Nolan watches the sinewy frame of his old friend storm into the room where they had met several years before.

Something's different.

Dark hair streaked with age outline the hardened features of someone who has witnessed the ugly truth of the world. The crooked nose of a recent break juts over a robust jawline, but it is his eyes that haunt Nolan. There was a light there once, a hope for change, but now Nolan sees only...

A complete stranger.

As he steps forward, a deep shadow cloaks an unknown scar on his forehead.

Drazen stops, his stale breath heavy against Nolan's face.

"Hello, Adam," Nolan says, refusing to break eye contact.

"Adam?" Drazen chuckles. "No one's called me that name in a long time. No one has called me anything. Thanks to you, I have been living in Hell, and all you can say is 'hello?'" Nolan remains silent, even as Drazen starts to pace around him. "Surprise. I've seen it countless times on the faces of the others before I killed them. They all knew. They must have known that I was coming for them. But, every time, they just give me that same stupid look like they had no idea. But you? No. You knew before I took out those guards, and even before that. Maybe you've always known. But here we are." He pauses, his eyes meeting Nolan's once more. "Why didn't you warn them? Why wouldn't you try to save them?"

"What makes you think I didn't or that you even *did* take them out? Even so, things are as they are."

Drazen swings around behind Nolan. "I see," he whispers before turning to face the machine. "'Things are as they are. Ha. You and your philosophizing bullshit. So, today's the day. I assume it's already done, huh?"

"We had no other option, Adam."

"No!" Drazen turns, his dark eyes bulging beneath narrow brows. "We had every option. I know you've seen the future. I've seen it, too. I've paid for it because of you. So don't lecture me about making the right choices while also just letting things happen. You may have fooled the others with your garbage, but not me."

"It's not garbage."

"No? Then what?"

"It's a paradox," Nolan says, watching the veins expand on Drazen's forehead.

Drazen whips out his pistol and pulls back the slide, allowing a bullet to enter the chamber. He grabs Nolan by the jaw and presses the barrel against his face. Nolan stares into his hollow eyes as the icy steel digs into his cheek. Terror grips his thundering heart.

"I heard a gunshot before you walked in," Nolan says as he feels his own quivering voice vibrate against the gun. "Yet, just now, you had to chamber a round into that cold barrel. Does that sound consistent? What would you say that is?"

Drazen lowers the weapon, smirks, but says nothing.

"A paradox, always true but rarely right."

Drazen looks away yet again to gaze at the machine. "You've always been observant when it comes to the details. Could never get the smallest one past you. That's what's so funny. You get obsessed with the smallest things and miss the big picture in front of all of us." As Drazen's eyes move from the base and work upward, he smiles. "Just imagine. The events, the world, time itself. No more war, poverty, sickness, famine..." He turns back toward Nolan and pauses. Nolan does not see anger in his dark eyes per se but rather sadness and disgust. "But all of you self-righteous pricks would rather see humanity destroy itself."

"Changing events doesn't change people." Nolan's voice

grows firm. "Has it changed you for the better?" As he says it, Nolan can see Drazen's gun hand shaking.

Drazen lets out a deep sigh and loosens his grip on the pistol. "You know, I really did like some of them, even thought of them as friends. I considered you a friend too some time ago. I didn't want any of this, but I couldn't just let... I couldn't." He lays his other hand on the machine's platform. "Once I knew what had to be done, I did it. Never hesitated. Not once, except now."

"Why?"

"You know why. Things are different now. I'm different. With the others, it wasn't personal. And when you look at the alternative, it had to happen. I never liked it, but we both understand why I did it, why I killed them. It wasn't personal." He turns, grabbing Nolan by the collar, and drags him onto the machine's platform. "But with you?" Drazen clenches his teeth and grips his pistol tighter as he returns the barrel to Nolan's head.

Nolan steadies his breathing.

Any second now.

He takes a deep breath, the air sweet on his tongue.

How many breaths have I taken for granted? Why is it always the last that makes you consider?

The picture of his son races through his thoughts, tumbling over memories and life itself. As he looks down with the gun to his head, his eyes meet the face of his watch one final time, unticking, unchanged, and lifeless. Before exploding gunpowder can be heard or a recoil felt, Nolan and his watch become one.

2

OUT FROM THE GARDEN

Sky watches as the bearded man approaches her. The moon's light creeps through the window and glistens against his full white beard, yet his face remains hidden in shadow. She hears his voice but fails to see his lips move at all.

"I've been waiting for you," he says.

Sky looks past him, ignoring his words as her eyes dart around the darkened room, struggling to recall how she arrived here. Silhouettes of bulky furniture stand between them. Shadows of trinkets and antique art rest along the pinstripe wallpaper. She can just barely make out the pink and navy patterns as they stretch into the halls beyond. The man moves around what appears to be an armchair and sits in it. The leather stitching groans as he adjusts himself.

"It's old and worn but fits like a glove," the man says. "Will you join me?"

Large, bony fingers wave her toward a nearby chair in the shadow.

Who is this guy?

And where the hell am I?

Her heart thunders as the adrenaline rages through her veins. It's opening night, and the primal stage of *Fight or Flight* is set before her. Dress rehearsals are over, and the show is ready to begin...

Only it doesn't.

The lights dim, but the curtains fail to roll back.

Sky looks down at her stilled hands as they refuse to reach for her holstered pistol. Muscle memory and years of training beg for her to reconsider.

But she doesn't.

Instead, she inches toward the strange man as if being compelled to do so. Her heartbeat is slow and calm; her breathing is smooth and restrained. The man isn't a threat, and she knows it, though she doesn't know why.

"I'm afraid our time here is very limited," he says. "Please, come sit."

Sky obliges and takes the chair directly across from him. Even sitting mere feet from him, she still cannot see his face.

Only darkness.

His vocal inflection is enough, however, to paint an impression of him in her mind. Calm. Commanding. Almost comforting, yet frighteningly sober.

"You have questions." The man strokes his bushy, ivory-colored beard. "I've not brought you here to answer them."

"Brought me here?" Sky asks, her voice scratchy. "Where is this place? And who—"

"Doesn't matter. What matters now is time."

Sky shakes her head. "Time?"

"Yes. It's how we make sense of things. It binds everything, you know?"

"Ah, okay." Sky raises her eyebrows. "What does this have to do—"

"You cannot exist outside of it..." He pauses, tilting his head into the shadows beyond. She follows his gaze to the far corner of the room. There, covered in shadow, stands a monstrous grandfather clock, its base twisted into a large, sculpted knot. "And, in many ways, I can't either. But very soon, you will be pushed to the limits of what that means."

Sky stares, his words twisting in her mind like the knot on that clock. She takes a breath and does her best to wrap her head around the man's words. "I'm sorry, but could you be any vaguer?"

"I could, yes."

Her nails clench, digging into the leather armchair. "No, I was being—"

"Sarcastic," he interrupts. "Yes, I'm aware. I'm sorry, but specificity right now will undo the very reason you're here. Not that you're going to remember any of this."

"Why wouldn't I?" she asks, her heart skipping.

"For the same reason you can't recall how you got here. You're not meant to know right now. But this I promise, you'll see soon, and you'll know. You've felt things. You'll continue to feel them. Don't be frightened of it. You're worried right now, but you shouldn't be."

"What, you're here to tell me everything is going to be okay?"

The man's beard quakes like flimsy bushes in the wind. "No. It's not my place to say that. But when you return, you'll know where you need to go."

"You just know that?"

"You won't remember it, but I need you to know it."

Sky leans in just as a loud ringing fills the room. Her shoulders flinch as she turns toward the sound, watching the pendulum of the strange clock break from the knot, break from its shackles. It tumbles over, face first. Glass shatters as it collides with the ground, spewing pieces of itself throughout the floor and onto her boots. Without warning, a spark ignites from the corner of the room behind her. The air rushes past her, desperate to feed the ever-growing flames. Sweat trickles from her pores as the flames inch closer. She whips back around to find the faceless man standing, his back to her and the fire beyond. Firelight shimmers against his polar hair.

"It's already time," he says.

The flames rage behind them, its tendrils reaching out as though to ensnare her.

"Time for what?" Sky asks aloud but already knows the answer.

The flame is closer now. Sky can feel its heat breathing down her neck, eager to sear her flesh. She holds up a hand against the blinding light, but it is no use. A part of her wants to be frightened, but she isn't. Even as the fire grows around her, there is no pain.

Only warmth.

She watches through squinted eyes as the man turns toward her once more, his face now blinded by the raging inferno surrounding them. She may not be able to see him, but she can hear his voice and feel the weight of his words.

"They, looking back, all the eastern side beheld," he begins, almost in song:

Of Paradise, so late their happy seat,
Waved over by that flaming brand, the gate
With dreadful faces thronged and fiery arms:
Some natural tears they dropped, but wiped them soon;
The world was all before them, where to choose
Their place of rest, and Providence their guide;
They, hand in hand, with wandering steps and slow,
Through Eden took their solitary way."'

THE HEAT WITHERS and the light fades. Sky's eyes open as she awakes.

* * *

"THEREFORE THE LORD God sent him out from the garden of Eden to work the ground from which he was taken." The minister's voice breaks through the mild gusts of wind. "He drove out the man and, at the east of the Garden of Eden, he placed the cherubim and a flaming sword that turned every way to guard the way of the tree of life." As the minister closes his Bible, Reuben can feel the shards of stares from behind him. He gazes toward the coffin, his chest tightening. His jaw clicks between breaths, the sound of grinding teeth a soft whisper compared to the turmoil of his father's death.

"Paradise was lost," the minister continues. "And death had now found a home on Earth where its curse would continue to plague mankind. Today, we are reminded of this curse as we commit Nolan Greyson's body to the ground."

What was it we had said to each other?

The words yelled nearly a decade ago rush through his mind, too blurry for him to recall correctly. It's as if they're encrypted somehow, protecting him from something.

From what exactly, he's not sure. Maybe it's from the pain, or worse yet, the truth.

He rubs his fingers together, reminiscing the smooth card stock letters his father would send him on each birthday. To this day, he doesn't know why his dad left, only that it had to do with work.

He shakes his head, the minister's words penetrating his thoughts once more.

"Yet, you do not know what tomorrow will bring," the minister says, now quoting from memory the book of James.

"What is your life? For you are the mist that appears for a little time and then vanishes."

Reuben recognizes this verse as something spoken at his mother's memorial service nearly fifteen years ago. His eyes water, the salty grief trailing down his puffy, pale cheeks. Reuben doesn't wipe them, even as the December air threatens to freeze the tears on his face. Instead, he continues to gaze at the coffin, to gaze at his father, to gaze at death.

After several more minutes of stubborn grief, Reuben stands with the rest of the mourners in preparation to sing a departing hymn. Scanning the mostly empty cemetery, he only recognizes maybe a quarter of the few faces that have come to pay respects. Even the leaves, either dead on the ground or clinging for life on their barren hosts, are as scarce as the visiting mourners.

Reuben lowers his line of sight as the sun's rays burst through the openings between the bare branches. The minister's words start to pull him back once more when a man sporting a solid maroon tie and a symmetrical double Winsor knot draws him back. Perhaps in his sixties, the tall man is hugged by a custom-tailored suit and fastened by a clean shave and military-style haircut.

The man catches his eye and nods.

Must be a co-worker, Reuben thinks, watching as another man approaches the coffin to lead everyone in the hymn.

"Rock of Ages, cleft for me,
Let me hide myself in Thee..."

PEOPLE SLOWLY JOIN IN, their eyes trailing over the printed lyrics.

It was his father's favorite hymn for as long as he could remember and it's only now, in this moment, that Reuben finally ponders it. It's not the words that capture him per se. It's the melody and voices that bring it to life. It's the memories of his family gathering around the table and the precious time they shared.

It's gone now. The time. His mother and father. His own twenty-seven years. All of it, gone. Only this song and its power to awaken a heaviness in his being remain.

Fresh tears break through his defenses, defrosting the remnants of those before as he realizes for the first time that he is truly alone.

> "Could my tears forever flow,
> All for sin could not atone..."

WIRES GROUND as the casket starts its final descent.

> "While I draw this fleeting breath,
> When my eyes shall close in death,
> When I rise to worlds unknown,
> And behold Thee on Thy throne,
> Rock of Ages, cleft for me,
> Let me hide myself in Thee."

THERE IS a solid *thump* as Nolan's casket reaches its final resting place. Reuben wipes away his tears with his sleeve. He attempts to button his jacket, but the decade-old blazer refuses such tension. Falling to his knees, Rueben watches as the tears fall from his face onto the casket below. His hand fumbles toward the mound of earth next to him, meaty fingers recoiling before delving into the soil.

A sob shudders through him as he watches the soil slip between the cracks of his hardened hands to the casket below.

Above him, a cluster of clouds eclipses the sun's rays in an almost eerie display of lament. He stands, mouth open and speechless, struggling to fathom its finality.

"Good—"

But he can't say it, not out loud.

Goodbye.

The word floats in Rueben's mind, but his tongue refuses to give it purchase.

The burial closes with the minister's hopeful words of gospel, but Rueben doesn't register them. He is lost in his own mind, in the memories and unfinished conversations. He hears the condolences of those who pass him by, but their words are hollow.

What could they possibly say that would fix this?

It doesn't take long before the chilly cemetery returns to its former state, lonesome and soberly bound to its eternal gates of finality, void of everything but itself.

"Mr. Greyson," a voice calls out from behind him. Reuben turns to see the older man with the maroon tie. "I'd like to offer you my deepest sympathies."

The man extends his hand, and Reuben shakes it.

"Appreciate that," Reuben says. "Sorry, I didn't realize there was anyone left. I don't think we've met before."

"No, my apologies. I'm Paul Peterson."

"How'd you know my dad, Paul?"

"I work in D.C. overseeing a project your father was a part of. Nolan Greyson was one of this nation's finest physicists. He contributed to facets in our society rarely thought of but of vital importance. We are grateful for his service, and this government is in debt to your family."

"Listen," Reuben says, "I really appreciate you coming out here and paying your respects. I do. I've heard from plenty of people how brilliant my dad was. But none of them could ever go into why. And to be honest, I'm not sure you'll be any different."

He attempts to walk past, but a slight tug on his shoulder stops him.

"I understand." Paul lowers his hand. "'Why' is undoubtedly an important question to ask. It's one we ask ourselves each day. Sadly, we don't uncover all the answers."

Reuben nods before heading toward his car.

"That doesn't mean we can't get to at least *some* of the answers."

Rueben stops in his tracks. "It would be a start," he says, his eyes meeting Paul's.

"We'll be in touch," Paul says as he turns, heading in the opposite direction.

"We?" Reuben says, shaking his head in confusion.

On his drive home, he listens to the cold air streaming over his car. He contemplates turning on the radio but decides against it. Music has always been his greatest coping mechanism to the struggles of life.

But this is different.

No upbeat tempo would contrast enough, nor mellow song complement enough to change his mood or provide comfort. Only the static noise of the wind delivers any sense of feeling, but it's far from solace.

His rambling thoughts drive him forward as his foot holds steady to the gas.

Paul Peterson.

An empty fridge awaiting him at home.

The ibuprofen failing to ease his mild hangover.

These thoughts grip his attention, but only one thought tugs hard enough at his chest to send him gasping for air, and he can't even remember it. As much as he struggles to recall and tries to forget, it's that final conversation with his father, ten years prior, that haunts him and refuses to leave.

As he makes a turn through town, Reuben prolongs his trip, taking the scenic route. His eyes widen as they stumble onto an old diner on the street corner, reminding him of that famous old painting whose name fails to come to him. His stomach growls as he passes it, remembering the lone pack of noodles on his single-shelf pantry and its companion frozen hotdogs, waiting to be microwaved.

It's time to get home.

In the distance, he sees it, a scarce cluster of ancient stucco gray buildings, like dusty toppled cans in an abandoned grocery store. Reuben rolls down the window, the cold air chilling his fingers as he enters the gate code, but he barely notices or cares. The half-rusted gate groans to life before creaking open. Reuben lets out a breath as he engages the gas. It's not a smile nor frown that comes over him as he enters the apartment complex.

It's nothing, absolutely nothing.

If home is where the heart is, then where is this place?

A chill rolls along his spine like waves barreling toward the shore as he unlocks his front door. His muscles tense as he crosses the threshold, his eyes scanning for an invisible threat.

But there's nothing.

I'm alone.

He throws his keys on the nearby hook, ignoring the light switch as he makes his way into the dimly lit hall. Light leaks in from the single window in the living room.

Without warning, a shooting pain tears through his shin as his hand crashes against the nearby wall. Swearing, he kicks the laundry basket out of the pathway. A mixture of clean and dirty clothes fumble over an already crowded floor, littered with books and empty beer cans. The throbbing headache he woke up with returns in full force as if triggered by where it had begun. He can still feel the imprint on the side of his face where the worn carpet had become his pillow the night before.

The blurry scene plays out in his mind's eye like a heavily edited film, filled with sudden cuts, dramatic filters, and an ominous musical score.

Hand reaches for beer.

Fingers graze over dusty family photos.

Eyes skim over Dostoevsky's words.

Hand reaches for another beer and another.

Mind drifts to oblivion.

Legs tire and fumble.

Head collapses to sleep.

It plays over and over.

The wardrobe changes through days, weeks, months, and beyond, but the final cut remains the same. Reuben blinks, and the movie stops. Film analysis will be left for another day.

He continues to his bedroom, his fingers fumbling with the knot in his tie. As a teenager, Reuben could never tie his own ties. He had always relied on his father to tie the few he owned. For the longest time, he kept them pre-knotted so that he wouldn't have to learn. Then, one day, he opened his closet to discover that all his ties had been undone. Although Reuben's father never admitted to undoing them, he took the opportunity to teach his son the skill so that he could learn to do it himself.

Musk and plain popcorn walls welcome him into his bedroom. The disarray of clutter from the living room has found its way in here as well, snapping him continually back to his reality of hangovers and coffee-stained resumes. He folds his tie and sets it on the bed next to a wooden box on his nightstand. His fingers run against the box's frame, trailing along the superglued crack, recounting the day he let it drop. His heart sinks at the memory, but he quickly pushes it away.

There's been enough pain today.

He opens the box, setting his father's tie gently upon the collection of heirlooms. A shiny object from the bottom reflects into his eye.

His grandfather's dog tags.

Rueben smiles as he lifts the chain gently from its resting place, the cool metal a small comfort. Removing his own set from his Army days, Rueben dons the family memento before slipping his personal pair into the box and closing it.

With only an undershirt and his dress slacks on, Reuben gets a brief look at himself in the mirror and recoils. If it's not last night's cheap beer, then it's easily the old picture of himself beside the mirror. As his eyes alternate between the two, a bitter taste grows in his mouth.

It's not the scruffy, unkempt beard or the aged face that gets to him.

It's the weight.

Easily over thirty or even forty pounds heavier today, Reuben's always told himself that the steady weight gain had primarily been muscle. But after years of little exercise, a shit diet, and a stomach draping itself more and more over his belt, he can't keep lying to himself.

Reuben takes the small photo and stuffs it in his dresser.

If there's no reminder, then there's no lie.

He flops onto his bed, closes his eyes, and releases a heavy sigh. The sun may still be lingering outside but, for him, this day could, and should, be over. The tension in his stiff muscles begins to melt. Feelings of angst and grief take a temporary back seat amid relaxation.

A chilled breeze slides across his face and glides down his body, causing a jolt down to his bones.

Why is there a breeze inside?

He shoots up from the bed as his eyes dart toward the source. Curtains roll and flow against the cold wind as he rushes over to his closet, his instincts coming to life. He pulls out a small lockbox. His hand reaches into his pocket, recovering nothing but lint.

Damn.

He sees it in his mind's eye, watching in panic as the keys dangle near the entrance, far from reach and negligent to his needs.

Enclosed within the lockbox sits a .40 caliber Glock 23 beside a bulky magazine of hollow-point rounds. And it's useless without those keys.

"Shit!" he mutters.

The luxury of other options fails to materialize. He grips the box tight and moves toward the kitchen, each step emitting little to no noise.

Without warning, a pocket of air from the window wisps over his shoulder. He takes another step, the breeze steady against his neck.

His legs freeze mid-stride.

The breeze has gone.

Before he can react, a hand grabs his shoulder. His body tenses, but it is too late. A razor-sharp blade presses against his throat.

"If you don't play this right, the next move you make will be your last," a voice whispers in his ear.

"There's a hundred bucks on the counter," Reuben says, the blade shaving the hairs from his Adam's apple as he gulps. "Nothing else of value here."

"Not true. You're full of shit and don't even know it." The intruder pulls at Reuben's collar and leans further into his back.

He must do something.

Without hesitation, Reuben seizes the momentum and

lunges his head back into the intruder. At the same time, he grips the man's wrist just as the intruder applies pressure to the knife.

It slices through the first layer of skin.

Before it can cut further, he twists the man's wrist, jabs an elbow into his rib cage, and flings the man into a nearby wall. The knife tumbles across the floor. Reuben kicks it, recovers the lockbox, and sprints toward the kitchen.

Swooping the keys from the hook, Rueben dives into the kitchen to find what little shelter he can.

A gun slide pulls back, but it's not his.

Its operator has just welcomed a round into the chamber, ready to fire.

Reuben scours the key ring through ragged breath as his exhausted heart struggles to pump blood into his being.

I need to get my ass back to the gym.

A rampant succession of bashing noises rushes through the apartment.

What the hell?

Rueben jams the key into the lockbox and throws it open. Within seconds, he loads the magazine and chambers a round. Only a five-pound trigger pull now stands between himself and the intruder.

He flinches as a blast rattles through the small apartment. Terror courses through his veins even as his instincts harden his spine. The blasts repeat, flooding the apartment with sulfur and casings. Reuben pinpoints the sound to the living room and charges toward it. Muzzle first, he rushes into the living room.

Another gun points back at him.

It's not the intruder.

"Lower it," a woman in a suit says to him. Reuben grips his pistol tighter and glances over her shoulder. Another suited gunman faces away from them, toward the hallway where Reuben had fought the intruder moments ago.

His eyes go back and forth between the pair. The woman is tall and lean. Her bronze skin and smooth face seem to him delicate and warm, while the strength in her voice is as fierce and impenetrable as iron. Reuben's eyes meet the man's as they glare back at him. His short, bulky frame and pale reddish cheeks contrast his partner. Reuben can't help but notice the glaring differences between the two, opposite in every way yet united in their most defying characteristics.

The guns.

The suits.

The no-bullshit demeanor.

They share it, and they wear it unapologetically.

"Listen to her, Reuben, and lower it. We don't have much time," the suited man says.

"Make time," Reuben says, still holding the gun at eye level, flexing its crosshairs against the man's chest. "Why are you in my apartment?"

"Paul Peterson," the woman says. "He sent us."

"For what?"

The woman gestures to the hallway. Keeping his arm extended in front of him, Reuben steps forward and swivels his head toward the sight of bullet holes scattered up and down the walls.

"He escaped. Make no mistake about it, though, that man was here to kill you."

Ah, shit.

All the pieces start falling in place.

The armed intruder.

The government agents.

The bullet holes left from where they shot at the man before he escaped. They've not come to harm Reuben. They've been sent to protect him.

But from who? Who was that knife-wielding maniac? How did he so easily enter his apartment, and then escape bullets?

Reuben shifts his eyes to the faces of the strange suits in his home. "You lower, I lower." They nod and comply as Reuben mirrors, slowly guiding his muzzle toward the floor. "Who was he?"

The man steps forward. "Like my partner said, he was sent to kill you."

"Yeah, but—"

"There's no time for follow-up questions." The suited man leans down and pulls a small white box from a nearby back-pack. He tosses it to Reuben, who catches it and flips it around. A faded red cross marks the center. "Your neck."

Reuben reaches up. The light layer of wet glides along his fingers. It's a minor scrape, but the knife most certainly peeled some skin off. He smears the dab of crimson red against his palm, and it quickly dries. He uses the first aid kit to clean and cover the minor cut as the suits finish clearing the rooms.

The woman returns to the living room after a few minutes and tosses Reuben his own duffle bag. "Pack at least a few weeks' worth of stuff. Toiletries, clothes, shoes, whatever. Just no phone, tablet, or any electronic communication."

"Listen, I don't know what you think I do that I can just up and leave for—"

"You're unemployed." She looks around at the cluttered apartment, her nose wrinkling.

"I was going to get around to cleaning..." Reuben clears his throat. "But, you know, with the funeral and everything, it's been—"

"The guy who was in here earlier knows you live here," she continues dismissively. "It doesn't take a genius to see you can't stay here. You've got five minutes."

Reuben resists the urge to continue a semantical exchange with someone who has clearly saved his life. Instead, he grabs his gun case and moves toward his room and begins packing. His thirst for truth outweighs his discomfort in taking orders from strangers.

Who was the guy with the knife?

Why did he want to kill me?

What kind of a mess was Dad into?

Pulling open drawers from his dresser, he rips out articles of clothing and stuffs them into his duffle bag. No time to fold or sort. He rehearses the words of his packing philosophy in his head.

Gone for a day, pack for two.

With no exact timeline or known destination, he shoves all he can into the bag.

He condenses and tightens the duffel before glancing over at his nightstand. The open handgun case sits comfortably, dangling its corner over the edge. He pulls his pistol from between his suit-pants and boxer briefs and begins to unload it before stopping himself.

"You ready?" a voice carries into the bedroom.

Reuben places the loaded Glock into the case, secures the latch, but does not lock it. *Accessible. It has to be accessible.*

"Hurry the hell up," the other one shouts.

Reuben walks back over to the bag, bunches the straps together, lifts with his legs, and flings it behind his shoulder. The duffel drives its blunt mass into his traps like Atlas's globe, burdening his shoulders with the weight of his world. He uses his free hand to grab the gun case before rushing out the door. The man walks over to him as he enters, his hand outstretched.

"I think I can manage carrying it myself," Reuben says, still holding onto the straps.

"I insist." The man yanks the duffel. Reuben's grip unwittingly yields, and the man marches away with it. While distracted, the woman slides Reuben's gun case from his hand before his reflexes can counter. He looks up at her, stunned by her quickness and his own inability to outmaneuver either of them.

"Don't worry, you'll get it back," she says.

Reuben's shoulders tense as she unlatches the case and removes the weapon. One by one, she extracts the bullets from the magazine and drops them into a leather pouch. She lowers the gun back toward the case but pauses. Her eyes meet Reuben's, searching. He holds his breath, not wanting to confirm her suspicions.

She smirks, pulling the slide back with almost a maniacal glee. They watch as the unfired bullet ejects from the chamber. It spins and topples toward the ground. The woman flings out her leather pouch and catches the round before it can strike the floor. She returns the now unloaded gun back into the case, secures the latch, and smiles. "You really should keep this locked. Safety first, you know?"

"I've misplaced the keys." Reuben fights to keep the muscles in his face from giving away the truth. He doesn't trust them, but he needs them to trust him. The woman nods and joins her partner in doing a final sweep of the apartment. While standing alone, Reuben looks down at his hands, one stained with his own blood and the other rubbed raw by the friction of the duffel strap.

Definitely getting that gym membership.

"So, where do we go from here?" Reuben says, hoping one of them heard him. The man appears and opens the front door as the woman emerges from the hallway with a coat.

"You might want this," she says, thrusting the jacket at him.

Rueben nods and falls in behind her.

He hesitates before taking one final look at his apartment. It's not the fresh bullet holes or the dated clutter that gets to him. It's not any particular thing at all, but a feeling, rather. His stomach recoils as it hits him.

Emptiness.

Nothing and emptiness.

He's not sure why it's so hard to part from a house that was never a home but, somehow, it is. He exhales, shaking his head as he crosses over the threshold.

The frigid air outside welcomes him like a pilgrim with no destination, a traveler without a creed.

Past the breezeway, a dark blue SUV lies angled toward the building, with one tire completely covering the sidewalk. The woman opens the backdoor and nudges her head.

There's no turning back now, Rueben thinks as he enters the vehicle. The door slams behind him, locking him away into whatever fresh hell he has found himself in now.

He watches as the man loads his duffel bag and gun case into the trunk, then climbs into the driver's seat as his partner settles in next to him.

The woman turns to Reuben from the passenger seat and tosses him a black cloth sack. "I know it's not the first time you've seen one of these," she says.

Reuben shakes his head. "Not the first." He looks down at the cloth. "Just didn't expect to ever see one again." His eyes veer back toward her. "I never got your names."

"I'm Quinn," she says. "My partner here goes by Scott."

"Where are you taking me, Quinn?"

"Your future." She nods toward the sack. Reuben lifts it above his head and watches as the darkness drapes the sunlight.

3

PROPOSITION

The sun's rays brace against the window as its stray beams burst through the tiny spaces between the blinds, painting a series of diagonal imprints along a nearby wall. Particles of dust dance between the open slivers, venturing through the loopholes of dark and light.

He sits up from his bed, exhausted from nothing and excited by everything. Stepping over clothes and collectible action figures, he paces back and forth before veering toward a small desk in the corner of his room. A glossy brochure pulls at his line of sight. He sits at the paper-infested desk, reading the bold print at the top of the brochure.

U.S. ARMY.

His fingers trail along the bottom, the printed words forming on his lips.

"Army Strong."

A smile comes to his lips. Nothing but these words matter to him; nothing but his future and life away from this place matter.

His nose wrinkles as the previously unnoticed odor of dirty laundry, leftover pizza rolls, and body spray floods his nostrils.

Rueben sighs.

Everything is the same, but it all feels different. A sliver of heat etches into his skin, the relentless sun desperate to breach the drawn blinds. As its golden color continues to seep through the cracks, he, too, must bleed through his barriers. He takes a deep breath and smiles, this time knowingly, this time decisively.

It doesn't take long for him to run through each bulleted point in the brochure, highlighting the education and tuition incentives sections.

This will sell him.

He gathers the other materials into a neat pile, looking over each in turn. Among them sits a camouflaged pattern pen, a '*Go Army*' writing pad, additional brochures, and the recruiter's withered business card.

His wrinkling nose is a reminder as he turns, determined to face down that rancid smell. It's too much to know where to start but too insignificant to stand in his way. He takes in another gasp of air and dives in, grabbing the first thing he sees. Bundling the scattered clothing, he makes no distinction or discrimination between dirty and clean. All dive headfirst into the hamper near the door, waiting to be purged. Trash is compiled and discarded. The other random things, such as comic books, pens, and collectibles, are thrown into boxes, shoved into drawers, and tossed onto closet shelving.

After making the bed, he returns to pacing.

It's clean, he thinks as he maneuvers back to the window.

His hand grips the plastic wand, seeking to grant the sun access. He stops mid-twist.

It'll be dark soon anyway.

Releasing it, he moves toward his bed. Before he can plop on it, however, the floor rattles with a familiar vibration from below.

The garage door.

His heart drops.

His hands shake as he reaches for the Army brochure and rushes downstairs.

Smooth is fast, and fast is smooth.

He knows the concept but, at this moment, it's foreign to him. Time stands still, his nerves burning as dread fills him.

Why am I so scared?

Before he can think any more about it, the door opens, and his father enters.

"Good evening, sir," Reuben says, fidgeting with the brochure beside the dining room table.

"Hey, buddy. How've you been today?" his father says, hanging his keys, coat, and briefcase before looking at his son.

Buddy? This is exactly why I need to get out of this place.

"I'm good— I mean, well. I'm well," Reuben says. "I was just hoping to talk to you about something. Kind of important." He takes a seat at the table.

"Of course, Son. Is everything all right?" His father joins him in a nearby chair.

"Yeah, everything's fine. It's just..." He straightens his back with a deep breath, allowing the rehearsed script to come back to him. "I've been considering an opportunity. I want to serve in the military like grandpa did." Before he can open the brochure, his father's eyes narrow under a furrowed brow. He nods, and his son continues, "I talked to the recruiter, and he was telling me about all the benefits. There's plenty of money for college, healthcare, everything."

"Son," Nolan tilts his head slightly with leveled eyes and a strained smile, "I can see your enthusiasm for this. It's an exciting path. But there are many other factors to consider."

He is such a scientist. Cold and calculating. It's as if he doesn't understand what it means to dream.

* * *

WARM SAND COMPACTS between her toes as she walks the beach. Sunglasses protect her eyes from the bright solitary sun above as a passing breeze refreshes her skin. A brief sense of ease relaxes her shoulders, but it's short-lived. Sky sighs as the ease goes out with the tide, and her anxiety returns with the incoming waves.

A day at the beach should change things.

But it's changed nothing.

This isn't her. She knows this. Beaches. Sunshine. The artificiality of it all. Even the laughter of nearby children forming extravagant sandcastles, only to be swept away by the tides of time, is all fake and none of it is her.

The cool water of the ocean spreads across the shoreline. It glides up and over her feet, splashing seafoam and mist over her flowing swimsuit cover. Sky contemplates taking it off and diving in. Or just diving in carefree and wearing everything; swimsuit cover, glasses, and even her phone, tucked behind the small of her back.

But she can't do it.

None of it.

It's not real.

The sun can burn her. The ocean could drown her. But still, none of it is real, at least not in the paradigm she's come to accept. It's the paradigm that dictates reality as *creation in time* and not *recreation* outside of it. She can taste the all too stable consistency of the air, and that's enough. That's enough to remind her which realm is the source and which is a pale imitation.

Sky smiles briefly, moves away from the water, and treks back up the beach and away from it all. She looks at the face of her watch and double taps it. Suddenly, all sounds cease. The wisps of the wind, the roaring of the waves, the laughter of children, and the calls of seagulls are all—without transition—

completely mute. As if the Creator Himself commanded it, nothing in sight dares make a sound.

'*TRANSITIONING*,' flashes in bright yellow across her watch. The world around her brightens before fading from existence. The ocean, sand, and sky above fuse with one another, blending until they're indistinguishably one. She blinks, and the bright white everything vanishes into cold black nothingness.

Home.

Real home.

'*Section 7 Transition Complete,*' the display on her watch reads.

Sky leaves the empty section behind her and moves out toward the greater open bay within the facility walls. It doesn't take long for her to return to her quarters, shower, change, and eat lunch, all in an hour and under a single roof. She tightens her straight black hair into a ponytail, straps on her tactical combat boots, and cracks her fingers. What others may have called 'rest' is over. Decompression and recharging are about to begin.

Paneled LED lights and the chatter of passing coworkers breathes life into the chilly facility as Sky continues through the halls. Her fingers tingle with excitement as she maneuvers her way toward the shooting range. The lack of windows and natural light often unsettles new hires and visitors, but not her. The absence of both sunlight and clocks ironically lend the place a sense of timelessness for those who know it.

A brisk pace gets her from *A* to *B* in less than four minutes. She swipes her badge, hearing the *click* as she grips the heavy, armored door. A man stands behind the heightened counter within, his smooth dark skin stretched against his aged yet chiseled physique. Towering over her, his hardened eyes narrow on her as she approaches.

"What the hell took you so long?" he says as she passes him.

"Caleb," Sky says, glancing back with a smirk, "last I checked, this was my day off, and I can make my schedule as I please."

"You said thirteen hundred hours."

"I didn't give a specific time. All I said was that I'd stop by after lunch."

"Which ends promptly at thirteen hundred hours. Do you not see the posted—"

"Maybe this is your issue."

"Issue?" Caleb chuckles. "I don't have an issue, ma'am. I can make it somewhere on time. Which, to be clear, should be at a minimum ten minutes prior to the stated time."

"Umm, *A,*" Sky says, raising a finger, "there was no stated time. And *B,* this is exactly what I'm talking about. Your strict military Marine—"

"Careful."

"...discipline," Sky says after a brief pause. "Don't you ever get tired of it? I mean, most of us were in the service, but—"

"But what?" Caleb interrupts. "We become careless beautiful butterflies when it's all said and done? Damned be to order and structure? Let's just all walk around smoking and joking with hands in our pockets and pass off some ambiguous prayer to the god or goddess of chaos and do whatever we damn well please? That it?"

Sky smiles. "Well, let's not go overkill. I'm here for target practice, after all. Need at least some bit of order and structure for that."

Caleb returns the smile and pulls out two large cases of ammo, setting them on the counter. "Bet your ass you do."

Sky pulls the rounds from the boxes and verifies the count. "Too bad I can't just get these myself."

"You're telling me. It's not just your day off. And I've got multiple cervezas calling my name right now." Caleb pulls out a tablet and passes it to her.

Sky grabs it and taps the screen. "Looks like I'm not the only one who likes to flap my wings."

"Just sign so we can both burst out of our cocoons and be on our way."

Sky squiggles her signature and hands the tablet back to Caleb. As she passes it, her eyeline meets the back of her hand.

Thump.

Her heart skips before sinking into her stomach. Thin, pale, and mostly unnoticed, the tan line along her left ring finger glows against the dimly lit room. The reminder grips her to the core.

The reason she ventured to the beach.

And the reason she can never leave this place.

If ignorance is bliss, then remembering must be hell. And hell must be bound up, burned, and forever buried.

"The new guy is supposed to be coming in today," Caleb says, breaking Sky from her internal hell. "You know, if he agrees to it all."

"Why wouldn't he?" Sky says.

"Man's got a choice."

"To turn this down?"

Caleb smirks and strokes his clean-shaven chin. "Technically, yeah. But I guess we already know how this is all going to play out. It's just...just something about this kid I can't quite shake."

"Kid? He's twenty-seven years old. Pretty sure he has a 401k...or at least should. What do you know about him anyway?"

"Read his file. Or at least the highlights."

"And?" Sky raises her eyebrows.

"And what?"

"What can't you shake about him?"

"Shit. I don't know. Just something. Maybe because his story seems foreign to me. Or worse yet, too familiar. Did you read the kid's file?"

"Of course, I read it," Sky says. "I'm not some jarhead who can't read." She winks.

Caleb laughs. "Okay, she's got Marine jokes *and* bullets. Suppose you can't have one without the other."

"Suppose we both get on our way and enjoy this day off?"

Caleb pulls a beer from behind the counter. Its perspiration forms a ring as he sets it down.

"It's one o'clock somewhere, and I with all sobriety herby witnessed and confirmed your signing for two cases of ammunition for the official purposes of mission assimilation between the sanctioned periods thereby listed on the signed form. And now my task has ended." Caleb tips the mouth of the bottle toward her. "Fire away, Ms. Fernandes."

Sky nods with a smile, grabbing the cases of ammo. The gun range illuminates as she approaches. The bare concrete flooring and walls welcome her as she settles into her booth. The chilled air hugs her nose and eases her muscles as she loads the training rounds into her Sig 9mm pistol. She smiles as the smooth metallic slide forces a bullet into the chamber. The precise mechanical nature of it awakens something in her, like a conductor raising his baton amongst a stilled orchestra, awaiting the signal to rain down a magnificent symphony.

Crosshairs align against a distant target. Her breathing steadies its pace before pausing. In this single moment, all is calm and right with the world. Her finger squeezes, gentle but firm, easy yet confident. Then, the moment itself, a complete surprise, the gun goes off. The muzzle flash bursts in front of her as the explosion sets the recoil back in her hands.

The fury of it, chaos.

Its aim, strategic and controlled.

A paradox of precision.

Sky looks beyond at the silhouetted target. A gaping hole lies center mass.

She does this again and again and again, reloading seamlessly. The anxiety, the unease, the unknowing of herself and the world flee from her with each calculated shot. Hours later, the silhouette is unrecognizable, with more space than paper. She breaks for dinner, then returns with bandages wrapped tightly against the blisters on her hands, wearing them with pride like a badge for her hard-earned marksmanship.

Sky tapes a new silhouette to the moving target and sets the distance as far back as the range allows, hoping to kill off her last five rounds. After firing four of them, it hits her, the raw numbness of her now shaking hands. She breathes and struggles to steady them, watching as the gun trembles in her grips. Just one more round, and it's all over.

Just one more.

As her finger squeezes the trigger a final time, she sees it. The pale ringless tan line peeks through her bandage, bringing everything back. Past, present, and beyond. Sky steadies her breathing, pushing everything else back. Time pauses before slipping from her grip. The gun goes off a final time, and the bullet expels.

Redness flashes before her and encompasses everything. It pulsates over and over. Then the siren sounds. An alarm. Sky sets the gun down and smirks.

It's him. Must be him. He's here.

* * *

It's BEEN hours without light. The lines between open and shut eyes have blurred, bending the polar shades into a canvas of nothingness, unadulterated oblivion. The adrenaline may have worn off, but Reuben's heart continues to race. He wonders if Scott or Quinn can hear it above the engine. Alongside his heartbeat, he can feel the sporadic braking, sudden turns, and the constant shifting of gears. Diesel engines of passing buses wisp by between the angry horns of confined commuters.

We must be in the city.

Quinn mumbles something to Scott, but Rueben cannot make them out. Tires screech as its condensed echo carries into the vehicle.

We're in a garage.

"We're almost there," Quinn says as the SUV comes to a complete stop.

"Almost?" Reuben says. Both front doors open and shut simultaneously as if choreographed. There is a *click* before his door is wrenched open, two pairs of hands grasping to lead the blind. Rueben reaches to remove the sack from his face. A vise clamps onto his wrist, forcing it back to his side.

"Not yet," Scott's voice says. Gentle cues from the hands placed on each shoulder guide him as fluorescent lights peek through his restraints at regular intervals. Lefts and rights battle each other for dominance in direction. His muscles contract as frigid artificial air pierces through his clothing. The smell of pine oil welcomes him, its potency increasing with each step until he's compelled to breathe through his mouth. Rueben takes another step but is jerked to a halt as the grip on his shoulders tightens.

"All right, you're good right here," says Scott.

They wait for a few moments before the chiming of a familiar bell sounds.

An elevator.

He shuffles his feet, confirming his thoughts as he steps over the small gap in the floor.

"Listen," Quinn says. "In a second, you might start feeling like you want to puke. It'll only last as long as the ride. Less than a minute. After that, you'll go back to feeling normal."

"It's not my first elevator ride. Just tell me if we're going up or down." His brow scrunches with the blindfold at their chuckle.

"We're not in an elevator," Scott says. A brief silence follows the sound of the closing metallic doors. "Here." Rough hands grab ahold of Rueben's. He jerks away, but their grip is firm as they pull him to the side, making contact with a smooth metallic cylinder attached to the wall. He grips it tight. "It won't change how you feel, but it's something to squeeze."

"Why—" Before he can finish, the room warps around him, his every nerve pulsating under his skin, and yet, there is nothing.

Is this what death feels like?

The floor tilts forward as the guide rail remains in place. A subtle *creak* breaks the silence. Without warning, his stomach leaps to his throat, and then slams back down. The elevator twists as if coming undone from whatever tracks had previously held it. All the muscles in his body tense and flow at once. One of his hands slips from the rail and collides into the wall. It sinks in as if it were clay, malleable and yielding. Its surface pushes back like a pendulum before solidifying once more. Reuben's legs give way to the rapidly increasing weight of his body. He can feel himself spinning as he gains speed. His mind competes with his body for control. Both struggle to gain footing. He lets out a scream, but no sound comes out.

And then nothing.

The nausea, the spinning, and the twisting are all gone. Rueben's chest heaves as the doors open with a *ping*. He steadies his breathing, resisting the urge to rip off his blindfold. Instead, he continues in silence down another series of hallways.

He grips his stomach, thinking of the inertia-defying elevator.

What kind of physics were you into, Dad?

It's not long before they come to another stop. There is a

beep, and the *click* of a latch as a door swings open. They continue for a few more steps and stop again. Cold metal taps the backs of his knees as he falls back onto a hard surface.

Light pierces his pupils as the black mask is ripped away, bringing with it a few stray hairs. His hand shields him from the brunt of the unshaded fluorescent light, but it is no use. His stomach quivers as his fists clench, ready to combat the unseen.

"Hello, Reuben," a familiar voice says to him from somewhere close. "I apologize for the manner in which we brought you in. I believe you'll see it as a necessity in time."

"Paul?" Reuben squints, unable to make out anything but pure light.

"You remembered my name."

"It's not a hard name to remember."

"No, it's not. But the ability to recall it against a voice you've only heard once is...well, some might say it's impressive."

"Some?" Reuben manages to get his right eye open for a brief second, seeing Paul's stoic, deadpan face.

"Very little impresses me anymore. Your father did, though. His attention to detail, I'm told, was exquisite. It's only fitting that his son should receive remnants of that."

"Were told?" Reuben opens his eyes a bit more. White cinderblocks encase the pair, a single door on the opposite side. Paul sits just in front of it, a steel table the only thing separating him from Rueben. "You said..." He pauses. "It just seemed like you knew him. Going to the funeral and all."

"I didn't have to personally know Nolan Greyson to appreciate his brilliance and pay respects to his memory."

"What do you want?" Reuben looks around once more, enclosed in space and thought, sifting for answers. "Where the... What is this place?"

"This is home. Home to what your father and many others dedicated their lives to build. And to protect."

"You mean that elevator thing?"

"Goodness, no. That's what brought you here, but it's not what we're protecting. The device you're referring to is a relic of the Cold War. We use it today as means of transport to undisclosed locations. A layperson may confuse it as a teleport. But our physicists would say calling it a 'teleport' is too simplistic. Or something." Paul folds his hands. "It does bridge distances, I suppose. Much like the project your father spent years enhancing."

"What project?" Reuben says, the light no longer burning as he focuses on Paul. He is still wearing the same clothes from the funeral.

"Chronos."

Reuben leans forward. "Like the Greek god?"

"'Like,' yes, but not equated."

"I'm not following."

"Clearly."

"What the h—" Reuben bites his lower lip. "Please, elaborate."

"You know of Chronos, or at least the name. I'm impressed. Your years at the university are paying dividends."

"I'm—"

"Unemployed. Yes, we know. It pays in knowledge, saving us the time to explain what Chronos is."

"You mean, who Chronos is? The Greek god of time."

"Perhaps in mythology, but not here. Doesn't stop some from thirsting after myths." Paul reaches toward the corner of the table and picks up a perspiring pitcher of water.

Reuben's eyes dart toward it, not having seen it before. Paul pours the water into a nearby glass. The light above reflects from the pouring stream, and Reuben's throat grows unbearably sticky and dry. Reuben grabs the glass before Paul sets it down. He chugs the cold water.

"Not realizing our thirst doesn't negate its existence."

Reuben sets the glass down, leaving a few solitary ounces at the bottom. He looks back at Paul. "If you really know about me, then you know that I know what you're doing. The tiny, enclosed room, the water, the manipulation, all of it."

"Just because you know about someone doesn't mean you know them. As it stands, this is the only room you've been cleared to see, at least for now. Regarding the water, well, you've been taken from your home and blindfolded for hours. To not give you water would be inhumane. If I wanted to manipulate you, I'd treat you to a steak dinner. It wouldn't even need to be exquisite, especially given your eating habits as of late."

Reuben looks down at the metallic table for a few seconds, his shadow draped before him.

"You were talking about myths," Reuben says, averting his eyes.

Paul returns the pitcher to its corner. "We've abandoned the semblance of the myth and captured its essence. Chronos was only ever a personification of something greater. The god of time did not waste away counting the minutes of the day. Nor was he a slave to them. His power wasn't over fire or lightning. It was over the minutes, the hours, the years. It may not be a power we created, but it's one that we've managed to harness here at the project site."

"Power? You mean like—"

"Yes," Paul says.

Time travel.

Reuben shakes his head, his mind racing. "No... Sorry, there's just no way. You can't be serious."

Paul leans in. "Today, you attended the funeral of a father you've not spoken to in years. A strange man snuck into your apartment and nearly killed you. Government agents took you to an undisclosed location. You felt your own body come apart only to be reassembled, defying the laws of physics. Sitting in that chair, as you are, does it seem to you that any of this is not serious?"

Reuben says nothing.

"I understand how it sounds. But this is not some cult spewing its deeply held fiction with conviction. It's as real as this table, this room, and that scraggly beard of yours."

Rueben glances down. The imprint from his luggage strap has faded, the dried blood his only evidence of the evening.

"Why me?" He looks back up at Paul. "If this is true, I mean time trav—" He can't bring himself to finish the word out loud. "It's not something you share with civilians."

"No, it isn't." Paul leans back with a sigh. "You're no ordinary civilian. A sad, pathetic one, perhaps, but not ordinary. What's most fascinating about your military record isn't what it says, but what it doesn't say."

Paul pulls his phone out, donning a pair of glasses.

"An Army interrogator with an average number of reports in a few short years. Nothing special on the surface if you rely solely on the numbers. But if you dig deeper, you find more." He sets the glasses aside and continues, "And that's just what you're good at, digging deeper. You didn't just ask the questions. You searched for truth, and you connected the dots. Not just going after individual bad guys but collecting the kind of big picture information that helps to tackle entire organizations. We could use someone of your talents here on the project."

"Wait, you guys interrogate people here?" The memory of his past life leaves a sour taste in his mouth.

"Not exactly," Paul says. "I think you misunderstand me. We're not interested in extracting information from some enemy combatant. But we are interested in finding the truth."

"If I decline?"

"You won't. Even if you left this place intending to tell people of its government's scheming, all they would possess is the word of a washed-up, boozy, unemployed vet with no proof of any of it."

"Can I see it?"

"Doesn't work that way."

"Right." Reuben takes the final sips of his water and sighs. "Not until I've signed my life away. Is that it?"

"The start of it, yes."

"The last time I was naïve enough to take the word of a stranger, I got shipped to boot camp."

"And you regret that decision?"

"Of course not. It's just—"

"Just what?"

"It was the right choice, looking back. I was just fooled into making it. The recruiter put on a show. I'm sure you know this, but after I got out, I sold cars. At least for a couple of weeks. That's when I saw it, realized what the recruiter was doing. It was a different world, but the tactics were all the same. Smile, paint a picture of a bright future, and ask the chump to sign on the dotted line."

"I'm not smiling."

Reuben chuckles and bites his lip.

"Do you know why you were brought here today? Why I had my agents watch over you?"

"Yeah, you just said that you could use me."

"And we can. But that's not the reason. You were informed last week of your father's death, told it was an accident." Paul leans in, his hands folding on the table. "That was a lie."

"What?"

"Nolan Greyson was murdered."

Reuben's palms clench, his innards boiling. A sharp pain shoots up behind his ear as his teeth mash together. Shaking his head, Rueben pushes himself up, his fists slamming onto the steel. Pain pierces his bones, but he doesn't care. Nothing else matters except for Paul's last words.

"Stand down," Paul whispers into his headset as Reuben paces the length of the table back and forth.

"Why would you tell me it was an accident?" Reuben stops,

his whitened knuckles threatening to explode on the back of the chair. Paul says nothing and, for the first time, Rueben could swear that he sees hesitation in the man's eyes. Paul's frown deepens, the wrinkles in his forehead multiplying as he sighs.

"I advised against it," Paul says after a prolonged silence. His eye twitches as he strings his words together. "I would've contacted you as soon as your father..." His voice cracks before he can regain composure. "But it was not my call to make. I answer to others higher than myself. Even so, we knew that we had to bring you into the Agency at some point. It was your father's wish to have you here in the event of his death."

"He wanted me...here?" Reuben's heart falters, tightened fists subsiding beside him, easing away.

"Mr. Greyson, please, sit."

Reuben complies, and Paul pours him another glass of water. Rueben pushes it to the side, his thirst gone.

Paul proceeds to recount how Nolan was murdered by one of his former coworkers, Adam Drazen. For the first time since arriving, Reuben doesn't just absorb information and react.

He listens.

He listens with more attention than he's given anything in years.

His father. Betrayed and murdered by a coworker.

A Friend.

Adam Drazen.

The name fills Reuben's stomach with dread every time Paul says it out loud.

Paul, reaching the end of his sordid tale, takes a breath and adds, "I'm afraid your father wasn't alone. Both he and Drazen belonged to a twelve-person committee that oversaw the project. To date, each member has either disappeared or been recovered dead. Adam Drazen is the prime suspect. With your background and our resources, we can bring him to justice."

Reuben lets out a sigh as he ponders. "What did he take? Drazen."

"What gives you the impression he took anything?"

"If he didn't take anything, he was looking for something. Murdering all those people, people he knew well. He was after something. That...machine you have here, Chronos. I don't know how it works. I'm not really sure I believe it's real, but if it is, maybe he's trying to make one of his own. You know?"

"I can't speak to his motives or even entertain theories. At least not in this setting. If you desire to return to your one-bedroom dominion, eating your frozen pizzas and drinking your cheap beer, then I'll take you back myself. If, however, you'd rather pursue your father's killer through the vastness of space and time, well then, we can continue the conversation." Paul stands and pushes in his chair. "I'll return in twenty minutes. You have until then to decide which trajectory you prefer." He turns around and reaches for the door behind him.

"Paul," Reuben calls out. "What did Drazen take?" Paul sighs and opens the lockless door.

"Your father's life," he whispers.

The door *clicks* shut behind him. Reuben sits in the small room alone, tapping his fingers along the cold metal groves of the table.

Did he really work on time travel? Is that why he had to leave? Who were the other people who worked with him, the twelve? Can Paul be trusted? He's hiding something. What did Drazen take? What am I supposed to do, just go along with all of this?

His thoughts thirst for answers while his heart longs for solace, neither eager to wait until Paul's return. Only a programmed sense of conformity keeps him glued to his seat. He notices a mounted camera through his peripheral but refuses to look at it directly.

They're watching my every move.

Still seated, he leans forward, but the table blocks his view.

Reuben stands up slowly and stretches his arms. Using the motion to subvert suspicion, he seizes the opportunity to look downward at the small crack beneath the door. Just beyond it, two shadow streams lie swaying.

At least one guard, directly in front of the door.

He studies the shadow, ensuring that the guard is facing away from the door.

I need answers.

He looks down at his glass, filled to the brim. Instead of pouring it down his throat as before, he grabs the chilled water and takes two tiny sips. The first steps of a plan trickles into his mind as he moves to the other side of the table. He glances over his shoulder toward the door.

No hinges. Must swing out.

Sweat fills his palms, loosening his grip on the glass. Up until this point, each move has been inconsequential, like casing a bank without robbing it. There will be no reversing trajectory once things are set in motion.

Making up his mind, Rueben sets his plan in motion. He angles himself away from the camera and releases his grip from the glass. A flood of broken glass and water flows from its epicenter. The sharp echo pierces his ears as it reverberates against the cold cinderblock walls.

This is it.

No turning back.

Reuben swoops down to attend to the mess. He tilts his head parallel to the ground and watches as the water seeps under the crack beneath the door. Beyond the room, a radio broadcasts. Its muffled words obscure, its tone unmistakable.

"Shit," he whispers.

They know.

Reuben leaps up, grabs the handle tight, and throws his total weight into the door. The startled counter-resistance of the guard is no match for the force or puddle of water working against his footing. The guard slips, his body slamming against the wall behind the door. Reuben peers down the empty, narrow hallway before crouching toward the guard. Eyes closed. No wounds. Breathing. He's unconscious.

Holy shit, I knocked him out.

In a single sweep, he un-holsters the guard's weapon and takes his radio.

A dozen doors blur past him as he sprints down the seemingly endless hallway. Before he can reach its end, the piercing sound of an alarm batters his ears and jolts him to a stop. He pauses, shakes off the shock, and resumes his brisk pace.

No time for regrets.

Rueben stops several yards short of the entrance, his mind racing.

There're only two entrances. They'll be coming through here.

Pulling the gun from his waistband, he pauses just long enough to shoot out the cameras within range. Concealing his real-time location from the battalion of security forces eager to capture him may lend him the time he needs to find something.

Anything.

Answers.

With the cameras out, he runs to the nearest door, grabs the handle, and yanks down.

It's locked.

He goes to the next one—also locked. Panic shuffles his steps from door to door. As he approaches the fifth one, a tempest of footsteps roars down the hallway.

"Please," he whispers, his wrist twisting with a prayer.

It opens.

Without hesitation, he scurries into the room, closes the door, and locks it. Heavy footfalls, yelling, and rifle charging handles snapping forward come together at the hallway entrance, like a harmony of intimidation.

They're here.

Reuben looks down at the radio glued to his palm. It's off, likely from his altercation with the guard. He flicks the toggle and switches the radio from 'speaker' to 'headset,' sliding the earpiece in as the radio crackles. The transmissions are brief, but the messages are clear. They'll search for him, room by room. Lethal force is authorized if necessary.

It won't be.

It shouldn't be.

Feelings of fear and a semblance of remorse tempt him to turn himself over immediately, to cower, to reverse course, and plead for mercy.

But he can't.

Whether it's stubborn determination, a righteous quest or a stupid decision to keep going, he knows he can't turn back.

He moves to the nearest cabinet, careful to emit as little noise as possible as he rifles through the drawers.

Reuben's pupils expand to absorb any stray light stemming from beneath the door.

His sight calibrating.

Assimilating into darkness.

Finding nothing of value, he turns to discover a circular pattern of desks. A small light emits from the center of the first desk as he approaches. Beside it, a long thin plaque marinates in dust. Reuben rubs his finger against it, removing the first layer. Two more wipes, and he can read the name: *Frances Kent.*

"Room two clear!" a voice shouts from just outside the door.

Smooth is fast, and fast is smooth.

Reuben races around the desks and checks each of the names one by one: *Bruce Cobb, Steven Milford, Xavier Donald, Aperio Talesworth, Karen Oliver,* and so on. He comes to a halt, his father's name piercing through the darkness and into his heart. There isn't time to reminisce.

Time waits for no sentiment.

Rolling his body over the surface of the desk, he rushes to check the drawers, pulling them out quickly, too quickly, and finding nothing.

Smooth is fast, and fast is smooth, he continues to recite as a barrage of panic batters within, desperate to seize control. His hands move slow, but his focus sharpens as he runs through the drawers again.

"Room three clear!"

This time, he doesn't just search the drawers. He compares each, rolling them out two by two.

Nothing.

He repeats the action, this time with both eyes shut.

There.

The difference is so minuscule that a panicky scrummage would easily miss it. He glides the drawer out once more just to be sure.

This one's heavier.

Without hesitation, he rips the drawer free of the desk and sets it gently onto the ground. Rueben falls to his knees, his fingers removing a tiny paperclip before exploring the inside of the drawer.

There.

He can feel a crack in the back of the drawer where the bottom isn't flush with the side. He digs his tiny fingernail stubs into the gap and pulls up, but it's not enough.

I need a better grip.

A shine catches his eye, and he smiles.

The paperclip.

He grabs it, extends it, and shoves it into the crack. Bending the end of the paperclip, he pushes it into the corner of the drawer, and the false bottom elevates. He flips the drawer to its side. Its false bottom swings open like a door. Taped to it is a tattered leather journal staring back at him. Reuben pulls it out.

"Room four clear!"

With voices so close, his room must be next. Testosterone-fueled rage converges toward him just outside. He flips the journal, the pages flashing from one to the next as he searches for something, anything. At the center of what seems to be a continuous written narrative, he sees it.

A single underlined sentence screams for attention.

It all began with Croatoan...

Reuben flips toward the front of the journal with no time to read on, discovering sketches and diagrams mixed within the narrative. There's no time to absorb any of it, however.

Finally, he flips to the cover page and discovers his picture accompanied by writing just below:

To my only son, my most precious gift in life—May this guide you on your way as you surpass your most desired of dreams in pursuit of truth.

Message from the dead, words of life. His heart recoils as moisture glosses over his eyes before pouring out onto his palms. His fingers trail over his father's words, and then cringe, the once dried blood smearing across the page. His fist clenches as they wipe away his tears, and his resolve grows. His thirst for answers is no longer endless nor without direction.

"Prepare to breach!" the voice echoes into his headset.

Can't let them find it on me.

Reuben slams the journal shut, shoves it back into its hidden compartment, and pushes all the drawers back in place. He rolls back over the desk, gets on his knees, and slides the gun away from his body. The door implodes as a blur of black tactical suits swarm, pointing their semi-automatic rifles at his head, arms, and chest. He raises his hands high, ensuring his life but failing to guarantee a scot-free encounter.

They waste no time in restraining him, slamming his body into the ground. Knees to the small of his back, a retaliatory elbow to the rib cage, and a kiss to the dusty floor fails to distract him from what he found. It won't be today, but Reuben knows he must return to retrieve the journal his father left him.

"Have you secured our guest?" Paul says.

With half his face still lying flat against the floor, Reuben looks up, watching as Paul's expensive oxford shoes storm into the room. He crouches beside Reuben's head but says nothing, only stares. The ground muffles Reuben's voice. "He's not going anywhere now," Paul says to the tactical officers subduing him. They relieve the pressure against his back and pull him up to his knees, leaving the handcuffs.

A decade-long memory comes back to Reuben unprompted. It was the day he first talked to his father about joining the Army.

'Your grandfather did well for our family,' Nolan had said. *'He was honorable. But he never came home after Vietnam. I grew up much of my early years without him. The truth is, Son, every decision we make, for good or ill, has consequences. A man has to consider these things.'*

Reuben looks up, meeting Paul's hard gaze.

"I've decided."

4

RECEPTION

A bright spear of lightning tears open the night sky, its shuddering force far behind as it illuminates the path below. Damian exhales a frosty cloud and rubs his gloved hands in hopes of breathing life into his numbed fingers. The floorboards creak with each step, triggering his memory of the familiar path. A sharp pain pierces him as he rounds the corner, driving him to bite down onto his gloves for some semblance of relief. Another flash floods the hallway, illuminating Damian's shadowed assailant.

Who glues a damn table to the wall?

Damian squeezes by the table, his eyes careful not to meet the mirror alongside it. It's not his reflection that he avoids but what lies beneath it. The wisps of gray, scars, and muscle are only symptoms of the life that he lives.

No.

It is what lies beneath his hardened, sinewy skin. The past that denies him a future, the pain that has made him devoid of emotion.

I will fix this.

Damian stumbles through the labyrinth of misplaced

furniture, endless hallways, and a mesh of rooms. A small light glimmers in the distance, a lighthouse in a sea of lightning.

He pursues the source.

With each step, the objects around him become more and more pronounced. The curled, wooden handrail guides him up a steep flight of stairs. There is a gentle tug on his glove as a tiny splinter snags him to the rail. He removes it and continues, the creaking of his steps growing. His heart jumps from his chest as wood collapses beneath his step. Clutching the railing, Damian makes his way around the decrepit void.

A part of him wants to feel fear, the way he did when he was young. It was genuine then, tied to something beyond himself like love or sadness.

True emotion.

Hungry, cold, irritated, full, these are the things he feels now. Fear is only a survival mechanism. Hollow and without stakes beyond immediate physical harm. He knows he should be concerned.

But he isn't.

There are only two drives in his life now: the grand payout and feeding his baby, his bloodthirsty knife resting tight along his hip. He rubs the cold hilt, warmth spreading over him as he reminisces over their decade-long adventures beside one another. The blade is as sharp as ever, though the hilt is evidence of their journey together.

Aged but forever young.

His baby.

And babies never judge their caretaker. They marvel, play along, and grow but never judge.

At the top, Damian proceeds through a set of double doors and into a candle-lit library, the largest room in the monstrous house. An enormous mahogany desk lies in its center, showing no visual marks of entropy, no hint of decay, no sign of time's scar. Just behind it, a brown leather chair sits faced away from him, occupied and still.

"You're early," a voice calls from behind the desk.

"Trying to make some better habits, ya know?" Damian says as the chair rotates toward him. A bead of sweat trails down his forehead. A cloudy breath escapes from his lips. His hand fidgets at his side, the comfort of his knife calling to soothe him.

The man stands up, presses his fists against the surface of the desk, and leans forward. The candlelight dances across his worn yet youthful appearance, its flickering shadows deepening his scars like shaded canyons at dusk.

Damian forces himself to look into Adam Drazen's eyes.

"No, I don't know," Drazen says as he pulls back his straight, shoulder-length hair before moving around to the front of his desk. Damian twitches toward his baby once more, covering the move with an itch at his side. If Drazen notices, he doesn't let on as he continues, "Did you get it?"

"Uh, well…" Damian feels the back of his neck give way to the chill as his body shivers. It's not a feeling, no, it's a reaction, a struck nerve.

"Are you shivering because of the cold or because you failed to get what I asked for?" Drazen's tone isn't harsh, nor his voice raised, and yet, Damian's flesh raises as the chill pierces his bones.

"I mean, it is a bit chilly in here. I know there's no electricity, but can we at least get the firepl—"

"So, you didn't get it?" Drazen's eyes narrow, fingers tightening.

"I tried. I really did." Damian's voice trembles, his fingers desperate.

His knife.

His comfort.

He caresses the hilt, its warmth finding the words for him.

"I had my knife to his throat. You know how hard it is for me to hold it there without opening someone up. He got loose, and before I could get to it, two govies come bursting in shooting at me. I couldn't do a damn thing."

Drazen stares, his eyes an abyss.

Damian swallows, the ache growing. "I mean, I could've just slit his throat and taken it. I'll do that the next time—"

"No," Drazen interjects. "My instructions to you were clear. He can live...at least for now. We knew Paul was coming for him. We just weren't fast enough."

"It won't happen again. He won't be in that facility forever." Damian pulls out his knife, rips off his glove, and glides his frozen fingers along its razor edge. A tingling sensation spreads from his touch, his master's presence almost forgotten. "She's thirsty, too."

"Then feed her yourself. From here forward, I'll handle Reuben personally."

"Oh." Damian's face slackens. "All right, then." He slides the knife back into the holder around his belt. "What about all those funeral brochures?"

"You didn't toss them?"

"I would've, but it's, you know...a federal crime, taking it from the mail and all." Drazen closes the distance between them in seconds. Damian takes a step back, the hilt of his blade calling, but he resists the urge.

He needs me still.

We need each other.

Drazen's eyes search his own. Before he can react, there is a jerk at Damian's belt as his master rips his baby from his care. Drazen smiles, tilting the tip of the blade until it pierces into the point of Damian's nose.

"You carry around your murder weapon."

Damian's teeth clench as he huffs.

I can take the snips, but this? My baby? The sheer audacity of this man.

Damian's fingers twitch, a reflex to seize the blade back and end its captor. But he doesn't do it. He can't do it, and both men know it.

Adam Drazen lowers the knife and presses the handle against Damian's chest before releasing it. The blade falls straight down like a pointed dart, digging into the hardwood floor. Damian kneels to collect it, careful not to lose sight of his dangerous ally.

"That's different. It has sentimental value."

"And what does that serve?" Drazen stops short of his desk.

"I don't know. I guess it just keeps me—"

"Stupid. That knife ties you to every heinous act you've committed."

"Well, I wouldn't call it...heinous. Just seems a bit, you know, extreme."

"You butchered half a dozen people holding that knife."

"That was like ten years ago. And you told me—"

"To do what was necessary. And we've done just that. Most of them were proud, self-righteous, or just stupid. But you know what? Some of them were good people who didn't deserve to die." Adam Drazen bites his lip and, for a fraction of a second, Damian sees it.

Sadness.

Damian may not feel much emotion, but he knows enough to recognize it in others. And, at this moment, he sees the pain behind Adam Drazen's dark, hollow eyes.

"I know what they were," Damian responds. "I worked with all of them, even saved their asses a few times, but they stood in our way... They stood in *my* way. This knife represents the cost of standing between me and what is mine."

Drazen shakes his head, his eyes hardening once more.

"Trophies are for winners, Damian. There are no winners in

this battle. There is only the drive to get it done, to act where others won't. Don't forget what's at stake here because of your pride or that stupid knife." Drazen turns, his cold stare bearing down on him.

Damian's gaze falls, his hands fidgeting in front of him as memories long since locked off scream to be free. His wife's glowing smile and her beautiful pink dress. He can almost feel the flowy fabric on his fingers, thinking of how held her that night as they danced without music. How they stared into one another without muttering a word. She was the only one to ever accept him for who he was.

Tears pool beneath his eyes but he chokes it back, his breaking voice absorbing the grief. "You damn well know I haven't forgotten. Why else would I stay in this hell hole with you and do your dirty work? Sure, I'm no saint, and the work's been good, but even a murderous asshole like me has standards. I respected them, you know. Hell, I even liked some of them, too," Damian says, his voice cracking with the last words.

Drazen nods, though his frown deepens. "We may not do the pleasant thing, but we do what is necessary. I know your pain and the conflict you have, but they were not your friends. They looked down their smug noses and denied you the chance to make things right. They had the power to heal your pain and, instead, let you suffer."

Damian looks up, his eyes continuing to water even as he fights his inner demons back into their cage.

Drazen continues, "We are so close to getting it, to making everything right. Clear your mind, stick to the plan, and it'll be yours for the taking."

There is a moment of silence and, for a second, Damian swears that he can feel his master's empathy. The feeling fades, however, as Drazen's eyes narrow.

"Now, toss the knife, or you'll end up holding it the day you die."

"I'll find a place for it." Damian tucks it back into his belt.

He turns, heading for the door but stops short as Drazen says, "There's one other thing I need from you..."

* * *

"THIS IS BULLSHIT!" Kirk throws his arms up as he leans against her desk. "That asshole is gonna come work with us after pulling that stunt?"

Sky rolls her eyes before looking over at him. "It's not our call, and you know that."

"Yeah, but if I ever did anything remotely—"

"You've snuck fireworks and worse into the facility." Sky stands up from her workstation and tightens her bandages. She can already feel the soreness in her hands and arms. Tomorrow will be hell, and she knows it.

Kirk adjusts his posture, looking to his left and right before leaning in. "You know about that?"

"I'd be a pretty crappy supervisor if I didn't."

"Oh." He steps back, his shoulders shrinking and his hand coming to rest on his chin. "I mean, if you're waiting to report—"

"You launched the fireworks in Section 7," she interrupts. "It's stupid and against at least a dozen rules. But no one was hurt, and nothing was damaged. You're lucky I found out after the fact. Otherwise, I would've strapped you to them as they launched."

"Yeah..."

"Look," she says, eyebrows raised, "I'm giving you a second chance. Don't you think this new guy deserves one, too?"

"Deserve? We don't even know him. And I'm pretty sure I never knocked out a guard. I mean, it's hilarious, but that's some excessive shit. I would just think that you of all people—"

"What?"

"...wouldn't just let someone damage their home. That's what this place is to you, right?"

Sky let's out a sigh, fingers rubbing against her palms. "It's more than that."

"Then why not protect it?" Kirk says, hands flaring. "I know last year you went through some awful shit, but—"

"But?" The heat rises in her cheeks as her voice lowers. She knows he didn't mean it, but the fire within burns all the same.

"I'm sorry. I didn't mean it like that." Kirk takes a breath. "And maybe it's not my place..."

Kirk trails on as Sky lets out a slow breath. The anger lingers, but she can manage it.

Don't look at it.

Don't look at the finger.

It all fades in time.

"You're right," she says. "It's not your place."

"Look—"

"We've got less than a day to prep the environments," Sky says as she waves off his protests. "You've shadowed enough to take point on that. Don't let me down, okay?" Kirk nods, and Sky continues, "His accesses should come through any minute. When that happens, I have to go and give him the tour. Tomorrow's a big day. I'm counting on you, Kirk."

THE PIERCING SHOCK of instant cold causes Reuben to jerk the ice pack away from his bruised face. He reapplies in half-second dabs, numbing the skin's surface until it can accept a longer embrace.

"You're fortunate," Paul says, seated in a chair across from him. "On an average day, I may have rescinded my offer. On a bad day, you'd never see light again."

"And what kind of day is this?" Reuben sits up from the bed

and pulls the ice pack from his cheek. In the brief silence between question and response, the perspiring collection of droplets from the ice pack begin to hit the carpet. Its subtle, muffled tapping fails to cut the room's tension.

"Not an ordinary one. I understand your curiosity and determination. It's in part why my proposition to you stands. I feel compelled to tell you, however, that my tolerance for insubordination and cowboy antics is very limited. Do we understand each other?" Paul's tone is flat, yet there's something sharp in his words that gives Reuben pause.

He nods.

Peering over to the corner of the room, he notices his duffle bag beside a dresser. "So, this is where I'm staying?"

"These are your private quarters. Make it your own if you wish. Just ensure that whatever you do can be undone. Your access to the rest of the facility will take at least another hour. Until then, you can acquaint yourself with the room. My personal recommendation would be to get cleaned up. We'll begin with a quick reception this evening. You can rest after that." Paul glances over him with a smirk, and Reuben feels even more aware of his disheveled state. "I have no doubts you could use it."

Reuben looks back over at his duffel bag. "And my gun?"

Paul stands and soothes the wrinkles from his perfectly creased pants. "You'll be issued weapons as appropriate to your mission set. Jones will expand in more detail once you begin."

"What about my Glock? The one Quinn took from me."

"Security is inspecting it. Once cleared, it will be returned to you. The hollow-point rounds, however, will be destroyed."

"What? Why?"

"Having them on-site violates a long-standing policy."

"I didn't bring them on site."

"No, but it was your intention. Was it not?"

Reuben's fingers twitch as he stops himself from scratching his face.

It's his tell, and he was one mannerism shy from complete exposure.

As an interrogator, he learned to suppress it, but it's been too long. He's rusty, and Paul knows it.

"I didn't know where I was going or what your policy was."

"But you know now. Besides, being ignorant of the rules or their cost doesn't absolve you of them. I suggest you quickly learn and get on board. Things of far greater value than bullets have been lost here."

Reuben says nothing.

Exhaustion grips the gears of his mind, grinding until the fight has all but left him.

Paul departs, leaving Reuben to himself in his new quarters. He tosses his duffel onto the bed before peering around the room. The beige-coated walls stretch high, supporting a tall, smooth ceiling as it masks the size of the otherwise small space. A full-sized bed, nightstand, mini-fridge, chair, and dresser fill the room, leaving little space to maneuver between them.

He rips off his shoes first, allowing the soft gray carpet to hug the soles of his callused feet. The blood and sweat-stained undershirt follows, along with his dress pants. The stink of his body hits him at once and, for the first time in probably years, he hates it. He stumbles into the adjoining bathroom and turns the shower knob toward the red 'H.' The pressured stream beats against the top of his head as the water races to dilute the accumulation of dirt and sweat. The taste of salt hits his lips on its journey through his scruffy beard and eventually down the drain.

After minutes of vigorous scrubbing, soaping, rinsing, and repeating, he hops out of the shower and dries himself with the raged, Army-issued brown towel he'd brought from home. His towel then works to wipe the thick layer of condensed steam on the mirror.

Staring back at him, Reuben sees the same shaggy, pale face from this morning. The only discernible difference is the bruise along his cheek and the cut above his Adam's apple. It's a face he sees every day, yet the look of it unsettles him as his brown eyes stare into themselves. He could wear colored contact lenses, bleach his dark hair, and even lose all the weight, but none of it can change this haunting look. He glides his fingers through his unkempt beard, letting out a sigh before removing a trimmer from his bag.

It doesn't take long for the white sink and surrounding ceramic countertop to fill with hair. It takes even less time for the shaving cream and cheap two-blade razor to remove the stragglers. He rinses his skin, uncovering a clean-shaven face he's not seen in years.

Three knocks at the door echo into the room. Reuben rushes to throw on a clean shirt and pair of pants.

"Coming!"

Barefooted and half-wet, he opens the door to find a woman staring back at him, her greenish-blue eyes encompassed by full eyelashes. Her smile and smooth black hair are breathtaking but fail immediately to captivate him the way her eyes do. There's something beyond just the physical look of them. The words *soft*, *honest*, and *lovely* come to mind, but he dares not say them aloud. Instead, he stands in the doorway with a tilted head and open mouth as awkwardness fills the void.

"Ah..." he says, proud that he's managed anything at all, though disappointed it was shy of anything discernible.

"Hi," she says. Her voice is gentle yet firm. "I'm Sky, the senior navigator on site. Paul Peterson sent me to show you around. Is this a good time?"

"Uh..." He fumbles, desperate for some semblance of speech.

What's wrong with me?

"Yeah, that's...that's totally fine. I'm Reuben."

Sky smiles and nods as if to excuse his unexpected demeanor.

"It's nice to meet you, Reuben."

"Yeah, you too, Sky."

"Well, whenever you're ready, we can start."

Reuben nods and takes a step, stopping short when she doesn't move. She snorts, her eyes darting to the floor before meeting his once more.

"Don't feel rushed. You can put your shoes on. I can wait. It's not a problem, really."

He looks down at his bare, wet feet, heat rushing to his cheeks.

"I'll be right out."

He tears through his duffle, grabbing the first excuse for a pair of shoes he can find, and throws them on.

"Shall we start?" she says.

"Let's."

Sky takes a right down the hallway as Reuben closes his door and picks up his pace to catch hers.

"Oh, shit," Rueben says, realizing he doesn't have a key. "They don't happen to auto-lock, do they?"

Sky smirks before nodding.

"Damn."

"Don't worry about it. We'll get you a key."

Man, what is wrong with me today?

They walk side by side through what feels like an endless maze, depriving him of any sense of direction.

"Now, I'm not sure how much Paul told you about the place—"

"Enough to keep my mind boggling for a while."

Sky raises an eyebrow.

"I'm so sorry. I didn't mean... I've always hated when people cut me off."

"You're fine. It's been a long day. Your father's passing, someone trying to kill you, being blindfolded, and taken to a top-secret facility. And to top it all off, some guy you've never met tells you time travel is real. I wouldn't worry too much about etiquette right now. Besides, you'll probably be one of the more polite members of the team."

"Team?"

"Well, as I was saying before being rudely interrupted..." they share a brief smile, and she continues, "you'll be assigned to the Operations Team of our Collections Unit. We use Chronos to go out on fact-finding missions."

Before Reuben can ask any follow-up questions, they arrive at a guarded entrance. Sky swipes her identification card dangling from her neck against the scanner before showing it to the guard.

"And him?" the guard asks.

"This is our special recruit that Director Peterson brought in. His access just hit the system. Badge is being made as we speak. He's cool, Tyson. You can run the manual access check yourself if it'll make you feel better."

"I already did," Tyson says, deadpan. "He's good this time, but he better have his damn badge tomorrow. I don't care how special he thinks he is."

Reuben's jaw dangles, even as they pass the guard.

Is this dude serious? Why does he have to be such an— He sighs as it hits him. *Dammit. It's me. I knocked out one of their own.*

They proceed through a set of double doors and onto the lab floor. Reuben's knees buckle as he looks past the rows of desks, computers, and technicians. There, in the center of the lab, sits a metallic monstrosity that dominates every conceivable line of sight in the hangar-sized space. He only has eyes for what must be the legendary technology. Reuben's hand rises to meet it as his feet propel him forward. If there is a god of time, this is its sacred shrine. This is where it's made its dwelling.

His heart flutters and races as he stands before it, struggling to get out any words that would do the experience justice, or at least echo the thousand wordless thoughts streaming through his mind.

"Whoa," Reuben's tongue finally utters as his eyes take in the tiny minute details up close. Creaseless metallic edges. Seamless curved paneling.

Are there even any panels or is it all just one large piece?

This isn't just foreign to him, it's completely alien.

Otherworldly.

He tears himself from the wonder just long enough to find Sky. "Is this—"

"Yes," Sky says. "This is Chronos, the AIC's pride and joy."

"AIC?"

"Archive Initiative Center. The organization that brought you this," she says, pointing to the machine, "and so much more."

Rueben hears her words but cannot seem to make sense of them. He is lost in the robust platform, sharp lighting, symmetrical columns, and the smooth gray matte finish of his childhood fantasies.

It's elegant yet beastly. The construction of it seems to Reuben to not just walk a tightrope between sophistication and functionality but to redefine the terms altogether. A set of grated plexiglass steps invisibly support the path between ground and machine, almost flaunting the fact that grip safety can look cool. The lighting along the inner portions of the columns brings out the machine's unique contours while providing unadulterated visibility in every direction. There's no visible wiring anywhere, yet somehow the lab techs and engineers around them seem to have no issue accessing the random automated compartments that light up and open as they wave their hands in front of them.

It's not just the mechanics or the grandiose construction of the machine that grips him, but what he's been told about it. This isn't an astounding piece of modern art or some dormant extraterrestrial artifact. This is something more. It's the wildest theories of modern science and the most imaginative piece of fiction come to life.

"So, we can use this to time travel?" Reuben says, looking back at her.

"Kind of," Sky responds with her hands folded in front of her in a professional stance as if she were a time machine sales associate telling Reuben about its features. "We can't alter events or go to the future or some other things, but we can go back to observe and interact with the past."

"What's the point, then? I mean, going through all the trouble to build something like this and not change anything?"

"You don't have to alter the past to change the future. We believe that studying mistakes of the past is the best way for a better tomorrow. And I know it sounds kind of cheesy, but it's true. I think you'll see it, too. Just keep an open mind."

"I will. Or at least I try to." Reuben crosses his arms as the questions swirl in his muddled brain. "And I get it, with learning about the past and everything. But what about stuff like genocide? Do we learn from it or try and stop it?"

"Learning is part of how we stop it. Going back and erasing one genocidal event doesn't do much to stop the ones to come. I'm sure you know the old saying..."

"Those who fail to learn history—"

"Are doomed to repeat clichés." Sky winks at him as Reuben lets out a chuckle.

Reuben rocks back and forth on his feet, reflecting on it all. "It's funny, when I was in college, I was required to take this class. It was Science and Society, or maybe it was Science and Ethics or something like that. We'd argue all the time about all these moral dilemmas we could face in the future. It was easy to argue because everything was hypothetical." Reuben looks up at Chronos. "This isn't. This is a time travel machine hidden away in some...some... Where exactly are we anyway?"

Sky smirks. "I can't tell you the exact location."

"Can you give me an idea?"

"Afraid not. I can't tell you because I don't know. Few people do. We all transport in and out of this place. Some people, like you, have quarters and live here, while others go home at the end of the day."

"And you?"

"This is my home," Sky says. "I get to travel wherever I'd like to go without ever leaving."

"And the secrecy is to protect this place."

"To protect us." She shifts her focus to the machine. "And that."

"Is this the hero who's been causing all the commotion?" Rueben turns, his eyes widening as a monstrous hand juts out at him. Rueben takes it, doing his best not to wince at the firm grip.

"Reuben, this is Caleb Jones,"

Caleb, only slightly taller than Reuben, appears nearly twice the size. His arms are muscular and shoulders broad. His green T-shirt could pass as body paint over his chiseled torso.

"It's good to meet you, Caleb," Reuben says. "What is it that you do here?"

"I train sorry, pansy-ass punks how to fight."

"Caleb is the weapons, tactics, and security SME of our Collections Unit." Sky adds. "He's responsible for training and overseeing personnel as they prepare to make their trips through different time periods."

"That's right." Caleb smiles. "From Medieval weaponry to

modern combat tactics, I'll make sure you're ready for any mission and any century."

"Can't I just bring a gun wherever I go?" Reuben asks.

Caleb chuckles before turning to Sky. "Have you not explained anything to this kid?"

"He just got here a few hours ago," Sky says. "We haven't even gone over periodic jumps or déjà vu. Basics first." She looks back at Reuben. "Don't worry. We'll have plenty of time to go over everything. Alex will probably be the one to answer that question."

Reuben nods.

"You served?" Caleb asks.

"Eight years—Army."

"Ha! Army! What's the matter, Hero? Couldn't join the ranks of real warfighters in the United States Marine Corps?" He chuckles again. "I'm just busting your chops. In case my conceited demeanor hasn't given it away, that's where I served. Did three tours overseas. Force Reconnaissance."

"Yeah, I thought about the Marines, but my grandfather was Army. He gave his life for his platoon and was awarded the Medal of Honor." Caleb nods, and Reuben continues, "I always wanted to follow after him, so I went Army." Reuben pauses. "That and the Marine recruiter said I tested too high in my times tables." There is an awkward pause before Caleb doubles over, his booming laughter echoing through the lab. Rueben can't help himself and is soon doubled down next to him, their laughter as harmonious as children at play.

Sky smirks, rolls her eyes, and shakes her head.

"Oh, man, you crack me up!" Caleb gets out in between laughs before the two settle down. "I guess you're all right for a soldier. One fight."

"Yeah, one fight," Reuben repeats with a nod.

Rueben braces himself as Caleb claps him on the shoulder, nearly sending him tumbling to the floor. "All right,

Rueben, I've got to get to it, but I'll see you for training soon enough."

Rueben watches the man run off before turning back to Sky.

"He'll grow on you...hopefully."

"I guess time will tell." Reuben pauses before cracking a smile. "No pun intended."

"Believe me, working here all these years, I've heard them all."

She introduces him to some of the lab techs and assistants who run the domestic operations. After meeting several new faces, they proceed up the walkway toward the lab exit. "All right, there is at least one more person I'd like to introduce you to before we start your training. Since it's the end of the day and most people have gone home, you won't get the full introduction until tomorrow."

Reuben yawns before leaning against a nearby desk along the pathway. "So, what does my training look like?"

"Well, it's more or less meeting with the members of our team. Basically, we'll prepare you to go out on missions."

"These are the fact-finding missions you were talking about earlier?"

"For the most part, yeah. One thing you should know, though. Our parameters have changed some since your father's body was discovered. Before, the missions would be like we talked about, learning and understanding history. Recently, things have changed. Paul has made it pretty clear that anywhere we go using Chronos must meet certain...justification guidelines."

"What kind of justification?"

"Finding Adam Drazen. All of the Center's resources, including Chronos, must have a link in finding him."

"That's it?"

"Yeah." Sky looks down for a moment before returning her

eyes to Reuben. "Drazen's undermined everything this project stands for. It wasn't so bad all that time he was missing. Everyone just assumed Drazen was either dead or living some obscure life in South America. But your father's body turning up has stirred the pot. So long as Drazen's out there, it looks bad on the Agency. I see Paul's side of it. He wants to catch him and give some credibility back to the project. It's partially why he recruited you, I'm sure." She pauses again. "Reuben, I'm sorry for your loss. I hope we'll catch him. And when that happens, things might go back to how they were. And you'll see, then. You'll see the Chronos your dad fought for."

"Thanks. I hope you're right." Reuben looks back at the machine once more. "So, who's training me tomorrow?"

"We all are. I'm the team's navigator, so I'll walk you through time trajectories. Caleb, who you just met, will obviously go over weapons and tactics through time periods. He also accompanies us during trips as our security officer." As she's explaining, a slender man with glasses approaches. "Just the guy I was looking for," she says, turning toward the man. "Reuben, meet Alex Seung, our team's communications specialist."

"So sorry about your loss," Alex says. "He meant a lot to this place, your father. The project wouldn't exist without him."

"Thanks," Reuben says. "I wish I knew more about what he did here."

"Yeah, I hear ya, man. It's the line of work, though."

"So, communications?"

"Oh, uh, yeah, comms. We'll go over all that tomorrow."

They chat for a few more minutes before Alex excuses himself, saying goodbye. Sky takes Reuben to get his key before escorting him back to his quarters. During the walk back, Reuben feels his eyelids gaining weight. The day's overindulgence of emotion, fighting, and mind-warping thoughts have taken a toll. His mouth extends with a prolonged yawn. He fights for each step as his body aches and cries for rest. The mental struggle of comprehending Sky's instruction engages his mind enough to keep going.

"Like I said, have some milk in the morning to coat your stomach, and you should be fine," Sky says as they arrive at Reuben's room.

"Milk?"

"Yeah, most people really struggle with the queasiness their first time."

"Good to know," Reuben manages to get out between yawns.

"You should get some rest."

"I just had that same thought."

Once in his room alone, he nearly trips over his droopy legs on his way to the bed. Reuben's body collapses onto the mattress as the worn springs give way. He fades before his head hits the pillow. At this moment, a single thought carries him from wake to sleep. In Sky's gentle voice, he hears it.

You'll see the Chronos your dad fought for.

5

FORTY-SEVEN A

For a moment, everything around Reuben is entirely void. Neither dark nor light; time nor space; just emptiness. Then it fills. A room emerges and comes to life in an instant. Light blue walls fall into dusty, laminate flooring littered with action figures. This is his old room from when he was ten years old.

He sees a photograph in a gold frame atop his dresser and picks it up. Staring at it, the photo comes to life, pulling him into the memory. The sun's gentle rays warmed his skin and soaked the surrounding grass. The park that day sounded of chirping birds, buzzing bees, and passing cars. The air smelled of pending rain. His mother had packed a picnic, and his father brought baseball mitts to play catch. A passerby had snapped the photo of all of them before the clouds eclipsed the summer sun.

The smell of rain mixing with asphalt floods his nostrils as he remembers the panicked rush back to the car. In it, Reuben frantically searched the back seat, his drenched skin slipping on the leather as he looked for the tiny companion he'd brought with him everywhere.

A toy soldier.

He can still picture his father's eyes in the rearview mirror looking back at him. The soldier was everything to Reuben then. To his father, it was probably nothing more than a child's plaything, a replaceable toy. But as Reuben looked into Nolan Greyson's eyes, he saw a concern and care that solidified his love for his tiny friend.

Nolan rushed out of the car and back into the storm. Reuben doesn't remember how long it took for his father to return, but it felt like a lifetime to a child. Eventually, he came back into the car drenched. He turned back to Reuben and handed his son the tiny priceless companion. Nolan must've been cold and uncomfortable for the hour-long drive back, but Reuben doesn't remember any of that. All he remembers is his father's eyes in the mirror and the smile he gave him when he handed the soldier back to him.

Reuben looks away from the photograph to find that his room is gone. A blazing light fills his sight and vanishes, leaving behind a different space altogether. White cinderblock walls enclose around him, and his breathing quickens.

All the hairs of his body rise as if supercharged by static electricity. He can feel them coming off him one by one but there's no pain in the plucking. The sensation mirrors a mass exfoliation, leaving his bare skin to soak in the cool, tantalizing air. He reaches for the stray trimmings as they collect into a humanoid shadow before him. A jarring ray of light bursts through the room, and the shadow dissipates. Reuben's eyes shrink to squint before the light can dim itself back into a solitary lamp.

What the hell is this?

It's the first real thought he has beyond reacting to the strangeness.

A red button appears along the wall, paint dripping down from its edge. Reuben presses it, and the humanoid shadow reappears. It grabs him by the throat and fills him. Before he strikes, it's gone, and everything is back. The hair on his head. The beard on his face. All of it.

Seriously, what the hell?

The hairs rise once more, and his heart inflames. Dim, hair, shadow, white, fade, button, cease.

Repeat.

Finally, the lamp shatters.

"Hey, come on!" a muffled voice shouts.

Reuben's eyelids fling open.

He leaps out of bed as firm, sequential knocks echo into his room. "Time to start the day, man."

"Be right there," Reuben says. Rubbing his eyes, Rueben tries to shake the cloud of sleep from his mind as his fingers grope the nearby wall for a switch. His eyes cringe, the artificial light as blinding as the darkness before it. Yesterday's clothes are still wrinkled against him, a foggy reminder of everything that has happened. A knot coils his insides as the door shudders once more. With a tug, pull, and shake, he fluffs out his impromptu pajamas and answers the door.

"Dude, it's about time," the unfamiliar face says. Rueben rubs his eyes, searching his foggy memory for some familiarity. The stranger shakes his head, his red hair failing to waiver from its gelled formation. "Ah, man, you just woke up, didn't you?"

Reuben nods.

"It's all good. Believe me, I get how tiring everything can be. All this time travel shit..."

Great. It wasn't a dream after all.

"If that craziness happened to me all at once, I'd probably sleep eighteen hours, too."

"Wait, what?" Reuben's back goes rigid, and his eyes widen. "Eighteen hours?"

"Yeah, man. You're like five hours late for training. They

sent me to check on you. To make sure you're not dead or whatever."

Eighteen hours? How's that possible?

"Did Sky not show you the alarm clock? I know it's a little trippy with the warp-snooze invading your dreams and all, but it's pretty straightforward. Light means wake, red means snooze."

"Warp-snooze?"

"Yeah, they say it doesn't literally enter your dreams." Kirk looks around before leaning in. "But I think they're full of shit. That stuff is way vivid and creepy. I personally just unplug it." He pulls back and continues. "Anyway, why don't you get freshened up. Maybe a little caffeine." The man's nose wrinkles. "And, ah, some mouthwash."

"Who are you?"

"I'm Kirk," he says, handing Reuben a card attached to a plain black lanyard. "Here is your access badge. Should get you into the cafeteria and the training room." Reuben sees his picture on the translucent badge. "I mean, the guard will have to inspect it to go into the training area, but the cafeteria is only an easy scan... Oh, and you can ditch that temp key Sky gave you before. The badge should unlock your room, too."

"Thanks."

"You are welcome, my friend. The room is 47A when you're ready. Just don't take forever. You know with the whole five hours late thing?"

Reuben nods, shuts the door, and scrambles to get ready. Before he can ponder whether he feels well-rested, the thought of being five hours late to his first training session jets him into motion. A slap of toothpaste, a dab of deodorant, and a fresh shirt meet him in less than two minutes. He grabs the door handle but stops himself from opening it. Running to the mini-fridge, he looks for anything that can be inhaled in exchange for energy. His eyes meet a bottle of milk, triggering his memory of Sky's advice. He twists the cap, tilts the container, and lets it flow down his throat.

He pops a stale piece of spearmint gum and darts through a series of hallways looking for the training room. After several more minutes of navigating the labyrinth, he finds the plaque beside a windowless door reading 47A. Reuben scans his badge and opens the door to reveal a training area the size of a large warehouse.

How the hell does this fit in here?

"Can I help you, sir?" the guard says, startling him.

"Uh," Reuben shakes his head to attention. "Hi, I'm here for training."

"How about I see that badge?" Reuben hands it to him. "Well, I see you on the list, Mr. Greyson. Looks like you are a bit early." Reuben's eyebrows stretch into his hairline. "You're slotted for 9:30 AM. So, you have about fifty minutes to kill."

"Wait. Are you sure I'm not five hours late?"

The guard hands him back his badge and smirks. "Ha! Sir, the earliest we make this area available for training is eight. My old ass was still asleep five hours ago." Reuben sighs, smiles, and shakes his head in disbelief. "You're more than welcome to wait in the meantime. They usually leave out some training manuals if you want to study up."

"Yeah," Reuben says, still in shock. "I guess I'll, ah…thanks." He walks past the guard and into the massive space.

Eighteen hours? Not even college kids crack twelve.

A quick visual scan of the room fails to absorb everything in sight. The overall design reminds him of a sound stage that might shoot big Hollywood films, filled with a variety of lighting and able to quickly change its setting. The space appears to be broken up into six or seven distinct sections. Each section is fed with its own light source, its own layout, and its own interactive environment. The patter of his footsteps seems to only enter into whatever given environment he's walking by, somehow ignoring all others. The sections distinguish themselves only by lighting. There are no physical barriers or visible walls between them, only lights, and shadows.

Above him floats a single fully enclosed object, resembling a windowless telephone booth centering itself in front of the distinct sections at the room's base. Rueben circles the booth as it hangs fifteen feet above him. He searches for the source of its suspension but finds none as if it were a weightless chandelier hovering silently over its unsuspecting guests. Its unique vantage point likely gives complete visibility of the entire training room.

As he works his way toward the first section, a shadow materializes in his peripheral. His gaze shifts left to discover that it's not what's there that captivates him, it's what isn't there. His eyes widen as he circles in place to examine the shadow.

All of the other cells have vanished. It looks as if all the lights disappeared in the remaining sections, or a barrier fell into place when he stepped into this cell.

Taking a few steps back, Rueben watches as the different sections fall back into place. He scratches his head as he repeats the procedure, watching as the rooms disappear and reappear depending on his position. Walking over to the nearest barrier, he spots it. A thin layer of shadow separates them but is only visible when standing between two cells.

"You're early."

He turns to see Sky walking toward him from the entrance. Caleb, Alex, and Kirk follow behind her. Kirk struggles to retrieve his ID badge back from the guard in a fit of laughter before eventually catching up to the team.

"Early is on time, on time is late, and late is unacceptable," Reuben says, glaring at Kirk as Sky and the rest of the team approach. "Five hours, huh, Kirk?"

"Hey, man," Kirk gets out between laughs. "It's not my job to check the time for you. Besides, time is...totally relative here. Ha!"

"You're the only one laughing, Kirk," Sky says. Kirk's laughter dies under her stern glare. "And from now on, you're banned from using time travel puns."

"I second that shit," Caleb chimes in. "Gets old real quick."

"I'm sorry about him," Sky says to Reuben. "Kirk can actually be pretty helpful when he's not a total immature...jerk."

"Don't worry about it," Reuben says before looking over at Kirk. "Sometimes, a poor sense of humor goes hand in hand with high intelligence... Sometimes."

Kirk's solid grin remains as he nods toward Reuben as if to say 'touché.'

"Since you're here, we can probably get started ahead of schedule," Sky says.

"Yeah, sounds good." Reuben turns back toward the shadow border. "So, how does that work exactly?"

"It's diverted energy from Chronos," she begins. "You can't alter time without also bringing space alongside. We use residual energy from Chronos to create an invisible vacuum between each individual training area."

"Residual energy?"

"Yeah," Alex says, stepping up as if on cue. "Believe it or not, most of the facility is powered using that energy. Or at least most of the cool stuff."

"Like that teleport thing?"

"That, your warp-snooze alarm, the Observer's box above you," Alex says as Reuben peers back up at the suspended booth.

"It allows us to see and interact with all areas at once," Sky says. "But each area is completely separated in time and space from all the others. It's one of the ways we can train a sole individual in many different areas at a single time...at least from the Observer's point of view."

"Really helps with efficiency in training," Alex says.

"So, you're saying I can be in all these different sections at the same time?"

"From your perspective, no." Alex adjusts his glasses. "You'll go through them sequentially. But from the perspective of anyone in the front of this room, you'll be in each area simultaneously."

"Whoa," Reuben says with a breath. "That means I can get a week's worth of training done in a day?"

"Slow down there," Sky interjects. "In theory, yes, but remember your body is experiencing everything as it comes. It will still feel like one week, and you'll exhaust yourself quickly." She pauses and smirks. "But, yeah, we can definitely move quicker."

"Okay now," Caleb says, stepping closer toward the group. "We can spend all day talking about what we can or can't experience, or we can just go ahead and experience it. So, let's just get this thing going, huh?"

"Yeah," Sky says. Everyone else nods in agreement. "Reuben, go ahead and follow Caleb, and he'll get you started. After you're done with him, you'll move on to the next section."

"Come on," Caleb says. "Even if we have all day, I don't want to waste any time. Especially on Army folk who may need... additional remedial training." Caleb chuckles to himself as Reuben follows him to the first section.

As they cross into the final barrier, the sound of their footsteps changes direction—all other lighting vanishes. Reuben veers back to see the other members of his training team disappear into different sections.

"They are on their way to begin training you," Caleb says. "They'll be seeing you in just a few short seconds. But you'll have to take the long way to meet them. After my session, you'll move onto the next through the doors between the barriers."

Reuben looks over at the first area, seeing only darkness where the barrier should be. "What door?"

"The Observer will make sure you see it when you're ready to move forward." The two move to the center of the space.

"Who's up there?" Reuben asks.

"Doesn't matter. What matters right now is what's in here." The void begins to fade in on itself like a black hole forming in reverse. The previously empty black solidifies as if being summoned into creation, forming physical barriers. Without sound or warning, they take substance. Stone walls solidify and encompass them like hardening clay, surer of itself by the second. Reuben moves toward it and trips as a dull object jabs into his shin. The skin of his palms rakes against the jagged stone floor as he falls, the shock of it all quelling the pain. Hugged between his legs lies the wooden bench that brought him to his knees. He kicks it aside and comes to his feet.

That wasn't there a second ago.

A table, some benches, armor, chainmail, weapons racks, goblets, shields, and statues bloom from nothing as the room settles into its new décor.

"Wow," Reuben says as he maneuvers through the chamber. "Did we travel back to the Middle Ages? This looks so—" A glimmer of steel interrupts him as it races toward his peripheral.

He shifts his focus just in time to see the blade of an axe slicing through the air, barreling toward him. He's not sure what hits him first, the sudden jolt of fear or the instinct to react.

Fear and instinct.

He ducks and a wake of air rolls over his head. Caleb pulls back the axe as Reuben jumps to his feet.

"WHAT THE ACTUAL FU—"

"That's the wrong approach," Caleb interrupts as he winds

the medieval weapon to strike again. He swings toward Reuben's chest.

Reuben doesn't think.

There's no time for that. Instead, Rueben lets his instincts take over, fueled by his anger. He lunges back, avoiding the blow.

"Your first thoughts shouldn't be the time period." Caleb raises the axe again. "It should be situational awareness." Rueben darts to the side and wrenches a sword from the nearby wall. Caleb watches him, his axe settling into position as Rueben does the same.

He can feel his heart pumping the fear and rage into his hands, into the sword. The axe batters down, and Reuben raises his sword to block it, thwarting its momentum as sparks expel from the collision.

Is this how they train?

"Now we're on the same page," Caleb says with a toothy grin as he continues to strike. Whether by luck, reflexes, or stubborn rage, Reuben manages to hold his own just enough to ensure survival.

"You know the right muscles to use, but can they hold?" Caleb says and thrusts his weight behind the axe in a sudden jolt of force. Reuben stumbles backward, his legs and arms wabbling under the pressure as the strength and energy bleeds out of him. Caleb yanks Reuben's sword from his sweaty grip before dropkicking him without breaking a sweat. Wind, vitality, and any sense of orientation collapse as Reuben's back smacks against the ground.

The fight was in Caleb's hands the whole time. There was never any winning. Caleb sneers down at him before throwing the weapons onto a nearby table, leaving Rueben with nothing but rage and defeat.

The fight is over.

"What rank were you?" Caleb asks over Reuben's labored breath.

"What the—" Reuben tries to get it out, but there's no oxygen. He comes to his feet and just stares at Caleb, waiting for an explanation, waiting for something.

"Oh, wait, I think I remember from your file. E-6 type, right? A staff sergeant?"

Reuben nods, the lack of oxygen hindering all else.

"That's all right, Staff Sergeant. We'll just have to work on what y'all used to call 'Army Strong.'"

Reuben falls on a nearby bench and wipes the sweat pouring from his brow. Caleb smirks, his meaty hand offering peace within a goblet. Cold water rushes down his chin as Rueben inhales the goblet in one gulp.

"Situational awareness?" Reuben says with raspy words. He sets the goblet down and laughs as it tips over from shaky hands. It's the nerves, the edge, still lingering. "What the hell was that? Some sort of real-world lesson?"

Caleb smiles, almost laughing to himself. "No. That was controlled, believe it or not. I wasn't going to allow you to get hurt. A little roughed up, sure, but we're not here to hurt you. The missions, though. That stuff will be real. And you need to be ready for that."

"So, swinging at me out of nowhere is supposed to prepare me?"

"Truth is, most of us never see the first strike. We never get a say about that. It just comes. It's what we do about the second and the third attacks that will define how we win or lose. We're reactionary creatures. Can't always prepare for everything, but we need to be ready for anything."

Reuben's not sure what to think or if he agrees, but he understands. The brief anger and frustration give way as Caleb pours him another cup. The drink continues to quench his thirst but fails to ease his nerves. "I don't have experience with these types of weapons. Maybe we can work on that more?"

"I'll be sure you get the hours in. Few people walk through the door knowing how to wield these. But medieval soldiers spend hours a day practicing their tactics. We may not train as much to win a war, but I'll see to it that you can survive a battle." Caleb lifts his goblet with a nod and brings it to his lips.

"And who trained you?"

Caleb sets the goblet down without taking a sip. A frown spreads across his sullen face, and there is a heaviness in his eyes that sends a shiver up Rueben's spine. His brows dig into his nose, and he looks up at Reuben with eyes full of fire.

"Adam Drazen," Caleb says, the whisper echoing in the still chamber.

Reuben's heart collapses into his stomach. The name is like poison as it courses through his veins.

"It was before he lost his damn mind," Caleb continues. "He used to be a soldier, too, you know."

Reuben tries to imagine what kind of soldier would ever betray those closest to him and kill them. A soldier's duty is to protect his brothers and sisters in arms not slaughter them. Reuben tries to imagine, but he can't.

"Hey, man, we're going to find him. Don't worry about that," Caleb says.

"I'm not worried. It's just I... How do you face someone like that without knowing anything about them?"

"Knowing about him or actually knowing him?"

Reuben shrugs. "Both. Either. I don't know."

"Well, that's what all this is about." Caleb pauses to take his drink. "Basic time-traveling missions don't require a lot of training. But you see, this isn't about doing a few missions. This is about catching him. Adam Drazen is the fastest, most adaptable, smartest, strongest traveler who has ever come through Chronos. Hell, he helped put it together and named the damn thing. You'll learn how to fight him and, together, we'll work to beat him." Caleb grabs the sword from the table and throws it handle first to Reuben, who catches it. He then turns and reaches for another sword hanging on one of the walls. "How about I beat the crap out of you for a while until you can put up a decent fight?"

Reuben raises his sword and smiles. "I thought you said earlier that you didn't want to waste time?"

The two continue training for the next several hours, covering the very basics. Caleb goes over a broad spectrum of medieval weaponry, from swordsmanship to archery, to armored defense using a shield and even the basics of group line formations.

"All right, Staff Sergeant, not bad for your first session," Caleb says. "As the weeks go by, we'll get into some more interesting stuff. Wait until we start shooting muskets. Those things are a pain in the—" Lights pierce into the chamber as the weapons and other items begin to vanish, and the walls fade into the void. "It's about that time."

"Looking forward to next time," Reuben says, looking around the empty cell. "So, do I just wait for the ..."

Caleb nods toward a spot behind him. There, set against the vacuum in space, is a door. Its deep, walnut finish glows bright against the blackness that holds it. Reuben's legs push him forward without thought as his eyes marvel at something that would seem so ordinary in any other setting.

A burning sensation sears his flesh as he grasps the handle. The pain tingles to the bone but doesn't linger. He pulls away and inspects his palm. It's neither burned nor hot, or even warm. It's freezing cold touch and the surrounding balmy air only intensifies the stinging sensation.

"You're going to need that," Caleb calls out from behind.

Before Reuben can ask what he needs, he notices a coat rack to his left that had not been there before. He grabs the only coat there is, wraps it tight against his chest, and buttons it up.

Odd. No zipper.

Using a pair of gloves that he finds in the coat pocket, he opens the door and walks across the threshold.

It's white all around. The streaming winds sweep and batter his entire body with snow and ice, pounds at a time. The unforgiving gust forces itself onto him from every direction, compelling his eyes to a narrow squint. The dense air slices through his coat and gloves. His muscles contract violently for warmth. Blood retreats from his lips, nose, chin, and ears as they tingle in numbness. He struggles to keep his eyes open, the cold and wet flooding past his eyelashes to obscure his view. He steps back toward the door to regain his bearing, but it's gone.

Suddenly, something grabs his arm. He turns to it as he hears his name cutting through the wailing wind.

"Reuben," the muffled voice says over the blizzard's fury. He manages to open his eyes just long enough to see him. Alex's silhouette lies cloaked in layers of apparent warmth. Reuben can almost feel the heat coming from him.

"Follow me." Alex hands him the end of a rope tied to his waist. With Alex leading the way, the two of them begin trudging through feet of snow. Varying in depth between knee and thigh height, the snow layering the ground gives way to their movement but not without resistance. Every grueling step forces the accumulation of snow to compact. Each flurry that contacts Reuben's legs melts against his heat only to reanimate as ice moments later.

His thick wool coat works overtime to trap the heat so desperate to abandon him. His shoes, neither insulated nor waterproof, give way to the cold and wet until his feet lose all feeling.

Couldn't they have given me snow boots?

The hike continues for what seems to be an hour, though Rueben has no way to tell. Memories from his basic training flood his senses. Numbed fingers and air that pierced his lungs like knives. It was nearly a decade ago, seventeen degrees below at Fort Leonard Wood, Missouri. He can still picture the water canteens that froze solid in minutes. The voice of his drill instructor echoes in his head, yelling at him to, "Hurry the hell up." Only the misery of it all, the bitter relentless cold, had kept him distracted, kept him from panic.

And it keeps him still.

He had tightened his grip on his rifle and squinted down range, the pop-up silhouette against his iron sights. It was the bitter second before the trigger pull, when the frozen ground absorbed his shivering legs into frozen submission.

Embrace the Suck.

The ancient military mantra passed down to him from the aging careerists. It's never left him and is now the single thought gluing his eyes on Alex and driving his steps forward.

If warmth is life, then cold must be death.

"We're almost there!" Alex's voice carries to him. In the distance is a small lone cabin in the middle of an arctic plain. Its amber finish bleeds against the diverse colors of the looming sunset. In the misery and exhaustion of cold he sees it.

Beauty.

Splendor.

Light in the darkness.

They rush inside to be greeted by the flowing heat of the fireplace. Reuben tears off his gloves as he falls to his knees. A dull aching pain floods his limbs as they reanimate beside the fire. After a few minutes, he shakes it off and jumps to his feet. He finds Alex warming up a small kettle in the kitchenette.

"Where are we? Wait. Let me guess. 'It doesn't matter where you are. What matters is—"

"Situational Awareness," Alex interrupts. "Yeah, that's the

kind of thing Caleb Jones would say. And he's not wrong. That's part of why we got here, okay." He removes the kettle from the burner, pours the liquid into a mug, and hands it to Reuben. The steam hits Reuben's face as he looks down into the dark substance.

"It's black tea," Alex says. "It'll help to get your core back to temperature. You should also take those shoes and socks off and let them dry." Reuben removes them and lays his damp footwear beside the fireplace. "And it's okay to ask where you are. This session is going to be very different from what you and Caleb went over."

"And where is this place?" Reuben says, sipping the bitter tea as his pruned feet warm beside the fire.

"We're still in the training room."

"What? I saw the section before we started. It was the size of a room."

"And it still is...sort of. I know it looks like we traveled to a twentieth-century cabin in the Yukon, but we didn't. It's part of how the training room works. You see, the residual energy from Chronos doesn't only separate the spacetime between training areas, it can also replicate environments that we have previously traveled to."

"So, the medieval chamber and this Yukon arctic thing, these are places that you guys have been to before?"

"Exactly." Alex pours himself the remainder of the tea as Reuben continues to rub warmth into his fingers.

"Why not just make the entrance directly into the cabin?"

"Entrances and exits are usually fixed and based on where the initial travelers went. Technically speaking, though, it can be moved around, but Paul chooses to keep them where they are."

"So, trainees can freeze to death in a blizzard?"

Alex sighs. "In theory, it's supposed to teach you to adapt to the environment. Most of the time, we're prepared. Sometimes, we're not. It's why you were provided a coat...and, sadly, no appropriate footwear. I'm sorry about that part. If I ran the curriculum, I'd—"

"Don't worry about it," Reuben interrupts. "I get it. Sure sucks, but I get it."

"So, how much did Paul explain to you about our missions?"

"Not much. I mean, I think Sky told me more than he did. She mentioned that we'd go back in time to interact with people and places."

"How about the restrictions?" Alex asks.

Reuben shakes his head.

"Déjà vu?"

Reuben continues to shake his head.

"Man, we have a lot to cover." Alex takes a long sip of his tea and sets it back down. "Oh well, I guess we have time. Let's just start the communications training, and I'll fill you in as things come up. Sound good?" Before Rueben can say anything, Alex continues, "Good! Let's get started."

Alex walks over to a nearby closet door and pulls out a large, heavy-duty storage case. As he opens it, Reuben stands up to peer inside. Before he can get a good look, Alex tosses him a smaller hand-held black box.

"What's this supposed to be?" Reuben asks.

"Open it."

After setting the lightweight container on the table, Reuben undoes the latches and pulls off the plastic cover. Inside lies what appears to be a small earpiece and a remote transponder of some sort.

"The little one goes into your ear, and the bigger piece clips to your belt. This will keep you in touch with the team on the ground as well as HQ."

"So, it's just a headset?"

"Hey," Alex fires back. "It's a time-traveling headset. Give it some credit. Let's see what gadget you can come up with that lets you talk to people while traversing through spacetime." Reuben laughs as he puts on the headset. "Good. Now, the operation of that is straightforward. There are three buttons. The one closest to your belt buckle is the frequency that transmits locally to whoever is presently traveling with you, usually our team. The button in the middle will link you straight to headquarters, and the far one transmits to both. Easy enough?"

"Easy enough. So that's communications?"

"That is internal communication. The easy stuff. It's how we talk to one another on our side. The real challenge is what we'll spend most of our time on. External communications."

"External? As in the people we run across?"

"Exactly. Countless diverse types of people across many different periods and cultures. And it's not just how we talk to them. We have to dress the part and play the roles, blend in as much as possible."

"What's the point of assimilation if we can't change things? Wait, can we change things? Sky said that we couldn't."

"No, she's right; we can't alter history." Alex smirks before continuing, "This is actually where we diverge from your typical science fiction time travel nonsense."

Reuben leans forward, giving Alex his full attention.

"Changing things in time is not only dangerous but a theoretical headache. To keep things safe and practical, Chronos was written to ensure past events could never be altered. We go somewhere, we interact, we collect information, and we leave. History never records us. You could go back hundreds of years and straighten the Tower of Pisa, and by the time you returned to our time, it would still be leaning."

"Huh, I see. So going back and killing Hitler?"

"Ha!" Alex shakes his head. "Feel free, man. You wouldn't be the first to do it. Before the change in management, people would do it to blow off steam. Seems a bit morbid if you think about it. But, in the end, it doesn't change what happens to him, history, or the world. It's like being part of an interactive movie. You can pause, rewind, and take notes. But when it is said and done, beauty kills the beast, Dorothy wakes up, Bogie and Bergman will always have Paris, and frankly, my dear, I don't give a damn."

"So, why blend in?"

"Oh, right, sorry, your original question. It has no long-term impact. In the short term, though, people will always react accordingly. It is much easier to collect information and have a safe mission if the locals don't think you're a space alien or some magic sorcerer."

Makes sense.

"Now, there are plenty of other restrictions and such about Chronos, but we'll just have to go over them as they come."

Alex pulls out several items from the chest, including various clothing. For the next few hours, he trains Reuben how to blend into basic time periods. First, they walk through several adaptation methods followed by basic conversing.

"The key here is to be quick to listen and slow to speak. Don't be too eager to spout your mouth off about your interpretation of the time. Let the people speak for themselves. Observe first, then emulate carefully. For example, you travel to the Middle Ages in England, and someone tells you they've had an awful sweven. What are they talking about?"

"I don't know," Reuben says.

"A dream. They've had a terrible dream."

"How on Earth would I know that?" Reuben clenches his teeth in frustration.

"Lots of research. Books and the internet will tell you much of what you need to know. Just keep in mind that it won't tell you everything. History says that James Madison is the father of the Constitution. What history books seem to be shy about is what someone was like as a person. How did Madison treat his wife? Did he have nervous habits or quirks? Nothing substitutes being on the ground and learning firsthand. This is what's so groundbreaking about the project. It allows us to see things for what they really were. And hopefully, use that information to push congress members and other powerful types to make good decisions. Through political back channels, of course. This shit is super secret."

Reuben rubs his face, trying to make sense of it all as he stares at the line between floor and fireplace. Alex's hand greets his shoulder.

"Hey, man, don't let this overwhelm you. You'll have plenty of time to train and most of all you have us. We've all been through it, and we'll make sure you will too. Not even the Stewards figured all of this out in a day."

Alex's words bring a welcomed sense of ease. "Thanks," Reuben says, nodding. "I'm sure things will be all right. Just been a crazy week. You know?"

"No doubt, man. Believe me when I say the weeks get shorter from here on out."

"Yeah." Reuben smiles before pausing. "Stewards?" He watches as Alex's smirk dissipates, leaving his face's muscles lonesome in search of any way to mask its discomfort.

"Kind of a sensitive topic around here...for another day." Alex shifts his body toward the case, picking up the various items on the ground and placing them back into the container. "We should get going. There's still a practical exercise we need to get to before you move on to the next session."

"Uh, yeah, sure," Reuben says, tilting his head slightly. "Sounds good." He has to find out more....

I need to get to my father's journal... Just have to wait for the right time.

"All right, those boots by the door should be your size. They will keep your feet warm and dry."

Reuben grabs the boots, parts the laces, and slides his feet into them. He straps them tight, feeling its insulated warmth as he wraps the extended laces around the bases hugging his lower calves. Alex throws him a fuzzy cap with goggles that lands on his lap.

"There, that should do it."

Reuben slips on the hat and follows him out the door.

The thin cold air strikes his nostrils, the sharp chill piercing his lungs. He looks out over the tundra, less visible now. The color wheel sunset from earlier has faded. The blackness of the trees and the white of snow sweeping across them are the only colors that remain.

"The temperature drops to about negative forty at night," Alex says as Reuben investigates the dark. "Good thing you have that cap."

"So, the weather, sunlight, air, and everything else are recreated in this training room?"

"For the most part."

As they walk farther into the tundra, the visibility continues to diminish. Reuben turns his head back after what feels like an eighth of a mile. The cabin's light struggles to reach them. Eventually, only a faint glimmer glistens before vanishing altogether. The goggles allow him to keep his eyes open but serve little else. The constant flood of pounding snow against darkness fills much of his vision. The relentless wind sweeps across them like a river whose powerful current is forever fixed. If it weren't for the headset communication device, they would not be able to hear one another through the whipping of the wind.

They eventually reach the base of a tall rock formation. While looking up at the hundred-foot monstrosity, Reuben keeps walking before almost running into Alex. From a dead stop, Alex's shoulders go limp as he stares in silence at the wind.

"Hey," Reuben says through the headset.

Alex turns to him, opens his arms, and tackles him. They jolt back several feet, crashing into the ice and snow.

"What the—"

Before he can get out any more words, a thunderous wave of force shakes the ground and thrusts both of them back even further. Reuben's head spins as his fingers reach out to grab onto anything. He comes to consciousness with Alex pulling him out of a thick layer of snow.

"Are you okay?" Alex says.

"Yeah, I'm good." Reuben shakes off the snow as he attempts to regain his footing. Before he can ask what had happened, his eyes widen and jaw drops.

The path.

Gone.

In its place, a boulder the size of a pickup truck. His mouth somehow falls further as he continues to stare where they had stood only moments ago. Death had been lurking from above, patiently waiting to send its fury down on them.

He just saved my life.

"How did you know?" Rueben says.

"Déjà vu."

"What?"

"I saw it happening before it actually did. It's something that Chronos does at odd times. We're not really sure why. But, sometimes, it will give you a flash of what is about to happen. The thing is, though, you can never change what you see, what Chronos shows you. The only reason I was able to get us out of the way in time is because that is exactly what I saw happen. If I were to have seen us get crushed, then we wouldn't be talking right now."

A rush of blood pulsates through his body from the adrenaline. "This environment, it can kill us? Even if it's controlled?"

Alex nods. "History is written, and we can see its writing, but when we interact with it, when we move through it, we are the anomaly. We are the thing that introduces chaos to a world that we were never meant to be in. When we go on missions, there will be danger and possibly even death. At the end of the day, we are the biggest instability."

Reuben can hear his father through Alex's voice. After ten years, he can still recognize Nolan Greyson's deeply held belief in entropy. People have made a mess of history.

We should change that.

"All right," Alex says. "It's time to move on to round three of today's training."

"No practical exercise?"

"Will have to take a rain check." Alex flips a switch on his communications belt. "Phase three ready."

Looking over Alex's shoulder, Reuben no longer sees the enormous rock. Instead, a sizeable door-shaped void stands against the blizzard. "Yeah, no door handle this time. Just walk right through, the same concept as before."

Reuben moves past Alex toward the void, turning back at the last second. "Thanks."

"What for?"

"For that. You just saved me."

Alex smiles. "What choice did I have?"

6

A PARADOX OF TEMPESTS

The sun and wind compete to outdo one another. With no cloud in sight, the rays of the sun work to bake the flesh of anything in its path while the wind screams violently across the sea, sending massive waves to rock the large wooden vessel. Those on deck would be hard-pressed to hear anything other than the piercing sound of static force.

Sky can taste the salt in the air, and she hates it. She's an Air Force girl, destined to be among the clouds. Ships are a necessary evil, and unfortunately, one that she is forced to face in this line of work.

Clinging onto the wooden railing, Sky stares at the churning sea, and her stomach turns to butter. It's not just the boat that bothers her; it's the memories that the sea trudges up. He had proposed to her on the beach, and she said yes. They had stood in the surf. The waves swirled in chaos and went every which way, but her love for him was sure and solid. She was the immovable object and what was thrown at her was an unstoppable force.

It was a paradox from the start.

If either gave way, it would fail to be true.

"He should be here any second," Kirk says through the headset as they grip tight to the ship's mainmast for balance. Towering masts loom above them, propelling the sixteenth century longboat through the open waters. Sky's attention snaps away from the waves and fixates on Kirk.

"We couldn't have met him somewhere a little less..." Kirk pauses as the color flees his cheeks. His fist jerks to his mouth in a poor attempt to cork the bile, desperate to escape. Wiping his hand with a wave of disgust, he continues, "Sea-sicky?"

"That would defeat the point," Sky says, avoiding Kirk's mess lest she succumbs to her own nausea. "History is brutal. It's not always for the faint of heart..."

Kirk digs his fingernails into the wooden railing, leans over, and pukes into the sea.

"Or stomach, apparently. Besides, sometimes you have to be able to run before you can walk," Sky says, averting her eyes.

Kirk regains his footing and takes a few deep breaths. "I'm sorry," he says. "But let me see you try to run in this shit."

"It's just something people say, you know, a metaphor. Like killing two birds with one stone."

"I'd kill ten birds with a stone right now if it would make this boat stop."

"Don't be so dramatic. You're supposed to be a deputy navigator. I know you got out of training not so long ago yourself, but I wouldn't have picked you if you weren't up to it."

Kirk wipes his lips and looks down at the putrid mess on his hand. His nose crinkles as though he is just smelling the foul sick for the first time. His hand quivers as the color flushes from him again.

Sky pats his back as Kirk heaves into the sea below, careful to keep her eyes on the horizon. "Come on, Captain Kirk, just a few minutes, and we'll be on dry land."

A scream cuts through both wind and headsets. Kirk and

Sky look up just in time to see Reuben stumble-running across the main deck, barreling toward them, barreling toward the ship's edge. She watches as Reuben attempts to pull back against gravity as the waves tip the vessel in its favor. Sky extends her arms to catch him, but it's futile. He's unstoppable, like the waves crashing on the shore the day she said yes. They collide, and all go overboard.

She's weightless, and time is infinite.

The wind, sky, and sea fade into the background, waiting for the penultimate moment.

Then it comes.

Sky's back slams flat across the water, the surface burning into her skin. Then it takes her, swallowing her whole. Salt penetrates her nose, throat, and pores. Waves batter her body as she searches for the surface through a murky film of bubbles and chaos.

Then she sees it.

A stream of light piercing from above.

The surface, the clouds, and that sweet, sweet air guide her.

Sky kicks with all her might, only the drag from her cargo pants holding her back, but it's not enough. The water gives way as she inhales a large breath of fresh air.

A wave rolls over her face. It passes, and she opens her eyes, watching as Kirk himself breaks the surface, realizing that he, too, went overboard. Another wave passes, pushing her closer toward the ship. She resists and swims against it, treading further out to look for Reuben. Sky turns to Kirk. "Anything?"

Kirk burps up saltwater in response.

Sky sighs. "Go ahead. Double tap. I'll meet you there."

She returns to her search. The seconds grow long and slow as her heart races. If Reuben is underwater, then time is against them both. She shouts his name but no answer. She dives down below the surface.

Nothing.

Before panic can set in, she breathes. She doesn't think about it. She just breathes.

He was on the swim team. His file. It said he swam. He's disoriented, not drowned.

Still, no one can hold their breath forever. Another wave strikes her, and she embraces it, diving deeper this time. The salt stings her eyes, but now she barely notices. The murky water and seaweed may cloud her vision, but her sight is hyper focused. A glimmer dances in and out of her peripheral vision. Eyes narrowing, she pinpoints its source through the swirling murk and kicks with all she's got. A shimmer of metal materializes, clinging to a silhouette.

Reuben's silhouette.

He's treading water and disoriented.

Panicked and quickly losing oxygen.

But he's alive.

Sky reaches him, grabs his shoulder, and double taps her watch. A light comes over them as the water fades.

* * *

Reuben squints as the light consumes him. The roaring echo of waves ceases. His arms and legs move unrestrained by the drag of the sea. He's standing, feet on solid ground. In seconds, the light begins to fade in on itself. He's no longer underwater or anywhere near it. He takes a deep breath and looks around as the sun's rays warm his pruned skin. He crouches and rubs his hand against the rocky surface before looking out at the sea; its salty stench and hazel coloring remain the same, but its roaring waves have all but subsided. The image is peaceful but somehow manages to rope knots in his stomach.

He turns to find Sky directly behind him. Kirk stands only a few feet away from them, color returning to his pale skin.

Falling to the ground, Kirk clings tight to a nearby rock. "Thank you!" he yells. "Thank you for not feeling the need to rock and move and sway and throw me into the freaking ocean!"

Sky shakes her head. "Hey, if you are done being dramatic, we have some training to do." She secures her drenched hair in a ponytail and looks back at Reuben. "Excuse my deputy. He can get a bit motion sick. Are you good?"

"Yeah," Reuben says. "I had some milk earlier. It really coats the stomach." He cracks a smile.

"Told you."

"What the hell just happened? We were out there, and now...now we're...here. And the light. What was that?"

"Here," Sky says, handing Reuben what appears to be a black and white smartwatch. "That's how. And now you have one of your own." Both Kirk and Sky hold up identical watches on their respective wrists to show him. "This is what connects us to Chronos and the Observer."

Reuben wipes off stray water droplets from his left wrist and straps on the watch. "You mean the Observer from the front of the training room?"

"That's it," she says. "In order to go in and out of time periods, Chronos needs to be anchored to the Observer's perspective. Of course, since the Observer itself is in the motion of time, it's not completely fixed. But it does give us a frame of reference when traveling. The Observer's perspective, where Chronos is housed, is what we call 'present time.' What we are experiencing now in this environment is what we call 'local time.' These watches act as a link between the Observer and where we are now. It even displays both time periods."

"Huh, interesting." Reuben looks down at the sapphire glass display. "So, how was it able to pull us out of the ocean?"

"It's all in the linking," Kirk says, fumbling back to his feet.

"Linking to Chronos lets us travel within a period as well as *to* and *from* the Observer's point of view at headquarters. It's basically your time travel watch." Kirk pauses, smiling. "And it's all kinds of trendy, too. You know, like an urban hipster time traveler."

"Wait. Travel *within* a time period?"

"Yeah," Sky says. "Up to a one-mile radius and one hour forward or backward. We're about three-fourths of a mile from the ship and about an hour in the past before the wind picks up. That's why the sea is calm, and we're on land. The watch will take anything in contact with it. All I had to do was grab you and activate the watch to what I had preset it to."

"Preset? You knew we were going to be overboard?"

"No, not exactly. I was hoping to be on the boat when we time jumped, but I guess the lesson is to be prepared for anything."

"And just to let you know," Kirk says, wiping his mouth, "if this was in-mission Chronos, Sky wouldn't have been able to jump you without you also wearing a watch."

"Huh?"

"And not just that," Kirk continues. "Jumping within a time period is also something we're only able to do in a training environment. These features help us quickly change a scenario without moving to another section. It's a cool thing that trainers use, but don't get used to it. Once we start using Chronos's main portal to go on real missions, watchless travel is a no-go. We're stuck in a single local time until we get back. So basically, time elapsed in destination will be time elapsed when we return to HQ."

"Why is that?"

"Dude, I'm sure there is a reason for everything. But honestly, who the hell knows. Or cares. When it comes to Ops, we just learn the rules and play by them. Leave it to the lab coats to worry about why the rules are that way and how they work."

"Kirk's right," Sky says. "Chronos gives us time, just not all the time in the world." She walks up to Reuben and lifts his wrist so that his watch faces him. "If you take the time to play around with it, you'll see it's pretty intuitive. The Observer's present time is at the top and the local time is at the bottom. The green chain link you see between them lets us know that Chronos has authorized our location. If you try to put in an unauthorized time and place, it'll display a broken red link."

"Why would something be unauthorized?"

"Dang, this guy asks a lot of questions," Kirks says with an exaggerated sigh.

"They're good questions." Sky snaps back as she rolls her eyes before refocusing on Rueben. "This is another example of how the rules work. Some things are authorized, some aren't. Draw your own conclusions as to why. Just know what we do is heavily regulated."

As they continue training, Reuben's thoughts wander. The waters of the nearby ocean may be calm, but a tempest rages within him. Fantasies of changing history's past and his own begin to surface.

No Hitler, no Genghis Khan, no Adam Drazen.

But why would they put chains on something that could change the world for the better?

His mind jumps to the problematic issues of paradoxes, intersecting timelines, and butterfly effects.

But that's why you have a team of physicists, like my fa— *Maybe that's what he wanted. To change things. And Drazen killed him for it.*

The many suns of the training room set, closing out his grueling first day. Reuben spends the next few weeks sparing with Caleb, becoming more proficient in fourth-dimensional communications alongside Alex and time-hopping his way through different environments with Sky and Kirk. What would have taken months to accomplish in a traditional setting takes only a few short weeks from the Observer's perspective. Unfortunately for Reuben, the shortcut does not apply to him. The hours, days, and weeks stretch longer. He travels the long way, out-aging his trainers.

7

FINAL EXAM

The street buzzes with the hum of life in the city. Pedestrians brush past with hurried steps. Vehicles trudge along the roads in the jerking pattern of heavy traffic as horns voicing their displeasure. Steam vapors and carbon exhaust collide throughout the city before dissipating in its accent, racing to topple the steel beams of new skyscrapers.

"Chicago Municipal Airport, now open! Read all about it!" a boy says from the street corner, his voice rising above the cacophony of the vibrant city surrounding him. Rueben tries to slip past him, but the boy blocks him with the paper.

"Only two cents, mister. All your news right here."

Reuben grabs the newspaper from the boy and hands him a nickel with a wink.

"Don't spend it all in one place, kid," Reuben says.

"Gee, thank you, mister!" the boy says with a grin.

Reuben peers over his shoulder before leaning in toward the boy. "Listen, Son. Do you know where a man can get a drink around these parts?"

The boy mirrors Reuben's action before adjusting his flat

cap. "Down the next block," the boy whispers. "It's on Broadway. Look for the windmill. It's small, easy to miss."

Reuben tips his fedora to the boy, drops his newspaper back on the stack, and veers toward Broadway.

"Hey, mister!" the boy says, jutting out the paper. "Your paper!"

"Keep it. More inventory, more dough."

"You sure, mister? Lot of stuff happening this week. Feds really coming down on bootleggers. You should keep yourself informed."

"I'm not too worried about it, kid." Reuben smiles. "Different headlines, but the paper's always the same. Take care of yourself." He tips his hat and continues down the sidewalk.

The Windy City's winter air forces its pedestrians to huddle close to one another as they move along the sidewalk. Footsteps, Model T engines, and marketplace shouts fuse, replicating the rhythm of the era's early Jazz sound. Reuben's steps continue, but his mind pauses to admire the setting. No cell phones, social media, or other societal disconnects. The people around are engaging in conversations, aware of their surroundings. The city's sense of liveliness stirs up a feeling of nostalgia for an age he never knew. Its surreal vibrancy transports him from a once imagined black and white world to one of full color.

His suit is a custom fit, hugging his physique with quality, comfortable material. He looks around and sees it everywhere. Three-piece suits, leather oxfords, and wool fedoras. It's a fashion that sings of class among the commoners. A big band performance where everyone knows the beat.

How did all of this go out of style?

Strolling down Broadway, Reuben eyes a series of red brick buildings. He nearly passes it before doing a double take. Above a doorway is an engraving so small and inconspicuous that most passersby would think it were a chip if they'd even noticed at all. Stepping closer, the lines of the strange object take shape, forming the very thing his cold, shivering body has been searching for.

Windmill.

If the boy hadn't said it, Reuben might not have been able to recognize the shape.

He steps up to the door beneath the engraving. A small, eye-level slide opens.

"It's dry out today." A gruff voice says through the slit.

"Well, then, let us bring on the rain," Reuben says without missing a beat. The slide shuts and the clanking echo of unhinged locks releases the door into the darkness beyond. He steps inside and his pupils grow toward the dim lighting in the small closet-sized room. As he makes his way to the center, two men in pinstriped suits pat him down.

"Welcome," a third man says with a Chicago accent. Reuben peers over his shoulder, seeing the thick velvet curtain separating them from the forbidden haven.

"Guns and knives we don't care much about," the man continues. "So long as you check em in, we're good." The man steps forward, inches from Reuben's face. "Badges, on the other hand...uh, let's just say that would raise some serious concerns. You're not here to raise serious concerns to this fine establishment, are you?"

"No guns and no badges," Reuben says. "The only weapon I have is thirst."

"Ha," the man chuckles. "Kid, that may be the most dangerous weapon of all, according to Uncle Sam. That makes you family here." He pulls back the velvet curtain behind him. "Try not to get into too much trouble. Mr. McGurn expects all his patrons to be civil with their liberties, you follow?"

"Completely. No trouble here." The smooth velvet gives way to a plume of cigar smoke as he enters the speakeasy. Its tendrils grab ahold of him, desperate to fill every crevice of his suit with its bitter perfume. His nostrils flare as the hairs within start to char. He looks across the hazy space filled with tables, patrons, and malfeasance before fixating on the bar. The live jazz massages his eardrums, romanticizing the seconds it takes to reach the bar.

"I'll take a coffin varnish," he says to the bartender. The man nods without a word.

"Not a bad way to start the evening," the person beside him says.

Reuben turns toward Alex. "What makes you think I'm starting? It's also not quite evening." The bartender sets his drink down, pausing just long enough to look between the two. Rueben nods and lifts his glass to the light above the bar, staring at its foggy appearance. Alex smirks as Reuben tips it back. The drink scorches his tongue and throat. He neither flinches nor cringes, he only sighs.

"So far, so good. You're dressing the part and speaking the lingo." Alex takes a sip of his watered-down whiskey. "But like I said before, you need that little something else. You've been sitting in that seat for more than two minutes and have yet to light a cigar. You have to think about how people perceive your behavior."

Reuben pulls out two stogies from his vest pocket. "Is that your way of asking for one?"

"Hey, man, we'll encounter plenty of passive cultures. But this. This isn't it. I'll take one of those." Alex plucks the cigar from Rueben.

"You know, you've been sitting here longer than me. How do you think you're being perceived?" Handing Alex a match, the two of them light their cigars simultaneously.

"Not my final exam." Alex puffs his cigar. "Good catch, though. I was wondering how much you'd notice. Most people who come through don't think about that. They're so obsessed about how they're doing that they forget the world around them."

"Yeah." Reuben spits out tiny bits of tobacco from the poorly cut end. "I have to say, though. This is impressive the way you guys were able to capture every detail. At least it looks that way. Can't say I've been here, but it's almost like we really traveled to 1927 Chicago. How do you do it? I get the environment stuff—like before. But the people?"

"It's a carbon copy. Sure, there are certain things we tweak, but the people are as they were for the most part. I don't know exactly how it happens. The lab techs can probably give a better answer. I do know that it's tricky in the training environment to get it right. That's why we don't encounter many people in 47A. Things will be different when we start using the actual Chronos machine. You'll see, man. But for testing purposes, this is what we have."

"Why don't we just use Chronos for testing?"

"Well, for starters, we need a controlled environment. Something we can replicate again and again."

"We can't do that with—"

"No," Alex interrupts. "Even if we wanted, the rules are set up to where we can't. It won't allow us to go to the same place more than once, at least not within the same hour."

"Wait, why?" Reuben shakes his head with a grunt. "Never mind, I'm sure it's one of those 'it's just the rules' kind of thing that I have to accept and not think about."

"It is part of the rules. Just don't beat yourself up about your questions. I'd be more concerned if you weren't asking any. It lets me know that you're really thinking through things and not just going through the motions. And with three kids at home, I've gotten pretty good at distinguishing. Just remember, when we are 'out there,' it is the right questions that will keep you safe."

"In that case, how is my evaluation going?"

"You're a 'GO' at this station, Staff Sergeant." Reuben stops shy of taking the next sip of his drink, realizing that he never disclosed his previous rank in the Army to Alex.

"Jones?"

"No. But it doesn't surprise me that he'd know that kind of thing. And even though I, like everyone else, read it in your file, I'd still be able to tell. I was in long enough to know what a good NCO looks like. It's something that you can't hide, much like the fact your accent gives away that you are likely not from around here and might even be a Fed. It would explain why the mobsters here haven't been able to take their eyes off you since you walked in."

"You said I passed." Reuben glances around the speakeasy as stoic faces in pinstriped suits veer in his direction.

"And you did...at this station. This is a comprehensive exam. You still have two rounds left. What comes next is where Jones will pick up." Alex gulps the remaining whiskey in his glass. "I hope you've warmed up."

A stray hand rests on his shoulders. Reuben turns to find Caleb Jones donning similar attire as the other mobsters.

"Sir," Caleb says, "Mr. McGurn has requested to speak with you in the back." Reuben nods and stands up, following Caleb toward the rear of the room. "It'll be a combination of hand to hand and armed combat," Jones says, and Rueben is forced to lean in. "Whatever you do, I'll back you up, but it's your test, so you'll have to take the lead."

"So, I take it that diplomacy isn't an option?" Reuben asks. Caleb snorts, shooting a sly look his way.

"With these thugs? They only understand one thing."

The pianist on stage hammers away at his keys as the controlled riff fills the background. The saxophone cuts through it with ease, subduing the room with a relaxing harmony. Reuben hears the soothing music, but it's the racing of his heart that takes stage as they get closer to McGurn's table. Mobsters from every hidden corner of the establishment begin to emerge from the shadows, their eyes fixed on him. He counts at least five moving toward him, maneuvering as a pack of wolves forcing its prey toward the mouth of their alpha.

A puff of smoke blows out from a darkened table in the distance. Reuben's fingers tingle and his knees buckle as they arrive. The faint orange glow of a cigar's ember brightens then dims as the man behind it takes another drag.

This is him. This is Jack McGurn.

His heartbeat picks up in tempo.

"What's your business here?" the man in the shadows says.

"Just a man enjoying a drink," Reuben says back. The man blows a cloud of smoke into his face, its hazy presence lingering.

"What do you hear?" the man says.

"I'm not sure what—"

"No, really. What are we listening to right now?"

"Music," Reuben answers as a slick-haired man steps out of the booth into the light. His face matches the photo of gangster Jack McGurn. The notorious mobster blows another puff of smoke directly into Reuben's face before walking past him to face the stage.

"Yeah, that's right. Music," McGurn says. "Only something's missing, don't you think?" Looking at the stage, Reuben sees four musicians playing various instruments. "Vocals. It's all there otherwise. Style, form, content. Geez, it's even got some soul. But what it doesn't have is that guide. You know, leadership and a..." McGurn circles back to Reuben. "Structure... Do you know why there are no vocals?"

Reuben shakes his head.

"Because the man who usually sings here did not give me the right answer when I asked him a question. He didn't tell me the truth, so I slit his throat. Doctors think that he will recover, but that rich voice will probably never be the same. Forever gone in some sense. Sad thing, really.

"So, when I ask you what's your business here, I'm looking for the correct answer. I'm looking for a reason to not take away from you something irreplaceable."

Reuben can feel the weight of at least seven men longing to tear him apart, waiting only for the word of their master. "This is the last time that I will ask. What is your business here, Fed?"

"My apologies," Reuben says in between breaths. He knows he needs to calm, but his breathing is getting the better of him. "I'd prefer to talk in the back, in private."

"Few people in your position ask to be taken out of public view. But okay, just know that from here on out, only the right answers mean you leave as you are. Walking, breathing, and intact. You follow?"

"Understood."

Two men grab him from behind and walk him toward the back room of the speakeasy. Looking to his left, Reuben sighs as he realizes that one of them is Caleb. With McGurn leading the way, Caleb and the other mobster shove Reuben into a door. His shoulder breaks the momentum and causes the door to swing open, revealing a lonesome extended hallway. Reuben hears it close behind them.

It's just the four of us.

Not knowing how many of McGurn's men lie ahead, he realizes a two-on-two fight might be the best he'll get.

Without hesitation, Reuben tugs at Caleb's clothing twice. In a synchronized motion, they thrash their weight against the other guard holding Reuben. Before the guard can react, Caleb jabs his fist into the mobster's gut. He swings his elbow to the man's temple. The guard attempts a counterstrike but misses and shakes his head. Caleb leaps behind him and wraps the crease of his elbow against the man's throat, hugging it tighter and tighter until the resistance stops.

Reuben, now free and unbound, looks down the hallway. McGurn stares back at him from only twenty feet away. Any element of surprise fades with the consciousness of the guard.

Like with any exam, knowledge and preparation hold the key to success. Reuben recalls his test prep, learning everything he could about Jack 'Machine Gun' McGurn and prohibition-era Chicago. The countless hours of tactical training fade in thought only to reincarnate in muscle memory. The fears of unpreparedness and physical incompetence are at bay against a brutal gangster and professional boxer like Jack McGurn. He clenches his fist as he approaches his opponent.

McGurn throws the first strike. Reuben jolts his head to the side, evading McGurn's wrath.

He misses.

The window for a counter strike begins to flee. Reuben takes advantage of this window without hesitation and delivers the first punch to McGurn's jaw. An audible *crack* sends a shockwave up his arm. In rapid succession, he strikes McGurn again and again and once more.

McGurn retaliates, jabbing his knuckles into Reuben's chest. Reuben falls back. Before the wind departs him, McGurn's fist forces it back down, striking Reuben's nose and mouth. Reuben's back hits the ground as he gasps for air. McGurn jumps toward him for the finishing blow. Reuben kicks up his leg and thrusts his leather oxfords into McGurn's nose. He kicks again, this time to the chest and twice. Reuben leaps to his feet and forces all his energy behind his fist. It pummels into McGurn's temple, forcing his body to collapse onto itself before colliding with the ground.

He stays down.

Reuben falls back against the hallway's wall and slides down with a heaving breath. Before he can catch his breath, Caleb grabs him by his suit lapels and pulls him to his feet.

"No time to rest," Caleb says while dragging him back to the other end of the hallway. "Still gotta get your ass out of here."

Reuben regains his step, still gasping for air. "No Tommy guns, pistols, not even knives," he says as they approach a door next to the one they had come from. "Just hand to hand with a professional boxer?"

"Any fool can pull a trigger or stab someone. The real test is if you can make a weapon of yourself when you have nothing." Caleb opens the exit door to outside light. "Sky and Kirk are around the corner. You're a pass here. Good luck on the rest."

Reuben darts out of the building and down the alleyway. The late afternoon sun shines bright in contrast to the dim lighting of the speakeasy. His eyes race to adjust. While running toward the street corner, he can begin to make out two figures at the end of the alley, standing in the shadows.

It's Sky and Kirk.

He stops shy of colliding with his trainers. "We need to get out of here," he says in between gasps.

"Well, no shit!" Kirk snaps back. "Did you see the mobsters in there? Pretty sure they're not going to hesitate to slice us up and make us 'sleep with the fishes.'" Both Sky and Reuben glare at him. "What? I don't want to wait around for a horse head to come flying at me!"

"This isn't the freaking *Godfather*!" Sky snaps before turning toward Reuben. "I don't want to tell you how to take your exam, but those men are coming. There are worse things that can happen here besides failing a test."

Reuben nods. "Sitrep on Alex and Jones?"

"They got out."

"Okay, good." He looks around. "There's too much foot traffic and not enough signal to uncloak our watches. But if we run down two blocks north, it should be open enough to link to HQ and get the hell out of here." Before they can move, the speakeasy back door swings open and slams against the brick exterior wall. The shockwave of metal against brick amplifies in the narrow alleyway.

"Hey, there he is!" says a voice from the rear of the alley. A swarm of mobsters flows from the door, filling the space between the two buildings. Many of them fumble to pull out automatic machine guns from underneath their coats

"Go!" Reuben shouts, pushing Sky and Kirk ahead of himself. The bullets will have to strike him first. The metallic slides of Thompson submachine guns echo as they round the corner toward the main street. No one looks back. Rapid bursts send lead and chunks of wall and debris hurtling in their direction. They turn another corner. The intensity and sound of gunfire increases.

They're getting closer.

The veins on his neck stretch against his skin as his pulse quickens. They may outrun the gangsters, but nothing outruns bullets.

"Turn here!"

Sky and Kirk comply, veering into another alley. Reuben knows they must keep from the line of the Tommy guns' iron sights.

Taking the long way to the rendezvous site, he keeps his trainers in front, using his own body as a shield of last resort.

No one gets left behind.

They reach their destination just in time for Reuben to activate his watch, grab hold of Sky and Kirk, and transport out of the testing area. The light brightens and fades.

The amber dusk sky of the city disappears from his sight. The sounds of gunfire and city traffic go mute. The era, the mission, and the danger are all gone in an instant as a pair of soft blue-green eyes stare back at him. She smiles before breaking eye contact. Reuben glances around at the many faces filling 47A, and all fixate on him. On the ground, he sees Kirk lying on his back, curled into a ball. Reuben extends his hand to him, pulling Kirk to his feet.

"Congratulations." Paul Peterson steps forward from the gathered crowd. "You've passed your exam."

Reuben glances at his trembling hands before responding. "So, I can finally use Chronos?"

"Is that what you thought this was about? Anybody can put on a watch and play time-traveler. That isn't what we were looking for in a candidate."

"Candidate?" the question comes out before any possible meaning can sink in.

"Yes, you were it. And passed."

"What are you talking about?"

"We were looking for something more. Every other candidate in your position failed to do what you accomplished today. It wasn't for lack of knowledge or physical agility. They failed to keep the needs of their team ahead of themselves. We were looking for leadership, Mr. Greyson." Paul reaches into his pocket, pulls out a triangle-shaped badge, and pins it between Reuben's left shoulder and chest. "You're now ready to lead this team and hunt down your father's killer."

Reuben's smile fails to tame the angst raging within. He's not sure if it's something he wants or something he needs. All he knows is that he has it, and it scares the hell out of him. Forward, backward, and everywhere in between. Where he goes, his team will follow. And he better be right.

8

KEYS TO THE PAST

The door snags the draping bell as he enters the diner. Its sharp chime cuts through the mostly empty space like a knife through Styrofoam. Rueben peers over the counter before turning back to the window.

Closed.

It's the same diner he had passed following his father's funeral. Everything then had seemed crisp, sharp, and well defined, much like the famous Nighthawks painting, portraying a 1942 classic evening diner on a street corner. Cherry wood countertops, clean glass windows, and soft leather seating had enticed him to enter. He shakes his head slightly to dispel the image. Standing in the doorway now, he sees it was only a mirage, a beautiful vessel of false promises and dashed hopes. This is where he's come to learn the truth.

He takes two steps forward. The layers of grease and cleaners on the scuffed laminate floors tug at his shoes. He tries not to gag, but the evidence of age and disrepair are everywhere. Dust blankets the baseboards in a layer of neglect. French fry grease and mold mingle into its own exotically disgusting aroma. The few ceiling tiles that remain are worn with holes and water stains. If reality is gritty, this is as real as it gets.

"Sit anywhere you'd like," a voice says from beyond the swinging door behind the counter. Rueben looks across the sea of empty seats before moving toward a booth in the corner. He slides onto the farthest bench, careful to position himself so he can see the entire restaurant. His eyes wander as he makes mental notes of each exit, including the one just a few feet from him. The door behind the counter swings open, and a portly waitress walks through. A small hat is nestled in her peppered hair, complimenting the baby blue aproned dress.

"Can I get you something to drink for starts, darlin'?" she says.

"Coffee, please," Reuben responds with a forced smile. "Black is fine."

"You specting a friend, hun?"

Reuben's eyes dart toward the entrance, and his chest tightens. "I'm not sure."

The waitress raises an eyebrow and tilts her head.

"I'm meeting someone here." Reuben pauses, looking away from the door and back toward the waitress. "Just not sure if they're a friend."

"Well," she smirks, "I'll give ya some time to decide." She departs, shaking her head on the way back to the kitchen. Reuben cannot tear himself away from the front door. The flickering solitary streetlight beyond reveals only desolation. The small, nearly empty establishment appears to be the only beacon of life for miles around.

The waitress returns a few minutes later with a mug and decanter in hand. The sweet yet bold aroma strikes the tip of his nose as she fills the cup.

"Freshly brewed in house," she says.

"Thank you." The liquid within ripples as Rueben attempts to cool it down.

"That's a nice watch you got there." She sets a napkin and spoon beside him as Reuben glances down. "It's classic with the leather. Nothin' fancy, ya know? Just nice. Classic."

"Wish I could take the credit. It was my father's." He closes his eyes and strokes his beard, struggling to maintain composure. "He passed recently."

The waitress places her hand on his shoulder. "Sorry for your loss, dear. I remember when I lost my Pop. Ain't nothin' easy 'bout it. We all took comfort, though, knowin' that he'd always want to be the one to go first in the family. That's just parents, though. Always willing to lay down their life for their kin."

After the waitress walks away, Reuben looks back down at his father's watch. He undoes the clasp, feeling it tight against his wrist, and allows the straps to widen before refastening. As much as the watch means to him, Rueben would give it away in a heartbeat for just another second with its true owner. It's the impossible exchange, he knows. The watch can only now serve as a memento of things forever lost.

As Reuben waits, he thinks of her, and his insides recoil. Not because of her. It could never be her. But because of himself. His teeth chatter as he recalls the moment. She poured her heart out and told him everything. But he couldn't tell her this, at least not then and not now. He cares for her more than she knows, but he couldn't tell her about this meeting.

He couldn't.

The bell on the door chimes, snatching his attention.

It's finally time.

He looks up and sees the person he's been waiting for.

* * *

From beginning to end, I watch it all
Through the perils of venture since the Fall

Yesterday I explored the night
For tomorrow's protection, I bring my fight.

HE CONTINUES to recite the Traveler's Creed in his head as he stares at the words on the page. The crumpled, faded paper is from his father's era of AIC. At least, that's what Paul mentioned when he handed it to him after his final exam initiation. Its origin, its meaning, its purpose remains obscure to him. He folds it and tucks it into his drawer.

Dammit.

After a month of vigorous training and finally getting a day off, this is what surfaces in his mind. He wishes that his thoughts were blank, that there was nothing to dwell on, that he could relax, unwind, and enjoy his day off.

But he can't.

Not today.

Not while sweat oozes down his forehead in his overheated room. Not while the thought of leading his new team into unknown dangerous territories twists knots into his stomach. And especially not while his father's murderer, Adam Drazen, roams free.

Today is not the day.

Pools of perspiration continue to flow from his pores, cooling him down. Staring at the gray walls around him, anxious thoughts filling him, he manages to break a sweat doing absolutely nothing. Reuben paces the small space, trying to put himself at ease. But it won't come.

He must think.

He must work.

He must find Adam Drazen.

The organization is significant, and few of the people he's met had much interaction with Drazen. The person on his team who had spent the most time with him is Caleb Jones. But even those encounters seem to have been brief, inconsequential, and long ago. Unfortunately for Reuben, those who knew Drazen best—the people who may have understood the kind of man capable of eradicating those closest to him—are either dead themselves or missing.

Finding and defeating Drazen. The absurdity of restricted time travel. The grief of losing his father. These thoughts aren't scattered kindling for the fire. They are all branches of the same vine, leading his memory back to the handwritten words on the weathered page.

To my only son, my most precious gift in life.

The rest of the words are a blur. Reuben knows he must get to it.

His father's journal.

With every waking moment spent training, now may be his chance. Now may be the only opportunity to take back what's been hidden away.

Reuben breathes and thinks no more on it. Throwing on a fresh shirt, he dawns a baseball cap and makes his way through the facility. He's careful to keep the brim of his hat downward, concealing his face from nearby security cameras.

The excuses come to him as he strides along the hallways with ease.

The restroom in the cafeteria was too crowded, and I'm only looking for another one. I'm missing a sock and thought it might have slipped out in the facility's laundromat. The north end commissary was out of razor blades, so why not check the east end kiosk.

These will get him to the threshold but not one step beyond.

He knows that if he wanted to, getting authorization would be easy. Searching the shared office space of their fugitive is more than pertinent. It's obvious. But he can't bring himself to do it, to go through the proper channels. If he hadn't found his father's journal, then things would be different. But he did find it, the great secret that seemed to be preserved for Reuben's eyes only. And he must keep it that way, a secret. Opening the restricted space to scrutiny could undo all of it.

His stomach flutters as he approaches the double doors leading to the restricted wing. It's not anxiety that fills him. It's excitement. The adrenaline pumping in his veins and the truth waiting just beyond. If he can get by without an incident occurring and caught on camera, he may be able to slip by undetected. But if he's noticed, if they uncover his deception, it's over.

The doors swing out, and a gaggle of business suits strolls past him. Reuben keeps his head low and shuffles past them and through the double doors before they shut. No one stops him or even seems particularly interested. Even the security cameras he had shot down are still damaged.

Too easy.

In minutes, he finds himself facing the entrance to the restricted room, and his heart stops.

This is it.

With a quick look to either side, Rueben darts into the room. His eyes skirt the dimmed space, and it all comes back to him. The smell of mold. The dust-filled desks lined in a circle as if it were King Arthur's court, and the twelve mysterious souls were his knights. As he approaches his father's nameplate, Reuben's heart picks up tempo. Beyond the desk's surface lies the tangible proof of a truth he's always doubted and never known.

Reuben jolts the handle of the drawer back, pulling it to the floor.

No.

No! Please, no.

He scrambles for the paperclip. Wrenching open the secret compartment, Rueben lets out a muffled gasp. Staring back at him is the drawer's real and hollow bottom. It hits him like a punch in the gut.

"No," he says aloud, looking at the space where his father's journal should be. Time itself subsides from his mind as he grasps the drawer tight to his chest, its sharp metal edges digging into his skin. His one lead, the chance to understand his father, is gone. No answers or comfort could fill the emptiness of that drawer.

A muffle of voices echoes through the door, and time returns to him. He reassembles and returns the empty drawer before departing the room, taking only the tiny paperclip.

Questions surge through his head before reaching the safety of the common areas.

What happened to the journal? Somebody must have taken it. But when? And who would do that? Who else would even know about it?

His mind races to retrieve any remnant of memory from the journal. A single sentence returns to him.

It all started with Croatoan...

The floor squeaks as he stops on the balls of his feet, his mind churning.

The research lab.

During his early days of training, they had mentioned the lab in passing but paid little attention to it. It seemed more a footnote to the project than anything of significant value. But maybe the lab holds more than any of them know. Reuben doesn't hesitate; he barely takes the time to breathe. He just marches toward it, marches toward the research lab.

Though not as large as the 47A training room or as breathtaking as the Chronos platform, the research lab somehow manages to impress him. Housing all known historical, cultural, and scientific archives, Reuben knows he's arrived at the right place. Scattered in a checkered pattern throughout the room are large stationary kiosks, complete with a touch screen catalog that contains all available information from their explorations with Chronos. Reuben approaches the first one he sees and types a single word.

Croatoan.

Reuben's search yields a single result.

The Lost Colony.

Rueben glances to one of the many workspaces lining the wall, remembering Sky's brief. Those offices supposedly contain a three-dimensional workspace to interact with the maps, environments, and writing of anything the teams gathered within Chronos. Grabbing one of the provided green, translucent octagonal disks, Rueben saves the single file and moves toward one of the offices. A familiar voice stops him in his tracks, however. He turns as Alex approaches and tucks the disk into his back pocket.

"Are you seriously working on your day off? Do you ever rest, man?"

"Yeah, of course." Reuben forces a smile, his hand twitching toward his pocket.

"You know, some people like to watch movies or play a round of golf on their days off. Take a veg day, you know?"

"Well, I tried that. But it was too hot in the room, and the internet was out." Reuben glances down, watching as Alex fumbles his own translucent disk in hand. "And you? Why aren't you vegging out on your Saturday?"

Alex's eyebrows leap with a chuckle. "Ha! I wish, man!" After another laugh, he leans in and steadies his tone. "In seriousness, though, when you become a dad of three, vegging becomes one of those rare, unscheduled luxuries. Like finding cash in a parking lot. And believe me, if I didn't have these comlogs to archive," he waves his blue disk, "I'd be frying up some kalbi for our monthly Seung family Korean barbecue."

"That actually sounds really delicious right now."

"It's sure better than the grub they have here, whose molecules have been rearranged in transport. Anyway, we'll have to have you over some time for dinner. My wife will insist at some point...which means you'll come."

"Yeah, I'd like that." Reuben grins, almost forgetting the disk in his pocket as Alex looks past him at the sea of kiosks and computers.

"So, you decided to come out here and do some research?"

Reuben doesn't respond.

"Well, if you need help with anything, I have an eye for details. Not saying that to boast or anything. I just know the stuff in here can be a bit much. It's usually better to have at least two pairs of eyes to look over the archives."

The dance of risk and reward waltzes onto the floor. Trusting Paul is off the table, but could he share with his team? The dealings of this organization seem shady at best, but it's an organization he must work with to catch his father's killer. He looks up at Alex, studying his eyes and concerned expression.

His sincerity is genuine.

"What do you know about the Lost Colony?" Reuben says with a sigh.

"Of Roanoke?" Alex smirks. "I know it might leave you with more questions than answers. Whatcha got?"

Once in the private workspace, Reuben pulls the disk from his pocket and inserts it into the port nearby. The lights dim as a holographic ball the size of a marble appears in the center of the room. Its white surface glows brighter as it expands until it engulfs them in a three-dimensional map.

"Yeah, this is Roanoke, all right," Alex says.

"Why is it called the Lost Colony?"

"Well, it was one of the first English attempts at colonization in the New World. It was after Columbus but before Plymouth or even Jamestown. There were over one hundred settlers who attempted to make Roanoke a permanent establishment. However, when they were running low on supplies, and relations with the natives became more hostile, their leader and governor, John White, went back to England for help. England at the time was going to war with Spain and couldn't afford to send ships and resources back to Roanoke. It wasn't until years later that White returned to the colony, but it was too late by that time. The settlers were gone. No remains, nothing. It's as if they just disappeared out of history."

"How do you just know all that?"

"I was a history major in school. Keep up with it as a hobby."

"Huh," Reuben says with an impressive nod. "So, this is like a dream job for you?"

"Yeah." Alex smiles. "You can say that."

"It's funny. I would've guessed you were a—"

"What? A math major, racist." Alex chuckles.

"Ah, I was going to say communications. You know because you're the—"

"Ha! Can't find work with that degree. At least not in this economy."

Reuben smiles. "I majored in Criminology. And this is my first real 'career' kind of job outside of the uniform."

"Honestly, man, that's a lot of us here. There are some crazy stories of how people ended up at Chronos. I was lucky enough to stumble onto some Area 51 type shit when I was in the Navy. Turns out if you can sign *that* NDA, you're a damn good candidate for time-travel work. And I'll never complain. I can do my forty hours in half the time using the training room and make it to all my kids' events."

Reuben nods in astonishment. "Wait, Area 51?"

"NDA," Alex says, folding his hands. "NDA."

Reuben nods before directing his attention to the map. He stares at it for a few moments, noting the labeled geographic locations. "Where's Croatoan?" he asks. "Not seeing it on the map."

"That's because it's not a place. Well, technically it is, but it's also something else."

"What is it?"

"The million-dollar question."

"So, you don't know what it is?"

"It was a clue the settlers left. Or at least we think it's a clue. They carved that word into a post near the settlement. Many historians believe that it was a reference to where they might have gone. Croatoan was a Native American group that was south of their location. The Croatoan Islands is what they called it. But the truth is we don't know. The writing on that post, along with the letters C-R-O carved into a tree near there, were the only physical clues they left. Anything else is just speculation."

Reuben waves his hand, and the topographic perimeter of the settlement grows. After observing it for several minutes, he sighs and waves again, watching as the entire three-dimensional display collapses into its center like a dying star. The room's lights reactivate.

"They just disappeared," Rueben says, his fingers trailing his chin.

"Yep. And there are at least a dozen theories on that."

"If only we had a machine that would let us explore for ourselves." Reuben smirks.

"Good luck getting authorization. I couldn't even get Paul to sign off on a mission to the Galapagos to find out if Darwin was full of shit."

"I'm not asking for us to storm Normandy or anything too dangerous." Reuben pulls the disk from the port.

"You're not getting it. Paul has one concern."

"Finding Drazen."

"It's more than that, man. Just not less. He'd send us to Normandy on D-Day if he thought it would lead us to Adam Drazen."

"Huh."

"Listen, I'm not trying to talk bad about him. Paul's effective and cares about the project. He's just...particular. Now, if you had some sort of justification to visit Roanoke..." Alex pauses. "Actually, why are you so interested?"

Reuben's mouth opens, but no words follow. Awkward silence lingers, filling the fleeting seconds.

"Ok, I get it. You don't have to tell me, I guess. But whenever you talk to Paul, I hope you have something prepared. You'll have to explain why we're using precious AIC resources to go on the trip. If it has nothing to do with Drazen, you're better off trying to find a connection or forgetting the whole thing. I know it sucks, but that's how things are here now." He turns to exit, but Reuben grabs his arm.

"Alex," Reuben says as he steps around to face him, wondering just how much to tell him.

Then he says it.

"Croatoan." He pauses, the flutter in his chest growing. "It was a word I found in my dad's journal. One page said, 'It all started with Croatoan.' I don't know what else is in the journal. It was in a hidden place when I first arrived, and now it's gone. Someone took it, and I'm not sure who I can trust. I need to know what it means. I need to know why it was in his journal. It might even lead us to Drazen, but with the journal gone, the only way we have a shot at figuring out anything is to go to Roanoke, to the Lost Colony."

"Then to Roanoke we'll go. We may even solve one of this country's greatest historical mysteries on the way." Alex veers to exit again but stops himself. "I get being guarded around here. The truth is we all are in some way. A lot of people died in this place. When you talk to Paul, I would leave out the part about your father's journal." Alex departs, leaving Reuben to his thoughts and the disk dancing on his fingertips.

Less than an hour later, Reuben approaches Paul's office. A

chill of air hits the back of his neck. He extends his arm to knock but stops himself. His fist pulsates in rhythm with his heartbeat. He wiggles his hands free and winds his shoulders, hoping to evict the nervous energy from his body. A full gasp of air flows through his nostrils, filling and stretching his lungs. Reuben lets it out and knocks.

"Come in," a voice says from the other side.

Reuben enters with his back straight and chest out, leaving behind any signs of anxiety.

"Reuben, what do I owe the pleasure?" Paul says, raising his eyebrows even as his fingers fold just beneath his chin.

"Sir, as the new team lead, I've had some ideas about what our first mission should be—"

"Perhaps I wasn't clear earlier." Paul shuffles some papers in front of him before stacking them neatly to the side. "Missions will be dictated by the research findings of our intelligence capabilities. You oversee the operational aspects of the missions while I and others determine the direction we go based on what we know and what we learn. So, listen to me when I say that things will go more smoothly if you stay within your scope." Paul's tone stays flat as if he were reading from an instruction manual. "I apologize if this comes across as harsh, but I hope you understand the significance of these roles."

"I'm not trying to do your job or anyone else's. I came across something that couldn't be ignored. Did some digging and found that it may be worth looking into. I know it's not my forte, that's why I'm coming to you. You can have your other teams validate or whatever. I just wanted to pass off what I found. We may even get a mission out of it."

"Since historical academic research missions have been suspended indefinitely, I assume you're referring to something regarding Adam Drazen." Paul leans forward on his desk. "Well, what do you have?"

"Croatoan," Reuben says. "When that guy was trying to kill

me in my apartment, he whispered it under his breath. Like he didn't want me to hear it." Reuben maintains regular eye contact to conceal the lie. "The research from our archives points to it probably being a reference to the Lost Colony of Roanoke. It might not be anything, but I know what he said. Croatoan means something. This is the chance to find out what. Maybe Drazen's there."

"What makes you think Adam Drazen can time travel?"

"I mean, I don't know. Can he?"

"We're not sure. I am sure that Adam Drazen is a dangerous man who has managed to undermine, outpace, outmaneuver, and outsmart this organization's every task. That includes keeping the people here safe." Paul stands from his desk. "You're right. This may be nothing. It could also be an acceptable starting point. If I authorize this mission, what is the soonest you can have your team ready to deploy?"

* * *

"WE HAVE twenty-four hours to make this happen," Rueben says, addressing the team not long after his meeting with Paul.

"Dude, that seems a little rushed," Kirk says.

"There's an active fugitive on the run. We don't have the luxury of time."

"Really?" Kirk says. "I thought that time was literally the one luxury we do have."

"Look, whether it's time here or time there, time sped up or slowed down, it's all going. Now we can stand here arguing the semantics of time-travel, or we can work our butts off to make sure that we'll meet the deadline."

Kirk rolls his eyes and steps back.

"Hey, soldier," Caleb says. "I know this kid can be a prick, but he's got a bit of a point. If we cut corners in prep time, it could compromise our safety. Especially if we're going into a possibly hostile environment."

"Which is exactly why Kirk won't be deploying with us," Reuben says. "This may be a fact-finding mission only, but there is still a possibility of encountering hostile Natives or less than understanding settlers. So only those with combat experience will be authorized to go. That will be Jones, Sky, Alex, and myself."

Kirk's drooping face looks as if he were a puppy realizing his owner was leaving without him.

"We'll still need you to be our off-site navigator. I just can't put your life at risk," Rueben says, patting Kirk on the shoulder before turning back to the team. "As for the prep time, we can use the residual energy in this training room to turn one day into three. No cutting corners."

Immediately after the briefing, the team goes to work prepping for the mission. Caleb Jones gathers weapons for the period to include rifles and swords. Alex tests and prepares the communications equipment and gathers late sixteenth-century clothing that an early settler might wear. Sky familiarizes herself with the geography of the site of the Roanoke Colony along with the surrounding territory. Toward the end of the extended day, they gather at the front of the training room and take turns briefing each other regarding their subject matter. With weapons, uniforms, and knowledge of the layout covered, the team completes its preparation, leaving the remaining hours for rest.

"Hey," Sky says, locking eyes with him. With everyone else turned in for the evening, they are the last two souls in 47A. "I just wanted to say, you did a good job handling everything today. You put Kirk in his place, and let's face it. He needs that often. Plus, you got Jones to follow along with the plan. He usually doesn't listen to newcomers unless there is something about them that he respects. And Alex, I mean, he's probably the easiest of everyone. He'll go out of his way to be helpful unless you're a jerk, which you don't seem to be."

"And what about you? Why are you following me?"

Sky snickers. "Because you're the team lead." She pauses and looks to the floor. "Actually, I know what it's like to lose a parent, too. My dad was a maintenance worker here until he passed away from a heart attack some years back. It was the hardest thing I had gone through at the time, but I've been able to make peace with it. That chapter in my life is closed. Your father's killer is still at large. You can move forward, sure. But it's hard without closure. I want to help you get him."

"Thanks, that means a lot. I'm sorry for your loss as well. It's crazy both our dads worked here in this building."

"Yeah, it is." She twirls a loose strand of hair around her finger before tucking it behind her ear. "Well, I should get going. We have a long day tomorrow."

"Oh, yeah, of course," he says as she moves past him.

"Also, I have to say." She glances over her shoulder. "Roanoke seems like an odd place to start, but a cool one for sure. It's the kind of trip Chronos was made for. Just too bad we can't go back *before* the disappearance."

Reuben smirks. "Well, it's the rules, right? Those dates are locked out."

"Yeah, guess so. Makes me suspect you're actually on to something."

"Hopefully, the Governor will be able to give us enough clues."

Sky raises an eyebrow. "Clues to find Drazen or solve the mystery?"

"It's all a mystery. Drazen, my dad, Roanoke. Maybe it's all connected, or maybe none of this means anything. Maybe I'm still dreaming."

Sky chuckles.

"What? Too hypothetical?"

"No, it's not that," she says. "I mean, look around. This is where the hypothetical comes to life. It's just funny because I only ever have that thought on the outside. You know, about everything being a dream." Reuben nods, watching as Sky continues toward the exit.

"Uh, hey," he calls out. "Is there any place I could go to around here with a good view? I feel like most of the windows in the facility are small, and there doesn't seem to be anything but vacant flat farmland around."

"I've got a place in mind." She walks over to a rack near a bundle of training supplies. From it, she draws out two winter coats, tossing the larger one to Reuben.

Side by side, they wander from section to section through the facility. They say very little to each other as they walk, leaving a vacancy that Rueben's mind quickly fills.

Did I just do that? Plan a complicated multi-tiered time travel mission in a matter of hours? And they followed me. They listened, and they followed.

Reuben isn't sure why they trust him so easily or why they just went along with no pushback.

Is it my voice? Does it sound like confidence?

The more he thinks about it, the more terrifying it becomes.

Is this what power feels like?

The sound of metal clasping reverberates down the hallway as Sky pushes past a set of double doors. Reuben follows close behind. The hallway is unfamiliar to him. The walls, still cinder blocked, lack the familiar white coat of paint. Only the bare concrete encloses them. The floors, however, glisten and reflect the hanging lights from above. Less than five strides in, a potent smell strikes his nostrils.

Pine oil.

"What is this place?"

"You've been here before, but you were blindfolded at the time. It's how everyone gets in and out of the facility." They round the final corner and reach a set of elevator doors. Sky pushes a nearby button on the wall, and the doors open.

Reuben's stomach shrinks inward.

"No other way?"

Sky shakes her head as they enter. She swipes her badge and types 'Roslyn, VA' on the hologram keypad. Reuben grasps the hand railing tight as the doors close, allowing its steel edge to drive deep into his palms and fingers.

"I remember not feeling very well the last time," he says.

"Yeah, most of us get used to it after a while, but some really struggle. I know this guy who will stay in the facility for weeks at a time just to avoid it."

"Comforting." Reuben grips the railing even tighter.

"Sorry, I wasn't trying to make you feel worse. It'll be over soon. And believe me, it will be worth the brief nausea."

The elevator jerks, and his skin tightens as though a thousand hands are pulling at his flesh. His insides churn and bloat as though they are about to explode. The strange phenomenon is all too familiar, and yet something about it stings even more. He can see it this time.

All of it.

The walls buckle before stretching and twisting. In front of him, Sky appears as if she's walking through a series of funhouse mirrors that drastically alter her body in strange proportions. Looking down, he notices the same is happening to him.

Before his mind can comprehend, it's over. The stretching, the compression, and even the nausea are all gone. Rueben's heart continues to pound as his legs wobble like jelly beneath the now-solid ground. They both exhale deeply and exit the elevator. Reuben shakes out his hands in the best attempt to calm his nerves. A sharp chill of air sweeps across his neck.

The howls of the wind whistle against his ears before forcing its blood to retreat in search of warmth. Thoughts of cold and misery, however, quickly subside. In front of them, a collage of coloring fills the late afternoon sky. Soft shades of blue fade in the background as a warmer scheme of yellow and orange take the stage. The colors bleed from its canvas and onto the surrounding rooftop they now find themselves on.

They step forward, closer to the edge. A tall white obelisk begins to break the plain of sight as they move toward it. After a few more steps, Reuben recognizes it. Its shadow is heavy but fails to reach them or overcome the brightness between. The Washington Monument reaches for the burning light as the rest of the DC skyline begins to accept its fate in pending darkness.

"Wow," Reuben manages. The two of them sit down on a pair of lawn chairs overlooking the skyline from a rooftop across the Potomac River.

"I come here sometimes to be alone with my thoughts. I like the quiet, in sight but out of reach from the noise of the city, you know?"

"Yeah, it's just...beautiful up here." Reuben reclines in his chair.

"So, you joined the Army because of your grandfather?"

"At least in part. I guess I always felt that I needed to serve." He shakes his head. "I know it sounds kind of cheesy, but it's what I wanted to do. I still remember the stories of my grandfather fighting in Vietnam. I never met him. My father barely knew him either. But the man jumped on a grenade to save his platoon. Growing up, I looked up to that. He was honorable." Reuben pulls out the pair of dog tags around his neck and shows them to Sky. "These were his. They were passed on to my dad before he gave them to me." He tucks them back into his shirt. "So, I have to know. How did you get involved with the project? Was it because of your dad?"

"Kind of. I mean, I pretty much grew up around the Agency. My parents immigrated from Brazil before adopting me in the states. Since they couldn't have any other kids, they kept me close, especially my Dad." Sky rubs her gloved hands together and smiles while looking out at the skyline. "He'd bring me into work all the time. Even though he was just a maintenance worker, they treated him like family. Treated *me* like family. In some sense, I haven't known much else. It wasn't until after my time with the Air Force, though, that they offered me a position at the Center. I took it right away. It's not that I didn't give any thought to it. I just wasn't sure what else there was for me."

"Any regrets?" As the words come out of his mouth, he can see his answer in her face.

Hesitation and pain.

It's quick, but Reuben knows the look.

"Not one," Sky finally says. Minutes later, remnants of the sun's light fades into the skyline, overcome by night and the lights of the city. "It's crazy that something so beautiful doesn't last."

"What's even crazier is that with Chronos, we can travel back in time. We can slow things down or speed them up, but we can never stop it. The sun will always set just as it will always rise."

"After a month with us, you've finally seen it," she says.

"Seen what?"

"The irony."

9

ROANOKE

S ky jerks awake with a gasp. The sheets beneath her palms are cold, and her clothes cling to her skin in a sticky mess of sweat. The fog in her mind hangs over, obscuring her thoughts as she struggles to remember if she was dreaming. No details or visuals emerge. Only a dreadful knot in the fasted pit of her stomach remains. The gears of her mind grind as they come to life, and she knows it's too late.

Exhaustion be damned.

Sleep will have to wait.

The warp snooze can wake anyone, but not even Chronos can ease a burdened mind to sleep. She lays there in denial, refusing to look at the time. Looking will only make it real. Ironically, the only things she can think of are real things.

Not dreams or happy thoughts.

It's reality that keeps her up; tomorrow's mission, all the things that can go wrong, and the lie.

He asked her if she had any regrets.

Not one.

Her own words run over and over and over in her mind. He didn't deserve the lie, but he hasn't earned the truth. Her upbringing may have been why she came back to the Agency, but it's not why she stays. Her husband is the reason, and she knows it. She'll forever hate him and always be his.

He escaped. Why can't I?

Sky gives in and turns toward the clock.

3 AM.

Reality is here, and it's time to face it.

* * *

TALL BLADES of grass sway in the wind.

The sun melts behind a mountain range as its colors loom above, staining the sky in a reddish hue.

Cicada chirps surround him as he strolls through the valley.

As Reuben gets closer to the mountain range, the sun emerges again, and its light peaks onto his face. He sighs as it hits him.

Sunsets don't work backward. Not in the real world. Not up there.

The warp snooze pulls him from the dream, and he slaps the clock, knocking it from the table.

Why take me out of such a beautiful place?

It's a rhetorical question, but Reuben searches his mind for the answer anyway as he stumbles in the dark for the light switch. He flicks it, and his eyes retreat from the light before focusing on something odd and refreshing.

It's there, looking up at him in the mirror, a surreal sense of nostalgia. He rubs his clean-shaven face, smiling at the healthier-looking youthful skin and a beltline that no longer surpasses his shoes. Chronos hasn't just given him time as a means of travel. The ethereal project has somehow reversed time's effects on his being.

And perhaps his soul.

He doesn't know if it's the training room, the food they're

feeding him, or something else entirely, but something's changed him. Something has crept in made him whole, or at the very least, much less pitiful.

Purpose.

It must be purpose.

The training and the final exam, the speedy promotion, and today's mission. All of it drove him here. This isn't his youthful former self he sees staring at him through the mirror.

This is who he is now.

This is Reuben Greyson.

* * *

STANDING at the base of Chronos, Paul Peterson delights in its symmetry. Chronos's circular platform and metallic ring squeeze and bind its pillars into blissful infinity. Only the arches and staircase to the platform lend it any semblance of a starting point. Paul taps on a nearby railing, pondering if the lab techs scurrying around him ever grow disenchanted of the machine's might and majesty.

For him, however, it's the very presence of this incredible and terrifying power that reaffirms his resolve. The terrible things he's done and the awful things he must still do. The person he was and the person he must be. It was a choice, all of it. He knew that Nolan Greyson had to die, and that Adam Drazen had to go missing. He knows that Drazen must now be found and made to answer for his crimes. The thoughts, on their own, seem too convoluted and muddy. It's only when he stands in front of Chronos that it all makes sense. To do something good is to become someone fierce.

Forgive me.

He brushes the haunting plea from his mind. No one can hear his inner demons. No one will ever know what he's done or what he will do. Still, he prays to a God he's never known that someday they will understand why.

The sound of doors opening behind robs him of further thought as Rueben enters the lab with his team. Their arms are ladened with pre-colonial rifles and other such equipment. Paul smirks as he watches Rueben pulling at the uncomfortable-looking clothing needed to fit into the period.

"You've come to see us off?" Reuben calls out.

"Something of the sort, yes."

"I'm touched."

"Don't be. This is the first authorized mission in a long time. I'm here to ensure the operational safety of your crew and the mechanical integrity of the machine. I won't be here every time. Besides, it might make me feel uneasy if the machine's energy mistakenly vaporized you because someone forgot to update the algorithm that stabilizes particle transference."

Reuben takes a deep breath.

"Queasy?"

"I think I'm good," Reuben says with an uneasy smile. "I had some milk earlier."

"Great," Paul says dismissively while picking up a nearby tablet. "I assume that you and your team are otherwise prepared for this mission?"

"This team is ready to go."

Paul glances up from the screen and nods. "Very well. You may proceed."

* * *

As THEY APPROACH the steps to the platform, Reuben allows his team to go ahead of himself, performing a final spot check to ensure no last-minute issues with gear. His finger twitches beside him as if he were checking off invisible boxes. Before

Caleb can pass, the towering man grips Reuben and pulls him in.

"You good?" Caleb says, eyes fixed square on Reuben's.

"I'm good." He doesn't know if he believes it, but it's too late for self-reflection. It's t-minus right-the-hell-now, and his team needs him.

The steps illuminate as he climbs them, air expelling from his lungs as he meets the faces of each of his crew. On the lab floor below, Paul joins the technicians and a brooding Kirk, hunched over a tablet screen. Reuben smiles at him and nods. Kirk smiles back and thrusts out his middle finger.

"Okay," Reuben says as Alex lets out a chuckle behind him.

"Hey!" Sky's voice pierces through the lab as Kirk's head sinks behind his screen, like a turtle retreating into its shell.

Paul gives the team a thumbs up. The team flips their headset switches and syncs their watches. An anxious knot in Reuben's stomach tightens with each tick of the analog clock. A faint pulsating buzz pierces through the platform's plexiglass floor as its bright luminescence progressively fills their sight. The noise grows exponentially louder each passing second. The alien sound reminds him of a cross between an electric organ and a hurricane's wind tearing the panels off a house. Paneled lights lining the columns come to life, mirroring the ambiance of its accompanying sound. They spin and pick up speed, roaring in might and flexing their ferocity.

The lights become brighter.

The sound grows louder.

The fear in his heart permeates into his bones.

"Destination," Paul's voice crackles over the headset. "Eighteen August 1590. Objective. To collect any information that may lead to the capture of Adam Drazen."

The rotating columns pick up speed. Reuben looks on as each watch strapped to a team member pulses in unison. He looks into each of their eyes and sees the same petrified look on their faces as if peering into a mirror of his soul. He knows he can't allow them to see him cower.

Fear is rational.

Cowardice is death.

"We got this," Rueben says with a firm tone.

The light, sound, and energy unite, shedding autonomy and embracing its call. Ricochets of their union batter the travelers, blinding their eyes and piercing their ears. They instinctively cringe and cover, struggling to protect their senses from an untamed fury as it rattles to break from its chains and devour them clean from the fabrics of spacetime.

Suddenly, it ceases. Reuben's eyes open to find themselves on the other side. The smooth plexiglass floor is gone. Dirt, sand, and pine needles now pave a more rugged terrain.

"Team, are we up?" Reuben says.

"One up."

"Two up."

"Three up."

Reuben looks down at his limbs, checking that he made it in one piece before readdressing the team.

"Okay, if we timed it right, John White should have just arrived," Reuben says. "We'll make contact as planned and see what we can learn. Sky, how far out are we?"

She taps her watch several times. "About half a mile south of the site. If we stay along the coast on the other side of these trees, it should lead us straight there."

Reuben nods and turns to Alex. "How are comms looking?"

"We have a strong signal, at least where we're standing," Alex responds. "But there seems to be pockets where it goes in and out. If something happens while we're in a bad pocket, then we might not be able to make the link to jump back."

"Can we talk from a bad pocket?"

"To yourself, sure."

"All right, we'll keep an eye on the pockets and make periodic discreet radio checks to headquarters," Reuben says before turning his attention to Caleb.

"Point in the direction, and I'll shoot at it," Caleb says.

"Hopefully, it won't come to that. But we do need to proceed with caution. The relations between the settlers and some of the local tribes have...well, you know."

"Yeah, I know." Caleb rolls up a sleeve. "Gone to shit."

The team edges beside the tree line parallel to the coast. A mild breeze skirts along the Chesapeake, grazing the shore with its timid presence, failing to overcome the late summer sun as it beats down against their heavy fabrics. The humid air clings to any exposed skin, sporing sweat and breeding misery. It invites its mosquito companions to share in its spoils and drink of its harvest.

A ship lies anchored within sight, resting in the calm waters of Roanoke Sound, bordering the island's east barrier. Reuben suspects this to be the ship that Governor John White brought filled with supplies for the settlers of the colony. Perhaps it's the first ship that Roanoke Island has seen in three years.

With quiet feet and rifles raised, they close in on the settlement's perimeter. Silence looms between the buzzing of bugs and the crackling of stray twigs beneath them as they pass. A large tree breaks their path. Carved into its bark, the letters C-R-O stare back at them. Reuben raises his hand and grazes the engraving.

"Hey!" a loud but distant voice yells. The team immediately swings their rifles toward the voice in unison. "Who goes there?" a different voice calls out, this time even closer. They look up as a dozen men storm toward them with rifles of their own pointing in their direction.

"Friends," Reuben shouts back. "We are merchants loyal to the crown."

"Hold fire!" one of them yells from the rear, pushing his way past the others. The men keep their weapons poised on

Reuben and his team. A middle-aged man with a pale, bearded face rushes to the imaginary line between the groups. "British Merchants?" The man approaches Reuben. "It took years for the crown to authorize a vital supply run to a colony of dire necessity. How is it that you and your crew have been able to venture during a time of war when every able-bodied vessel is in need of service elsewhere?"

"I said we were loyal to Her Majesty," Reuben responds. "But our ship is our own, a private vessel searching the new world for goods to provide the homeland. We were running low on bread and ale and heard of the settlement here, hoping to make an exchange of supplies."

"Ah, well, I'm afraid you will have to continue your voyage elsewhere." The man signals his men to lower their rifles. "We only have enough bread and ale for our return voyage. I'm sorry."

"How about the settlers? Perhaps they can—"

"What do you know of them?"

"Only that there were near a hundred of them here on the island of the Chesapeake," Reuben says as the man glances down. "But they're not here, are they?"

"Why are they of interest to you?"

"Not of any particular interest. They just don't seem to be present. We can help track—"

"Help? Good sir, I do not know you or your crew, save your suspicious appearance moments ago."

"I said—"

"Merchants, right. Bandits and worse also roam these seas. I wish not to be rude, but I cannot in confidence trust that you are who you say, though you may be."

"Bandits and worse would not offer a helping hand. They certainly wouldn't approach an armed force such as yours outnumbered." Reuben looks sternly into the man's eyes.

The man yields and drops his gaze. "We arrived today to

find no one. No sign of battle or slaughter, not even a discernible message. The settlement looked much as it was years ago when it was established, only no people."

"I have some experience in tracking. We'll likely stay on the island overnight regardless. It would be no trouble."

"My name is John White," the man says, extending his hand. "I am the governor of the colony of Roanoke, appointed by Sir Walter Raleigh, a servant of Her Majesty Queen Elizabeth."

Reuben opens his mouth, but the words stick in the back of his throat as he considers them carefully. He's spoken mostly lies to the governor and now the greatest truth, his name, feels odd as it emerges on his tongue.

"I'm Reuben," he finally says. "This is my crew, or at least the best three."

"Including a woman, I see," White says while glancing over at Sky. "Not unheard of but certainly uncommon. Being in the presence of men in an uncivilized setting makes a woman strong and of virtue. Certainly not the norms of English women in the mainland. It takes a special type of courage to make such a voyage. She reminds me of my own daughter, Eleanor."

"Eleanor, she was among the missing settlers?" As the words carry from his lips, Reuben can see an uneasiness settle into White's eyes. The disappearance isn't just a mystery to him. It's a personal quest to recover his family, a longsuffering desperation to find his people, compelled to fulfill his obligation to their survival. The governor nods and escorts Reuben and the team to the walls of the establishment.

Bare and dismembered tree trunks huddle together in an unnatural display of force, creating a barrier between the untamed elements and the encroaching establishment of civilization. Reuben peers past the gates and into the settlement. Hut-like domiciles, carts, and fire pits rest along imaginary lines within the walls. Sackcloth and fur drape over posts and chairs. The colony's rugged interior is neither futile nor unkempt. As they approach it, Reuben half expects someone to come out and greet them. A gust streams in from the bay, brushing up sand along the pathways. Only whistles of wind welcome them at the gates.

Before entering, the governor takes them to a nearby post and shows them another carving. Reuben knows the word before his eyes can read it. *Croatoan.*

"What does it mean?" he asks.

"We're not quite sure," White says. "Perhaps a reference to that native tribe or the series of islands in which they reside. Before I left our relationship with them...it was complicated. There were some misunderstandings and casualties when we first arrived. But we had made strides for peace between our people and theirs."

"Maybe they went with the Croatoans," Alex suggests.

"We certainly desired to coexist," White says, turning to respond to Alex. "But we were never them, and they were never us. Peace was attainable. That's why I fought hard to achieve it. But beyond our desire to live alongside each other, there seemed an irreconcilable dispensation between our kinds." Governor White taps his fingers against the letters. "It is very unlikely that they went with the Croatoans...willingly."

"If you would permit us, Governor, we would like to survey the settlement," Reuben says. "There might be other clues that could help to paint a fuller picture."

The governor nods. "I will accompany you, Mister Reuben. I am at your disposal if you could help us find them."

* * *

ONCE INSIDE, the team splits up to explore the settlement. Sand and dirt strike the tips of Sky's boots as she makes her way toward the center. The wind ceases, and a single cloud blots out the sun's light. Her eyes meet the cold ash of an empty fire pit as a hollow knot fills her stomach. Hairs on the back of her neck spring up as the chill grips her spine.

What is this? Where is it coming from?

"Hey, are you okay?" Alex calls to her as he approaches.

"Yeah, I'm good." She turns to him, trying to shake it off. "I think it's this place... Just seems—"

"Haunting."

"Something like that, I guess."

"Or as Kirk might say, 'This place is creepy as sh—'"

"It really is. There's something else, though." She looks around before fixating on the fire pit. "It's a sense of something. Hard to describe."

"Sense of what?"

"I don't know." She shakes her head, unable to find the words to describe it. Sky shrugs it off and returns to the search.

* * *

REUBEN AND CALEB assist Governor White in searching the individual domiciles. Reuben opens the animal-skinned door flap, allowing Caleb to enter with his rifle at eye level.

"All clear," Caleb calls out.

"You and your African crew member have awfully peculiar means of...of...of I'm not entirely certain what task you're attempting to accomplish," Governor White says. "With the nods, shouts, and that rifle held up while walking. It's all quite bizarre."

"His name is Caleb Jones," Reuben says. "He's one of my most experienced people, and someone I call a friend."

"Yes, of course. I apologize. I did not mean to rob a man of any dignity."

"I'm sure that's the case, Governor. Perhaps we ought to consider where our actions and intentions can be more consistent." White nods as Reuben continues to speak, "As for our methods, they may be unorthodox, but I assure you my crew and I are results-driven." Reuben continues to hold the doorway open. "After you, Governor."

They enter to find Caleb squatting in front of a small, wooden crib lying desolate on its side.

"Everything about this scene is organized and in place," Caleb says. "Everything but this crib on its side like this." He reaches out and feels the material between his fingers. "This crib, it wasn't brought over. It was made here from local bark."

"You are correct, Mr. Jones," White says. "I built it for my granddaughter, Virginia Dare." White kneels beside the crib and stands it upright. "I can still picture holding her and seeing the way she would smile. It was mostly in her sleep as she was so young, a few weeks old, but she did smile. The winters were harsh, some native groups hostile, and our situation progressively growing in desperation. Many people were beginning to despair. So much so that I had to leave if my people were to be saved. And yet, here was this child in the middle of everything with that beautiful smile on her face. It's almost as if Virginia Dare knew what this place was and wanted to offer something. Hope, I think. I must believe there is hope. For her, my daughter, son by law, and everyone." White stands up. "I know it seems delusional to think hope could be found in a child."

"Not at all," Reuben says. "It seems, Governor, that you knew your granddaughter well. We will do all we can to get her back."

"You have my gratitude for your efforts, Mr. Reuben. It's her hope I'm holding onto."

As they exit, Governor White regroups with his men, leaving Reuben and Caleb to continue searching on their own. "What do you think happened here, Army man?" Caleb asks.

"Can't say. If it was an attack, there would be blood and

bodies. They didn't seem to migrate either. All the supplies are still here. Everything is in its place. Nothing damaged or taken."

"Yeah, everything except that crib."

"What's your theory?"

"Listen, Staff Sergeant, I'm no detective. My primary concern is safety and security. Sometimes, that means shooting. Other times that means not shooting. I make judgment calls about the way things are, as opposed to creating theories for the ways things might be." Caleb pauses for a moment. "Having said that, it is my judgment that the girl that crib belonged to had a different outcome than everyone else in this colony. What that outcome is, I sure as shit don't know. Can't even say if it's good or bad. But I'd bet Benjamins that it's different."

"Well, I guess we better work on finding out."

"Especially if it will help us find Drazen. That is why we're doing all this, right?"

"It is my judgment that that is exactly what we're doing." Reuben winks, prompting a muted facial expression from Caleb.

"Soldier..." Caleb lets out a breath. "I hope you understand there's a line. You can cover it with sand or dirt. Hell, you can bury it in concrete. But one day, a hurricane is going to blow away everything but that line. When it does, I hope for your sake you're on the right side of it." Caleb glances around the settlement before stepping closer to Reuben. "And one more thing. What you said back there to White- defending me..."

"Yeah..." Reuben's voice softens as Caleb locks eyes with him.

For the first time in months, Reuben can see something foreign in Caleb Jones. It's vulnerability and, for a second, he doesn't know how to react or what Caleb will say next.

"I appreciate it," Caleb begins. "You know it's not something enough people think about. There are so many places we go to where people like me don't blend in. Where people like me are treated like second-class citizens, or worse, not even human."

"Caleb, I'm sorry. I—"

"This project, Chronos. It lets us see what history really is, not just some sugar-coated version of it. What White said, how he behaves, how he might feel, that's ingrained in the time, you know? We can't change that, can't alter history. The least we can do is go back and educate ourselves and make it known to these politicians in the shadows that this is precisely the kind of thing that people do to each other when we live in ignorance.

"You know this isn't just some cushy government job for me. Yeah, the benefits are great, but that's not what this is about. Paul Peterson. Say what you will about the man, but he fought to have all of us on this project. Even though it makes blending in a lot harder, even though the missions are extremely sensitive, he chose us. Not to some desk job, but Ops, the pride and joy of the whole AIC. That shit means something."

"Of course," Reuben says.

"Which is exactly why you need to keep your mouth shut sometimes. When you go spouting off trying to call out every racist and sexist comment we encounter, you compromise everything. You get that, right?"

Reuben shakes his head for a moment in confusion before it hits him. "Caleb, I was just—"

"Not thinking. This isn't the training room. Here, we only ever get one shot at a mission. The Governor here was agreeable, so not a big deal. But who knows about the next person we come across that's not from our time? It sucks, but we have to keep rapport if we want to get the information we need."

"I get it. It just doesn't seem right."

"It's not right. It's messed up, but it's what we have to do."

Rapid patters of crushing dead leaves and twigs storm in their direction. Reuben and Caleb turn as Alex rushes toward them from across the settlement. He halts a few feet shy of them, bending toward the ground to catch his breath.

"Hey," the word spews out in between giant gasps. "We found... You need to see what we found."

They scurry to the other side, shuffling between barren huts and lonesome openness, lining the wall's inner perimeter. Sky peeks from behind a nearby structure and signals them over.

As they approach, she pulls out what appears to be a leather-bound book. Reuben notices an inscription of two letters etched into the center on the outer cover, reading *TH*.

"You sprinted all that way to tell us you found a book?" Caleb says, glaring at Alex.

"Not just any book," Alex says. "It's a notebook, likely belonging to Thomas Harriot."

"Thomas who?"

"Thomas Harriot. He was an ethnographer, astronomer, mathematician who came over on the original passage. He studied Roanoke and helped build this place. Did you not pay attention when I gave my briefing?"

"Hey, man, that was a very long day of preparation for this mission. Forgive me if I can't recall the name of every dead white guy in history."

"You don't have to remember every name, but at least have some familiarity with—"

"Okay," Reuben interrupts. "For the sake of time and team cohesion, I'm going to ask that we skip to the part where you tell us the significance of the notebook."

"I don't know," Alex says.

"You don't know?"

"Well, yeah."

"Just spit out what the hell you do know," Caleb chimes in.

"That's the thing," Alex says. "No one knows what is inside of this notebook because it was never recovered. It was rumored that Harriot had writings lost in the Roanoke Colony.

It's speculated that it might have had a detailed history of the colony to include the relations with the natives, how they survived the harsh winters, and much more. It may even hold clues about the disappearance itself."

Reuben's eyes widen. "Have you opened it?"

"Uh, no. Not yet. I was walking, and then accidentally kicked it up from the dirt. It was buried a little. I was so excited when I saw his initials that I ran to tell you."

Reuben quickly flips through the pages. Specific words such as *agriculture* and *Manteo* jump out to him. Sixteenth Century sentence structures fail to piece together a coherent thought in a quick skim. He knows that it will require time and research to uncover anything from the notebook. He shuts the pages and hands it back to Alex.

"Maybe we can get John White to help us with it," Sky suggests.

"He probably could," Reuben says. "It could be time consuming, though. And if it proves fruitless, we're back to square one. Plus, he's already suspicious about how we're handling things. I'm not sure how he'll react if I bring him Harriot's notebook directly." He looks at Alex. "If need be, can we bring it back with us?"

"Yeah, it's inorganic, so we're good to go."

"Okay, good. I'll go and see if there's anything else I can find out from Governor White. In the meantime, find someplace quiet to review the notebook. Let us know if you find anything useful."

"Will do."

* * *

ALEX TUCKS the notebook into his loose garments and departs. He begins to circle the inner perimeter of the settlement. Around each curve and corner, sets of eyes belonging to

White's men dart up to meet him, branding his presence in suspicion.

Yeah, let's all just stare at the skinny Asian dude lurking around.

He wants to enter one of the domiciles but stops himself. He knows any concealment gained would only deny him foresight of unexpected visitors. He continues to search but finds no immediate haven.

The smell of dead fish clings to the heavy wet air around him.

Stupid low tide.

The scent draws his eyes outward toward the front gates. Beyond the entrance, he can see the water pulling back on itself, revealing a series of large rocks along the shoreline. He unslings his rifle and strides out of the gates. Several yards outside, he veers back to see no eyes staring at him. A sizeable pale rock beside the shoreline snags his attention, and he leaps behind it. His hands slip against the rock's jagged edges as its cold soaks through his garb, bathing it in a salty stench. He finds the vantage point suitable enough to look out for White's men.

As he draws out the notebook, a sharp beeping sound echoes into his ears. He pulls back his sleeve, taps his watch, and lets out an expletive. "Of course, it is," he says, staring down at the display.

Bad pocket or not, I probably won't find a better spot.

* * *

INSIDE THE WALLS OF ROANOKE, Reuben reunites with Governor White. They stroll along the perimeter, continuing their conversation.

"Autumn delivered the greatest sobriety," White says. "It became evident then who among us was wise and who the fools were. The former prepared while the latter squandered. You could imagine which group survived that first winter."

"And what do you believe of their fate now?" Reuben says.

"I know not, Mr. Reuben. I only pray it was something they could prepare for, or at best could endure."

What if no amount of preparation could cause them to endure?

He bites down on his tongue, forcing it not to utter the callous thought. He knows time is fixed. Nothing could ever change the fate of these people, whatever that might be. And yet, Reuben's chest can't help but sink into itself as he looks into the Governor's eyes. It's not a tenderness or weakness that's evident. If anything, there is a stoic hardness to them. But just beyond, there is a glimmer of the very word that White himself used while kneeling beside the crib of his missing grand-daughter.

Hope.

Maybe they did survive. Maybe they're just waiting to be found somewhere in history.

"When you left for England, did anyone else from Roanoke return with you?" Reuben asks, attempting to shift the conversation toward Harriot's notebook. He smiles to himself, realizing that his once rusty interrogation skills have come back to him.

"Yes. Although most stayed to preserve and grow our settlement, a few accompanied me on the voyage back to England. It was a select number who had already finished what they had sought, and it was time for them to return."

"There were some with you that were never intended to be permanent residents of Roanoke?"

"Quite. Believe it or not, there was even a man among them that desired to stay. Even throughout the harshness of life here, he was fascinated by this land, the natives, and if our nation of Great Britain would have longevity in the new world. Thomas Harriot, he was called."

"Fascinating," Reuben says, recalling the initials on the mysterious notebook.

"Indeed."

"Someone like that must've made a lot of contributions."

"If only I could list them all."

"I'm sure that type of man would keep a list himself."

"Oh, yes. Harriot was obsessive over his writings."

"I respect men like Mr. Harriot who seek to benefit future generations. What types of things did he write?"

"Many subjects. One could spend years reading his works. He even recorded much of what he encountered here. The colonists, the natives, the vegetation. He even wrote of bizarre experiences, he claimed."

Reuben's chest tightens as a heavy breeze sweeps sand across his boots. "Bizarre experiences?"

"It was nonsense mostly. The man is perhaps the most brilliant I've come to know personally in my years. But as you may know, not all that is brilliant is true, or sane for that matter."

"Yes, of course."

"It's interesting. He once came to me claiming there were other peoples in the land that were distinct from ourselves or the natives." White laughs. "As I said, the man is brilliant but, sometimes, I wondered if he ate bad vegetation unbeknownst to himself."

"What did he say about the other peoples?"

"It was the most peculiar description. He said that—"

A scream pierces from above. Reuben looks up as the man posted on the wall's overlook clings to his chest, an arrowhead protruding from his back. Fear and agony bleed from his eyes. A stream of crimson pours down the arrow's shaft, saturating the instrument of his demise with his own life's blood. His hand fumbles to pull the arrow from him but fails. His body weight shifts as his boots snag against one another, and the man tumbles over the railing. Reuben lunges forward to catch him, but it's too late. Sand and pine needles erupt and displace. The *thump* echoes deeper than the man's final scream.

Reuben immediately flips him over to check his vitals but can already see that he's dead. Without hesitation, he exposes his watch and begins to call out on his headset, "The settlement is under attack. I repeat, we are under attack!" Reuben knows that their cover with White is now blown. "Provide sitrep, over!"

"Jones up."

"Sky up."

"Alex, where are you?" Reuben says. "Alex!"

More of White's crew fall from their overlook posts, descending like fruit from the overburdened tree of time. The remaining men aimlessly return fire.

"He's not showing up on the nav schematics," Sky says through the headset. "Must be in a dead pocket."

"Dammit," Reuben mutters as every muscle goes into rigor. His jittery fingers struggle to tap the watch. The screen illuminates, but Alex is nowhere to be seen. Reuben can feel the panic crawling just beneath his skin, fighting to latch onto anything and everything. Leaving immediately means survival. Leaving a man to die, leaving *his* man to die, is an internal death, a worse death.

He lets out a breath, keeping the angst at bay while orders he's never pondered emerges from his lips.

"You two take cover against the interior wall and hold the entrance. I'll find Alex, and we'll get the hell out of here."

"Wilco."

"Roger."

Governor John White stares at him, speechless as his crew continues to get hit with arrows. "You're one of—"

"I'm sorry, Governor," Reuben interrupts. "I'll search for your people, but they won't be found today. Keep against that wall, and you'll make it out of this." He leaves White behind and sprints toward the entrance of Roanoke, searching for Alex on the way. As he approaches the gate, he sees Caleb and Sky taking cover. "You guys good? Anyone hurt?"

"We're good. Still can't find Alex," Caleb says.

"He probably went outside of here for privacy," Sky says.

"Then that's where I'll go."

"I'm right behind you, brother." Caleb motions to follow.

"No. You're taking Sky, making the link, and jumping back to HQ. Alex and I will be right behind you. Besides, a single load rifle is no weapon for cover fire, especially when you don't know where the enemy is."

"Glad to see you've paid attention."

Reuben sprints beyond the gates, darting from tree to tree as arrows whoosh all around the settlement.

He looks out and sees no one. Not a soul.

A branch rustles beside him, and his heart stops. He swoops his rifle toward it and lunges forward.

Nothing. No one.

The wind blows again, and more branches give way. He lets out another breath, then continues running forward toward the beach. His eyes scan the shoreline, and he sees it. A head is peeking up behind a large rock. Reuben opens his mouth to call out to him when something in his chest tightens.

They'll hear it. If I scream, they'll hear it and start shooting.

He looks back toward the settlement one final time, then out to Alex. Sand and fractured seashells are all that stand between them: no trees, no other rocks, no cover.

He slings his rifle, recites an unintelligible prayer and, with all his might, sprints toward the rock.

A flash comes over him, but it's not light.

It's Alex. His face, now inexplicably in front of him.

Reuben doesn't think. He can't think. Or even process any of it. His legs and back go stiff in the shock of it.

And yet, somehow, he does it. He moves. He tackles Alex as an arrow zips past his ear, strikes the rock, and ricochets into the sea. They slam onto the shore, and a wave rolls over them, saltwater flooding his nose.

The wave pulls back from his face like a curtain, and he sees it. The rock, Alex's head peeking over it, and the vast distance between them.

He's running toward Alex. Again. Somehow, it's all happening again. Reuben's legs wabble as a knot grips his stomach. He nearly trips and pukes before reality sets in.

Déjà vu.

Tackling Alex wasn't something he did. It's what he will do. Reuben reaches the rock in time to rip Alex from the arrow's trajectory. As the wave passes, he grabs him by the collar and yanks him to his feet. As they sprint back toward the walls of the settlement, Reuben pulls his watch in front of him, trying to steady his arm between strides. The display flashes from red to green as they escape the snarling grips of the pocket. He taps the watch and clutches Alex's shoulder. The bright light streams over them and sizzles their eyes as its sharp electric pulse pierces into their flesh.

The past fades, and the present emerges.

The columns slow as Reuben's eyes adjust to the lighting. The fierce roaring of the beast subsides as voices and chatter fill the room. Reuben dries his sweaty palms against his clothes and jumps to his feet. He pulls up Alex alongside him, who struggles to catch his breath.

As they stumble down the stairs onto the lab floor, he can see Sky near the entrance. Their eyes meet, and he lets out a sigh.

They made it. All of them. Alive and in one piece.

Frantically rubbing his fingers together, Alex mulls in silence before opening his arms and embracing Reuben. "Thanks, man," he says. "If you didn't come when you did, I'd be...I'd be..."

"You're not. That was never in the cards." Reuben pulls back from the hug after a few seconds.

"Déjà vu?"

Reuben nods.

Alex reaches into his vest, and his face goes pale.

"Oh, shit." In a frenzy, he rips off the vest and pats it down, his fingers frantically pulling along the seams. "No, no, no, no... Please..." He looks up at Reuben, eyes wide, face drooping in defeat.

"The notebook?"

"It must've fallen out."

Reuben's heart skips a beat as time itself stands still.

10

REMINDERS AND RECOUNTINGS

A variety of food clutters the dining room table; mixed green salad with goat cheese and dried cranberries, cilantro topped chicken curry, and a tapas assortment of sliced fruit, exotic cheeses, and chilled meats. Yet silence is what dominates the table. Only the ticking clock on the nearby wall makes a sound.

"Can you pass the dressing, love?" he asks, looking beside him to his wife.

She passes it without a word.

This is not like her. This isn't her.

In twenty years of marriage, Mira Greyson has always been the outspoken one, the extrovert. She has been the life of any room she walked into, and people gravitated toward her. She'd speak with her hands and pull you in with her laughter.

And her smile.

At least she still has that.

This sickness may have taken everything else from her, but it hasn't taken the one thing that defines her to the world.

At least not yet.

The thought terrifies him. He can transverse worlds and

time itself. He can recreate and redesign reality, but he can't save her.

Not from this.

There was a time when that unnatural power was in his grips before the Stewards sealed it away. It had proven too much for them to play God. He believed long ago that he'd be disciplined enough to control it, disciplined enough to control himself. He found out the hard way that it was a lie. And the terrifying truth stays with him today. There is no controlling it, no overcoming the temptation, no taming the beast that tears the flesh from the fabrics of spacetime.

As he remembers what happened, Nolan hears it in his mind. The faint cry and the impossible choice. He'd done every calculation, foresaw all outcomes, and yet nothing in the world and nothing in himself could ever prepare him for that moment when he heard the helpless weeping.

Nolan's heart crumples as it all comes back to him. It's not dread, he knows. It's gravity. It's the weight of the choices he's made and how it changed everything. Before taking the first bite of his salad, he looks to Reuben and smiles. The greens may nourish his body, but this meal and this time with his family fills his soul. It may be quiet, it may be different, and it may be fleeting, but it's precious, and nothing on earth would ever make him wish it away.

The sharp spices of the curry chicken tickle his nose as its steam fills his glasses. As it dissipates, Nolan can see his son's drooping face, hovering motionless over his empty plate. Were the other kids picking on him at school again? Did he embarrass himself in front of a crush? Or is he just a moody thirteen-year-old boy who's learning how awkward and cruel life can be?

Nolan's mouth opens, desperate to comfort his son, but no words follow. Instead, he clears his throat and takes another bite from his plate. How can a man who knows so many words lack the ability to string them together when his son needs him the most? The thought doesn't just pique his curiosity. It bothers him, twisting his insides into a Gordian knot of angst and shame.

"Reuben," Mira says, breaking the silence as she places a gentle hand on his. Her voice is soft and warm but firm. Nolan sees it in Reuben's eyes as he looks up at his mother. It's a tenderness that only she can expose. "There is plenty for all of us," she adds with a smile as she places the bowl of pulled chicken in front of him. Reuben picks at it with his fork before scooping a chunk of it onto his plate.

It's so subtle, so brief, and it impresses Nolan how well she does it. Mira doesn't interrogate or jump to a lecture. She engages with him. She brings their son into the fold with a few words, a touch, and a smile. It's not a skill. No, it can't be. It's magic, a gift.

"Your mother is right," Nolan says while passing him the bowl of spinach. Reuben looks at his father as he takes the bowl from him. It's not defiance or disgust in the boy's eyes, but something else. Could it be disappointment? Has he already grown old enough to see his father's shortcomings and follies? For a moment, Nolan thinks of the great and powerful Oz and how it was only ever a thin curtain that separated legend from truth. Maybe the curtain is time itself, an inevitability that reveals everything eventually.

Maybe I can quantify it. Perhaps I can use it to—

"Nolan," Mira says, touching his arm.

The thought flees him: time travel, physics, the meaning of it all. So often, these thoughts consume him, and she knows it.

Her voice, her touch.

It always brings him back and keeps him grounded. She doesn't say anything else, and she doesn't have to. Nolan lays his hand atop hers and spills aloud his one remaining thought.

"I love you."

Mira smiles and almost chuckles at her husband's lack of self-awareness.

"I know."

The weary sun of early evening begins to disappear, mirroring the food on Nolan's and even Reuben's plate. Nolan glances at his wife's setting. The steam from the warm foods has ceased while the cold foods have begun to wilt. He leans over and lays his hand on her shoulder. "I can warm it back up for you. It'll only take—"

She grabs his hand, squeezes, and kisses it. "It's okay. I guess I'm not that hungry."

"You should still eat something. I know this is draining, but you really should—"

"Maybe later." She stands from her seat with plate in hand. Her eyes meet Reuben's. "We won't waste, though. These will make for good leftovers."

"I'll take care of that." Nolan pulls the plate from her grip.

"All right, I'll start on the dish—"

"Will take care of that, too. I have help, you know." He nudges in Reuben's direction. "You should go upstairs and rest." She nods and lays her palm against his chest before departing toward the stairs.

"Feel better, Mom," Reuben calls to her.

"Thanks, sweetie." She turns back to him. "I will. Now, help your father with cleaning up. I'll see you in the morning."

The men remain at the table finishing the remnants of their meals. Silverware scrapes against their plates substitute for conversation. Nolan wants to tell Reuben something encouraging, to assure him that everything will be okay, but it's too hard. Thinking of his wife's condition, feeling his heart grow heavy and eyes fill with moisture, how can he tell his son something he doesn't believe? He swipes off his glasses and tosses them onto the table. His fingers wrap around the straps of his watch as his eyes shut, and his breath leaves him.

Suddenly, he hears it. It's not their breathing or the noisy air conditioner or the evening cicadas outside. No. It's something much more subtle and far more powerful.

His watch and its metronome-like tick.

The sound is as faint and pronounced as it was that day when he heard the helpless cry. It was a decade ago when the winds blew fierce, and the people shouted, but it's the cry he heard, and it's the cry that gripped him. That sound will always be tied to his watch. And now, it's his watch that reminds him of real weakness, true strength, and the paradox that binds them.

"Son," he finally lets out.

Reuben wipes his mouth and crumples his napkin onto the empty plate before looking up at him. "Yeah."

"I just want you to know that I'm here for you. So, if you ever need to talk about school or what's going on with your mom, I'm here. I'll admit I'm not always the best one to talk to, and there's so much that I don't see. But I do see you..." Nolan studies his son's face, hoping to see a thoughtful reaction, looking for anything to pierce the barrier between them. "You know that, right?"

"Uh...okay," Reuben says after a brief pause.

Nolan doesn't press him on it, choosing to shift topics instead.

"You finished your greens."

Reuben shrugs. "Yeah. I mean, what choice did I have?"

"Every decision is a choice, whether or not we're the ones who make it."

"Sure, Dad." Reuben rolls his eyes.

They work together clearing the table, rinsing the dishes, and stacking them into the washer. Reuben fills it with soap and turns the knob. Nolan tears a disinfectant wipe along its perforated edges and begins cleaning off the sticky food residue clinging to the granite countertops.

"Why's Mom been sick?" Reuben asks.

"I don't know, Son," the unfamiliar words pour from Nolan's mouth. He uses his elbow to catch stray beads of sweat on his forehead and continues wiping. "In my work, I've discovered that most everything has answers but, sometimes, we can't find them." He looks up at his son. "Sometimes, we're not meant to."

"I hope we can find out what's wrong. I don't like seeing her like this."

"Neither do I." Nolan dries his hands and hugs his son.

He reaches toward the garbage bin to toss the grease and food-stained wipe. Reuben's hand intercepts. "I can finish up," he says, pulling the wipe out of his father's hand. "You should relax and read one of your books."

"And you should do your homework."

"I will. Soon."

"I'll check on your mother."

In the darkened bedroom, he sees her motionless silhouette on the bed. As he gets closer, the features of her face come into view. Her lips are dry, and her thin cheeks droopy.

And her eyes.

Even closed shut, they look unbearably heavy. He's watched her age over the years, but not like this. In months, time seems to have taken away years. How can this happen? This was never the way things were meant to be.

In sickness and in health.

Nolan Greyson said the words, then, and they've never weighed as much as they do now.

A deep grief fills him quicker than the tears, but they all come out together. He tries with everything in him to cry quietly, to not disturb her sleep. The floors creak beneath him as he escapes to the closet and collapses to the ground.

Mira. Oh, Mira.

His wife's name is as sweet on his mind as it is on his tongue.

Nolan recomposes himself and walks back out to the bed one more time to check on her.

"Hey."

He hears her voice before seeing her big, bold eyes open in the dark.

"I'm sorry, did I wake you?" he whispers.

"Yeah." Mira smiles as she reaches for him. Nolan crouches beside the bed and takes her hand. "I heard you crying like a baby."

"Ha!" Nolan chuckles a bit as a few more tears find their way out. "Sometimes, I feel like a baby."

"I know. Keep it to yourself," she says jokingly. "Seriously, though, Nolan, you're never alone. I know you're scared—"

"I am scared. I'm scared because you're scared. You're the most fearless person I know. What am I supposed to do?" The question has been circling his mind, orbiting like an inescapable gravitational force, and now it's out. "Mira, I need you. I'll always need you. Reuben will need—"

"Reuben has you," her weary voice lets out before he can finish.

His chest sinks as it hits him. "He needs more."

"What he needs is the same thing we all need. He needs love and to know he's loved. That's all..."

"You've been on a Beatles kick lately, huh?"

Mira pinches him deep in his arm. "I'm serious."

"I know. I know."

"And what about the dog tags and your journal?"

"I'm prepping it, all of it, you know that."

"Just don't wait forever. We don't have all the time in the world." Mira squeezes her pillow and burrows her head further into it.

Nolan kisses her forehead. "Believe me, love, that is the one thing I'll never forget." He tucks the thick blanket around her shoulder. "Now, get some rest."

"I will if you promise to keep the crying down." Mira's smile widens as her eyes narrow and shut.

"I'll do my best," he whispers and shuts the door behind him.

As he walks past the empty family room, he imagines what this evening would look like if his wife weren't ill. Every night after dinner, they would unwind next to one another, holding a book and occasionally sipping a glass of aged merlot. Today there is no wine and only one book sprawled open on the coffee table—John Milton's *Paradise Lost*. Its words are open to any passerby. He doesn't believe in bookmarks when it comes to hardbacks.

Nolan runs into Reuben in the hallway.

"How is she?" Reuben whispers. Nolan ushers his son away from the bedroom door so as not to disturb his wife.

"She's resting," he replies once they are far enough away. "You should start your homework."

"Yes, sir," Reuben says as Nolan starts toward the family room. "Hey, Dad." Nolan turns back to acknowledge him. "I don't get it. How—"

"Like I said, Son. We don't know why she's sick."

"I know. It's not that. It's just you...and her. You're so different."

Nolan smiles. "It's a paradox. Always true, but rarely right."

* * *

REUBEN TOSSES a rock into the lake, watching as the ripples make their way to shore. A few of the sun's rays pierce their way through the tall branches beginning their bloom, warming his skin. As birds chirp in the distance, he strolls along the shoreline, smiling and taking it all in. There are no cars or buses, no streetlights, or pedestrians. Almost no civilization at all.

Almost.

A puff of smoke expels in the distance, drawing Rueben's attention. About a hundred yards from the lakeshore sits a small log cabin, nearly camouflaged into the wooded scenery. If not for the extended dock running between them, Reuben might walk by it without notice. As he gets closer, he recognizes the man sitting on the porch's rocking chair smoking a cigarette.

"Not a terrible way to spend a lunch break," Reuben calls out to him.

"Well, I don't come out here for the company," Caleb says as Reuben walks up the steps. "I suppose I don't mind it every now and then, though." Caleb nods to the empty rocking chair next to him.

Reuben takes a seat. "So, this is Section Seven?"

"That's right. The only part of the training room not used for training. Accessible 24/7."

"I guess it makes sense to set aside a place for recreation."

"Yep. I like the cabin, Sky usually does the beach, Alex likes to watch old Babe Ruth games, and I don't even want to know what the hell Kirk does in his spare time." They both share a laugh. Caleb pulls out a cigarette box, opens the cover, and motions toward Reuben.

Reuben shakes his head. "Thanks, man. I'm good, though."

"I keep forgetting your generation doesn't take well to these. Suit yourself, I guess. One more for later."

"You're probably the first person I've met in years that still smokes classic cigarettes. You know they have the synthetics, right? And it's not like the electronic stuff they tried in the early 2010s. Seriously, two decades later, and you're not supposed to be able to tell the difference."

"Well, I can tell," Caleb's voice cuts through as he inhales a puff. He blows the smoke out the side of his cheek away from Reuben. "There's nothing like the real thing. Besides, a good time traveler needs to be in touch with what's real."

"Coming from a man sitting on a fake porch in an artificial environment?"

Caleb smiles to himself. "Touché, sir. I guess it's hard to put something down that you spent so much time picking up. You know?"

"Yeah."

Caleb spends the next several minutes telling Reuben stories of a similar cabin he and his family would vacation annually. Reuben smiles and takes in Caleb's nostalgia, accepting that things have changed in one sense yet paradoxically clinging to its memories in another.

"I like this, but it's not the same," Caleb says.

"Feels pretty real."

"But it's not. Looks like it. Even that lake smells like it was, but I know it's fake. Just knowing makes all the difference."

"Like synthetic cigarettes."

Caleb smirks. "Exactly." He drives the amber glow into the chair's arm, putting it out. "You know, maybe one day I'll give it up and just smoke cigars. Better on the lungs if you don't inhale. Classier, too."

Reuben nods. "There's a thought."

"Tell you what, soldier. The next time people are shooting at us, and it looks like we may just pull through, I'll say goodbye to the menthols forever and kiss the sweet binder of a Nicaraguan stogie."

"I may just join you there." Reuben looks down at his watch and reality sets back in. "We should probably get back. Paul is expecting us for the debrief."

Caleb double taps his watch. The sun's reflection against the lake fades first. Its light subsides from the trees and, eventually, the entire environment, disappearing without ever setting. In a few seconds, only the porch remains illuminated. Caleb faces the cabin's entrance, opens the door, and walks into its darkened interior. Reuben follows him into the open bay.

They make their way across the facility to a conference room, where Paul and the others await them. Reuben enters first to find an oval-shaped table stretched from one end of the small space to the other. Black leather chairs line the table on each side. The alien sense of ordinary chills his spine in a building where warp-snooze alarm clocks, teleport elevators, and spacetime-defying environments are considered normal.

"Welcome, gentlemen," Paul says from the table's head. His hands clamp against one another at its center. Reuben and Caleb find their seats, joining Kirk, Sky, and Alex. "You two are prior service, are you not?" Neither responds to the rhetorical question. "Is punctuality something we've allowed to retire as well?"

"We still have two minutes." Reuben motions toward the hologram hovering over the table; its digital display reading '13:58.'

"And this is adequate time to get accountability of your team? To ensure each member is prepared to deliver their debrief statements? I believe the custom is a minimum of ten minutes prior to the meeting time. Even Kirk, a lifelong civilian, met this—"

"Sir," Caleb interrupts. "We're late because of me. Reuben spent his lunch break tracking me down. Poor kid has nothing in his stomach."

The grinding of Paul's teeth cuts through the silence. "I appreciate the candor, Jones. But ultimately, a leader is responsible for his subordinates and their actions."

"I get it. But come on. In all these years I worked here, do I seem like the type to be subordinate to some young scrawny Army kid? Don't get it twisted, though, sir. I respect the hell out of this kid, but you can't blame him for my stubbornness."

"In your twenty years of service, I know you're not that naïve. I won't allow you to cover—"

"And he won't," Reuben chimes in. "You're right, Paul. It's on me. This is my team. And as you can see, we're all here, and it's exactly two o'clock. So right now, I'll exercise my responsibility to actually starting on time instead of wasting any more of it."

Paul's eyebrows contract as tension fills the silence.

"Hey, okay," Kirk attempts to cut the unease. "So, ah, this is my first official debrief thingy. Do we each take turns talking about our shit, or only one person tells the whole thing, or is there some sort of reenactment?"

No one responds.

"Or is it like *Jeopardy*? Cause I'll take 'Awkward as hell, for a thousand, Alex.'" Everyone stares at him. "Not you, Alex. The old *Jeopardy* Alex. My grandma loves binging those."

"Kirk," Sky says, refusing to look in his direction. "Please, stop."

"Yeah, no, I'll shut up."

"Let's begin," Paul says.

The team goes on to recall the events at the Roanoke Colony as Paul asks follow-up questions.

"That's when Caleb and I heard Reuben's transmission after the scream," Sky says, retelling the portion of events from her perspective. "We knew then that we were under attack. Everyone but Alex showed up on the nav schematics. That's how we knew he was in a bad pocket."

"Why weren't these pockets identified and mapped ahead of the mission?"

"It was a new destination," she responds. "If there had been travel prior, it was before the data breach. Rough geographical information aside, we had very little else of the environment beforehand."

Paul nods. "Ah, yes, the Day Zero breach that's caused us a decade's worth of headaches."

"If we conduct another blind mission, I'll need my backup navigator on-site."

"Yeah, no shit," Kirk interjects.

"Regardless," Paul says. "We need to find ways to improve safety measures. You won't always have déjà vu on your side." Paul swivels his chair in Alex's direction. "And this notebook belonging to Thomas Harriot, what were you able to extract from it?"

"It was absolutely fascinating. I mean a long-lost piece of history that people weren't even sure existed. I had it in my hands." Alex sighs. "I can still feel the inscriptions of his initials. And it was—"

"Fascinating," Paul interrupts. "Yes, you've said that and made evident its significance. Now, what did you find *inside* the notebook? Anything of use?"

"No. Before I could really explore, Reuben tackled me. Not that I'm complaining. That may have been the single best moment of my life. But right before I hit the dirt, I did see a sketch on one of the pages. I couldn't make out what he was trying to draw. It looked like a circle shaded in black, and there were a series of lines or maybe dashes drawn either going in or out of the circle. I'm sure the notebook had notes about it. Even if the man was mad, we might've been able to decipher it."

"And this is where you found it?" Paul points to a spot on the three-dimensional map over the table.

Alex nods.

"Are you certain?"

"Yeah, of course. I remember it stood out to me because of where it was. Harriot left the island years ago. That notebook should have been kept in one of the domiciles. And even if Harriot himself wanted it hidden, it would've been buried outside the settlement. But it was right there, with only a thin layer of dirt on top of it. I know this might sound weird, but it's almost like someone wanted us to find it. It was too easy."

"We all know that isn't possible. Not unless someone here brought it and placed it there." Paul shifts his gaze to each member of the team. "Did anyone here plant that notebook when you arrived?"

"I know, I know. It's crazy. All I said is that it *seemed* that way."

"Well, since no one was able to conduct a nav sweep while you were there, I'm afraid we can't replicate it."

"Can't we just go back the hour before and retrieve it?" Reuben asks.

"If it were there, yes."

"I'm telling you," Alex says. "That's the place where I picked it up. I may be off a few square feet, but it wouldn't be hard to—"

"Harriot's notebook isn't there or anywhere inside that settlement," Paul says. "I made the trip myself."

"That's not possible."

"You and I are in complete agreement, Mr. Seung."

"Maybe it was one of them. They—"

"They?" Paul interrupts Alex. "They are no longer with us. Even if they were, it couldn't be done."

Reuben leans forward in his seat. "You're talking about the Stewards. My father, he was one of them, wasn't he?"

"It doesn't matter," Paul says. "Adam Drazen ensured their disbandment. We must work more diligently to find him and spend less of our time chasing historical pursuits. I don't know what's in Harriot's notebook. We can't recover it. Therefore, its contents are no longer pertinent. Now, Reuben, you spent some time with Governor White before the attack. Did he say anything of significance to you?"

White's words ring in his ears.

You're one of—

Reuben can still visualize his pale expression.

"Not really," Reuben responds. "He went on about wanting to find his family and how harsh the winters were. Nothing much outside of that."

"Write up a report of your conversation. Perhaps in doing so, it will encourage your brain to recall more specifics." Paul stands from his seat, now addressing the entire room. "You ought to follow in your leader's footsteps and formulate similar reports. Once that's complete, we should be able to identify if there are any gaps or additional clues. From there, our research team will assess everything, and I will determine your next mission. Thank you all. Good day." He pushes in his chair and proceeds out the door.

"Damn, I didn't even go with you guys, and I still have to write a stupid essay," Kirk says.

"It's report writing, chump," Caleb says. "It's no big, just comes with the territory. Given that Alex here was almost shot, I'd say that we all got off pretty easy."

"Caleb's right," Reuben says. "Things could have been much worse. We need to be more vigilant moving forward about watching the six of the person next to you. And, hey, that goes for me, too. I'm responsible for keeping you all safe and the mission going."

"We're all responsible," Alex says. "We'll do better. I'll do better and try and not get myself stuck in a bad pocket away from the team."

Reuben smirks and pats Alex on the shoulder before turning toward the rest of the group. "All right, everyone. Get some rest if you need it and start those reports."

The team disperses, leaving Reuben to wander down the halls alone with his thoughts. His interactions with White.

The misplaced crib.

Déjà vu.

A group of other mysterious people on the island.

Who were they? Could it have been other travelers? How much did Thomas Harriot really know? What did Dad mean about how it all began with Croatoan?

His fact-finding mission only served to multiply questions.

The desire to learn, to find out, drives him to pace laps within the facility. '*Sometimes, we're not meant to,*' his father's words rattle within, unable to quench his parched longing for answers.

"Reuben," a gentle and familiar voice soothes from behind. He turns to meet her gaze.

"Oh, hey." The muscles in his face contract without his consent, painting an infatuated smile. He knows this dance may dwindle, but it's not today.

"I just wanted to say. I hope you don't feel too bothered or anything by Paul. He's smart and knows how to run the AIC effectively, but he also likes control. You challenge him. Some people don't know how to handle that."

"Do you trust him?"

Sky looks down, her eyes dancing as though in deep thought. "With some things, I guess," she says as she looks back up at him.

"Do you trust me?"

"Well, I could answer yes, but who's to say I'm being truthful." Sky strokes her hair. "The real question is whether or not you trust me to answer you honestly?"

"I'd answer yes. But is that because I'm a good judge of character, or am I just naïve with…" The words 'beautiful women' dance on his tongue, but he bites down on it and swallows instead.

"With?" Sky blushes slightly as if reading his mind.

Silence lingers as each second grows more and more awkward. Reuben rattles his mind to think of something passable, anything.

"…damn good navigators," he finally says.

"Seems like a question for self-reflection." She bites her lip and smooths her hair as if trying to iron out the strange tension between them. "Well, anyway, I should go and write up this report. I'll see you around."

"Yeah, I'll see you."

Reuben continues to his room. The thoughts of Roanoke have all but eroded. Instead, he wonders if his flirting was too overt, too soon, or completely inappropriate.

It just happened.

He arrives at his door and a chill shoots from the back of his neck to the base of his spine. The handle is warm, hours since he had last been to his room. He unlocks the door and enters with a clenched fist. The lights flicker on, illuminating a made-up bed, shut closet, and opened bathroom. His room radiates in an undefiled gesture of calm.

Just as it was.

The words fail to warm the chill. Instead, he searches his room for any subtle hint of disturbance. Suddenly, the dresser pulls his attention. Something about it is different. Sitting on top lays a small cardboard box. He picks up the foreign object, rubbing his thumb against the clear plastic tape imprisoning its contents. He tilts the box onto its side and reads his name, written in black marker.

Reuben.

11

CHEAP BOOZE, PRICELESS ENDEAVOR

Falling snowflakes brighten the evening sky as they float down from heaven, filling the small town's empty streets and buildings.

Adam Drazen crushes them beneath his boots, dwindling and liquefying them between layers of rubber and salt. Cold and bitter is the air around him, gloomy is the sky above, and unforgiving are the icy sidewalks that rob his steps of stability.

He hates these things.

It doesn't just surround him. It *is* him, a reminder of who he fears he's become.

What choice did I have?

A heart was never required to make the hard choice. It could only be a setback, a weakness that clouds sharp judgment and sentences the blood of the innocents to uphold the egos of the arrogant. For Nolan, Aperio, and the others, it must've been easy.

Life without sacrifice. A feast without a slaughter.

Even Nolan himself knew that if a balance were to be reached, it must be paid for, and blood is the only currency. Nolan Greyson could never do it himself, though.

No.

It had to be someone else, someone with grit and determination and none of the other things that weigh a person down.

A heart.

A conscience.

They didn't believe Adam Drazen had them, but they never knew him, not really.

The countless lives lost to genocide, war, and famine. Where was Nolan Greyson's heart when he had the power to overturn injustice? And yet, Adam Drazen is the one being hunted as a cold and heartless killer.

This world deserves better.

It's the only truth he's managed to hold onto in all these years as his reputation and life's work were stripped from him.

There is now only one person who holds the key to everything in her hands, and she doesn't even know it. She may know it's valuable, but there's no way she truly understands what she's guarding. He's come here, to this barren, podunk town to find her and retrieve the Chártis, the key of keys.

He trudges up to the liquor store, the doorbell chiming as he enters the warm space. No displays or décor greet him at the entrance of the state-run establishment. Its meticulously clean yet deteriorated environment reminds him of a well-maintained hospital that hasn't seen a renovation in fifty years. Faded blue shopping baskets and stacks of paper bags loiter by the door. Only the gloss from the yellow hue of the once-white floors provides any semblance of welcome.

What the store lacks in flare, it compensates for in selection. Eight aisles of shelving line the space from floor to ceiling as if they were hallways paved by a collage of glass. Bottles of every size, shape, and color occupy each shelf. Drazen ventures to the back, beginning his self-guided tour through spirits and scotch. While browsing, he peers over at the register near the front of the store as a group of three young men approach the lone store clerk. He'll need to wait until they're gone.

A towering step ladder lies along the back shelf near the store's corner. Above the final step, Drazen can make out the exquisite bottles locked behind a pane of spotless glass. They glisten like prized trophies on display. He climbs to the top and glances over the sea of valuable spirits, admiring and desiring them.

He peers toward the front as yells break out to find three men harassing the clerk. His muscles tense as the scene unfolds, and his knuckles turn white as the ladder seethes with his anger.

The bullying. The disregard. The disrespect.

Not your concern, he tries to tell himself.

"You gotta pay for that!" The clerk's voice cracks. The men pay him no mind as they continue to shove miniature bottles into their pants. Drazen's heart thunders as it picks up momentum, a raucous drumline goading him into action.

"I don't think so," one of the men retorts. "I come in here and buy your expensive ass booze all the time. The least you can do is to let us get some free samples." The young men laugh as they knock over shopping baskets and some of the remaining miniature bottles at the counter. "Besides, you're not gonna do jack shit." The man leans his head over the counter, only inches from the clerk's face. "Isn't that right?"

The clerk opens his mouth to respond, but no words follow.

From the ladder, Drazen's legs fill with blood and wrath, propelling him down the steps and onto their level, down to where spectators dare not venture. Intervening could cause a greater commotion. Someone could call the police and burn his location, but it doesn't matter. He cannot sit idly by and watch this poor man be ridiculed like this. It goes against his very nature, against everything he is fighting for, even if it is but a drop in the ocean compared to his true purpose. Still, thoughts of doubt creep into his head as he nears the counter.

Why should I risk everything for the good of one?

He stops mid-stride as the answer comes to him.

The Stewards.

Passive and passionless.

They saw the world end many times over and did nothing. Nolan Greyson cowardly hid behind a philosophy of inaction, convincing all the rest that history was just there to learn from. That somehow, we had to allow millions to die so that we could take away some vague lesson about senseless violence. Drazen saw through the bullshit then and sees the truth now. The only senseless violence is the one that you allow to continue when you have the power to stop it.

Drazen looks up as the man shoves the clerk. People dedicated to inaction are who the Stewards were.

Not him.

He can't stand by and just let terrible things happen.

None of the men, including the store clerk, notice him at first, each distracted by their adrenaline-fueled tasks. The shortest of the three barks orders at the other two, waving his arm toward the entrance. They comply without debate, going to the door, and locking everyone in. Drazen looks back at the shorter man, the leader, as he balls a fist, cocking it back to strike the clerk.

"I wouldn't," Drazen says. All four men veer toward his voice in stunned silence. "How old are you?"

"Old enough to whoop your ass, Grandpa," the leader responds. "Now, why don't you mind your own? In case you can't tell, I'm in the middle of getting some damn customer service." He turns back to the clerk.

Drazen's hand flexes, the overwhelming desire to tear them apart screams to be heard, but he pushes it down. It's what makes him different. Not the rage but the patience. "Nineteen? Twenty?" he says.

The leader veers back toward him and steps in his direction. "Listen, Gramps. I only give one warning." He reaches the small of his back, whips out a pocketknife, and ejects the blade. "How old are you?"

"Old," Drazen says. "Older than I even look. And I see what you're doing to that poor man behind the counter. You think because you and your friends can come in here and push him around that he'll fear you. You think you can control him. You can't. Not like that. He is afraid. We can all see that. Your mistake is to think that it's you he's afraid of. If you controlled him, then he wouldn't be clenching so hard to that handgun just under the counter. He's more afraid of what he can do to you than what you can do to him."

All three men turn at once to see the clerk's right hand resting beneath the countertop.

"He doesn't want to hurt you, and neither do I," Drazen says.

"Bullshit," the leader says. "There's nothing under there. You think I'm some punk? Like I wouldn't check before taking my samples?"

"Is that really the gamble you want to make?"

"Man, we're about to whoop yo—"

"You already gave me your false warning."

"False?" All three step toward Drazen.

"I'll show you what a real one looks like. No one here's been hurt. I'd prefer it stays that way. Dump out your pockets and walk out the door. You won't be pursued. No one's coming after you. I sure as shit have much better things to do. But if you do something stupid—especially with that knife—I'll make sure it pierces your skin. This is not a joke. One of you might die. I can't promise otherwise. What I can promise is that one way or another this ends."

The leader nods. His two followers rush Drazen. One swings his fist toward Drazen's face as he lunges back and crouches. He drives his shoulder into his opponent's gut, grabs his knees, and launches him over his back and into a nearby shelf.

Glass shatters, liquor spills.

Before the other man can strike, Drazen grabs him by his wrist, extends his arm, and jabs his fist into the outside of his elbow. His scream muffles the sound of shattering bone. Drazen winds his leg and drives his boot into the man's hip, sending him tumbling to the ground in a gurgle of tears and agony.

Adam Drazen glares at the leader. But before he can move, there is a crackle of glass from behind. He turns just as his attacker lunges from the bed of broken bottles. His breath leaves his body. The world spins before exploding with searing pain. Drazen lifts a hand, pulling a shard of glass from his cheek. Whiskey and vermouth seep into the fresh wound with a sterilizing pain.

His attacker mounts him, fists flying. Drazen raises his forearms, shielding himself as best he can as blood, glass, and booze rain down among a fury of strikes. His opponent swings again. Drazen catches his fist and drags it down. He latches onto his upper arm with a free hand, swings his hips, and thrusts the attacker off balance, slamming him to the floor.

Drazen counter mounts before the man can react and drives booze-soaked fists to his face. Each strike is met with a grunt. Again, again, and again Drazen hits him. After thirty seconds, the grunting stops, but the punches continue.

They could've stopped.

Why should I?

His knuckles throb in pain as he clenches them to strike once more. He comes down and the motionless man's face cracks beneath his fist. Blood spatters across the floor and onto the shoes of the stunned leader. Drazen stands and meets his terror-filled eyes, pleading for deliverance.

I warned them.

"N-n-now," the man says, stumbling and dropping his knife. "Y-y-you don't...you don't..."

The man just stands there, nearly motionless as Drazen grabs him by his jacket collar and slams him on the ground. Drazen can feel the man tense under his grip, horrified shock flooding his eyes.

Almost done.

A small miniature bottle pokes up from the leader's pocket and Drazen smirks, pulling it free and shattering the bottom against the ground.

"No," the man says.

But it's too late.

Drazen lifts the glass to the man's eye, cupping it and applying pressure. Screams pierce and fill every crevice of the store. Tears and blood unify, the fruit of his agony streaming down his face.

After a few seconds, Drazen stops and chucks the bloody broken bottle across the room. He grabs the sobbing yet still conscious man and drags him to a nearby wall, sitting him up. The leader clenches his hand over the battered eye, and looks up at Drazen, now towering over him.

"You see that?" Drazen says, sensing the exhaustion in his voice as he points to the leader's fallen followers. "That's what you did. You could've walked out of here." He spits up a cocktail of saliva and blood. "I didn't want to do that. You get that, right? Now, you must wear that scar around your eye. You're lucky it'll heal." He wants to say more but has no wind to say it.

He turns his back on the wounded leader and moves toward the front counter. The clerk jolts back, revealing a tightly held revolver shaking in his hand. Drazen says nothing as he reaches him, blood and booze dripping onto the counter. The clerk releases his grip, and the revolver drops.

"Please," the clerk says, "I don't want any of this."

"Of course not," Drazen says. "None of us want this. I'm..." he takes a brief pause to refuel on air, "I'm sorry for the damage."

The clerk nods. "Are you okay? You're bleeding every-where." He reaches for his phone and begins to dial. Drazen raises his hand, clenches the man's wrists, and pulls his phone away. "Sir, I need to call the police—"

"You will." Drazen sets the man's phone face down on the counter and slides it back to him. "You have to. Look at this place."

The clerk stares at Drazen wide-eyed, shaking his head. "I don't understand."

"I just need something from you first, and I'll be out of your hair. Will even help compensate for the damage."

The man's eyebrows raise, his face becoming more puzzled.

"I'm just an employee. The state owns the store. They'll be going through insurance and all that. I don't need compensation."

"Insurance?" Drazen chuckles. "Insurance companies are professional. Too professional if you want my take. They'll scour through every detail of the police report, conduct their investigation, and find some way to screw over the least powerful party involved. Who do you think that would be? The commonwealth of Virginia that owns this store?" Drazen nods toward the man's revolver. "Or the lawyerless store clerk ille-gally carrying a firearm on the property?"

The man drops his head and lets out a deep breath. "Shit."

"The key," Drazen says. "To the cabinet in the back."

He unclips the set from his belt and flips through them. Seconds later, he removes a single key from the ring and hands it to Drazen.

"Thank you," Drazen says before walking to the aisle with the rolling safety ladder. He climbs up, unlocks the glass door, and slides it open. A single bottle calls his attention. Its upscale yet common name does nothing to sway him. Its printed age, however, promises to pass on its forty years of wisdom. He smirks and takes the priceless bottle of scotch.

Advancing back to the register, he stops at the whiskey section along a nearby aisle. His knees crack as they bend to support the weight of his squat. Plastic bottles on the bottom shelf glisten as he reaches for the nearest one. He tilts the label toward the light. The small cursive name brand is illegible. The word 'Whiskey,' however, lies large, centered, and bold across the front. He secures his grip on both bottles and sets them onto the register.

Two of the men remain unconscious. Their leader stares in silence as Drazen pulls out a cloth sack from his inner jacket pocket. He dumps the contents across the counter.

"Oh shit," the clerk says as paper bills collide and scatter everywhere. He shivers as a variety of countless green faces stare back at him.

"I'm looking for someone," Drazen says. "She wouldn't be a regular. Not much of a drinker either. All she might get is a single bottle like this." Drazen holds up one of the miniatures beside the register. "It would likely be schnapps or vodka."

"We get a lot of people—"

"In this shitty little town? C'mon, man."

"You'd be surprised. What do you think people do to pass the time in a place like this? Plus, we're not far from the highway. Plenty of out-of-towners."

"All right." Drazen nods before picking up one of the bills. "Do you have a pen?"

"Yeah." The man hands him one from behind the register.

Drazen scribes a series of numbers along the outer borders, above Franklin's face. He sets it into the clerk's hand. "She's young and pretty. Might seem a little off or on edge. When you see her, give that number a call. My associate—"

"Sir, I can't...I can't do that."

Drazen plops the sack on top of the money and lets out a sigh. "Well then, go ahead. Help me scoop all this back in."

"Sir—"

"These two bottles and the cloth bag. I'm leaving with them. I can leave with an empty bag or a full one. These bills are a collective thing. If any of them stay, they all stay. That includes the one you're holding."

The man pauses, but Drazen can see in his eyes that he's already decided. "How old is she?"

Drazen smiles. "Late twenties, early thirties." He grabs the two bottles and the cloth bag and motions to the door before looking back. "Remember, that's the number you need to call."

Before leaving, Drazen stops in front of the injured leader, who only stares at him for a moment before averting his eyes.

Drazen smirks and continues to the exit.

Snowfall ceases by the time he arrives at his safe house. The boarded steps bend and creak with the slightest shift in weight. Inside, Drazen lights a candle and maneuvers through the labyrinth before reaching the mesh of kitchen and greenhouse, an unorthodox collision of two spaces once unacquainted.

He sets down the two bottles on the counter and pulls out a single glass. Candlelight gleams against the crystal, outlining its wide bottom and narrow mouth. He opens the cheap whiskey and pours a few ounces into the glass. Others may have gone for the priceless scotch first, but not him. Cheap things are taken and consumed while precious things are earned. And he hasn't earned it, not yet.

Drazen takes a sip, embracing the harsh burn of the bottom-shelf spirit. It warms his throat but soothes nothing.

This world deserves better.

* * *

KIRK PULLS UP to the house and parks on the street. Heavy raindrops batter his red Chevy Camaro. He's half-relieved it's getting a much-needed wash but irritated he'll have to haul multiple bags of groceries in the cold rain. He takes a moment to blast the last few lines of an alternative rock song on the radio before cutting the engine. Over the years, he's come to realize the behavior makes him look like a complete tool. But he doesn't care. He doesn't do it for himself or even to tick off the neighbors nearby. He does it for her.

It's his grandmother's house, and this is their tradition. He's been dropping groceries off for her since he could ride his bike. She would always give him grief about his taste in music, and he'd always turn it up. As a middle-school kid, he'd do it to annoy and taunt her but, as time went on, it evolved into something more. He'd play the music, she'd complain, he'd turn it up louder, and then they'd share a smile. For the first time in years, Kirk takes the time to think about the tradition. On the surface, it was a battle of generations. But, to them, it's something they shared, an endearing way they found to connect and know each other.

He slings every bag onto his arms. It offsets his balance and nearly pulls him to the ground, but he doesn't care. There will only be one trip. Halfway up the driveway and completely soaked, it hits him.

The mail.

He veers back and trudges toward the mailbox. With arms and hands completely utilized, Kirk grabs the two pieces of mail with his teeth. By the time he gets to the front steps, she already has the door open for him. He rushes in and beelines for the kitchen counter.

"Take your shoes off," she calls to him as he struggles not to drop everything. Kirk lets out a frustrated sigh and kicks off his shoes in the middle of the hallway. Finally, he gets to the kitchen and hurdles the bags onto the counter. "You got teeth marks on my letters," she says as he begins putting away the food.

"Well, what the hell do you want from me? I've only got two arms."

"Hey," she snaps. "Watch the language. You know, when your father spoke like that, we washed his mouth out with soap."

"That is some cruel sh-shtuff." He smiles at her, and she pulls down her glasses, staring at him as if waiting for something.

"Do I have to beg for a kiss from my grandchildren now?"

Kirk kisses her on the cheek, and she plants one on his forehead.

"It's good to see you," she says. "I was getting worried when you didn't show up earlier. I had to put your lunch in Tupperware."

Kirk sighs. "Yeah, sorry about that, Grandma. I got held up at work and—"

"That job of yours again, huh? Is it that pretty lady keeping you?"

"Who? Sky?" He chuckles as he finishes putting the groceries away. "She's my supervisor. And no, she hasn't. She's been great about me taking a longer lunch to stop by here. It's just other stuff that's been going on."

"Careful with the pretty ones."

Kirk rolls his eyes. "Okay, Grandma."

"And you also shouldn't work your life away."

"I don't plan on it..." Kirk pauses before pulling a crumpled brochure from his pocket. He looks at it, admiring the palm trees in the sand beside the beach, then he hands it to her. "I was going to surprise you next week, but what the hell. It's just outside Tampa, near the water. Figured it would be a great way to celebrate your eightieth. Plus, we can go down and see your sister while we're there."

She reaches for her chest as if to feel for her heart. He sees it on her face: surprise, bewilderment, joy. "Kirky...is this real?" They share a smile.

"Yeah, Grandma, it's real."

She hugs him and squeezes with all her might. "And you're coming, too?"

"I put the leave request in today," he says.

"And your father? Is he coming?"

Kirk feels it in his chest, the pain as if someone just drove a dagger into his heart. "No," he lets out quietly as he thinks of how much her son, his father, has neglected her. "He's got a work trip, a congressional retreat or something and can't make it. Besides, we'll probably be better off anyway. When he's not yelling at his aides on the phone and actually graces us with more than five minutes of his attention, he's like zero fun. A complete buzzkill."

"Ah maybe, but at least he doesn't use foul language."

Kirk shakes his head. "Yeah, Grandma, but he's an asshole. Last time he ate all your food and almost gave you the wrong medication."

She smiles. "I hope those people you work with see how sweet you are."

Kirk laughs. "No, there they think I'm the asshole...which I kind of am."

"You know, Kirky, it makes me sad that you two barely talk. None of us will be here forever. Life's too short to hold grudges. I'm not blind. I know what a piece of work that son of mine is, but he's my son. And he's your father. He's made mistakes, but even good things can come out of mistakes. Look at your job, the government thing. That was your father who helped you get your foot in the door, didn't he?"

Kirk says nothing.

"All I'm saying is that forgiveness isn't that bad," she continues. "It's a good thing. That's the thing that'll last. It's like the priest said in mass the other day, 'the grass withers, the flower fades, but the word of the Lord will stand forever."

Kirk wants to roll his eyes at the religious reference, but he doesn't. "Okay, Grandma," he says finally.

She pulls out the leftovers from earlier and heats them up for him. Kirk eats it with a smile before heading for the door to return to work.

"Oh, wait!" she calls to him before he can leave. "I almost forgot. You have a package. Some man left it at the door."

"Man, what man? Like a postman?"

"No, I don't think so. I know Mr. Walters, and it wasn't him. I saw him from my bedroom window. He was gone by the time I got to the door. It had your name on it, so I put it in the spare bedroom, meaning to give it to you when you came over. Can you believe it slipped my mind till just now? You know your father would always say that there's nothing I'd forget." She laughs slightly to herself. "Maybe it should be, 'the grass withers, and the mind fades.'"

Kirk smiles. "You're hilarious, Grandma." He walks back toward the spare room until, stopping short as his phone vibrates. He reads the display and sighs. "Ah, shit, it's work."

"Maybe I should've set up a swear jar years ago. Could you imagine? I'd have a nice retirement home in Tampa, all thanks to that mouth of yours."

"I'm sorry, Grandma, the package will have to wait. Something huge just happened."

12

FORTY-EIGHT MINUTES

Reuben's heartbeat pulsates in his hands, time slowing in anticipation. The cardboard box sticks to his sweaty fingers as he opens it and peers in. A sigh escapes him, leaving a disappointing hollowness in its wake.

Nothing.

Is this some strange joke? Is someone just screwing with me?

Reuben slumps onto his bed, staring at the emptiness inside. It's been months, and everything about the AIC, his father, and Chronos remains shrouded in mystery. His chest had tingled only a few moments ago, filled with the excitement of finally getting answers. It was premature.

He sits there holding it in his lap for what feels like hours, unable and unwilling to part with it.

No, it can't be nothing.

His father's journal is gone. Roanoke was a dead end. No one knows anything, and everything is a mystery. He needs something, anything.

He looks down at the box before releasing his grip in defeat, watching as it tumbles to the ground, landing on its side. His eyes blink, and there it is. As if being pulled, the box reverses course and flops onto its bottom.

The realization comes to him at once.

No, not empty. Hidden.

He leaps from the bed and rummages through his dresser. A piece of metal nicks his fingernails, and he takes hold. In an almost déjà vu-like fashion, he unfolds the end of the paperclip, slips it between the box's inner edge, and exposes its false bottom. There, in its center, a taped-down antique key lies waiting. He removes the tape, picks up the key, and examines it. The key fits perfectly in his palm as if it were meant for him, as if it had been waiting for him. Reuben smiles and squeezes it. He can feel his thoughts take him.

Journal. Drawer. Box. Key. The paperclip was a key to the journal and a key to the key. But what is the key a key to? Are you doing this, Dad? Is someone else? Who else?

He knows that hours of meandering contemplation will lead only to more hours of meandering contemplation. So, instead, he just holds it. The questions subside, and a greater truth sinks in. The box was never empty, and hope is with him still.

* * *

DAYS LATER, he slouches over his food in the cafeteria, still pondering the key. The steamed broccoli and mystery meat cool before he can take the first bite.

"And I thought I was anti-social."

Reuben looks up as Alex approaches.

"Where've you been, man?"

Sky comes from behind with her tray.

Reuben straightens his back and smirks. "Been around. Busy with this report, mostly."

Alex shakes his head and takes his seat across from him as

Sky joins them at the table. "Don't get me going on that," Alex says. "At least you don't also have to take your three kids to swim practice, soccer games, and every other extracurricular their schools offer."

"Fair point."

Rueben glances at Sky as they attend to their meals. In between bites, she looks up, making eye contact with him before glancing away.

"What about you?" he asks. "Were you able to start your report?"

She smiles and nods. "Uh, yeah, almost finished. It's easy once you've figured out what to say."

"And what are you going to say?" Alex interjects.

Sky turns to him, grinning wide. "That I didn't get trapped in a pocket."

Alex lets out a laugh. "Ah, shit, I have to include that part on mine, don't I?"

Reuben smiles as their playful banter continues, relishing in the company of people who have somehow become more than just members of his time-traveling team. They've become his friends. The smile erodes, and a heaviness fills his chest. He takes a sip of his lemon-lime electrolyte beverage, washing out the artificial taste of the food, hoping that the discomfort is only heartburn.

It isn't, of course.

Reuben sighs, but Sky and Alex barely seem to notice. It's not the food that gives him pause. It's them. In a matter of months, they've managed to do the one thing that no one has been able to do since his discharge from active duty. They've earned his trust. And yet, he can't bring himself to do it. He can't open his mouth and tell them all his secrets.

I should tell them.

"What do you think, man?" Alex says.

"What?" Reuben snaps to attention.

"Look at this guy," Alex says with a playful nudge and continues, "off in his own world. The game this Sunday. Do you think Virginia will pull it off?"

"Uh, I don't know. Maybe."

"They will," Sky says.

"Seriously?" Alex glares at her. "Look at the stats. It's completely against them. They need it, sure. But the chances are slim at best."

"Well, that's how I know they will. If stats proved everything, people wouldn't watch. They wouldn't place bets either. When the cards are stacked against you, you turn to the bleachers. The fans are loyal, and it's a home game. They'll be there to push them. And it's times like that, when everything is against you, that you turn to your fans for help. Stats can't measure that."

"No, but they don't hurt either." Alex crumples his napkin. "Wish we could forward travel, though. Then we'd know for sure."

"Hey, guys," Reuben says. "I need to tell you both something, and it has to stay between us." His eyes scan the room and meet no less than four security cameras. "Not here. Section Seven in twenty minutes."

* * *

ALEX AND SKY enter the training room and stroll toward the rearmost section less than half an hour later. Moonlight greets them as they cross its barrier. Crickets chirp while the dew resting on the grass clings to their shoes. They approach the front steps to a wood-paneled home. Its beige coloring and freshly painted white trim bathe its aging body with a taste of youth. Sky rings the doorbell. Reuben answers and welcomes them into the house.

"I don't recognize this setting," Alex says. "Was this in the archives?"

"Yeah," Reuben replies, "but you would never know to look for it." He leads them to the living room.

"How were you able to find it?" Sky asks.

"Because it's my house. When I learned about Section Seven, I found out that only a limited number of locations were archived. Each one of them being an hour-long loop of a single setting. It's why everyone comes here for their breaks. It's predictable and as relaxing as you'd want it to be. This is a carbon copy of our house when we must have been away on vacation."

Alex glances up the stairs. "That explains why no one's home."

"I think my father archived it when he worked here. It's not one of the generic or pre-programmed settings. That's why it doesn't come up. I spent hours playing around with the archive until I finally searched manually for it. The house only came up when I searched for the exact name of the street we lived on."

Sky strolls through the living room, observing the family photos on display. She stops at the fireplace and smiles at the portrait above its mantle, strokes of green and dots of red and white paint form the setting of an outdoor picnic. At the center of the impressionistic painting, Reuben, as a child, sits with his parents.

"You didn't keep the bowl cut?" Sky remarks.

"If my mom had her way, I'd still have it." Reuben motions forward and takes a closer look at the painting. "I remember this day. We took a picture before it started raining. My mom loved it so much that she had a local artist paint an impression of it."

* * *

THE THREE OF them eventually take their seats as Reuben gets them up to speed on all that transpired leading up to the mysterious key.

"It has to be someone who works on Chronos," Sky says. "With all the security, it would be impossible for someone from the outside even to find this place, let alone break into restricted areas."

"I'm not so sure," Alex says. "I mean, yeah, some random guys couldn't, but maybe someone who knows the systems. Even our engineers constantly complain about not being familiarized with all the capabilities. Ever since the data breach, we've been working with remnants of the old project trying to put the pieces back together."

"Who on the outside would know about the project?" Reuben asks before answering his question. "Drazen. Do you think it might be him?"

"If it is, then we have larger problems. Plus, if it were, why wouldn't he slit all our throats at night? It could be one of the other Stewards."

"Aren't they all dead?"

"Maybe. That's the thing though, man. I know for a fact that—"

The lights in the house start to pulsate bright red. A deafening buzz follows suit, matching the red light's intensity. As they run out of the house and down the porch steps, the moon bleeds blood red as if wounded. The crimson coloring radiates down onto the trees while Paul Peterson's face cuts through the branches.

The house, trees, and grass all fade from existence.

Paul's mouth moves as if yelling, but nothing else is audible above the buzzing noise. Seconds later, the noise ceases, and the red light fades to white. "You three follow me. Now!" They arrive at the front of the training room to find Caleb and Kirk awaiting them.

"Sir," Reuben says while running to the front of the pack. "You have to understand—"

"No, it's you that must understand," Paul says. "On its last objective, your team found itself in peril due to a lack of communication. It has since been addressed. Today, the three of you have the audacity to turn off your headsets to indulge in Section Seven recreation. An urgent matter comes to fruition, and not one of you can be found."

Reuben, Sky, and Alex sigh near unison.

"Even Kirk kept an open line of communication from his grandmother's house."

"Hey, I resent that sh—" Kirk pauses as Paul and the others glare at him. "Whatever, I'm here."

"Urgent?" Reuben says.

"We've been hacked," Paul says. "An unknown entity broke into Chronos to link to July of 1943 in Sicily during the Allied assault against the Axis powers, known as Operation Husky. There will come a time to investigate *how* and *who*, but it's not now. This may be related to our ongoing mission to capture Adam Drazen, or it may not. What is certain is that we've not seen a breach like this in over a decade."

As Paul speaks, Reuben can feel the angst in his chest, but he's not afraid. No. He's excited. A key intended for him, friends he can trust, and a real lead to Drazen all find him in a single week. "What are our orders?"

"The intruder made the jump twelve minutes ago. You all know well what happens to the link outside the span of an hour. You and your team now have forty-eight minutes to make the link if we're ever to find out who's behind this. Otherwise, our mystery person becomes a ghost."

Sighs and murmurs echo from the team. Reuben's excitement quickly fades as the reality of the mission hits him.

"Forty-eight minutes?" Reuben repeats in disbelief. "That's barely enough time to pack the necessary gear. And that's just packing. That doesn't even include site exploitation, safety briefs, assimilation training, nothing. I understand how significant it is to find out who's on the other side. Believe me, I want to know more than anything, but you can't expect me to drop my team in an active war zone without the proper preparation. The four of us going—"

"Five," Paul interrupts. "Kirk goes, too."

"What?"

"Sky said it herself, you can't properly navigate an unexploited site without a backup navigator."

Sky's mouth opens, but no refutation comes to her lips.

"We don't have to do this mission. We can wait until—"

"*You* don't have to do this mission," Paul says. "Your team, however, will go, and you can decide whether or not you want to lead them."

Reuben argues no further. The safety and wellbeing of his team are at stake. The only way for them now is forward.

"It may even be Adam Drazen on the other side. This might be our only chance in catching your father's killer," Paul says, letting the following silence flood Rueben's mind with the idea of catching his father's murderer.

Reuben steps forward, aligning himself beside Paul to face his team.

"Alex, prep the comms and find out what military units supported the operation. From there, we tailor our uniforms." He looks over to Caleb. "Collect the appropriate weaponry from the era. Rifles and explosives are primary. Sidearms, only if we have time to grab them. Collaborate with Alex on the armor." He shifts to the remaining two. "Set the sections of the training room to carousel, like we did for Roanoke. Once we've collected our gear, we can start to prep in there. It will buy us some time, but we still need to move quickly. Pull the most recent maps for the location. Once deployed, we'll calibrate the navs."

The team nods before running in every which direction. Reuben pulls Paul aside before he can leave the training area. "If anything happens, you won't get to lecture us on safety protocols."

"I don't intend to." Paul's stoic face fails to display any emotion. "I trust you'll return each body. And hopefully an extra."

"Do you really think it's Drazen?"

"It's possible, yes. Although it's strange he'd make such a high visibility move."

"If it's really him, then he could be testing us to see how we'd react. Or worse, setting a trap."

"Let's hope that's not the case," Paul says.

"Hope? If any—"

"Careful," Paul says with narrowing eyes.

"If the Agency has our best interest, it wouldn't knowingly send us in as bait."

"That sounds like an irredeemable act, one reserved for people like Adam Drazen."

"That's right."

"Perhaps it's not him on the other side," Paul says. "Maybe it's one of the people who have been reported missing from the project. There was a lab tech that worked closely with your father. Her name's Nea, and she's been missing for a long time, so long that we presumed her dead. It might be her." Paul walks toward the exit before stopping mid-step. "Oh, and I'd be very careful in the future about delivering thinly veiled threats...I may be direct, but when it comes to how we do business here, I expect nothing short of professionalism." Paul walks away, leaving Reuben to prepare for the impromptu mission.

Reuben eyes his watch. Forty minutes remain on the countdown. A surge of questions assails his consciousness.

Who's hacking into Chronos? How are they doing it? Is there anything else that Paul isn't sharing about this mysterious link?

These and more rattle the barrier between thought and the outside. He rushes to secure the mental barricade with the task at hand. The questions will have their day. They will flood, pummel, and overcome any obstacle in their path, but it won't be today. Every thought, breath, and movement bring the team closer to their deployment, closer to war, and hopefully, closer to finding Drazen.

With another twenty minutes elapsed, Reuben helps Alex to drag in uniforms to Section One.

"I tried my best to get the insignia right," Alex says. "But wasn't able to confirm the specs with the time constraints." He tosses Reuben a sack containing his WWII Army uniform. Reuben pulls it out and inspects it, noting a multi-layered triangle—colored red, gold, and blue—on the left-hand shoulder of the jacket.

"It's the insignia for the US Seventh Army, led by Patton. 'Pyramid of Power' was the official motto. 'Seven Steps to Hell' was the unofficial," Alex says.

Reuben nods. "Looks good to me. And if it's not quite right, then hopefully the gunfire and explosions will be more captivating than our appearance."

"I'm not sure that's comforting." Alex tightens the straps of the other sacks. "Jones should be here soon with the weapons and helmets. Unfortunately, we don't have much as far as body armor. We're being dropped in decades before they used Kevlar in the military. All we can really use is the snakeskin stuff under our clothes."

"Will it stop a bullet?"

"Yeah, depending on the caliber, it can. It'll do nothing against close quarter melee attacks, though. Also, if you do get shot, it'll only stop the bullet from puncturing. Your body will still absorb the full impact of the round. So, expect broken bones if that happens."

"I'm not sure *that's* comforting," Reuben says, regurgitating

Alex's own words. "Hey, real quick while it's just us..." He glances around the voided barrier, verifying no one else can hear them.

"What? About Paul busting in on us earlier? Man, that was close. I thought for sure he knew about the—"

"No, not that."

"Although I'm not sure that us going into a war zone is much better."

"How is it someone can link into Chronos from the outside? I mean, if you don't physically deploy from the platform, how can you use Chronos to time travel?"

"I don't know," Alex says. "I've never actually seen it before. From what I understand, the platform is the gateway. You would need an elaborate shortcut. The only way I could think of is if that person had a modified watch." He holds out his watch. "It's probably the reason that tampering with the mechanics of it is heavily restricted. I mean, you have to fill out scores of paperwork just to change the battery. Personally, it seems like the watch does more than linking. Think about it, man. All these things you see in the training room come from only Chronos's residual energy. Now, imagine what a modified watch can do when it's directly linked to the machine."

Footsteps patter just beyond the barrier. "Okay, carousel mode is set for section one," Sky says as she passes the threshold with Kirk and Caleb. "It will reset every five minutes. That should stretch our fifteen minutes to an hour and a half."

"That's great. Thank you, Sky," Reuben says before turning to address the whole team. "Okay, you heard it. That's time saved, but we're still short. Each person will have to give their brief while the rest of the team changes and packs their gear. I hope you guys can multitask. Since we're going to an active combat zone, Caleb Jones will begin first with the weapons and tactics."

"All right, everybody. Listen up, and this won't take long."

Jones drags out a chest of rifles, grenades, and other explosive ordinances. "Today, you're going to get a taste of what it means to be a Marine." He explains each one as the rest of the team scurries to pack their equipment and put on their uniform.

Ex nihilo, concrete floods and hardens around them, forming from nothing and creating the walls of a briefing room bunker. As Caleb continues his brief, Reuben walks the room and checks on his team. Metal clanks and echoes across the floor as Kirk fumbles to catch his tumbling canteen. It stops shy of Reuben's boot. He picks it up and hands it to Kirk, who neither makes eye contact nor responds.

"Hey, man, how are you holding up?" Reuben asks.

Kirk's fingers shake as he attempts to shove the canteen into its cover. "Just peachy."

"It's okay if you're nervous. Pretty sure we all are. Except maybe Jones. This kind of thing excites him."

Kirk snickers, his eyes darting around the room.

"Listen, I know that this isn't the ideal place to get your feet wet with hostile environments. War is an awful thing that we have to do sometimes. Just remember your training and try to keep your head down as much as possible. We've got your back." Reuben grabs Kirk's other canteen, drapes its cover, and tightens the straps before handing it back to him.

"I've got your back."

Kirk looks up at him, smiles slightly, and nods. They spend the next few minutes packing the rest of his equipment.

Eight minutes to deployment, the now packed and somewhat prepared team makes their way out of the training area toward the Chronos lab floor. They arrive and rapidly climb the steps to the platform of the machine.

* * *

PAUL APPROACHES THE BASE. A large digital clock at the rear of the lab reads *01:56*, counting down by the second. "Is your team ready?" he asks, and Reuben nods. "Very well."

The columns begin to spin as Chronos awakes. Its light pierces the team from ever-moving angles, and they vanish before Paul can recite the destination. He glares at the nearest lab tech.

"I'm sorry, sir, but we had to. Didn't want to risk any of them getting caught between the two locations."

Paul sighs. "Next time, please provide me the courtesy of notification before cutting me off, Jefferson."

"Yes, sir," he answers. Less than five seconds later, a rapid, repetitive beeping sound emits from Jefferson's workstation. "Ah, sir...we've been hacked."

"Yes, of course, we have. It happened an hour ago. The whole reason for this mission—"

"No. This is something else." Jefferson swivels his screen as Paul approaches. "It linked on almost immediately after deploying the team. The signature is different and everything."

Paul covers his mouth and steps away from the screen.

"Sir, it's almost as if whoever it is...it's like they were waiting for us."

13

FIELD OF BULLETS

Reuben's eyes remain shut, and he covers his ears as he does his best to shield them from the chaos of light and electric sound. As if taking a natural pause between breaths, the massive energy shifts and begins to quake from the ground below.

Boom!

The ground trembles as his knees hit solid ground. His eyes dart open with a sharp intake of breath, and his hands fall forward into the thick muck that surrounds him. Shards of green grass pierce through the mud to tickle his palms.

Boom! Boom! Boom!

Heavy fire tears through the summer breeze. His hands fly into the mud with eyes frantically searching.

Come on! Where is the damn thing?

Mud flies with bullets as Rueben searches for his only saving grace. Just when he thinks all is lost, an anomaly in the earth catches his eye.

Gotcha!

Rueben grabs ahold of the rifle and brings it close with a

sigh of relief. He's unsure if the trembling ground is because of the nearby artillery rounds or his pounding heart.

"Provide sitrep, over!" he says over the local network.

No one answers.

"Provide sitrep, over!" he repeats the message, this time to all channels, including headquarters. Silence looms over the headset. Not even static returns to him.

Nothing.

The heavy artillery ceases, giving way to more concentrated bursts of machine-gunfire as if passing the baton to a more focused lethal force.

They're closing in.

He props himself against the muddy hill and dares a look. Gunfire bursts, sending muck and grass flying overhead.

Dammit!

"Provide sitrep, over!" Nothing. No one. If hope were a person, she wouldn't be here.

Not in hell.

Not in war.

Rueben pushes himself further into the hill with his rifle pressed close to his chest. Low voices can be heard in the distance, faint but drawing nearer. He listens intently to make out the language. Anything other than English likely means danger knowing the Axis's hold on the island. His knuckles are pale against his rifle as the group starts to close on his position. Still, Reuben can't make out the language. He cannot wait much longer. The closer they get to him, the harder it will be to sneak away.

Rueben turns to find a small shed-like structure sitting in the distance. Near the wooded tree line, it reminds him of a toll booth into the wilderness, a means of escape whose cost is unknown. Between him and the structure lies fifty yards of open land. The hill might be able to conceal him for the first twenty yards or so, but anything beyond that will be fair game to those beyond.

Reuben takes a deep breath, his mind swimming with risk and benefit.

There isn't time. If I wait, and they aren't friendlies, then it's over. Who am I kidding? It's probably over anyway.

Seeing no other alternative, Rueben kicks himself up from the mud, slings his rifle, and runs. At ten yards, silence. Twenty yards, twenty-five, still nothing. More than half the distance across and completely exposed, Reuben picks up his sprint.

Almost there.

Dew, drag, and the weight of his boots pull at him, but he refuses to let it slow him down. He can feel his heartbeat pick up, but not out of dread.

No, not dread.

Not fear.

Something else.

It's the shed, coming closer and closer to him as if reaching to pull him into safety. It's hope, and he can almost touch it, almost taste it. Almost there.

Then it hits him.

As if daggers were being shoved into his ears, he hears it. Sharp, cruel, and unmistakable, the shouts cut through the air behind him. They are not English, not friendly, and most certainly are aware of him. The shed, which seemed at fingers length only moments ago now stretches farther and farther from his grasp. It's as if hope is nothing more than a cruel joke, only ever existing to tease him.

A blast billows from behind. Mounds of dirt spring up from the ground as enemy bullets shadow his footsteps. Splinters of wood ripple and burst as full metal jackets strip the structure of its edges. Reuben does not drop, he does not stop, and he does not turn around. Forward is the only way. It's either forward or die. If hope is more than a joke, then it can only exist ahead of him.

Just a bit farther. Just keep running.

He closes the gap, diving behind the shed just as a hail of bullets tears into the corner. His veins throb beneath his skin. He pauses to breathe, to find relief in the fact that he made it, but there's no time. Crouching low, Rueben eases his rifle around the corner. Muscle memory seizes his shaky hands as he recalls the technique from basic training, slicing the pie. Before his iron sights can peer around the corner, a bullet scrapes by, inches from his barrel.

Without waiting for an opening, he returns suppressive fire. The casings ricochet against the structure and nick his cheek as the scent of gunpowder lingers beneath his nose. He may not see his target, but perhaps it will be enough to keep his opponents at bay while he bides his time.

A few more shots expel from his rifle before retaking cover. Looking around, he sees no other structures, only the wooded area. He may buy more time by running into the woods, but it would only prolong the inevitable. Bullets may not run to infinity, but he knows his opponents are closer to that number than he is. He must do something.

He veers to return fire but falters as something snags his ankle. Looking down, he notices the sole of his boot partially covered by the shed. Crouching beside it, he examines a small opening just beneath it. His instincts plead with him to hide in it. It's small enough to evade immediate detection, though a closer look from the enemy may prove lethal for him. He resists, knowing the greater danger of being discovered.

"Come on, Reuben, just make a damn decision," he mutters under his breath.

Unless...

He pivots around his cover, lays down more suppressive fire, and runs. He looks back, ensuring his body peeks out far enough to be seen headed for the tree line. Once out of sight, he doubles back to the shed and slides feet first through its opening.

The pounding of footsteps rushes past seconds later. Rueben counts six, maybe seven of them. Tucking further in, Rueben listens as the footsteps fade in the direction of the woods.

It worked.

A pair of voices just outside dashes the thought as he swallows the premature sigh of relief. Rueben doesn't understand what they are saying, though he recognizes the language is German. Laughter rings out, and Rueben pulls his weapon closer, readying himself for a final fight. Feelings of past combat experiences return to him. Even as a 'non-combat arms' soldier, he still experienced it. Gunfire, explosions, adrenaline, taking cover, suppressing fire. Its haunting familiarity becomes engulfed by a strange, more surreal reality of his situation.

I'm hiding from Nazis.

Time slows to a near stop. The men above continue to jabber overhead, and it becomes apparent that they are awaiting the return of their comrades. If true, it means their rendezvous will happen inches from his head. His heartbeat pulsates into the handguard and lower receiver. He slows his breathing, raises his rifle, and begins switching out his magazine for a full one, clamping onto it in hopes that his palms will buffer the sound of sliding metal.

If they discover the opening, he will be ready. He won't die without taking some Nazis with him. A thought tries to take him, but he keeps it at bay.

Yes, in history, they're already dead...but I'm not. Not yet, I'm not.

One of the men's voices shifts from casual to alert. The sound of sliding metallic rifle bolts erupts in near unison.

This is it.

Rueben lifts himself just enough to guide the barrel of his rifle to the edge of the hole. Rueben jumps as gunfire erupts around him. He pulls the trigger with no target in sight. Bursts of muzzle flash fill the cramped space, blinding his line of sight. The miniaturized explosions batter his ears as they bounce around the compacted hole. The stench of sulfur grips the inside of his throat.

"Cease fire!" a familiar voice cries over the chaos.

Is that English?

"Cease fire!"

Reuben lowers his weapon, his eyes searching through the fog of war until he sees him. There is a sigh and smile as the man walks toward him, the butt of a cigar jutting from his toothy grin.

It's Caleb Jones.

Deus ex Machina my ass. Caleb is the machine.'

14

OPERATION HUSKY

Sky taps her fingers on their cozy, foldable dining table as the food cools. Though not much of a cook, she gives it her all for him—her husband. Looking over at the seared T-bone steak and grilled vegetables sitting lonesome on his plate, Sky sighs before cutting into her baked chicken breast. This isn't the first time he's been late for dinner. It seems that it's been happening more and more often. Work goes late, or a buddy asks him to get a beer. But it's not the lateness that bothers her.

It's the unknowing.

A phone call or text ahead of time would go a long way. At least then dinner wouldn't be cold. And yet, here she is, wondering what the story will be today. Will it be how the boss made him stay for an unexpected meeting, how there wasn't any cell phone service to send a text, or how he meant to call, but time just got away?

Her stomach growls, and she rechecks her phone.

Nothing.

I might as well enjoy what I can.

A glimmer of light strikes her eye, and she looks down. Light reflects off of the diamond in her ring from the chandelier above, and she smiles. The food may be cold, but a warmth grips her heart. He convinced her to leave the Agency, to experience the real world, to grow old together. He's sacrificed so much to be with her, even taking on overtime hours at work to make ends meet as she searches for a new job. He loves her, and she knows it.

The minutes grow shorter, and before she knows it, she's finished her plate. It doesn't take long for Sky to clear the table and place his food in leftover containers. She pours herself a glass of wine as she finishes cleaning up. One glass of wine turns into two, the sun is far set, and her butt lies snug in her comfy pajamas on the couch.

She glances around their modest one-bedroom high-rise apartment, again wondering where he could be. Her phone lies next to her, its black screen taunting her with no news. Reaching for it, Sky taps its glass surface as though sure she must have missed a notification. But there is nothing to see other than some article highlighting the world's chaos. She slides the phone away from her and curls up, the temptation to call nagging at her insides.

I hope he's okay.

Sky takes another sip of wine, but the warm red fails to soothe her nerves.

Stop worrying so much. He's done this before.

But as the minutes turn to hours, she realizes the clock is against her, and the clock never loses. Her heart races as she imagines all the terrible things that could've happened—an accident, a mugging...just about anything could have gone wrong, and her mind is thinking of all of them.

Setting her glass on a nearby coaster, Sky stands, pacing from one side of the room to the other. Her stomach quivers and flips as the possibilities simmer in her mind. Her eyes dart to her phone, and she rushes over, snatching it from the crevice of the couch.

At least the weather keeps me updated.

Opening her call log, she clicks the first name and places it on speaker. She starts to pace again, waiting for the call to go through.

It rings.

And rings.

And rings.

He's everything to her, and right now, she doesn't care where he is or what he's doing. She just wants him to answer. She needs him to answer.

* * *

SKY SHAKES HER HEAD, the fog of the worst night of her life drifting into the abyss. She hasn't thought about that night in a long time. So, why now?

It's Reuben.

Sky, Kirk, Alex, and Caleb continue marching with Captain Adam's platoon. They arrived together several hours ago at the rendezvous site. Everything and everyone had made it; everyone but Reuben. Sky looks at her watch once more, hoping to find the flashing beacon she's been desperate to locate. But the only beacons to be seen are that of the team around her.

"He's not new to combat," Caleb says as if reading her mind. "I'm sure he can handle things until we find him."

"*If* we find him," Kirk chimes in. Sky's eyes narrow as Caleb smacks him upside the head.

"Ow! What? We all know it's a possibility. I mean, I'm hoping he's all right, but you heard what HQ said. There's someone else here, and chances are it's either Drazen or one of his goons. They've tried killing him before. It was only a matter of time before they came after him again."

"Dude," Alex says.

"What?" Kirk quips back. "We're all thinking it. I'm just trying to be—"

"I'll tell you what I'm trying to be right now," Caleb interrupts. "I'm trying to be damn well positive that we do everything in our power to get him back. You hear me? I don't have time to talk that pessimistic shit. Reuben's out there, and he's counting on us. Now, shut your trap and do something productive to help."

Kirk's eyes fall.

"I'm sorry," he finally says. "I didn't mean to— You know I would never want... I'll do what I can." Kirk steps away from the platoon, his eyes focused on his watch.

"You didn't have to be that hard on him," Alex says.

"He's working right now, isn't he?" Caleb says.

"Well, yeah, but—"

"But there's nothing else to it. This is combat, and every moment is precious. We don't have time to think the worst. I'll be more sensitive when we get back, but now's not the time nor place for it. Death's a bitch, and she loves war. So long as she's lurking, I'll do any mean ass shit I can to keep her away from this team."

"You're right," Sky says. "We have to find Reuben. He needs us." The words seem to comfort the team more than herself. She can't shake that similar feeling, taking her back to that night with her husband, to their final night.

It started with worry and ended with dread. Like déjà vu, it's returned to her. Ray was her love and companion in time and life itself. Reuben is a man she barely knows. And yet, her heart drops as she thinks of how he may be hurt, how he may need her...how he may want her.

This is too much. We just need to find him...and everything will go back to the way it was.

As they continue to march down the path, Sky notices the men from Captain Adam's platoon staring at her. She rolls her eyes and pushes on.

"Hey!" Kirk calls out from behind the platoon as he runs to catch up. He pulls the team to the side with a smile from ear to ear. "Guys, I did it. I know how to find him."

Her heart flutters as an unstoppable smile streaks across her face. Since arriving in Sicily, she discovers the most significant distinction between her memory and her present for the first time. Hope.

* * *

"Hold your damn fire," Caleb Jones calls out to the platoon behind him. "He's one of ours." Caleb leans down and extends his hand to Reuben, pulling him out from underneath the shed. Reuben peers over Caleb to see the rest of his team among a platoon of American soldiers. "Don't worry. Everyone is accounted for, Staff Sergeant." He taps on the stitching lining Reuben's shoulder. The triple chevron and single rocker face out, displaying his rank as they walk toward the group. "We found our squad leader," Caleb says to the rest of the platoon.

"Two less Nazi pieces of shit in this world," one of them remarks.

"There are at least five more in the wood line," Reuben says to the man. "There's more over that hill, too. Or at least there was. They're bound to follow the gunfire."

"I doubt that very much." The man spits brown as Rueben eyes the bulge in his cheek. "Given our numbers and fire superiority, if they'd seen us, they're running shit scared."

"Staff Sergeant," Alex says, stepping forward, "this is

Captain Adams. He and his men are with the Third Infantry Division. We were just explaining to him that our squad got separated from First ID on our way to Enna."

Reuben nods. "Sir, what my soldiers have told you is accurate," he says to the captain. "It's important that we regroup with our unit."

"I'd say," Captain Adams responds. "Staff Sergeant, you and your team are welcome to accompany us on our way to Caltanissetta. It's about two miles north of here. Any assistance in taking the city would be much obliged. From there, it shouldn't be too much further to Enna."

"Roger that, sir. Just need a few minutes with my troops, and we'll fall in with your formation." Reuben signals to his team to gather off to the side of the platoon. "Is everybody good? Any injuries coming in?"

Kirk laughs. "Dude, you're the one hiding from Nazis all *Inglorious Bastards* style."

"Your poor sense of humor made it, too, huh?"

"More than that," Sky says, "Kirk's the one who found your location and directed this Third ID platoon your way."

Reuben tilts his head. "Man, that, ah... You did good," he says to Kirk. "You're becoming a hell of a navigator."

Kirk's eyes widen, and he smiles in response.

"We belong to First ID, huh? Anything else pertinent I should know?"

"Yeah, sorry about that," Alex says. "I mixed up the Army Divisions in the briefing. I know that I had said the reverse before we launched. Once we saw the Third ID insignia on that platoon, I realized my mistake."

"Don't worry about it. We didn't exactly have adequate prep time for this mission. It's impressive, though. Meeting up with another unit and directing them over here in less than fifteen minutes."

"Fifteen minutes?" Kirk's mouth gapes.

"Reuben, we arrived five hours ago," Sky says. "After getting here, we thought maybe you were left behind at HQ, but they said you weren't there. I was worried that... I mean, we were all concerned that—" She breaks her gaze.

"Concerned that what?" Reuben asks, and silence follows.

"Somebody, hurry up and tell the man," Caleb says.

"Fall in!" Captain Adams's command echoes along the wood line as his soldiers make their way to the formation.

"We're not alone," Sky says. "Somebody else hacked in after we left but before the window shut."

Reuben's heart falls to his gut. The short-lived relief of being found and rescued is all but gone. "Well then..." He pauses, knowing what he wants to say, but struggling to deliver with conviction. He breathes and straightens his back. "We better stay vigilant. Complacency isn't an option."

As the rest of the team rushes to join the formation, Reuben pulls at Sky's shoulder. "Hey, are you okay?"

"Yeah. I mean, all right, for the most part, considering. The adrenaline distracts me from all these men staring at me. Thankfully, the shooting distracts them from asking."

"Asking?"

"I'm a woman in combat. This is World War II."

Reuben smirks. "And you're a badass. Probably a better shot than most of them. Besides, we'll be out before you know, and no one will remember we were here."

"Sometimes, I wish they would remember."

"I thought—"

"I haven't changed my opinion," she interrupts. "It's not our place. I know that. Just a feeling I get sometimes. But like everything else, it passes."

Rueben nods as the platoon continues marching toward Caltanissetta. Tilting his helmet, he admires the sun's light as it basks over the vast Sicilian countryside. The Mediterranean breeze streams along its rocks and hills, bringing with it a sweet relief. Vines trail beside the ruins, breathing life into destruction once more.

Beautiful.

The thought fades as the city's walls grow with each step, the greenery disappearing with it. Reuben peers forward from the rear of the platoon, squinting to see the first cluster of Third Infantry Division troops secure the perimeter of the small city. His breathing is restrained, and his heart calm. The jitters from his earlier encounter seem like such a distant memory. A series of tanks leading the invasion churns the narrow gravel road ahead, the sound of their engines so faint.

Still so far.

"Caltanissetta," a soldier beside him mutters as the city grows closer, as the battle draws near.

Subsequent units approach the perimeter, preparing to breach the enemy-held haven.

He can see it now—the cracks along the stone walls, the broken windows, and the fascist flags draped beneath them.

A deafening silence lingers, and his heart rate spikes slightly. His fingers clam up as they draw his rifle in closer.

Almost there.

Gunshots erupt and fill the air. His ears pop, and his boots tremble as artillery rounds quake the earth below.

"Incoming!" voices cry.

"Enemy fire one hundred meters north!" another voice yells before echoing down the line. Machine gun fire hails down on the platoon like lethal rain. They scurry to take cover behind rocks. Men in the platoon instinctively look to their captain for instruction.

Smoke and dust billows around them as Rueben stumbles for cover. Shouts cry out through the chaos, and bodies fall with a thundering finality.

Rueben watches as several of the men nearest him quiver

from impact and crumple. He sprints to the closest body, clamps onto his collar, and drags him into an adjacent ditch from the middle of the road. Rueben tries to prop the man up against the gravel lining but loses his grip as the soldier slumps to the ground. Rueben shouts for a medic and tries again, though he knows it's too late. His hands are slick with blood.

Too much blood.

Dust settles on the lifeless face of Captain Adams. He closes the captain's eyes and turns toward the rest of the leaderless platoon.

"Return fire!" Reuben shouts, his heart thundering. The soldiers adhere to his command as if he sounded a war cry through a Viking horn. As the platoon exchanges suppressive fire, Reuben switches his comms set to internal.

"Sitrep, over!"

To his surprise, responses from each member flood his headset.

"Bound forward with the platoon. Sky, Kirk, select a safe rendezvous within the city and send the coordinates to the team. Alex, relay our movements to HQ. Jones, make sure everyone gets there safely."

The team pushes forward toward the city entrance and begins to creep out of Reuben's sight.

A light flashes, and his face burns.

Dirt and debris crush him as black smoke fills his eyes and lungs.

He coughs and gasps, searching for light and direction, his ears ringing from the blast.

Pulling himself from charred earth, Reuben regains his footing as muzzle flashes burst through the dense smoke.

"Sitrep!"

No response.

He feels for his ear. Nothing. No headset. Gone.

Shit, the blast.

The wind shifts, cleaving a path through smoke and sulfur. He sprints over the fresh crater, its heat baking his boots below. Bullets graze past him. Screams are cut short.

He ducks behind a large rock and peers through his iron sights toward the city. Clusters of allied soldiers overtake the walls.

Where the hell are you guys?

He looks down at the cracked screen of his watch. Only half the display works, and there are no dots, no sign of his team.

They must've made it through. I have to get to them.

As he bounds his way toward the entrance, the firefight continues. Rounds zip by from all directions, delivering death as each side fights for life. An agonizing scream bellows out beside him. Reuben turns to find a man with a gaping hole in his belly. Blood drenches the man's hands as he struggles to keep his innards from leaving him. He tumbles toward the ground, and Reuben catches him. Tears and shock pour from his face.

"Medic!"

The man passes before anyone can respond.

"Dammit," Reuben mutters to himself as he looks into the eyes of the now lifeless corpse. He lays the man's body down gently before springing back onto his feet. Fighter planes race above him, dropping bombs into the city ahead. Soldiers scurry around him in the chaos. These men are dying, and he can't think. He only watches as the faces he'd marched alongside only minutes ago get battered and broken.

I can't just watch.

He pulls his rifle close and aims its barrel downrange. His heart and breath steady as a fire ignites in his chest, as a Nazi soldier appears in his iron sights. The trigger squeeze is slow and methodical. The bullet is fierce and unforgiving, painting crimson behind the Nazi before his body hits the ground.

With each shot fired, smoke and chaos dissipate. The

glowing heat from his barrel radiates warmth into his fingers. He continues firing, watching as SS uniforms collide lifelessly with ash and dust.

A lone stray bullet grazes the neck of an allied soldier.

Blood spews onto the gravel.

Reuben's distraught eyes sink, and his stomach turns as the man gasps in pain.

No!

He sprints to the man and yanks out a med kit, fingers trembling as he applies pressure to the wound.

"Medic!"

A hand touches him from behind. Reuben turns as the figure motions around, sighing and grinning as his eyes meet the sweet and glorious red cross on the man's helmet.

"It's okay, I got this," the medic says.

Reuben squeezes the injured soldier's hand, nods, then motions back toward the gate. He lays down suppressive fire as he integrates back into the platoon. The inner fire rises to fill his lungs, projecting his commanding voice through the gunfire and artillery, leading them perpetually forward.

Toward the city walls.

Past the cost and toll of war and into its end.

Into victory.

There must be victory.

Then it happens. Mortar rounds blast the walls into rubble. Allied troops swarm every pathway and breached barrier. Nazis pull back, firing panic shots through street corridors as they flee.

Reuben smiles as he counts the blackened, bloody, and ragged faces marching beside him.

We've made it.

The wind shifts again, blowing dust and the scent of death toward their fleeing enemy.

A thought strikes Reuben, and his chest fills with lead. The lives of these men. Their agonizing trauma and suffering. It's not just real and happening. It's already happened. Sealed in history, a history he's been told cannot be altered.

As Reuben helps to pull troops up over the breached walls, he doesn't see Chronos or nihilistic determinism. He sees bleeding and battered men, eyes heavy with war, backs burdened by killing and dying.

The rules of Chronos tell him his actions today are inconsequential, that they don't matter. But his gut, and the uneasiness that grips it, can't reconcile these things. Somehow, all of this matters.

It must matter.

Varying units regroup around him. The fog and intensity of battle begin to subside. His eyes widen as it hits him. The narrow view of here and now erode in an instant, leaving the panoramic reality of why he's here.

The hack.

My team!

Reuben shuffles past a cluster of soldiers treating wounds and redistributing ammo. He glances at the faces and insignias, hoping to find them, to see them walking about, to hear their voices.

The only thing he hears are echoing commands from strangers. All he sees are the faces of Patton's Army, the barren streets of Caltanissetta, and corpses of Nazis who signed up for the wrong side.

"Sir!" one of the soldiers from the platoon says to Reuben as he runs up to him. "We've secured the southeast end and stand ready to advance on your command."

"It's Sergeant," Reuben says, "and you should report to your commanding officer or NCOIC."

"But, sir— I mean Sergeant. Captain Adams is..."

"I'm sorry for your platoon's loss, Corporal." He takes note of the soldier's rank and name.

Clemens.

"Do you all have an LT or another sergeant?"

"We did, Sergeant, but now it's only us. I'm just a squad leader."

"Not anymore, Corporal. As I see it, you are the highest-ranking man in your platoon, making you its leader." Reuben slaps the corporal's shoulder as he exhales. "If I were you, I'd get accountability of your men and report back to your company commander."

"Roger that, Staff Sergeant."

"One more thing, Corporal. Have you seen the members of my team?"

Clemens shakes his head. "I suppose we both need to get accountability for our people, huh, Sergeant?" They exchange smirks.

"I suppose you're right." Reuben walks toward a nearby alleyway before turning back to Clemens. "Hey, after this island is completely secured and this operation is over, drop and do a hundred."

"We might not see each other again. How do you know I'll do it?"

"Because you have to. Leading this platoon will take a lot out of you, but it demands integrity. It's the kind of integrity that will make you kiss the ground a hundred times." They nod at one another and depart on their path.

Once around the corner and out of sight, Reuben pulls out his watch. To his surprise, a point appears on the undamaged side of his screen. It's the coordinates for the rendezvous site, pointing to a building only four blocks away. With rifle held at the ready, he maneuvers through narrow streets of rubble, smoke, and exposed brick. The strain in his muscles grows, but he refuses to slow down. Reuniting with his team is the priority.

Slicing pies and bounding forward, he scans continually for any cowardly Axis forces waiting amongst the civilian population to ambush Allied troops. The white noise of distant shouts and sporadic gunfire looms in the background as he advances further into the eerily quiet city.

His silhouette shades the back steps to the building as if it were royal carpet being laid down for his grand entrance. Vibrations from the watch rattle his wrist. He's arrived. With a gentle turn of the knob, Reuben pulls the door open. Its ominous creak echoes into the seemingly hollow and lifeless interior.

Inside, unsettled furniture and scattered debris greet him. Beginning at the kitchen, he explores what was once someone's home. He searches each room for his team and finds no soul but his own staring at him through dusty mirrors. After an initial sweep through each floor, he verifies the coordinates.

Where are you?

Back in the kitchen, a sliver of space protrudes between a door and its frame. Believing it to be a pantry, he slides his fingers into the crack and opens the door. A flash of white sweeps his eyelids and vanishes as if it were a single subliminal frame, spliced into a film only to be seen and quickly forgotten. Downward steps unravel themselves into what seems to be a darkened basement. He reaches for a light switch but finds none. With an emergency flashlight in hand, he ventures down into it.

Each step immerses him further into the darkness and silence. A chill pricks the back of his neck, and his entire body tenses. It's not the change in temperature or moving into a strange space. It's the eerie feeling within his gut as if he crossed into a realm that he doesn't belong.

He reaches the bottom, and everything in him wants to turn around, to run.

But he can't do it.

The only thing worse than fear is giving into it. Reuben's heart races, but he can't look back. He won't look back.

Each step forward makes it more challenging to see the fading kitchen light from above. He's abandoned that light to wander further and further into the darkness. He shines his light into the open darkness, finding no end.

The sharp sound of grinding metal cuts through the chilly stale air. It reverberates against the dusty concrete floors. Reuben raises his rifle as the metallic clanking maneuvers through the dark. Heavy breathing fills the air, but it isn't him. An unseen figure tags along the mysterious sound as it shifts beyond sight. The grinding sound intensifies, moving left then right, closing in, encircling him like prey.

His heart pounds, nearly breaking free as he steadies his aim. His finger slides onto the trigger, a nanosecond from pulling it and filling the space with lead.

Before he can fire, a hand grasps his shoulder and pulls.

He veers to engage, but the figure slams his body to the ground, dragging him against the concrete. His finger slips in the commotion, and the rifle goes off, the bullet cracking and echoing in the seemingly endless black space.

Reuben thrashes his bodyweight back and forth along the stairs as the hand continues to drag him up. The more he resists the grip, the tighter its hold grows. Like a Chinese finger cuff of steel, defiance only strengthens its resolve to hold him.

A flash of light overwhelms his eyes before adjusting to the bright kitchen. Reuben looks up from the ground, watching the face of an older plump man smiling down at him. Rushing to his feet, Reuben swings his rifle up in front of him, holding it firmly between the strange man and himself.

Must be a local national.

"Why didn't you evacuate?"

The man says nothing, only continues to smile.

"*Evacuare!*" Reuben says, meaning '*evacuate.*' No other Italian words come to his lips or mind.

"I don't think you want me to do that just yet, Reuben," the man says.

Bewildered and taken off guard, Reuben lowers his rifle before catching himself and raising it again. "Who the hell are you?"

"Other than the man who just saved your life down there?"

"That was you? But how? You're—"

"Old, yes, I am aware. Although I only noticed well after it happened." The man chuckles. "I've also been waiting a long time for us to speak. You need to listen to me because your team will be bursting in here very soon. Not to mention that you and I were not alone down there."

"Who are you?"

The man steps forward. "Lower that," he says, pointing at Reuben's weapon. "Don't worry. In a few minutes, you're going to have to raise it again." Reuben complies and lowers the rifle. "There is a cupboard to your left. Please, open it and hand me the contents."

Complying again, he opens the nearby cabinet door. A small wooden box sits in solitary among dust and rotted shelving. Keeping one hand on the pistol grip of his rifle, Reuben grabs the box and tosses it to the strange man. The man sets the box down, opens it, and pulls out a cigar and matchbook. He smells the cigar, smiles, cuts the end, and lights it.

"Really?" Reuben sighs and shakes his head. "You had... You..." He lets out another sigh. "You made that seem important like—"

"It is important," the man responds in between cigar puffs. "Your friends will be here any minute, and they likely won't allow me to start smoking this once things get rolling. Otherwise, it might seem awkward or even rude." Reuben detects his mild Sottish accent.

"Uh," Rueben utters, unable to find the appropriate words. He hopes for other discernible words to follow.

Nothing does.

"Oh, yes, forgive me. You had asked who I am. My name is Aperio Talesworth. I'm a Steward of Time."

15

THE GRASS WITHERS, THE FLOWER FADES

ow the hell did I get here?

Kirk watches as the team shuffles through the war-ravaged city. He knows that Reuben and everyone else doesn't really want him here, but here he is— inexperienced, burdensome, and near useless.

Near useless, but not completely.

He found Rueben after all, and even now, the team is depending on Kirk to find a rendezvous site. He's never been particularly smart and always struggled to get along with others. His resume could easily fit on a Post-it note with only his father's name.

That's how. That asshole is the reason I got here.

Nepotism be damned and the truth with it. Kirk can feel his chin strap loosen underneath his helmet as his jaw clenches tighter and tighter. Senator James Fowler is only a name to him, a stranger, the kind of man accustomed to using his family as a mere photo op. Building relationships with his children, remaining faithful to his wife, and caring for his widowed mother never seemed to fit the senator's long-term strategy to climb the political ladder.

Image seems to be the only thing the senator truly cares for. Completely absent is the essence of family life—the joys of gathering, laughing, and bantering—and the sacrifices of time and self. He's never cared for these things.

Why would he?

If cameras aren't there to capture him helping his wife with the dishes or witnessing him attend his children's school plays, why would he partake?

It's the image that matters most to him, the façade of perfection. There are twenty-four hours in a day, and Senator James Fowler uses all of them to preserve that image as the objects of the image wither and fade.

The grass withers, the flower fades.

His grandmother's words. In war, chaos, and bitterness, why have these words come to him now?

I may be a screw-up, but screw him. This team needs me, and my loudmouth ass is going to help them.

"Move!" Caleb shouts as he holds his rifle outward, pointing to a seemingly empty alleyway. He provides cover as the team continues bounding forward before pausing behind a wall.

Caleb takes a defensive position. "You've got less than ninety seconds. Any longer, and we'll be begging for Nazis to swarm this spot."

"I'm sure they're running scared by now," Alex says.

"And you're the expert, Mr. Blindside?"

"Hey, man, I—"

"Can we please get to it?" Sky interrupts.

Caleb breaks with the sights of his weapon to look at the rest of the team. "All I'm saying is that a man is most dangerous when he's afraid." He brushes his chin before returning to the iron sights. "Now, hurry the hell up."

"Where are we at with the rendezvous site?" Alex asks, looking to Sky and Kirk.

Sky shakes her head.

"Great."

Kirk peers down, tapping his watch. His eyes widen as his breath leaves him.

"Naw, man, it's not like that," Kirk mutters to himself, feeling the large beads of sweat flow down his face.

"What is it?" Alex says.

"It's these maps. I calibrated them when we got here, and now they're all screwy. It's harder to tell what's what the farther we get from where we came in."

"Can we set up a meeting spot closer to the entrance of the city?"

"No," Sky interjects. "If we go back that direction, we'll risk being caught up in the crossfire."

"Wait." Kirk smiles, still looking down at his watch. "Found a spot three blocks away. It's about the same distance from the entrance and is away from the main street. So, if we're quick—"

"Then we can meet up with Reuben while evading the crossfire," Alex says.

"Yeah, no shit. That's what I was going to say before you interrupted me, prick."

"You know, just when I think you're coming around and finally being a decent dude—"

"Hey, boys," Sky says, "is now really the time?"

"Not anymore." Caleb stands and lowers his rifle. "We need to move. We can send the coordinates on the way."

The team shifts their direction and begins to move toward the rendezvous site. Gravel and dust collide with their boots as they bound from building to building. Kirk can hear his thoughts through rhythmic panting.

Meet up with Reuben, track down the mystery man, and go home.

They just need to get through this mission, and Kirk can step away for some time. He can take his grandmother on that trip to Florida, sink his toes into the sand, and forget this grueling day.

Almost there.

"Rendezvous set, over." Alex transmits to Reuben with no reply. He looks down at his watch, and his eyes widen. "Seriously again?"

Caleb holds up a hand, directing the team to a pile of rubble. They take cover, positioning themselves around Alex.

"It's Reuben's comms. They're down again."

Sky taps her watch, and worry fills her eyes. "I can't see him in the nav schematics either. I thought you said that there were no pockets in Caltanissetta," she says.

"There aren't." Alex turns to Kirk. "See if you can resend him the coordinates directly to his watch."

Kirk complies without hesitation. "Done," he says seconds later. "He should be able to use his watch to get there now."

The city lies in shambles as they move to the site. Smoke stains run up the battered buildings like blackened oil on torn canvas. Broken doors and crumbling walls break up the sea of debris and rubble. Waves of ash grip onto the team's uniforms as they approach the rendezvous site.

Kirk lets out a breath, staring at the barren, abandoned restaurant. He scurries up the steps and opens the door. Before he can cross the threshold, his collar yanks him backward.

"Hey, what the—" He regains his footing and turns to see Caleb holding him back. Caleb releases him and nods toward the foot of the entrance. Kirk leans in as a glare of light slices his line of sight. Focusing, Kirk gasps as the thin wire stretching between the doorposts comes into view. Caleb steps in front of him and crouches to inspect the tripwire before cutting the line.

Kirk stands near the doorway, perplexed whether he should feel relieved or embarrassed. "Well, I guess that means no one's inside if they planned on blowing this shit up," he says.

"Maybe." Alex peaks into the restaurant. "I mean, we're dealing with two different Axis armies. One could have set the mine and not told the other. Communication quickly breaks down when one of your cities is being invaded." The team enters and glances around at primarily empty space. "Doesn't look like Reuben's here yet."

"We should clear the building," Caleb says.

"The whole building?" Kirk's voice shrieks.

"Listen, chump. It only takes one hidden enemy and timing to do what can't be undone. There are three floors with an unknown number of rooms, closets, and other hiding places. We search them all. That's non-negotiable."

"If we split into pairs, we'll cover more ground," Alex says.

Sky sighs. "Kirk and I—"

"Uh-uh," Caleb interrupts. "You've babysat enough. The kid will come with me. Maybe he'll prove my daddy wrong and learn some common sense."

"He's all yours."

Kirk's heart sinks.

It's like I'm a joke to them.

He waves his hands. "Hey, ass—"

Alex lays his hand on Kirk's shoulder and whispers, "I wouldn't pick this battle."

As the team splits, his heart sinks further.

Kirk shrugs to himself. "Un-freaking-believable."

* * *

THIS IS BULLSHIT.

Kirk follows Caleb through the darkened halls, leading them past knocked over tables and shattered chairs as if touring through a haunted crime scene. They clear each room in short order before reaching the final door in their section. Caleb jabs his elbow into the cracked door. It swings open violently as if a battering ram struck it. The dim lighting from the restaurant's front creeps into the room, causing the shadows to retreat behind the bathroom stalls, like cockroaches scattering upon discovery.

"Ah, finally. I have to piss!" Kirk says as he runs past Caleb.

"Hurry up." Caleb steps out as Kirk walks into the first stall.

Kirk slings his weapon behind his back and relaxes his shoulders. Before he can relieve himself, a sudden squeaking sound breaks out from the stall beside him. Every muscle tenses in his body. He wants to move, but he can't. Another squeak breaks out, this time closer, this time behind him. He can feel his heartbeat race as it throbs into his face.

Footsteps.

It's fight or flight, but he can't do either. If he turns, if he acknowledges, then it's real. If he doesn't, then he may be dead and never know it.

Coward.

Senator Fowler's words come to him, taunting him. Kirk spent his life fearing the man and hating him. At this moment, he's terrified that this man, who never really knew or understood him, has pegged him in a single word; and that perhaps his final thought will be that word.

"No," Kirk says aloud as his motor functions come back to him. Reaching for his rifle, he swings around to face the sound. He sees the barrel first, pointed at his face. The Nazi soldier holding it grunts and slips his finger into the trigger guard. Kirk freezes, and his eyes convulse before sealing shut. A loud gasp slices the tension.

Gunfire erupts.

Splinters of wood and rushing liquid strike Kirk's cheek. He opens his eyes.

The Nazi stares back at him in horror as blood gushes from his neck. Caleb pulls out the knife and releases the corpse. It flaps before Kirk's feet in a pool of rushing pipe water, blood, and shattered porcelain.

"You okay?" Caleb straightens his back with a breath.

Kirk glances down at his body, then back up at Caleb. With his jaw dangling, he nods and says nothing.

"All right, like I said. Hurry up and piss." Caleb wipes his knife and leaves.

"I think I just did," Kirk mutters to himself. Moments later, he exits, joining Caleb to search the next section.

* * *

As they search their sectors, Sky and Alex bound past one another in a symmetrical feat of efficiency, reading and responding to each other's body language as if they were symbiotically one. Sky's eyes shift between her rifle's iron sights and the unexplored unknown in front of her. She doesn't think about it. She doesn't have to. It's more than muscle memory and quick reflexes. She didn't just train for this; she lives for it.

The accident took everything from her, but it gave her this, the sure solace of knowing it won't ever happen again. Whether it's the elite marksmanship skills she's earned since Ray's passing or the wall she's built around her heart ever since, she knows it won't ever happen again.

It can't happen again.

As they continue clearing rooms, an inexplicable feeling grips her as her thoughts ravage within. It's not about Ray or the accident. After a year, she's managed to channel and control those thoughts. This is something else altogether. A feeling she can't control. Thoughts she doesn't understand.

It hits her like goosebumps in the night.

What's wrong with me?

The unease grips her stomach, making her nauseous. They clear their final room, and she sighs.

"You okay?" Alex says, slinging his weapon and motioning toward her.

"What?" She shakes her head, hoping he won't pry more. "Yeah, I'm fine. Why? What's up?"

"That look." He points his finger, almost wagging it.

"Look?" Sky raises her eyebrows in contrived denial.

"Yeah. The same one you had back in Roanoke."

"Are you archiving my looks?"

Alex chuckles. "No, I'm not some creep—"

"Is exactly what a real creep would say." She smiles.

"Ha." He rolls his eyes and continues, "You know, it baffles my wife, too. All the little things I notice. Not sure who hates it more, her or the kids."

"Her."

"You think?"

Sky nods with a grin. "Oh, yeah. Your oldest is what, fourteen?"

"Fifteen. Alicia's birthday was last week."

"Kids are used to adults noticing things. Plus, she's only got a few more birthdays before she's gone."

"Ugh, don't remind me."

"My point is that Sherry is a grown woman and mother, stuck with you for who knows how long."

"God bless that woman. Don't know what I'd do without her." Alex turns to exit the room before jolting to stop. "Hold up a sec! You almost made me forget... Seriously, though. Back in Roanoke. You said before something felt off there."

"Yeah." Her smile fades, and she sighs. "I don't know what it is. I mean, I guess I do. Reuben's comms, getting split up, the mystery person. It's all so..."

"Freaking weird."

"It's more than that. Roanoke was weird. Not sure why that turned my stomach, though. It was a different kind of strange, like déjà vu or something. I don't know. But this here..." Sky looks down at her boot print in the dust-filled floor, and her nausea grows. She takes a breath before gazing back up at him. "Whatever's going on here in Caltanissetta doesn't just turn my stomach. It boils my intestines, and I can't shake it."

"Because you think something bad is happening?"

"Or will happen. Or has happened. I don't know."

"Ah, like some crazy omen stuff." Alex smirks as Sky shoves past him.

"This is why I didn't say anything."

"Hey," Alex says, jumping in front of her. "I'm sorry I was an ass." He adjusts his glasses. "In all seriousness, though, I get it. You're not the only one who thinks this place is off. This mission's been a cluster from the start."

Sky feels her heartbeat against her breastbone, marking time in a surreal sense of hyper-focus.

"So, Roanoke wasn't a bad type feeling like this? Just weird?" Alex asks.

"We really don't have to talk about this."

"I know, but—"

"It was mixed, I guess. Almost bittersweet. Like...like..." She shakes her head. "I don't know. I'm not much of a metaphor person."

"Simile," Alex lets out.

Sky glares at him but says nothing.

"But, yeah, I get what you mean. Like looking at stars millions of lightyears away, knowing that no matter what kind of technology you had, even traveling as fast as physics allows, you'll never reach them."

Sky raises an eyebrow.

"Okay, that was a nerdy example."

She smirks. "I didn't say anything."

Several loud crashes tear through their conversation. Sky raises her rifle, directing Alex to stay behind her with a gesture before advancing. A series of corners and a surge of adrenaline lead them to Kirk and Caleb.

"Are you okay?" Sky says. "We heard the shots. What happened?"

"Yeah. Uh, yeah, we're good," Kirk says. "That freaking Nazi that Caleb just stabbed in the neck isn't."

Alex veers toward Caleb. "In the neck?"

"I had two options," Caleb says. "I could let that asshole kill one of our own, or I could take him out and watch Kirk piss himself. The latter seemed like a win-win." Everyone but Kirk snickers.

"Hey, I didn't actually..." Kirk pats his trousers, causing them to slush liquid. "That's from the stupid busted pipe when the Nazi shot his gun. Water went everywhere. Really!"

Silence looms.

"You know what? I don't have to defend myself."

"Uh-huh," Caleb says, winking.

Alex clears his throat, garnering the team's attention. "So, it doesn't look like Reuben made it here. Kirk, are you sure these are the coordinates you sent him?"

"Yeah, positive." Kirk glares down at his watch before tapping its surface. "Wait, no. That can't be right." He looks back up at Alex. "I swear I sent him this location."

"What?"

"It's showing that I sent coordinates to some house a few blocks from here, but that's not what I typed. I vividly remember—"

Everyone else sighs.

"Guys, you have to believe me. I would never."

"We don't have time for this," Caleb says. "What are the other coordinates? We need to move there now."

* * *

THE TEAM MOVES toward the restaurant's exit. Kirk snags Alex back as Sky and Caleb continue forward. "You believe me, right?"

"Doesn't matter right now," Alex says. "Listen, man, I know we're all under a lot of stress. It's a combat situation, meaning life and death is at play. You saw that yourself two minutes ago. Just stay alert. Okay?"

Kirk's head sinks to the ground. He can feel the weight of Alex's words and the team's disappointment crushing him.

Shouts and indirect gunfire grow louder as they get closer to the site. Kirk's breath grows heavier through the seemingly endless city blocks, ravaged by smoke and rubble.

They eventually stop at a series of connected housing, strung together like a quilt of multicolored rags. Kirk glances down at his watch, and all the dots align. He smiles and nods toward the team.

"All right," Caleb says. "Let's go." He storms up the front steps, and the team follows, Kirk lagging in the rear.

"Damn, locked," Caleb's voice carries back.

"No worries." Alex reaches into his pack. "I have a set of lock pickers that should—"

Before Alex can finish, Caleb kicks the door. A crackling sound breaks the silence as the door bursts inward against the might of his boot. Caleb rushes inside, and the team follows.

Kirk's heart races as he crosses the threshold. He raises his rifle, sweeping his sights past debris and battered furniture. In seconds, they reach the kitchen. Kirk drops his aim and grins as they encounter the familiar face.

"Stand down!" Reuben shouts, his rifle pointed at an older man with his hands suspended, holding nothing but a half-smoked cigar. "Guys, this is—"

"I know who he is," Caleb interrupts, tossing Reuben a pair of flex cuff restraints, weapon now pointed at the man. Reuben takes the cigar out of the man's hands and applies the restraints. He places the still-lit cigar onto the countertop.

Caleb lowers his rifle and steps toward the man. "What's it been, Aperio, ten years?" He picks up the nearby cigar and takes a drag. Kirk convulses as he thinks about the slimy tobacco paper sliding against Caleb's lips. "Ugh. You know this isn't a lollipop, right?"

Aperio smirks. "I thought you only smoked cigarettes. Marlboro, wasn't it?"

"Camel," Caleb corrects while rubbing the tip of the cigar against his sleeve to dry the saliva before taking another puff. "Or at least I did. As it turns out, I recently quit cigarettes. You see, I made a promise that the next time shit hits the fan, and there is a light at the end of the tunnel, I'd make the switch. This may be my second cigar today, but I'd say bringing in one of you troublemakers seems like an even better occasion." He grabs a nearby chair and forces Aperio down onto it.

Across the room, Kirk watches as Reuben's eyes meet Sky's, greeting one another in a blissful glance. Reuben turns to the rest of the team. "Let's regroup in the dining room before we roll out."

"Y'all go ahead," Caleb says. "I'll keep our guest company."

"He's tied up."

"These guys are slick, believe me. Don't let that jolly old man routine fool you."

Reuben nods and exits with the rest of the team.

* * *

CALEB PRESSES the cigar against his mouth. Its amber glow glistens. His gaze pierces through the thick layer of lingering smoke and into the Steward's eyes, into Aperio's eyes. Caleb never thought he'd see one alive again. But here he is, looking at a man who can bend time in a way that he can't even understand. And now? Now, the man can't even bend his way out of a pair of flex cuffs.

"You're nicer than I recall," Aperio says.

"I take my aunt to church now that my uncle passed. She makes me stay and listen to the message."

"Some of that must be sinking in."

Caleb shrugs. "Yeah, I don't know about that, old man."

"The Caleb Jones I once knew wouldn't hesitate to slam an opponent to the ground."

"Don't get it twisted. I still don't hesitate for anything." He pauses and rubs the cigar. "I just might feel bad about it later, is all."

"Well, that slow, gradual change is what we might call a character arc and—"

"If I were you," Caleb interrupts, "I'd wait to tell someone who'd actually give a damn." He wants to say more, to interrogate the man, to find out where he's been and how he hacked into Chronos. But he says nothing. It's not his place, and he knows it. Safety and security, that's his mission, that's his role. So, Caleb just sits there and watches as the old stalky Steward swings his boots back and forth.

Kirk stands in silence on the other side of the wall as Reuben shares with everyone how he came to the house via the coordinates.

"Those aren't the coordinates I sent you," Kirk says aloud. Silence lingers for a moment.

"I think he's right," Alex finally chimes in, addressing the group. "I mean, think about it. Reuben being separated from the rest of us at the start of the mission almost got him killed. The comms were going in and out despite being clear of pockets. Oh, yeah...and we just happen to run into Aperio. It's too much going on not to be connected. If the Chronos platform can be hacked, then why not our watches?" Alex looks over at Kirk. "Sorry I didn't believe you earlier."

Kirk stands there in disbelief.

An apology.

A thump of the heart.

"It's...it's fine," Kirk says. "I mean, I get it. I'm always joking around or whatever. And I know I'm not experienced like you guys. It's just—" He exhales and rubs his temples, feeling the tears wanting to come but holding them back. "Sometimes, I just want to contribute, to be part of the team, you know?"

"You are a part of the team," Reuben says. "Messing up or getting things right doesn't make you more or less a member. You're a part of this team because you're one of us. We're all travelers. We're in this together from the moment we hop on that platform until we arrive back at HQ. And even outside of all this time travel stuff. Besides, man, you're the one who helped find me when Nazis were shooting at me. You're more than a member of this team. You're a friend."

The words pierce Kirk as his eyes fill with moisture. He wants to fight it, to deflect and tell a stupid joke, but he can't. He won't.

His father's name comes to his mind without warning and, for the first time, a smile emerges. It isn't the man or what he's done. It's his name, only his name. Suddenly it all makes sense somehow. Senator James Fowler may be a name typically responsible for turning his stomach, but it's the reason he's here. It's the reason for this strange calling. It's the reason he is with these people, his friends, who have said the words that the Senator would never think to utter, '*We're in this together.*'

James Fowler may have made the call to AIC out of guilt, Kirk may have taken the nepotism in shame, but these people have accepted him in love.

'*Life's too short to hold grudges.*'

His grandmother's words. A part of him wants to ball his fists and allow the anger toward his father to seethe through clenched teeth.

But how can he?

Standing here, among the people who genuinely care for him, knowing that his father is the reason they're in his life. James Fowler, name and all, is a part of who he is, a cornerstone of his journey.

Okay, Grandma, maybe you're right.

* * *

REUBEN SCRATCHES his head before readjusting his new earpiece, trying to think if there are any other details he may have left out of his story. His heart drops as he recalls the moments before they busted through the door with rifles drawn. He didn't say a word then, and he can't say anything now.

Must keep it a secret.

"I think we can safely say that Aperio was the one who hacked into Chronos," Sky says.

"Or at least one of them," Alex says.

"So, then who's the other hacker?" Kirk says. "Didn't Paul mention that lab tech chick who worked for your dad?"

"Nea," Reuben says. "Her name was Nea. I don't know if it's her. I couldn't find anyone when I came into the house, so I started exploring the basement. It was dark, and it looked endless. It's almost like it covered all the surrounding houses. Was really weird. I knew I should've waited for you guys to show up, but I couldn't help it. I had to go further in. So, I went. There was just something about the dark unknown that kept drawing me in until I couldn't see anything else. I heard sounds of something or someone, can't really describe it, but I felt like it was coming for me. Before it could reach me, Aperio pulled me out. When we got upstairs, he said that we weren't alone down there and that he had saved my life."

Sky motions forward. "That noise could've been Aperio. You said yourself you didn't actually see anyone."

"Right but—"

"I'm with Sky on this man," Alex says. "He's been gone for too long. Who's to say what he's been up to or even where he's been. Conveniently *saving you*," he says, holding up air quotes. "Just doesn't sit right."

"If I were in your shoes, I'd see it that way, too. I know how it sounds. And I'm not denying that something strange is going on. I'm not even saying we should trust him. But having been there, I know in my gut we weren't alone. And the look Aperio had when we were back in the kitchen... I've looked in the eyes of a lot of lying men. That's not what I saw with him."

"Well, I guess we'll know soon enough," Alex says. "Paul's going to want to put him in the interrogation booth as soon as we get back. I'm sure he'll be excited about it, too. I don't think he's ever met one of them."

Distant gunshots ring through the outside streets. Reuben looks out toward the window. An eerie sense of fear sits like bricks in his stomach. He turns back to the team. "The invading forces are getting closer. The opposition is pulling back in this direction. Won't be long before this house becomes part of the battlefront. If we're bringing Aperio with us, then we need to leave ASAP."

"What about the other dude?" Kirk chimes in. "You know, the second hacker. Shouldn't we at least try and find out who it is?"

"Not today. Aperio will have to be Paul's consolation prize for now. We can't jeopardize the mission searching endlessly for someone we might not find while the invasion continues around us. Alex, report our status to HQ. Kirk, conduct a quick nav sweep so we can archive some of this for later. I'll question

Aperio for a few minutes while we prep for departure. Sky, how much time do we have?"

"Our calibration is off a bit." She taps her watch. "But from what I can see, we have at most ten minutes before the firefight arrives...but..."

"What is it?"

Sky looks up at him, and he can see the uneasiness in her eyes. "Reuben, this whole thing is twitchy. If our watches really are being hacked, an estimated time...it could be wrong. *I* could be wrong."

Reuben can sense it, the weight of an impending decision. Leave now or stay the ten minutes. He's been making life and death choices all day. Why does this one tie a knot in the pit of his stomach? Reuben is close, and he knows it. Just a few minutes of questioning Aperio may give him all he needs. He feels a slight hesitation in his shoulders as if someone were pulling at him, begging him to leave. But he can't. Answers lie on the other side of the door, and he knows it.

"We've made it this far," he finally says to her. "I know we can do this. We'll get what we need and get out of here in less than ten."

"Okay," she says, with an almost worried look as if trying to reassure herself. "I trust you."

The team breaks away to perform their assigned tasks as Reuben looks down at his watch, his chest tightening as he ponders the decision. It's not just the choice to leave or stay that causes his breath to grow short and his palms to clam in sweat. It's the flex cuffs and the strange man bound by them.

Reuben enters the kitchen, and a cloud of cigar smoke flows into his eyes. "We need to talk."

"So, talk," Caleb says in between puffs as he continues to stare down Aperio.

"Alone."

"Gracious," Aperio says. "I'm a tied-up old man. Surely you

can talk to your friend here while I sit moping about how you stole and smoked my cigar." Jones takes a final puff and sticks the remaining quarter cigar in Aperio's mouth. "Much obliged," he muffles, now puffing the cigar with his hands restrained behind him. Caleb and Reuben proceed to the living room, ensuring enough distance not to be heard.

"We need to leave," Reuben says. "This place will be under heavy fire in less than ten minutes. I'm going to ask him some questions before we head out. I need you to secure the perimeter and help the rest of the team with a quick inventory check."

"Be careful, Staff Sergeant. Don't underestimate the man. You weren't there when everything went down. You don't know what they can do. Shit, I don't know everything they can do. Not even Paul knows. That's my point, though, you follow?"

"My father was one of them, a Steward."

"And he was a good man. I'm not just saying that. But things aren't like they used to be. Paul Peterson runs things now, you understand?"

"I understand that we don't have much time left."

Caleb nods before departing to join the rest of the team.

Reuben returns to the kitchen as Aperio sits and puffs the final remnants of the cigar. Reuben pulls it out of his mouth. "You have five minutes."

"That's not enough time, and you know that."

"More time isn't mine to give. This place is about to be filled with gunfire."

"You don't need to tell me that. I know what's coming, and it's far worse than gunfire, I'm afraid. Five minutes is barely enough time for you to ask the questions you've wanted answers to."

"Maybe. But that's all you have to make your case."

"Well, as you may be able to tell, the sun is on its way down.

If we had more than five minutes to speak, you and I would be a couple of nighthawks." Aperio winks.

"I don't know what you're talking about."

"No," Aperio smirks, "but you will when the time is right."

"Who's the other person who hacked into this time period?"

"If that's not a rhetorical question, then your father spoke more of you than what was true. You know who the other person is. The reason the Agency detected him is the same reason why you've encountered me here."

"Why's that?"

"C'mon, Reuben, we've both done this dance before and are quite good at it. You know why." Aperio's eyebrows elevate.

The cigar slips out of Reuben's fingers as it hits him. Its embers collide with the ground and dwindle. "Because...you wanted to be found." He can feel the shock as his voice strikes his ears.

"I've managed to remain a ghost for over a decade and, believe me, this is not the first time I've hacked Chronos. But it is the first time I wanted to be detected. I was waiting for them to bring you in. You are the son of the First Steward. Both me and the other may have wanted to encounter you on this mission, but as you'll come to see, our motives could not be more diametrical."

"He was the one in the basement earlier?"

"Was? Yes."

"Where is he now?" Reuben asks, and Aperio shakes his head.

"I'm sorry, Reuben, I truly am. I did everything in my power to stop him. But I am not God and can't change what happens next." As he finishes his sentence, loud gunfire ensues just outside the house.

Reuben grows queasy, and he wants to vomit. Aperio's face turns to cold stone, a sadness residing in his eyes.

Reuben needs to get his team out before it's too late.

It can't be too late.

He leaves Aperio and says nothing, boots fumbling along the dusty floors, running to get to them in time.

"Is everybody ready?" He enters the room, and the world goes black. The shock strikes him in his gut, the heat and debris searing his skin as he launches backward. He gasps for air, but there's nothing. His wind is gone, and his chest collapses.

A faint ringing vibrates from everywhere as he comes to. Oxygen flows back into him, though he coughs most of it back out. He peels the dirt from his eyes and comes to his feet, the world spinning around him.

Dust and sulfur fill his lungs as he regains his footing. A cloud of ash engulfs the living room, swirling through piles of rubble and fire.

"Sit—" he dry coughs over his own words. "Sitrep!"

Pop, pop, pop!

Gunfire bursts continue around the house. Reuben glances up as the sun cuts through the gaping hole left by the mortar. He slips a fresh magazine into the weld and charges his rifle.

"Jones up."

"Alex up."

"Kirk up."

Silence looms as he waits to hear her voice. It doesn't come. "Sky, sitrep, over!" Nothing. He shuffles through the ruins toward the front of the house. Through the dust, the faces of his team come into view; everyone but her. His heart races before sinking into his gut, unraveling within itself.

"Sky!"

His joints rattle with each step. He must find her. The smile that greeted him at the door. The voice that told him he'll see the Chronos his father fought for. The soul that showed him the joys and ironies of time from a rooftop. All of it had warmed him, had touched his heart, and at this moment, all of it is terrifyingly absent.

I trust you, she had said only minutes ago.

He must find her.

Before reaching the next room, a gentle tap warms his shoulder. He turns and sees the reflection first, tiny points of the sun's light resting along her irises as they radiate. His heart fills as he sees them, as he sees life, as he sees her. Dirt and dust cover her face, but her eyes shine on. The toll of war has given her greasy hair, clothes reeking of sweat and sulfur, and a face filled with cuts and bruises. Yet, she is beautiful and precious to him, perhaps more than she's ever been.

He embraces her, gripping her back and pulling her close. She mirrors the affection, allowing her shoulder blades to rest firmly into his palms.

Gunshots erupt from outside, and they break away.

"My headset got smashed when the mortar hit," she says. "I heard your voice through the rubble."

The dust settles further as the rest of the team converges on them. "We leave now," Reuben says. "Jones, grab Aperio so we can get the hell out of here." Caleb complies and runs to the kitchen. Reuben looks across the dining room at the ruins. Kirk leans against the staircase, kicking dirt off his boots before slinging his rifle and moving closer to the group. Reuben watches as he strides toward them. Without warning, Kirk's shadow diverges from his steps.

Not shadow.

Reuben's heart sinks as he watches it from across the room, powerless to stop it. His muscles tense, and dread fills him, burning a hole in his gut. He wants to shout, to run, and to stop it, but he can't.

He raises his rifle, but it's too late. A long blade pierces through the front of Kirk's chest. Shock and fear pour from his face.

No, no... Please, why? No.

The blade retracts, and Kirk's body collapses to the ground.

Tears fill Reuben's eyes, and he wants to run to him, but he can't.

He's there in the shadow. That monster is right there.

Reuben shifts his rifle's sights. The blood-soaked sword retreats into the darkness as its beholder moves his head into the light. A chill grips Reuben's spine as he sees him, as he immediately recognizes a face he's never met but always known. The incarnation of all the stories and terror stands there expressionless, glaring into his eyes, piercing into his soul. He lines the crosshairs against Adam Drazen's forehead and pulls the trigger. The muzzle flash pierces shadow like a torch igniting in darkness. Gunpowder and dust settle, revealing nothing but a lone bullet hole in the wall, an emptiness, a void.

Adam Drazen is nowhere to be found.

Reuben's brain races to find an explanation, to think of a way to turn back time and stop Drazen. But there's nothing.

No explanation. No reversing the last twenty seconds. Nothing.

Reuben runs to Kirk and crouches as he pulls his limp form closer. Blood spurts from Kirk's wound, drenching Rueben in his friend's fading lifeforce. Reuben grabs his hand tight as tears fall freely down his cheeks.

Kirk's mouth opens before choking on itself. He gasps for breath. "We—" Coughs of blood break his speech.

"Hey, buddy, no, no, no. It's okay," Reuben says through sobs. "You don't need to talk. You have to save your energy. We're about to get out of this place. You hear me?" He can see the devastating doubt in Kirk's eyes as if they were mirroring his thoughts.

"We're a team," Kirk gasps as he squeezes Reuben's hand.

"Yeah, man! We're a team, and we gotta get out of here as a

team," Rueben says even as Kirk's grip starts to fade. He watches as his teammate's eyes begin to glaze over, and a bloody smile crosses his lips.

"The grass withers," Kirk says through a bloody cough. His smile never falters as he continues, "The flower fades." The last word trails on rattled breath before Kirk's body slumps into lifeless slumber.

16

TWO MONTH HANGOVER

It's early morning, and Reuben can still taste the whiskey from the night before. Its numbing effects, gone. Its consequences emerging and in full force. The weight of his bloodshot eyes becomes borderline unbearable. The dangling lights above feel like they're microwaving his head as he maneuvers down AIC's infamous maze of hallways. He's not walked down them in months, nor does he miss them. A solemn emptiness fills him as he gets closer.

His arms droop and sway like lifeless pendulums. Whether it's the hangover or the extra pounds he's gained back, the weight of his being seems too much to walk such long distances.

A part of him wants to break down and cry. But he can't, not today. Self-pity has held him hostage too long. He's nearly numb to it. Before he can make the final turn toward 46B, he recites the promise he made to himself when he woke up, knowing he'd return.

Keep it together.

Reuben arrives at the entrance to 46B and swipes his badge, waving it in front of the reader as if saying a halfhearted hello.

A high-pitched beep denies him entry. Again, he swipes his badge, attempting to access the room. The sound emits once more. Before he can grab the handle, the door opens from within.

"Can I help you?" a familiar face says to him from the other side.

"Hey, Tyson," Reuben says, feeling the hoarseness in his throat. "I think there's something up with the scanner. I'm supposed to be in a meeting—"

"Badge," Tyson interrupts, and Reuben complies, handing it to the guard. Tyson's eyes dart several times from the ID to Rueben, as though he couldn't comprehend how the clean-shaven man in the photo could be the same man standing in front of him. "That scanner works just fine. It's your credentials. This area is for navigators only."

"Since when?"

"Listen, Greyson. You're smart enough to know that things are changing around here."

Without warning, Reuben hears her voice for the first time in over a month, and his heart drops.

"Tyson," Sky says as she approaches the doorway from inside the room. "I'll sign as his escort."

Reuben steps toward her, the warmth in his chest growing as if she were a blazing campfire in the frigid cold wilderness of his lonesome existence. His eyes come up to meet hers, but she doesn't look at him, as if intentionally averting her gaze. The inner fire freezes over, and a dreadful pit forms in his stomach.

She's angry.

"Very well," Tyson says as he hands Sky the tablet to sign. "No more than twelve feet and always in eyesight. New reg."

"Hope you don't mind being so close," Reuben says, trying to break the tension as he and Sky walk into the space. "I'll try to keep the bathroom breaks to a minimum."

She snickers politely but says nothing.

Okay, then.

His heart crumples deeper.

Open and large, the room mirrors the ambiance of 47A. Desks, chairs, and cubicles take the place of vacuum barriers and ever-changing environments, but its smell, feeling, and essence are all the same, as if it really were the training room, only wearing an office as a disguise. Moments later, they reach one of the sub rooms and enter, closing the door behind them. At the room's center lies a hologram of a three-dimensional map, encompassing much of the space.

"Navigators only. Can't say I'm surprised."

"Paul announced it at last week's all-hands meeting as part of the new security measures," Sky says, finally meeting his eyes. "You'd know that if you were here."

Her words pierce him, and he glances down, scratching the back of his head. "Uh, yeah," he says. "I know. Listen...I want you to know I really am sorry—"

"I'm sure you are. And I understand. You needed some time. You were never a prisoner here. It's just..." She shakes her head as if trying to maintain her composure. "You said that we were a team."

"I did. And it's true."

"Is it, though?"

Reuben says nothing.

"Listen, I'm not here to give you grief. I know that we're all going through this in our own way. But walking out on us like that when your team needed you the most, it just didn't seem like you."

Her words sink into him, and he drowns in his own doing as if he had tied a cinder block to his feet before jumping into the deep end.

"It is me," Reuben says as he gathers his thoughts. "You know, I remember coming here for the first time. I had quite the hangover and hadn't showered in a couple days, looking all scraggly. Kind of like today." He smirks to himself before continuing, "Then I'm told about time travel and read some note in my dad's journal. Suddenly, I wanted to clean myself up. So, I shaved, put on a nice shirt, and got back in shape. Paul gave me a badge, and I played the part. It wasn't until after everything happened with Kirk that I saw things clearly. He bled out, and I couldn't stop it. We should've left the moment everyone got to that house. Any good leader would've done that because that's what you do. Safety of your team comes first. I knew that. It was somewhere in my head. It was clawing at me, but I just brushed it off. And Kirk paid for it."

Keep it together.

The tears begin to glaze his eyes. "Truth is, beard or no beard, hungover or sober, stained undershirt or a team lead badge, I was the same person. Can't change that with a shower, fresh clothes, and a can-do attitude. Never could."

Sky looks down as if collecting her thoughts before turning back to him. "That's bullshit," she says.

Reuben can only stare in shock.

"What?" he lets out.

"Sorry, not trying to be harsh, but it's bullshit."

"Ah— I know that... I mean, I don't doubt that sometimes I —" Reuben shakes his head, still surprised. "You know, I've never heard you curse."

Sky smirks. "I usually don't, but I don't know how else to say it. Seriously, though, do you know how many of us were questioning your leadership after what happened? No one. Not me, Alex, Caleb, nobody. What happened to Kirk was awful, but Drazen's the one who drew the blade. Reuben, you saved lives that day. And you're constantly thinking of others. That's who you are. I don't care how hungover and pathetic you feel. Nobody cares about your bullshit pity party. We've all made mistakes, but it's not about that. It's not about you, and it's not about me. It's about us, our team, and we needed you. We still do."

Reuben thinks back on it but can't let go. Regret. Sadness. Failure. Sky's words move his thoughts, but his heart can't let it go. He knows she's right, and the guilt of leaving his team during grief pierces him even more.

"I'm sorry," he says finally. "I should've been here."

Sky sighs with a frown. "It's fine." She pauses for a moment before reassuring him with a subtle smile. "You're here now."

They continue to share what's been going on in their lives. Reuben explains to her where he's been. "...I even tried staying at my old apartment, but it wasn't the same. Looked the same, smelled like it did, but it was different somehow. It's great that AIC's been paying the rent but, honestly, it's just an overpriced storage bin. So, I put everything in real storage and terminated the lease. Been staying mostly in cheap motels. And sure, the coffee's stale, and the mattresses are as rough as rock, but at least there's no history there. None that I know of anyway. A stained but clean slate."

"Very poetic." Unmasked sarcasm fumes from her tone. Reuben smiles, shedding for a moment his self-seriousness. "So, no razors in these crummy motels?"

Reuben strokes the mesh of hair covering his face before smirking. "Haven't really seen the point lately."

"Please, don't tell me that's a depressed beard." She smiles.

"Ha! No, nothing like that. It's just, ah...I don't know. I kind of missed it. And it's a lot easier not to shave every day. You know, like 'why change out of your pajamas if you're just going to stay home all day and drink whiskey?'" He pauses for a moment, then smirks. "Gosh, maybe it is a depressed beard. Anyway, how've you been holding up?"

"I'm okay." She nods and clenches her teeth into her lips.

"It's not just you. We all felt some responsibility for what happened. He was my backup, my deputy. I trained him. I remember when people were testing to fill the position, and Kirk came along."

"He scored the highest?"

"Ha, no. That's the thing. And it wasn't the nepotism thing either, with his dad being a powerful senator. Paul told me that we had to give him a shot like everyone else, but that I'd make the final call. There were plenty of others that did much better, but he really wanted the opportunity. Didn't take long for me to see past the sarcasm. I noticed that he had something no other candidate had. An eye for detail and potential. Everyone else was at the top of their game, not willing or wanting to learn much more." Reuben watches as her eyes begin to fill with moisture. "That's all Kirk wanted, though: to learn, contribute, and be part of something. You know?" Her tears begin to pour out, and Reuben embraces her.

"I know," he says, feeling the warmth of her head against his chest. Her tears soak into his shirt, and a more profound sadness grips him as if she's transferred her pain to him.

"He was there and was fine. And then...and then."

"I know," he says again. "We're going to find Adam Drazen."

She breaks away from him. "I know he'll be found. We just have to make sure he doesn't kill anyone else again." Sky steps back and wipes the tears with her sleeve.

"He won't. We'll make sure of it. Were you able to dig anything up?"

She nods. "Now that all missions have been suspended indefinitely, it's given me some time to look through the schematics that Kirk obtained from the nav sweep." They both turn toward the hologram.

"This is what he got?"

"Mostly. It was a large and diverse geographical area with a lot of personnel and systemic events. Most of the fragments he got were from the house and a few surrounding square blocks, some with a lot of detail. Either way, it will probably take several more months before we can duplicate everything he captured in the training room."

"At least we were able to get something. Having an actual nav sweep puts us leaps and bounds ahead of Roanoke."

"True," she says. "In the meantime, we can examine the map itself." Sky waves her hand over the hologram, her brows furrowing. "That's odd." She zooms in on a particular region. "When we were in that house, you said that Aperio pulled you out of the basement."

"Yeah, that's right."

"Reuben, this house didn't have a basement." Sky points to a space on the three-dimensional map.

"What?" He leans in, turning the map in every which direction as though it might appear. "That's not possible. I went down there, through the door. You saw it when we were there, the basement door in the kitchen."

"I remember the door, I guess. It's kind of foggy. We were all in a hurry. According to this map, it leads to some sort of closet or pantry."

"I'm not crazy or making up what happened. You said that Kirk's nav sweep was incomplete. Maybe it didn't pick up the basement?"

"If it's what you described, it should've picked up some part of it." She stares at the space before turning toward Reuben. "I know you're not crazy. But I don't think the map is lying either. Drazen or Aperio may have done something to the place itself. It's impossible to tell without going back. Reuben, you know Paul has access to the same schematics that I do. When he sees on here that the basement you described in the debrief doesn't exist, he will suspect you're lying."

Reuben just stands there, staring into the void of the missing basement.

How can a basement just disappear? What aren't they telling me about the Stewards?

Instead, he says, "You're right, he will. I'll have to catch Drazen before then to make my case."

"*We* will catch Drazen before then. It's going to be harder, though, without Chronos."

"I think I may have a workaround. What time is it?"

"10:50."

"I'm sorry, Sky, I need to go."

✳ ✳ ✳

REUBEN MAKES his way down the sidewalk, appreciating the day's sunshine and beauty while dreading each step he takes as he gets closer and closer. Leaves stretch and expand as if awaking from a long hibernation. Pollen clings to the blades of fresh-cut grass, spreading the seeds of life in a place that only knows death. The lifeless quiet seems peaceful to him, but he hates it still. It's not the graveyard or the tombstone he's come to see that he hates. It's not even death itself. It's the years that it robbed. Too few years lived and too many taken. That's what he hates.

The path eventually leads him to a tombstone. Trimmed flowers stand guard beside it, shedding their petals as if in mourning. He grips his chest, his breath void as he reads the inscription on the tombstone.

In Loving Memory, Kirk Fowler.

The grass withers, the flower fades——*Isaiah 40:8a*

"I failed you, Kirk." Reuben crouches beside the gravesite, thinking of the day everything happened, almost feeling Kirk's hand in his as he squeezed it a final time. A young kid at war, younger than him, bleeding out as the terror of death took him;

this is what haunts him. Sky reassured Reuben that what happened to Kirk wasn't his fault. He trusts her words, but he can't shake the guilt. Words are meaningful, but experiences are everything. Kirk Fowler died in his arms. There's no forgetting that. Living with it, maybe, but not forgetting.

Reuben pulls out a flask from his jacket and takes a swig. The bourbon stings his throat and warms his chest. He chuckles for a moment, thinking about gravesite scenes from the movies where a character would sip a flask while visiting a deceased loved one. He takes another quick sip and looks back at Kirk's name.

"You really helped kick a lot of ass that day and saved mine. I won't forget, and I promise you...he won't either." Reuben reaches into his pocket and lays his team lead badge against the tombstone.

"I think your friend would want you to keep that," a voice says from behind. He veers as a strange woman approaches. A gust of stray wind captivates her straight blonde hair. "I'm sorry. I wasn't trying to sneak up on you."

"It's fine," Reuben says. "How do you know he'd want me to keep this?"

"I don't. I mean, not really. I just thought... It's not my place. I'm sorry for your loss." She turns and begins to walk away.

"Hey, it's okay, really. I only asked because I thought maybe you knew him. Are you here for someone else?"

She turns to him and nods. "I am, yes. And having a hard time facing him."

"I understand. My friend, his name was Kirk. This is the first time I've visited his grave in almost two months. There's nothing easy about coming here."

"No, it's not... You misunderstand me. I'm not here for someone who died. I'm here to see you, Reuben."

His heart begins to race as he stands, recalling the concealed 9mm on his right hip. "Who are you?"

"I'm Nea," she says, looking around. Reuben's back straightens at the name, and he tries to control his breathing. "I worked with your father before he passed. I was his lab tech assistant. I'm taking a huge risk seeing you, but with how they're changing things at the Agency, I might not have another chance."

"How do I know—"

"What? That you can trust me? That I actually am Nea? You don't. And you also don't have time to ask me a whole lot either."

"I should take you in with me."

"You weren't able to take Aperio in, and I won't let you take me either."

"How did—"

"I know about that? Stop asking dumb questions! Like I said, we don't have time."

"I won't force you, but if you come with me, we can protect you from Drazen."

"You can't." She sighs. "None of you at that stupid Agency can see what he's doing. I didn't see. At least not until your father. He saved me. Got me out the door before Drazen came in. He saw it then; I see it now. You'll all see it soon. You think that you're looking for him. You think that you will find, kill, or capture Adam Drazen, but you won't. Drazen is the one who has been playing all of us. He wants to make you believe that he's on the run. Can't you see that's part of his plan? Your father, the other Stewards, and now your friend. He didn't just happen to kill them. They were his targets, obstacles in the way of what he really wants."

The veins in his neck spasm at the mere mention of Drazen. "What does he want?"

"It's about time you asked one of the right questions." She looks past his shoulder. "Not here. Looks like one of your friends is walking up." Reuben turns to see Alex approaching in the distance. "For my safety, for his, and for yours, you can't mention this meeting to anyone. I know you don't fully trust me, and that's okay. I also know you really distrust Paul. Stay that way. If I'm not in touch before your scheduled meeting, then something's happened to me."

"You know about that, huh?"

Nea winks at him and departs.

"Who was that?" Alex asks, approaching seconds later.

"Someone in grief," Reuben responds. "Did you bring it?"

"Oh." Alex shakes his head as if to welcome a fleeting memory. "Yeah. It's right here." He pulls out a manila envelope from his jacket pocket and hands it to Reuben. "We have to be careful with it, man. If Paul even suspects that we have something like this, we'll be in the same boat as Drazen."

"That's the idea." Reuben unclasps the prongs and peeks into the bulky envelope. He sees it at the bottom and smiles. "It doesn't look any different. That's good."

"Yeah, getting it to appear the same was the simple part. Just remember that you can never turn that into maintenance. We have to destroy it once we're done. It'll be too risky to keep it around."

"Shouldn't be too much longer."

"Does Sky know?"

Reuben shakes his head, thinking of their conversation today, about all the things he told her and about the one thing he didn't. "I saw her today for the first time in over a month. I thought about mentioning it, but..."

"But?"

"Time got away from me. I had to leave to get here on time."

"That's not the only reason, man." Alex's eyebrows stretch toward his hairline.

A part of him knows he should've told her what he's been up to. She opened up to him, trusted him. "Yeah, I know. It's probably for the best, though. I want to make sure she's safe."

He knows it's not a lie, but there's more to honesty than not lying, and he can't for the life of him pinpoint the truth of why he didn't share it with her.

Alex smirks. "Well, thanks for that same consideration. If only I had long, pretty black hair." They share a laugh.

"Have you seen Jones?" Reuben changes the subject. "I was meeting with him pretty regularly up until a couple weeks ago."

"Yeah, he was in the dining hall the other night. I spoke with him for a few minutes in passing. Something's bothering him, but I can't tell what."

"Are you sure that's not his normal self?"

"No, this seems different. I know he's usually, well, you know...Jones. But I've never seen him as pissed as he was that day in Caltanissetta. It was bad enough what happened to Kirk, plus learning that Aperio escaped really set him off. It looked like his eyes were going to burst from their sockets."

"I remember. That first week was pretty rough for everyone."

"Yeah, well, when I saw him the other night, the conversation was pretty standard and civil, but he had that same anger in his eyes. It looked like he was struggling to hold it back. It's hard to describe. You had to be there. It was as if he forgot that anger for a couple months, and then something reminded him of it again. And usually, I'd ask, 'What's up?' over a beer, but things have been crazy with this assignment and trying to squeeze in time with the fam. You know?"

"Yeah, man. And I hope you know how much I appreciate your help with this. The last thing I'd want to do is take time away from your family. It's just there are very few people who can get their hands on something like this. And even fewer that I could trust."

Reuben breaks eye contact as something else comes to mind. "Hey, do you remember the basement in that house?"

"Uh, yeah, I guess." Alex's cheeks twitch with the sudden change in topic. "What about it?"

"No, I mean, do you remember seeing it?" Reuben watches as Alex struggles to recall the memory.

"I guess I don't. The door was closed when we got in. Why?"

"Sky couldn't find it on the schematics from Kirk's nav sweep. She said that, according to the map, the basement didn't exist."

"Huh," Alex lets out. "These Stewards, man. I feel like they're playing this game on a dimension we'll never get to."

Reuben raises the envelope. "This is a start, thanks to you."

Alex squats beside the grave and picks up Reuben's badge. "What you're holding is just a means to an end. This here, though," he waves the badge, "it means more than that. This is the real start."

"It didn't do anything for Kirk." Reuben's jaw clenches.

"And it won't do anything for him collecting dust. Kirk was a loudmouth who didn't respect many people, but he respected you. More than that, man, he followed you and made sure that you could be found when we got separated. He didn't want your badge then, and I don't think he'd want it now. You need it. We need it. The whole incompetent AIC needs it."

Reuben's stomach flutters as if it were filled with anxious butterflies. "What if I can't live up to it?"

"I'd say you're probably right. But if Kirk were still with us, I know what he'd say. He'd probably say something like 'Well, that's too freaking bad.'" Alex tosses him the badge.

Reuben runs his thumb against the engraving as the grooves of the Chronos symbol contour around his skin. The nerves pump up higher, but he can't give into them. He knows Alex is right. He hates it, the anxiety of it, and the fear of failure. But he knows that Kirk's dead voice has more truth than his live feelings, and he can't turn his back on his team.

No, not again.

"I guess he'd be right to say it."

"He definitely would be, even if that means we die trying to stop Drazen."

There, in the graveyard among the dead and the living, Rueben hears his father's words as though his ghost is standing right beside him.

You can't really live until you know there are worse things than death.

17

A DREAM OF BEASTS

The might of the current pulls at Reuben's feet like a hellhound attempting to haul him into the pit, ripping him further and further from shore. It drags him down into the icy deep, hoping to devour his soul and spit out his carcass. Terror grips him, but it doesn't take him.

It can't.

He fights, kicking and stroking with all his strength, feeling a massive wave forming behind him. The water pulls and stretches like a slingshot, building its tension as it rushes past him, collecting as much of itself as it can in preparation to strike.

Reuben fights forward as his lungs grip the walls of his chest in search of more air. He swallows a large chunk of it, dips his head down, and strokes forward with what little energy he has left. His body resists the wave's gravity, yearning to swallow him as it draws his body closer and closer into its orbit.

He eventually breaks the surface for air, and his heart pauses. The sharp tips of the wave protrude from above, spanning the horizon like shards of liquid glass raining down from the heavens. The terror grips his chest, and all he can do is flap his arms and kick with all his might.

It isn't enough.

The massive wall of force breaks him, and the wave knocks any air he has in his lungs out toward the shore. From above, behind, and in every direction, the wave pounds and crushes him.

Each second previously spent defying the force returns for revenge. The water expands and solidifies. He stiffens, but it's of no use. His bones batter within his flesh as the wave continues to tear him in every direction as if a pack of wolves is picking him apart. With no air or might, without options or hope, he yields to the will of the wave in hopes that submission will constitute mercy.

Moments later, the wave slams his body against a rock. Its jagged edges scrape and jab into his ribcage.

The wave lifts him once more and gently lays his body on another rock near the shore without warning. Saliva and salt-water spew from his lungs in a series of coughs. He's too afraid to be relieved, too skeptical to be grateful, and too confused to have his mind on anything but the shore.

His arms and legs tremble, dragging himself further onto the rocky beach before rolling over to face the sea. It stares back at him, still and calm, only gentle ripples remaining. It's as if it were a beastly lion, capable of tearing him to shreds, but beyond reason has released him and spared his life. Even stranger, the lion has come beside his battered and naked body to speak comfort through its stillness.

Reuben sighs, and his shoulders relax.

It's a mystery to him, all of it. But he can't help it: the sudden ease in his breathing and being. Perhaps it is mercy that has led to his submission.

Moments later, Reuben turns and begins making his way up the rocky beach. He stumbles forward and trips, using his hands to break the fall. Cold, wet sand sticks to his palms and fingers as if it were grained tar. He comes to his feet only to find that it's all changed. The rough pebbled beach is now soft cold sand. A towering cliff sits off in the distance, but he can't remember ever seeing it until just now. The bizarreness of it grinds the gears of his mind, and the questions come.

He can't remember the reason, the journey, any of it. It's like a mystical blur surrounding him, a curtain veiling the truth of why he's here. It's within grasp, the truth behind the curtain, but he doesn't reach for it. There's a tight feeling gripping his heart, pleading for him to carry on with the mission, to forget about the curtain.

Trust your gut.

It's a clichéd thing to think, but Reuben can't help it. Progress. He knows he's made it, and if he wants to continue, he must go forward and not look back.

Reuben finds himself at the base of the cliff. The blackened, moist rock formation stretches from the sand upward into the clouds as if the Earth were reaching for Heaven. Its shade drapes him in cold and darkness. He begins to make his ascent, the slipperiness of the rock giving him pause as he struggles to keep his footing. His eyes peer upward, and the blood-red sky skirts his peripherals. Aches begin to permeate into his arms, and he hums a tune to distract himself from the distance to the top. Yet the more he looks upward, the further it feels and the more everything aches.

Seeing a thick root, Reuben reaches out to grab hold. In a single swift motion, the root dodges his hand and lunges its head toward his arm. Before he can register, it sinks its teeth deep into his flesh. The pain, shock, and terror of it unite, and he screams. The word '*snake*' bubbles into thought as expletives flow from his lips. The riled reptile throws itself onto him and coils its body around his forearm. Reuben lets out a deep grunt as his foot slips out from the rock.

The snake constricts tighter.

The pain pules deeper.

He uses what remains of his grip to pull his body toward a better footing as the pain grows sharper. If he falls, then the curtain will take him, and there will be no return. He must move forward.

With both feet planted firmly, Reuben uses his free hand to grab the snake by its head. He secures his fingers at the snake's jaws and squeezes. The snake constricts tighter, the loss of circulation in his arm helping to mute the pain. He squeezes the snake's head harder. Finally, its teeth begin to break contact with his skin. Pulling the snake's head further back, he slams its body against the wall. The snake loosens its grip enough, and Reuben yanks it from his arm, tossing its coiled body to the ground below.

He gasps, hugging the cliff wall as though in the arms of a parent. But the danger is not over, and reality strikes as he examines his throbbing arm. Blood seeps out along the bite lines in a pulsating rhythm. Reuben arches himself against the slanted rock once more and pulls a bandage from his medical kit. The wound will have to wait until he can properly clean it. For now, it is enough to stifle the blood flow and keep him from slipping. Tying off the wrap, he continues the ascent toward the cliff's peak. His arm throbs with each pull, and his veins start to darken as they bulge beneath his glistening skin.

He wants to stop, rest, and examine the wound, but he knows that he can't. It will take just as much energy to hold himself up as it will to keep going. His stomach churns, and his eyes turn upward, hoping to see an end approaching.

But the end is still a journey away.

Reuben's only option is to move forward, perhaps infinitely, in hopes of finding the peak before physical exhaustion takes him or his wound proves fatal.

With what little strength he has left, he pushes and pulls through the searing pain until finally rolling over at the peak.

Reuben lies on his back for several minutes catching his breath. Stars shoot across his hazy vision, and he considers making a wish to be out of this dreaded place. Sweat and exhaustion flow from his pores as he wipes the salty concoction from his eyes and sits up. Grabbing his medical kit, Rueben starts to unravel the makeshift bandage on his arm. The final layer bonds to his skin, the dried blood an unyielding glue. He rips it from the wound but feels no pain. His eyes widen, and his breath lodges itself in his throat.

The bite marks are no longer visible.

In its place is dead, blackened, and festering skin. He gags as its smell strikes his nose.

"It's infected," a voice calls out to him. Reuben looks up to see a familiar face walking toward him.

"Corporal Clemens?" Reuben responds, recognizing the man from Operation Husky. He can feel his eyes widen with excitement at the sight of an acquaintance and the relief of seeing another soul.

How long has it been?

Clemens kneels next to him while looking at the snake-bitten arm. "I'm sorry, Staff Sergeant. I have to take that arm." Reuben's heart drops as Clemens loosens his belt and pulls a hatchet from the small of his back.

"Whoa!" Reuben jumps to his feet. "No, we don't have to do that. It'll heal, man. I don't even feel it. I can just wrap it back up, and I'll be good to go in a few days."

"It was a snake, right?" Clemens asks, and Reuben nods. "Hanging around the rocks, pretending to be a root or something?"

"Yeah, how do you know that?"

"Because, Sergeant, that's what it does. It waits until you need something, and then acts like that thing so that you'll reach for it. It was probably waiting there for days, knowing that you'd be coming up that cliff. It was patient and only struck when you were most vulnerable. But it doesn't end with a bite; that's just the start. I bet it hurt like hell for a little while, but then you can't feel it no more. That's how the poison works."

Reuben grabs the used bandage and begins to rewrap his wound.

"You see," Clemens continues. "That's what the poison is doing. Making you numb so that you'll just wrap it up and forget about it. All the while, it's eating your flesh and won't stop spreading until you're dead." Clemens holds up the hatchet. "That's why I have to take it."

Reuben tries to think of something, anything, but nothing comes to him.

No solution.

No response.

Nothing but the image of an axe severing his arm. His stomach turns, and his head becomes light. "There has to be something else we can do," he finally says.

"Staff Sergeant, I know it's scary and will hurt more than anything you've ever felt, but that pain is much better than getting used to the smell of dead flesh following you around as you die."

Then it hits him. Like the Dues ex Machina that had been waiting for him, it hits him. "Time," Reuben lets out. "We don't have to do this now, or ever, if I can just control it. I'm working on a way. All we need is time."

"Don't you see? That's how you got bit in the first place. Time won't fix that."

"I'm sorry, I can't. I won't." Reuben sees a rucksack a few feet from where the two men are standing. "Is that for me?"

"I guess," Clemens says. "It ain't mine."

Reuben reaches for the bag and begins to rummage

through it. Inside, he finds a fresh pair of clothes and boots. He puts them on and tosses the rucksack to the side. Rueben starts for the wooded area ahead but is blocked as Clemens throws out his arm.

"At least take it with you." Clemens hands him the hatchet. With a moment's hesitation, Reuben reaches out and secures it to his belt.

"You can come with me, Corporal," Reuben says.

Clemens shakes his head and smiles.

"Don't think so. I still need to do my hundred push-ups."

"Oh, yeah. I completely forgot. When did I tell you to do that?"

"You never did if you think about it."

"I guess you're right. I could, though, you know? If things could change, there's a lot I'd be able to do."

"Well, if that's what you really want, then the man in the woods is the only one that can make it happen. I don't think you should, though, Sergeant. Like I said, that's how you got that snake bite."

"What snake bi—" He looks down at his arm, and it comes back to him. For a moment, he had almost forgotten. The dread of it had gripped him and, in minutes, he completely forgot as if he had temporary amnesia.

How?

The woods open before him, and the curtain drifts from memory, forgetting again something once painful. Reuben nods at Clemens and continues his march forward.

The icy wind cuts through his thin layers, summoning dead leaves to tumble over his boots. They crackle beneath his heels with a final breath. Surrounding trees watch him as they tower in their unashamed nakedness.

It must be close to winter.

Pausing, Rueben listens and hears nothing but air streaming over dead branches as it intoxicates the wood with its lifelessness. The moon's light creeps into scene. Its pale blaze carves through layers of shadow and night. Reuben recalls the overcast daylight from the start of his journey but fails to remember the transition to night as if moving from wake to sleep.

The night looms in deafening silence, permeating between the rustlings of his footsteps. His thoughts expand to fill the void.

This is strange. I don't remember what I'm doing here. I don't even know where here is. I thought it was sunny not that long ago. There hasn't been a sunset. Was I swimming earlier? Why would I be swimming?

The questions continue to pour over, tempting him to look, to peak beyond the curtain. He knows he can have the answers. They're just in reach. But those aren't the answers he's looking for.

No.

It's only curiosity.

The real reason he's here is for something bigger. He can't for the life of him remember, but he knows. It may not be destiny or fate, Heaven or Hell, or even the grand mysteries of the cosmos. But he's here, and it's for a reason.

He continues making his way through the peculiar environment and the dead quiet. There are no crickets or animal noises; nothing but the crushing of lifeless leaves beneath him. His eyes shift downward, meeting his boots, still and planted against the ground. The rustling noise, however, continues.

He turns and sees nothing. The sound shifts to his left, then his right, his heart picking up pace alongside it, rattling within. His pupils dilate, inviting the moonlight to reveal the source of the sound.

But again, he sees nothing. The sound speeds up and encircles him. It's all familiar, and none of it eases him.

Like déjà vu.

The crackling grows sharper and faster as it begins to mirror the sound of grinding steel.

Suddenly, the noise stops.

Reuben's shaky hand removes the hatchet from his belt. Its grooves contour into his sweaty palms as he raises it to shoulder level, ready to strike. Several quiet seconds elapse as he remains still, gazing into the dark woods. All he can hear is his own rapid breathing as he struggles to control it. Fear has him in a way he's not experienced in a long time.

Two tiny beacons of red light emerge side by side, glowing brighter and expanding as its beholder grows closer to him. War is terrifying, but this is something else. This feels like hell.

He watches and tightens the grip on his hatchet as the crimson eyes dance in the darkness. Reuben fails to make out the creature beyond the red. Shadow cloaks its figure. Its eyes pierce his own as if they were emitting deadly radiation directly into his soul.

The eyes do not cower.

They do not waiver.

They do not blink.

He winds his arm as terror pulses through his veins. The beast growls and lunges toward him. Displaced air and a festering stench pummel his face.

He swings the hatchet at the body of the shadowy creature. It misses. The red eyes squint in anger as they converge on him. Reuben gasps as the creature sinks its claws into his chest. He looks down to see a blackened void where its arm should be as the shadow drapes the moonlit ground below.

His eyes move upward to meet the red glow. The creature's claws dig deeper into his chest, forcing skin and flesh to mesh against his sternum. Reuben screams as the pain and dread take him. The hatchet's handle nearly slips his fingers before regaining the grip.

He raises it above his head, aims at the creature's eyes, and swings. The heel of the bit jabs into the creature's face. The shockwave from the strike shoots up his arm.

The creature's eyes continue to stare without flinching, its claws expanding further into him. Reuben feels his feet leave the ground as the beast lifts him, but he continues to swing the axe.

After five blows, the claws begin to retract.

He swings three more times, and the beast growls, dropping him to the ground.

Reuben takes the hatchet, now with both hands, and drives it between the creature's eyes. There is a satisfying crunch as he forces his entire bodyweight behind the hatchet and into the beast's skull. The creature snarls and counterforces himself toward Reuben while swiping its claws against his chest and face. The warmth of Reuben's blood quickly cools as it greets the night air. He can feel his life pouring from the open wounds but does not stop driving the blade into the creature.

Suddenly, a *crack* breaks through the grunting. The slashing ceases. Reuben sinks to the ground and watches as the glowing red eyes dim into the night. He pants in exhaustion before coming to his feet again.

Reuben reaches for the axe and retracts it from the creature's skull but fails to hear its body drop. Using a green glow stick from his pocket, he searches for the body but finds nothing, not even a trail of blood. Realizing his own pain has vanished, he pats himself down to find that he is oddly dry.

No blood.

No gashes.

Not even a scratch.

He moves the glow stick along the ground as he continues to walk through the dark forest. The ground ends as its flat and darkened replacement displays the moon's distorted reflection. He approaches to find the shoreline of a lake. The green of the glow stick bathes along the ripples of the water. Tiny splashes subside beside the bank.

As he raises the light to scan the edges of the water, something captivates him. With each step and swipe of the stick, his surrounding reflects the green light to him.

He scans again and sees it: nothing. Several feet into the lake, a dark vertical sliver of emptiness consumes his light along the shoreline. Only by the edges where the green reaches can he see the outline.

The voided space reminds him of the sections in the training room, separated by a vacuum in spacetime. Stepping into the water, he walks toward the vacuum but stops just shy of reaching it. Rueben shivers, the icy water settling around his waist as its chill works to penetrate his bones. He watches as the ripples from his own movement vanish into the void in front of him. The glow stick dips below the surface, and his fingers release it. Reuben watches as its light floats toward the empty sliver of nothing. In moments, the stick is gone, and the green light with it.

He inches closer to the vacuum and reaches for it. Before he can touch it, something snags him by his shirt collar and down into the water, dragging him toward the shore as he struggles to free himself.

"No," a strange voice says.

Reuben's eyes open as his body rolls onto the shore. He comes to his feet and turns to the figure that removed him from the lake. The dim moonlight dances on the man's grandfatherly white beard but fails to reveal his face.

"Where am I?" Reuben asks.

"A dream," the man responds.

The curtain. I wasn't supposed to know.

"Don't worry," the man says as if reading Reuben's thoughts, "this is not a typical dream. You'll find what you're looking for."

"Who are you?"

"I am no one."

"So, you don't have a name?"

"I never said that."

"If this is a dream, then none of this is real."

"I never said that either." The man turns from him, walking toward a nearby sidewalk along the lake. Reuben stands in stunned silence.

"Wait," Reuben says, running up alongside the stranger. "You're the man in the woods that Clemens was talking about, right?" he asks, but the man doesn't respond. "Maybe you can help me."

The man stops in his tracks and turns his bearded face toward Reuben. "Help you? Do you even know what you're looking for? You're lost, boy. And worse yet, mortally wounded. It's only a matter of time now."

"Time," Reuben says, recalling more of his previous conversation with Clemens. "He said that you could help me master time, to control it. Is that true?"

"What else were you told?"

"I don't remember."

"Nor were you meant to," the man says as they continue to stroll along the sidewalk. "There are things that have been locked away from some so that they may be found and entrusted to others. There are also things, however, that have been locked away so that they can never be found. Do you know which of these you seek?"

Reuben shakes his head.

"Neither does that red-eyed creature you encountered. He's smarter than you. Make no mistake. But you must be wiser. That's the only way you'll ever beat him."

"So, I didn't just beat him back there?"

The man laughs. "Have you not learned anything? That's his trick. I bet you felt great when you drove that axe into his head, thinking you've finally rid the world of him. That's what he wanted, for you to feel like you're more powerful than he, but you're not. You're playing into his hand. The moment you think that you finally have him is the moment that the tides have truly turned against you."

"How did he get here?" Reuben asks. "Is he dreaming too?" The man stops dead in his tracks. Reuben can feel it somehow, the expression on the faceless man, a sadness in him.

The man turns to him. "No," he says. "There is no dreaming or sleep where he is. There's only misery." The man pauses and looks directly at Reuben. "Do you understand?"

Reuben shakes his head in confusion. "No."

"You will."

"How do I stop him?"

"I can't answer that for you. I suppose you can stop trying to walk into voids, for starters. And your friend was right about that arm. Keep the axe handy."

Reuben looks down at his bandaged left arm.

"I know you forgot about it and will continue to do so. But remember this, the poison never forgets."

They reach a set of iron gates at the end of the path. Chains wrap and cling to the opening, sealing the entrance shut. A nearby series of lampposts illuminates the walls surrounding the property. Glistening in the light is an old plaque reading:

34 Canto Lane.

A thin layer of fog loiters beyond the gates, clutching to a darkened structure in its midst. Reuben squints past the iron bars, noting a large house without lights.

"What is this place?" he asks.

"It used to be my home. Now, it just sits lifeless, rotting away in time."

"No one owns it?"

"There is one that has taken up residence. You drove an axe through his skull." Reuben turns to look at the man. "Don't worry, though. He's not there now. So, you should be able to find it without him getting in your way."

"Find what?"

"You're looking for many things. While some of these things may be dangerous, there is something you were meant to have, and it's in that house."

"Well, what is it?"

The man says nothing.

Reuben grabs at the thick set of chains holding the entrance closed. "Can you open it?"

"Do you not know how to climb?"

He makes his way over the gate before turning back to look at the man through the bars. "You coming?"

"I said *you* were meant to have something in there. My path to this place ceased a long time ago." The man hands him a lamp through the bars. "You'll need this. It's darker inside than it is out here."

Reuben holds up the lamp to get a better look at the man's face, but it's too late. Its light glistens against the iron bars before spreading into open darkness.

He's gone.

Reuben veers toward the house, cleaving a way through the fog. The frazzled structure reveals itself more with each step. Waterlogged and rotting plywood clutches onto most of the windows. Dirt and mold lie seeped into the panel siding while spider webs embrace the entranceway, guarding against squeamish intruders. As he approaches the run-down structure, staring at its ugly battered exterior, he can't help but smile. Somewhere within the rotting walls of brokenness lies what he's been searching for. More than a dream, it's the very reason he's come here, and it's just inside.

A splintered strip of stair sits against the steps to the entrance. He picks it up and forces the shard to part the cobwebs before reaching the front door. He opens the door, dangles the lamp before his feet, and enters.

The scent of mildew and rot fill his nose as his light pierces into the darkness through debris and broken furniture. Reuben steps further and further into the labyrinth, his shoulders tensing at the chilled air. The buzzing of hanging fluorescent lights strikes him as he rounds a corner. His mouth drops as the light reveals the battered shelves of what appears to be an abandoned convenience store. He shakes his head, reminding himself of the dream.

It doesn't take long for him to work his way deeper into the house, every passing second unraveling more out-of-place and bizarre rooms throughout the maze-like structure. Finally, he reaches a small library and makes his way past the desk and toward the room's center. An out-of-place object snags his attention.

The light strikes it, his heart skips a beat, and a smile comes to his face. Tucked against the far wall, an antique safe waits for him. Its ascetics are cold and metallic, but its meaning is everything. He knows it. He knows this is what he's been looking for.

The journey.

The reason.

All of it.

He doesn't know how he knows, but he does. It's as if his eyes have just found their sight for the first time since entering the dream.

He runs to the safe and sets the lamp beside it. His fingers trail through grime and dust as they inspect it. They catch on something, and Rueben wipes away the filth to reveal a large keyhole.

"Of course!"

The ground quakes beneath him, and the lamp tumbles over, shattering. Its light flashes like lightning, illuminating everything before catching its flame on a nearby set of curtains.

Reuben struggles to maintain his footing as the earthquake intensifies. Paintings rattle against the wall and fall. Books tumble and leap from their shelves as the expanding fire works to consume all. A crack breaks through the ground between Reuben's legs. He tries to jump from its path, but it's too late. Like the delayed but sure sound of thunder, the ground shatters, and gravity swallows him.

A scream pierces from the bottom of his throat as he shoots out of bed. Heavy breathing ensues, his hand shaking as he knocks over the nearly empty bottle of whiskey beside him. He turns on the light, and his breathing slows.

It was a dream.

His heart flutters, and it hits him.

Not just a dream.

Reuben stares at the bulky manilla envelope on his nightstand, and a pit forms in his stomach. The profound discomfort only grows as he shifts his focus to the whiskey, grabbing the bottle and tasting his nausea.

He's not sure if it was the envelope or the drinking that had taken him there. The dream, its all-too-real feelings of dread, and the answer he found. Something brought him there, and it's not a force to be taken lightly. Reuben keeps the envelope but tosses the whiskey into the trash. One, he still needs. The other can go to hell for all he cares.

After spending the next few hours regaining his thoughts, Reuben leaves his room and makes his way down the hall toward the training room. Before he can reach it, he runs into Sky, coming from the opposite direction.

"Hey," she says with a smile. "You're up early. You know it's five AM, right?"

"I know," he says. "I woke up and was going to go back to sleep, but I remembered that you get up early to go to the gym. I need to talk to you, Sky. It's important."

"Yeah, of course. Are you okay?"

Reuben looks over her shoulder to the camera pointed in their direction.

"I'm good. I was actually on my way to Section 7 if you'd like to join?"

"Uh, sure," she says, tilting her head in confusion before they both make their way toward the training room.

Once in section 7, Reuben sets the setting back to the hour-long loop of his house.

"Okay, no cameras in here," Sky says. "What's going on?"

"The key that someone left in my room," he says. "I know where it goes."

18

UNOFFICIAL BUSINESS

"Shouldn't Sky be helping you with this?" Jefferson asks as he strokes keys on his tablet. "I'm just a lab tech. Seems like this would fall under nav tasks."

"Wrong," Caleb retorts. "This would fall under deputy navigator tasks. In case you missed it, we've been down one for a couple months."

"I know that, Mr. Jones," Jefferson says, pausing to look up at Caleb. "I was there. I was the one who warned you guys... You know? Of the other person."

Caleb grips the handle of his knife as memories surface from the day that everything happened. He unlatches it from his belt and pulls it free, holding the knife up between himself and Jefferson.

"Yeah, and I saved the man's life using this blade, jamming it into the neck of a Nazi son of a bitch who snuck up on him. What good did that do, huh? Less than an hour later, he dies anyway." Caleb slides the knife back into the leather holster and lets out a sigh. "Right now, it doesn't matter what you did or what I did. It doesn't change what happened to Kirk. The only thing that counts right now is what he got off that sweep. He's gone, that's that. Let's not make it in vain. Okay?"

"Yes, sir, understood."

"Don't call me sir. I work for a living."

Jefferson nods and returns to poking away at his tablet as Caleb gazes into the empty first section of the training room.

"I'm sure Sky told you that we can't get much right now," Jefferson says. "I might be able to pull a few cubic feet, but it'll take at least until the end of the month before we can duplicate the whole room. And that's just the non-organic materials."

"A few cubic feet are all I need right now."

"Did you review the hologram in the nav room to see which part you want to duplicate?"

Caleb nods.

Jefferson taps the tablet a few more times and hands it to him.

"That's it." Caleb points to an area near the corner of the dimly lit screen.

"All right." Jefferson retrieves the tablet back. "Looks like I can duplicate the five seconds before the blast of that particular spot."

"Perfect." They step away from the center as the environment materializes, dust and light skirting the edges that form the space. Caleb immediately recognizes the kitchen floor of the house in Caltanissetta. Flakes of dust hover and reach for the ceiling as it comes into existence, paused in time. Two legs of a chair form, firm and un-splintered.

Before the blast.

"Can we get the rest of this?" He points to the created half-chair.

"I'm afraid not, Mr. Jones. It looks like it's in between two different sectors. Maybe in a couple days, we'd be able to see more of it. Just let me know when you're ready, and I'll set the loop."

"Go."

Jefferson taps the center of the screen.

They watch as air and dust sway and come to life, shaking off the restraints of suspended animation. Caleb focuses on the opening between the seat of the chair and its curved wooden back, waiting for it to come to life, to move and tell him if he's right or just crazy. Just as the five-second loop begins, two plastic circles generate behind the seat, slowly forming into a complete set of flex cuffs. Caleb's teeth grind as the inner fire comes back to him, watching as the cuffs twist and fall to the ground.

The scene repeats.

Air and wrath flare from his nostrils each time the cuffs collide with the ground.

"Pause it right there."

Jefferson taps the tablet as Caleb approaches the center of the section. Squatting beside the chair, Caleb reaches for the flex cuffs. The plastic is light and artificial, while the weight of his suspicions is too real to ignore. He takes a breath and pushes everything down, everything but the cold logic he knows will lead him to the truth. Inspecting the cuffs, he can feel the accumulation of sweat lining the inside. It takes minimal effort to force his large hands in and out of the restraints. He grips both his hands around a single oval cuff and pulls with all his might.

It doesn't give.

Caleb tightens the cuff a few more notches and attempts to pull it apart once more. Again, the restraint does not give. No defects, no issues.

Son of a bitch.

Rage fills him as the realization hits him. Fooled. Manipulated. Lied to.

"I can forward these findings to nav and intel while we wait for more of the environment to materialize," Jefferson chimes in.

Caleb flings the restraints, watching as it vanishes into the section's barrier. "Hold off on that." He takes a moment to collect himself before coming to his feet.

"But, sir... I mean, Mr. Jones. This can be used for—"

"It will be used," Caleb interrupts. "And I can do without that 'mister' shit. It makes me feel like a useless civilian." He lets out a breath and smirks as a chilling comparison comes to him. "You ever seen combat, Jefferson?"

"No."

"Well, let me tell you something about it. A lot of times, things go down, and you have no say in when, where, and how it happens. It just does. When I was overseas, we'd be in our tactical convoy on patrol, day after twelve-hour day, mostly trying to stay awake. The hot ass sun and air trying like hell to cook you alive while you keep an eye out for the enemy. To pass the time, we'd smoke and joke. Not to where we'd be complacent, but just enough to ease ourselves. A man has to hold on to himself somehow, you know?

"Being in a foreign place where so many hate you, away from family, and getting shot at. It's enough to break anybody. I don't care how tough a chump says he is. That's why more than anything, we'd look for those times where we could just laugh with each other. And a lot of times, we'd be laughing at some pretty messed up shit. But that's how it goes. It kept us sane. But, sometimes, it made us vulnerable, and the enemy knew it. It's like they sat waiting for the exact moment for someone in the convoy to light a cigarette, say something funny, or to take a dump. That's when they usually chose to strike. It never took us long to return fire, but anything we gained out there was paid for by blood."

"So, they'd always wait to catch you off guard?"

"When they had the opportunity, yeah. But that's the thing,

opportunity was everything out there. And like them, we had our turn, too. I was a part of recon, and we lived to have our turn. Intel would collect information, leaders would dictate who the target was, and people like me would facilitate the raids. There was nothing better than being steps ahead of your enemy and catching them with their pants down. It's a rewarding thing. But to have that, sometimes you had to be patient, and you always had to think ahead. Same goes with this," Caleb nods toward the empty chair.

"What do we do?" Jefferson asks.

"Let me worry about that."

* * *

RUEBEN FLINCHES as a loud knock breaks through the void of silence. He turns to the front door, wondering who it could be.

Is it time already?

"Coming!" he shouts before running to the dresser and removing his pistol. It could be anyone on the other side of the door. What Reuben learned, what he knows, and what he yearns for is paramount. For some, finding the answers is a cause worth killing for, but it's worth dying for him. He knows he can't be too careful. Safety is a habit; paranoia is an addiction. And he's not addicted.

I guess it's hard to put something down that you spent so much time picking up.

Caleb's sober words ring in Reuben's hungover mind. Pistol tucked behind him, Reuben opens the door.

As the edge of the door swings past his peripheral, he sighs and smiles, welcoming her into his room.

"Who'd you think it was?" Sky asks.

"I wasn't sure," Reuben responds. "You're early."

"Like you told me once, 'early is on time...'"

"On time is late, and late is unacceptable. Yeah, I remember that. I said it after Kirk played that joke on me, making me think I was hours late to training." They chuckle, though the laughter is short-lived as Rueben's thoughts turn to Kirk's grim fate. "This key," he says, holding it up, "I know it's connected to everything. It has to be."

"How do we know it's not another trap?"

A sudden image of Drazen's blade going through Kirk splices into his mind as his hand grips the phantom aching of his own chest. "We don't," Reuben says, feeling the sadness in his voice. "But we can't sit here and do nothing while he runs around toying with us. Maybe it is a trap. Maybe he kills me. But it sure beats waiting around for him to come to us." He slips the key into his pocket. "You don't have to come, Sky. If this is a trap, it's better that you stay safe."

"I didn't follow you into Roanoke or Caltanissetta because it was safe."

"I know that. You went because we had a job to do. But it's not like that anymore. You heard Paul. Missions are suspended indefinitely. And where I'm about to go isn't exactly sanctioned—"

"Us having a job to do is why I went, but it's not why I followed you. Reuben, I believe in what you're doing. We might not be able to use Chronos right now, but we still have that same job to do, sanctioned or not. Drazen must be caught, and you can't do it all by yourself. So don't tell me after everything that I don't have to come."

Reuben smiles and nods, filling himself with her confidence. It's not that she just believes in the mission, but that she believes in him.

"Okay," he says. "Let's do this thing."

Sky pulls a paper map from her backpack. She unfolds it and lays it across his bed.

"This is some ancient stuff," he says.

"Low tech is the only way to stay ahead...and undetected. I

must admit, I haven't used one since nav school. Should be the same principle, though." Sky points to a dot on the paper map and circles it in pencil.

"This is the place?" he asks.

"Not exactly. This is the nearest transport station to the spot. From there, we grab an Agency car and drive three hours."

"Agency car? That means we can be tracked. What happened to low tech?"

"They will only know where we are at a given time if anyone is even paying attention. But no one will know where we're going."

"Really?"

"Well, at least not until after we arrive. Also, our badges will register at the teleport station."

"I guess there's no avoiding that part. We could swap the Agency car for a civilian rental."

"And draw even more suspicion?"

"Yeah, I guess you're right. I just don't like the idea of being watched. If this place is what I think it is, the Agency probably doesn't know about it. Once we get there..."

"I know. But I'm not seeing a better option," Sky says. Reuben picks up the manila envelope on his nightstand as she asks him. "Unless you've got something better?"

He feels it like a dagger in his chest. He won't lie, but he can't tell her, not yet. Reuben tucks the bulky envelope into the breast pocket of his jacket. "Better? No." He's sure to face away from her as he says it.

It's not a lie.

What he has isn't better, and in many ways, he knows it's a stupid plan. But he's hiding it from her, and the reason he's doing it finally hits him. She'll talk him out of it, and that can't happen. He has to do it. There's no other way.

Sky folds up the map and returns it to her backpack. Reuben grabs his pack by the door, and the two proceed out of his room toward the elevator transport station. They arrive, and Reuben grasps his backpack straps tight as they enter.

"I can hear your breathing from here," she says. "Has it at least improved?"

"Improved..." Reuben feels it in his stomach, the looseness as if feathers filled his core. "Yeah, I don't think so. I mean, maybe I've gotten used to it. Or maybe it's my hangover I'm worried about."

Sky glares at him. "Geez, another one?"

"The last one."

"Good," she says as the doors shut.

Reuben shifts his grasp onto the railing as Sky enters the destination. The memory of their first transport trip to view the rooftop sunset surfaces in his mind. It fails to ease his nerves at the thought of watching his body twist, stretch, and jumble like gelatin. The memory does, however, give him control over his breathing. He manages a steady rhythmic pace of inhales and exhales as his bones and being come undone. It ends quickly. The doors open, and the pair step out of the teleport into an underground parking garage.

The chilled air hits them first, filling the void of the mostly empty space. A few scattered cars parked between faded and chipped white lines separate the spaces. Their footsteps break the static noise of half-shattered fluorescent lights as they make their way toward the Agency car. Reuben notices the charcoal gray paint and black tinted windows before being drawn to the bulky, outdated body cloaked in a layer of dust.

"Dodge Charger," Reuben says. "I thought the government stopped purchasing gas vehicles years ago."

"They did. There aren't many of these dinosaurs left. We only really keep them around for emergencies, especially in more rural areas where EV infrastructure is less reliable. Every now and then, someone will stop by to check the fluids and take it around the block." Sky tosses Reuben the set of keys.

"Don't I need authorization to drive it?"

"What, now you're concerned with the rules?"

Reuben shrugs.

Sky sweeps a loose lock of hair behind her ear as she approaches the passenger's seat. "They converted all of their vehicles to manuals years after all the manufacturers stopped giving people the option. Since low-tech, gas-powered sitting cars tend to be thief magnets, AIC had to find a way to repel would-be carjackers. Like much of the population, most criminals can't operate a manual to save their lives. So, if you can drive stick, you have all the authorization you need." She opens her door. "You can drive stick, right?"

"Yeah... I mean, I haven't done it in over ten years, but I think I remember." They enter the Charger in unison. "It's weird, though. My father taught me how about a month before he left."

"Why's that weird?"

"I remember it seeming so random at the time. He just came home one day with this old Toyota. He said that he borrowed it from a friend to teach me to drive a stick. When I asked why, all he would say is, 'You never know.' It was strange, but my dad said and did strange things all the time, so I just went along with it. We spent weeks in that car, and I eventually learned it. I was surprised that I didn't ruin the gearbox with the constant stalling. He was always patient with me and made sure I not only knew how but that it was instilled in my brain. You know, like muscle memory? Anyway, I never thought that I would ever be behind the wheel of a manual. And here we are."

Reuben engages the clutch, shoves the key into the ignition, and turns. The starter clicks but refuses to turnover, returning instead to its slumber. He removes his foot from the clutch for a moment before reengaging. Sky glances at him, her eyebrow rises. Reuben takes a deep breath, closes his eyes, and turns the key again. The starter yields as pistons fire, breathing life into all eight cylinders, roaring like thunder. Within moments, they're out of the garage and onto the nearby road.

He glances in his rearview mirror at the office building they had just left from. "Does the Agency own that building?"

"I think so. Technically anyway. They lease it out to local businesses so that it doesn't sit dormant and suspicious. Many of the other transport stations work the same way. That's why most of us won't go to one of the outer teleports unless it's a weekend. The fewer questions from civilians, the better."

"I guess that makes sense. The out-of-order sign on the elevator door is a nice touch."

Sky pulls the map from her backpack. "Okay, turn left up here," she says, and Reuben complies. "All right, we should be on this road for the next forty miles before the next turn."

The scenery continues miles on end as it drags the minutes and hours alongside it. Reuben glances down at blades of grass overtaking the edges of the asphalt. The mostly empty road doesn't behave as an intrusion into nature but rather a pathway into a forgotten spring. He recalls the history of interstate highways and how before that time, this is how people would travel.

Nature, small towns, and vast farmland would routinely greet travelers. Today, even interstate highways have become too burdensome. People seem to prefer flights for domestic travel. Now with Chronos, spacetime's bridge has grown even more. However, with a map in hand and a full tank of gas, Reuben and Sky redeem the time.

Clusters of trees tower alongside the road as the Charger roars past them. Their branches arch over the car, creating makeshift tunnels lined by full, green leaves. Reuben rolls down the blackened windows, allowing them to see the weary sunlight as it breaks through patches of vegetation. For him, a ride in the car had always been a place of solitude and meditation. But today, with her, it's not about him or his thoughts.

It's about them.

It's about their journey to find the truth, Adam Drazen, and all that comes with it. The heavy drinking and hangovers. The self-pity and guilt. The cynicism that had been killing his soul and the joylessness that had haunted him for years. All of this had been part of a cold and terrible inner winter. And now, a warmth grips him as he stares into the lush, life-filled vegetation around him. Just a few weeks ago, the trees were bare and the air cold. But that time has passed. Winter is over, and spring has begun.

He looks away from the road, his eyes drifting toward her. She turns to meet him as if feeling his glance. Their gazes lock onto one another and, for a few split seconds, Reuben feels as if he knows the world and yet can't recall a single thing about it. He's mesmerized, unguarded, and vulnerable. He wants to speak and tell her anything and everything. But he doesn't say a word, and neither does she. The moment is bliss and, for him, that's enough.

Less than an hour later, Sky points to a nearby sign and shuffles the map. "Yep, that was mile marker forty-five. It should be right around this bend."

The steering wheel resists as Reuben holds it inward, the tires hugging and pulling into the winding road. Gravel suddenly kicks into the undercarriage, and Reuben's rearview mirror fills with dust as the Charger's shocks adjust to the unpaved pathway. An eerie sense of familiarity tingles into the back of his neck, and then he sees it. It's not a hallucination or a dream. It's as real as the trip itself. There, in the shadow of dusk and the beam of the car's headlights lies the set of iron gates the old man had taken him to.

No flipping way.

Reuben slams onto the brakes.

"What the—" Sky says as she grasps her seatbelt and the two of them jolt forward.

"I'm so sorry," Reuben says. "Are you okay? I didn't mean to. I saw it and just—"

"I'm fine." She grips the back of her neck. "It's only a bit of whiplash. Nothing a bag of ice can't fix." Reuben places his hand on her shoulder. "I'm fine, really. The shock was the worst part, and that's over now." They unbuckle their seatbelts and get out of the Charger. Reuben pops open the trunk as Sky looks toward the house, less than a block away from where they stopped. She turns back around to face him. "What are you digging around for in there?"

Reuben closes the trunk and walks toward her with a white, liquid-filled plastic bag in his hands. He slaps the pouch and shakes it before pressing it against the back of her neck. Her shoulders and neck cringe as the numbing cold pierces into her skin. "It's an instant ice pack that was in the first aid kit. Hopefully it helps. Sorry again about the brakes."

"Thank you," she says. "That's really sweet. But, yeah, don't worry about it." She takes hold of the ice pack and forces it deeper into her neck as she looks upward. Reuben looks up as well, realizing that it's nearly twilight. Sky removes the pack and tosses it into the passenger's seat of the car. "I'm sure it'll still be cold by the time we get back." They grab their backpacks and walk toward the gate.

"I can't believe it," Reuben says as they approach the gates. He brushes past her, running his fingers against the plaque. "34 Canto Lane," he whispers to himself before elevating his voice. "This is it."

"Just like in your dream?"

"Yeah." He scratches his beard. "I mean, kind of. In the dream, it was a sidewalk that led to the house instead of the road. Everything else looks a little bit different, but the feeling, it's..."

"What?"

"Exactly the same. I don't know if it's the smell or what, but

I've been here before and can't shake that feeling... There's just something about it." Reuben droops his shoulder, allowing the backpack's strap to fall into his palms, and tosses the bag over the gate. Muscle memory pulls him to the peak of the iron bars before Sky yanks at his ankle from below. He looks over at her and watches as she pushes open the adjacent gate. He jumps down and follows her through the entrance. "Well, that part was definitely different."

They make their way up the long sloping driveway as the day's light continues to drift toward slumber. Its afterglow, not eager to linger, fades as the landscape begins to cloak itself in shadows. One of the larger shadows creeps up over the top of the driveway. He doesn't recognize the shape at first. It's only when they finally reach it that he can make out the rust-covered car sitting atop fractured cinder blocks in the absence of tires.

Reuben approaches the car first, with Sky not too far behind. The windows welcome the early evening breeze through its hollowed-out openings. Shards of glass and debris litter the seats inside. A hazy web of fractured windshield lies along the dash, altogether divorced from the frame.

Reuben reaches for the door handle but finds none, only the gap of space where it once resided. He works his way to the front of the busted-up vehicle and sees that the hood has been torn off completely, exposing the naked engine bed. Yet there, front and center, he can see it.

The Toyota logo.

He looks up and sees Sky peering into the interior. "I can see why someone retired this old thing," she says.

"Retired? Looks like they gutted it alive before finally putting it out of its misery."

"Can't say I blame them. Old manual transmission. The resale value must've been terrible. You're better off scrapping it for parts."

"Manual?" Reuben walks back toward the driver's side door and sees the stick shifter. An unexpected thought hits him, and his heart stops. "I'm sure it's not it. I mean, what would be odds?"

"Odds of what?"

Reuben steps backward away from the car.

Sky glances at the shifter, then back at Reuben. "Wait, do you think..."

"I don't know. It's been ten years, and my memory of that car is... Even if I could remember the car... I mean, look at it. It would be like trying to ID a witness that the mob got to first. Completely unrecognizable."

"You said it belonged to your dad's friend, right?"

"Yeah. At least that's what he said."

"Do you remember his name?"

"His friend? No. I don't think he told me. And I never would've asked."

The wind shifts, and a chill fills the air. Reuben stares at the car intensely, pondering how it may have gotten here. He sighs as he realizes that the answer is as clear as how he got to where he's standing.

34 Canto Lane.

The key in his pocket.

A killer in hiding.

And a mesmerizing dream.

It's all a mystery, still. And the answers, if ever they come, drive him forward.

* * *

SKY LOOKS AT HIM, watching his eyes jump back and forth, perplexed by the ravaged car. She parts her lips to speak, but the words don't come.

Instead, an intense weight twists her gut in an instant. Her blood runs cold, and her heart slows. She feels herself return to Roanoke, Caltanissetta, and the puzzling unease gripping her spine and imprisoning her mind to wonder what the source may be.

Reuben's face drops as if he can see the fear and discomfort in her eyes. "Hey, what's—"

An agonizing scream pierces through the heavy air, but it isn't her.

Sky's eyes dart toward the source, toward the house. She doesn't think. There's no time to think.

They draw their pistols and sprint to the entrance, the porch steps rumbling as they rush up to the door.

With one on each side, they plant themselves beside the entrance. Sky pulls the slide back on her pistol, ready to fire.

The scream emerges once again, this time fainter and briefer. Reuben and Sky lock eyes and nod. After a year's debt of promises, it's time to collect, and she must deliver.

Game time.

Reuben kicks the door, and it gives, bashing the inside wall as it swings open. With pistols at the high-ready, they sweep past the entrance and into the dark.

Game time.

19

TARE

Nea pulls the door open from the inside and peeks her head out. Motel guests splash and shout from the pool next to the open courtyard below. Seeing no one else, she steps back into her motel room, shuts the door, and fastens the guard lock with trembling hands.

Is this what it's come to?

The life she had is forever gone: promising career, great benefits, and a German shepherd pup who loved her.

It's all gone.

Images of that day bubble to the forefront of her mind. The computer screens going black, the power cutting off, and the fear in Nolan Greyson's eyes as the gunshot echoed through the lab floor. There are two instances that Nea will never forget from that day, the feeling that something is terribly wrong and the awful realization that she can never go back. She knows she could do nothing when Nolan infected the network and its central archived database with the Aion malware. But when Nolan gave her the disk, that was a choice, and she chose to take it and run. So here she is, sitting in another run-down motel room.

Always running.

She sits on the worn-down mattress with eyes fixed on the entrance, even as her hands reach for the nightstand's drawer. A tiny vodka bottle rolls along the bottom as she opens the drawer, knocking into the edges of its resident Gideon Bible. She sets the miniature plastic bottle onto the nightstand, exhales, and allows herself to fall back onto the mattress, half hoping that it welcomes her like a fitted glove. Instead, the stiff springs jab into her back as the bed creaks, and its stale smell makes her gag. This is the life she never wanted but must always choose.

Nea tears off the aging dust cover and tosses it across the room. The now-exposed white sheets welcome her body as its potent bleach stench assures its sanitation. Comfort may be a luxury, but cleanliness is a must.

In less than thirty minutes, she relaxes enough to nearly drift into sleep. Meandering thoughts of nothingness pull her into a brief dreamlike state.

Can't let my guard down, not now.

Laying there, she thinks of all her belongings, taking a mental inventory of the items scattered throughout her room. The pair of tennis shoes, lying perfectly perpendicular to the foot of her bed. Neatly packed toiletries beside the sink, just outside the splash zone.

And her suitcase.

Her blood recoils as she thinks of the luggage, half-packed with the disarray of uncommitted clothing.

But she knows it's necessary and therefore pragmatic. At the threat of life, she may have to leave any moment. Time, like comfort, is a luxury. One, she knows, can't be wasted on last-minute packing.

She springs up from the bed, quickly relinquishing the façade of relaxation.

I need something better.

Nea pulls out a portable kitchen scale and sets it next to the vodka before grabbing one of those plastic cups, individually wrapped. Adding four large ice cubes, she sets the cup on top of the scale and hits 'tare,' allowing the digital display to read *0.00 oz*. The numbers grow as the stream of vodka collides with the ice before the reading hits *0.48 oz*. Nea stops for a moment and allows one more drip to strike the cup. The display holds at *0.50 oz*. She smiles and returns the bottle to the nightstand.

Before she can reach for the cup, her eyes stumble back onto the reading, now at *0.51 oz*. Her heart drops, and her chest tightens even as her breathing quickens.

It has to be exact.

Impairment is not an option. Since being on the run, she's had little control over anything. But these stupid numbers on the scale are the one thing she has power over. Nea closes her eyes and focuses on her breathing, remembering the exercises she learned from a quick internet search. Her heart winds down as she dips her index finger into the cup, pulling out slowly a single collected drop of vodka, dangling between nail and skin. She deposits the drop back into the bottle and looks again at the scale.

0.50 oz.

She sighs and pulls out a single-serve cranberry juice from the mini-fridge. Filling the cup to the rim, she stirs, sips, and sighs once more.

It doesn't take long for her to finish it. The tartness and potency linger on her tongue, cooling and relaxing her mouth as it doses her muscles with a mild semblance of ease. She tosses the empty cup into a nearby wastebasket and shuffles back to the bed, first stopping at the suitcase and grabbing a book from the larger compartment. She reads the title to herself aloud, "Paradise Lost." Instead of beginning at the book-marked spot, she flips through the first few pages before a set of words catches her gaze:

Who first seduced them to that foul revolt?
Th' infernal Serpent; he it was whose guile,
Stirred up with envy and revenge, deceived
The mother of mankind, what time his pride
Had cast him out from Heaven, with all his host

THE WORDS ARE meaningful to her, even if she doesn't know *what* they mean. Her engineering degree didn't require many in-depth literary courses, not that she had much interest. But this book, these words, and everything it represents, it means something. It belonged to Nolan Greyson, and it must mean something.

Nea pauses before flipping to the bookmarked page. On the left-hand side, the John Milton poem continues. On the right, his words go on before lying gutted and hollowed out at the center of the section. In its place is an octagonal cutout, preserving the very reason she's endured chaos and cheap motels.

Molded into the hidden space, the translucent orange disk stares back at her. Nolan Greyson's sacrifice and her promise to him stare back at her. The promise, she never muttered but made, nonetheless. The promise, she knows, must be fulfilled.

'*Give the disk to Aperio,*' Nolan's voice echoes in her head. '*He's the only one of us left you can trust. Until then, disappear.*'

I have disappeared. And so has Aperio.

Even though she has communicated with the Steward, she has yet to meet him in person.

Even Reuben managed to get a face-to-face.

Nea knows she must get it to him before it's too late, before

Drazen can get to Reuben and the others, and before time runs out altogether.

She glances over at her modified watch centered on the nightstand. Lying in hibernation, it's been the instrument of her evasion from Adam Drazen and her contact to Aperio, a shield and a bridge. Defense and hope meshed in the fabric of space and time. Spacetime. Two facets of the same diamond. The same but in opposition. Always true but rarely right.

A paradox.

Nea knows that every run-down motel room, stale cup of coffee, and paranoid glance over her shoulder in all this time is not in vain. It can't be. Nolan Greyson laid down his life to get her here, tasked with preserving the disk inside of this *Paradise Lost*. She may not know what's in it, but it must be worth fighting for and dying for.

She closes the book and returns it to the suitcase, securing it to the innermost compartment. Of all her belongings, that disk, whatever it is and whatever it may hold, is the most precious thing she carries. And it must be protected.

The heat of the sun bakes her room's window and the thick curtain covering it. A pocket of warmth clings to her skin as she pulls it back and looks out, gazing at the crystal-like ripples of the pool water, allowing it to entrance her.

This is just what I need.

A good book. Lounging beside the pool. An escape.

It's not the alcohol that moves her to pull out her bathing suit. If this were her first or second day in hiding, she knows it would take so much more to be so careless. But after too many days and too many motels, even her paranoia needs a break.

So, she does it.

She lets out a sigh and pulls out her keycard holder from the nightstand drawer.

It's time for a break.

As she opens the paper holder and removes the lone keycard, her heart pauses.

I had two cards.

She races back to the drawer, fingers trembling as she yanks out the Gideon Bible and two neatly stacked receipts, leaving the drawer empty. She pats down the bottom and sides for good measure before completely detaching the drawer and tossing it onto her bed.

It may have slipped out and is sitting tucked away.

She inspects the small space between where the drawer was sitting and the inner back lining of the nightstand.

Nothing.

Where is it, Nea?

Within minutes, she tears apart the rest of the room, dissecting each piece of furniture and every square inch. She retraces her steps, hoping to jog her memory, but nothing comes to her. As she reaches the door, a thought hits her.

The holder.

She doesn't remember the keycard, only the flimsy paper that held that. Running back over to the nightstand, she picks up the holder, puts the lone card into the paper slot, and clings it tight in her hand—the sense of the weight, the feel of the bulkiness.

Is *this how it felt when I walked in with it?*

Her mind jolts back prior to entering the room itself, back to the lobby only a few hours ago.

She recalls the smell of stale coffee, the mediocre customer service, stained carpets, and dated wallpaper. The memory of helping an elderly woman through the front door jumps to mind.

Where was it during all of this?

She continues to think it through before it hits her.

I set it on the counter.

Her eyes widen as she recalls setting the keycard holder down when she saw the woman struggling to open the door.

It wasn't there long, less than a minute probably. Just long enough for someone to—

A swipe and a *click* pull Nea from her reverie. Her eyes dart the door as a sharp *beep* echoes, sending a chill down her spine. The door handle moves down, and she gazes motionless, in shock as outside air flows into the room through the broken seal of the door. A silhouette fills the crack, blocking the sunlight. Nea still can't move, her feet remaining planted in a stunned holding pattern. The door opens wider and, for a split second, she sees one of his eyes staring back at her. Murderous rage pierces out from it, into her room, into her eyes, into her soul.

Suddenly, a snapping sound breaks out. The door snags as it collides with the bold resistance of the additional top lock. She gasps in silence. The intruder slams his weight against the door as the lock and frame absorb tension. It holds but fails to dissuade the intruder.

He continues to bang, kick, and slam his body against the door, each time more violent than the last. Still motionless, Nea's heart races, outpacing the veracity of the door. She tries to move, tries to run but can't. Fear clenches her muscles still.

"Now is not the time, Nea," she manages to whisper to herself.

The door suddenly stops its motion, and Nea exhales, her hand reaching to cover the noise.

Bang! Bang! Bang! Bang!

The stranger pounds the door in rapid succession. In defiance of her fear, she rushes to pull out her suitcase, tossing her remaining items into it.

Where is it?

She shuffles to recover the book holding the octagonal disk.

Wait, it's already in here.

She physically checks, zips up the suitcase, and runs for the window at the rear of the motel room.

Bang! Bang! Crack!

The impact against the door begins to bypass the lock, targeting its frame. Nea can feel it, but she doesn't look back.

She can't look back.

She uses a chair to reach the small, elevated window in the rear of the room. Her adrenaline-fueled hands unlock it in a single swipe before she uses her suitcase to brace and pop the screen.

Bang! Crack! Crack! Splat!

The doorpost gives and breaks apart, splintering like a pair of chopsticks. The intruder enters, and Nea trembles.

The suitcase drops from her hands, tumbling into the alley beyond. She can feel the panic begin to take her, knowing it will only be a few seconds before he reaches and does God-knows-what to her before taking the disk. This can't be how it ends, not after everything.

Her body convulses, and her mind stalls.

Then clarity.

She knows she can't opt out of what comes next. One way or another, it's coming. Just below is a two-story drop. Just below is her suitcase. Just below is freedom.

There is no thought or debate. She doesn't even feel herself do it, but she does; with all her might, she does it. The ground comes at her quick as she tightens herself, bracing for impact. Shoulder first, her body slams down against the pavement. The *crack* of bone hits her ears first, then an instinctive scream. Adrenaline surges to intoxicate her nerves, subduing and quenching as much of the pain as possible.

She jumps to her feet, grabs the suitcase, and runs. The intruder races through the motel room to reach her. She can see it in her mind but doesn't dare turn back. She picks up her speed to a sprint. She knows she must take advantage of any distance she may have, or there is no chance.

Nea turns a sharp corner and then another before darting in the opposite direction, each veer increasing her chances of escape, every new choice stacking the odds in her favor.

At least in theory.

After a few more sporadic turns, she pauses to catch her breath against a wall. Bursts of gasping air rush to fill her lungs. Beads of sweat pulsate from her forehead with each violent thump of her heart as her shoulder throbs. She struggles to tune out the sounds of her heavy breathing.

Sharp gusts of wind and car engines from the nearby street flutter just beyond sight. Cocktails of rotting garbage and urine fill the air throughout the narrow alleyway, but she barely notices. She peeks around the corner before quietly maneuvering around it. Taking each step with care and precision, she avoids the shards of broken glass scattered across the ground, petrified that a careless slip of the foot will give her away.

Nea's uninjured arm begs her to roll the suitcase, but she resists the temptation to emit unnecessary noise. The intruder may be near, and she can't afford to compromise her position. She's come too far and given up everything. He can't get to her. She'll die before she lets him take it. Around the following corner, her eyes are drawn to the sunlight reflecting off the shiny coat of a fiberglass sign, centered in the distance beyond the alleyway walls. A few steps further and she can read the sign along the storefront of a street just out of reach.

'Fresh Coffee.'

Just another thirty feet, and she'll be in the haven of public view.

The muscles in her cheeks pull back a smile of hope as her strides pick up speed toward the diner. Only a few feet from the street, a noise breaks out from her peripheral. She turns to meet it, but it's too late. Before instinct can counter it, the fingers of fear grip her shoulders, pulling her from the light's reach.

Her heart recoils as she tries to scream, fear and dread filling her. Only timid muffles make their way through the intruder's hand clasped tight against her mouth. He yanks her into the doorway, and her arms flail, trying to grab onto something, anything. Her eyes cling to the diner's sign, but it's not enough.

The sunlight abandons her as the intruder slams the door behind them. She can feel his violent breathing against the back of her neck and can only imagine the murderous eye that stared into her soul minutes ago. A sharp prick pierces the base of her neck. Her body relaxes against her will while the dwindling light beyond dims itself out of existence.

An extended slumber ensues, with time stretching and stopping before commencing once again. Nea struggles to part her eyelids as if held by a pair of clamps. She tries to lift her head, but it's too heavy. Consciousness slips in and out of her as feeling and motor function slowly seep into her muscles.

She can feel herself seated with hands bound together from behind, sending a tingling sensation from her shoulder blades down to her fingertips. No memories of how she got this way come to her; only a fog of fear lingers.

Footsteps and the rummaging of objects strike her ears as more strength returns to her. She manages to sway her head, feeling it jerk sideways. With eyes now vertical, they open with ease. A crouching figure stands and moves toward her.

"Finally," the man says. "For a while, I thought that maybe I gave you too much knock out juice."

Knock out?

Then it all comes back. Thoughts of terror resume, sending chills back through her bones. The man stops a few inches from her, his breath warm against her cheek. Nea looks up, and her eyes widen. This is not the face that she expected, the face of the man that has haunted her dreams all this time.

No.

This was someone else, someone that she knew and trusted all of those years ago. But, then again, hadn't she trusted Adam Drazen as well? While time had been kind to her, the years hadn't been so generous with her captor. She couldn't have been much younger than him then, and yet now, the sorrow etched into his face tells a different story. His clean-shaven cheeks are marred by a scar running from the edge of the bone to the tip of his nose.

"It would've been a shame if you signed off too soon on me," he says. "We've got quite a bit to catch up on." Her head droops, the exhaustion taking hold even as fear settles in the pit of her stomach. She knows what this man is capable of, the reasons he was assigned to the project. Hired to protect because all he's ever known is the kill. A guard dog. One who now seems to have gone rabid, now emerging from the deepest depths of Hell.

The man grabs her head and straightens its orientation. "Don't worry, Nea. In a few minutes, you'll be able to hold it up on your own. More importantly, you'll be able to talk, sing even." Nea glances around the large room, unfamiliar and mostly darkened. The only source of light appears to be a cluster of candles on top of a nearby desk. Next to it, her belongings lie littered around her scavenged suitcase. "Oh yeah, I already got acquainted with your things. Figured I could get started with something while you were out. You got some interesting shit, my dear."

Oh, no. Did he find it?

"You hear me?" he says, now crouching to look into her eyes. Nea manages to open her mouth, but no words follow. "Come on. You got this. Let it out." She opens her mouth again, this time managing to spit out the little moisture between her lips, flinging it in disgust at the man. He wipes the scattered saliva from his face with his right hand before using it to slap her in retaliation. "That isn't how you want to play this, Nea. You're not like me or Caleb Jones. You were one of the smart ones—an engineer. Remember? I know you have brain, and it's time we kick into gear."

"What do you want from me?" Nea finally lets out her first words since waking.

"What do I want?" The man laughs. "No 'hello' or 'how have you been'? or 'hey, it's been a while, not sure why I'm tied up right now. Let's talk.'" He lets out a sigh. "Pretend like you know me, at least."

Nea remains silent.

"Well, shit. I'm sure you already know what I want." He walks over to the desk, picks up a glass of water, and brings it to her lips. Her dehydrated body doesn't allow her to protest. She locks on to the glass as he tips the liquid toward her. The chilled water fills the crevices of her parched mouth, quenching the undeniable thirst. She drinks it quicker than gravity can serve. In seconds, it's empty.

She locks eyes with him once more, her mind bursting like rapid-fire as she tries to piece it all together. Then it comes.

"He got to you..." she says, barely a whisper. "Adam Drazen."

The man's face hardens as his hands press on her own.

"Dammit, Damian. Really? I mean, why on...why would you...what could he even offer you? To do all of this, to turn on us, your colleagues...your friends?"

Damian turns away, setting the glass onto the ground near the chair. "Friends. Is that what you call them because, in my mind, they're traitors."

"What are you talking about? They would've never—"

"Oh, but they did." He sighs, a hand coming to rest on his forehead. "You may have seen everything they did, but I don't think you understand. They were traitors to the world, and more than that, my trust. When I needed them, where were they? When Jenny...when she..." He chokes and sadness fills his voice as he struggles to get the rest out. "When she died in that accident, which of the great and noble Stewards stood up to offer use of their discovery? They could've brought her back. We both know it."

Damian turns, and for a moment, the killer is gone. All that is left is the pain from his loss, the anger from betrayal, and the sorrow of what must come next. Nea can see it in his eyes, and she knows that there will be no stopping him even as his eyes fade into those of a killer once more.

"Only one person came to my defense and offered me a path forward. Only one provided more than an apology and some damn flowers or a nasty ass casserole. Even when I begged, Nolan didn't help me, at least not in that way. The only way that he and the others could. The brave and powerful Stewards." Damian chuckles as he says it. "Reigning in their graves. Is that what you want, Nea? Living in run down motel rooms, and looking over your shoulder until the day comes where you can reign beside them?"

"I'm sorry about your wife, but this isn't—"

Damian holds up a hand, and she falls silent.

"He's been looking for you a long time. I never understood it, though. We got really good at Steward hunting. Not many of them left. But some unremarkable lab tech manages to stay hidden all this time. I knew you were smart, Nea, but not even you could avoid him for a decade. But we will get to that later." He pauses, lowering himself to her level as his nails dig into her skin. "Do you know what your mistake was?"

"No."

"You went and saw him. You know, at the gravesite. Shouldn't have done that. It was very risky and just plain dumb. But you couldn't resist, huh?"

"He'll find you. And Drazen. Reuben will stop whatever it is you think you're doing."

Damian laughs. "Is that what you think? I'm not even going to slap you for that bullshit." He returns to the desk, opens a drawer, and retrieves a black leather bag. He opens it and pulls out a long stainless-steel knife. "You know, I can kinda see your line of thinking. He's a smart kid. I'll give you that much. The problem is, though, he's just not equipped. If you want to fix anything, you need the right tools," he says while tapping the tip of the blade against her nose. "More than that, you need to know where to find the tools. We both know you have an essential one...something you've been hiding for a while."

He must not have found it.

"Listen, I know you want to resist me and not say anything. I get that, really I do. Nolan Greyson saved your life so that you could protect it. The sad truth is that I'm going to find it, and you can't stop that. I'm sorry, but you just can't. Look at you." He waves his knife at her in disgust. "What you can do is make sure that his sacrifice to keep you alive wasn't in vain. I've been doing this a long time. Believe me. I've cut up prettier, younger, and more vulnerable."

"I lost it a while back. But even if I told you where it was, you'd still kill me."

"You think your chances are better that way?"

"It doesn't matter. Like I said, it's lost."

"Nea, there are three types of people who sit in that chair. The first type is your run-of-the-mill average joe or jane. They've got little to offer and everything to lose, so they squeal like a pig and tell me everything. Even dumb little shit that I don't care about. The second type knows more but feels like they've got nothing to lose. So, they resist until convinced otherwise." He runs his finger along the side of the blade. "Do you know who the third type is?"

She shakes her head.

"The third person is the disillusioned. They seem to believe that they have the upper hand. These jerks are so full of themselves that they think they can lie their way out of the situation. Basically, they're bullshitters. Do you know which type is best off?" He brings the blade along her neck, his breath warm against her ear. "It's not a trick question. It's the first one. You see, for the most part, they don't get hurt all that much. Maybe a few slaps for fun, but that's the most pain they feel. You talk now, I'll even hold back the slaps just for old times' sake. But if you keep on this course, don't think that our past friendship will save you, Nea. I will hurt you. I will make your life hell until you beg for death, and then I will hurt you some more. And then you will tell me, and all of this pain will be for nothing more than your silly pride."

"You wouldn't. I know you, Damian. What you did before coming to the Agency, why they recruited you. You left that life, remember? You traded it for something better, where you could use your weapons to protect people...not hurt them. What happened to your rules? You know, the things that kept you from becoming a monster?"

Her heart races as her words hang in the air.

"I know you may have done a lot of awful things out of pain, but this? This isn't you."

Damian pulls back as he locks eyes with her and smiles.

"In a past life, maybe you'd be right." He laughs, his smile growing. "But what you don't seem to get is that I would do anything for Jenny."

Nea watches in horror as the knife rushes down and plunges deep inside her thigh. Her scream cuts through the room and beyond as the excruciating sensation of cold metal splicing through nerves, tissue, and flesh cultivates agony to her core.

"Does it feel good to lie?" Damian pulls the blade out of her leg. He runs the flat end of the blood-soaked knife against her face, its warmth cooling to form a crust on her cheek. Damian takes the point of the blade and presses it against her bare shoulder. "We can end this now. Just say the word"

"Go…" A lump pulls at her throat, but she forces out. "Go to hell."

Damian smiles and says nothing. Instead, he puts pressure on the knife, causing its point to break the skin. Blood flows over the blade and down her arm.

She lets out another scream as tears stream down her face.

The terror of helplessness as this deranged man slices into her.

The excruciating pain of the knife tearing into her nerves.

She's not sure which is worse. And, at this moment, it doesn't matter.

She can't escape this, none of it. The taste of blood and tears fills her mouth, and she spits it up before screaming again. It must stop. She'll do anything to make it stop.

Nea opens her mouth to tell him everything: Reuben's plan, Aperio's location, and the disk. But before she can summon the words, it hits her.

Hours ago, she was staring at it, touching it. Nolan Greyson gave her the disk, and it means something, even now. He didn't leave her with lofty and inspiring words or confidence in some greater cause. He was terrified when he gave it to her, just as she is terrified now. But he laid down his life to give it to her, to save her. Words, feelings, grandeurs, and even her own life; it's all fleeting. But what Nolan Greyson left her with was tangible and real.

A physical disk.

His actual life and blood.

What did he do it for? What on earth is she even protecting? The answer is a mystery to her, but the reason couldn't be more straightforward. Agony, terror, and pain will leave her eventually, but it's the reason that has gotten her here, and it's the reason that will outlive everything.

A faint yet powerful crashing sound echoes through the room. Damian pulls the knife out of her shoulder and looks up. Moments later, Nea hears the door to the room behind her burst inward. Damian raises the knife to her throat.

"I'll kill her right here and now! Don't think that I won't!" he yells. "Ah, what the hell." He presses the blade to her skin as if preparing to slice. She knows it will be less than a second before it takes her life.

Damian tortured her, and yet she didn't say a word. He may take her life, but her soul was never his. She closes her eyes as a loud noise and physical shock pummels her being. Again, it repeats, and her body shakes involuntarily, her rapid breathing increasing.

Wait. I'm breathing.

Nea opens her eyes to find Damian's lifeless body lying on the floor. Blood pools underneath him, seeping out from the two open chest wounds.

Gunshots. It was gunshots.

A warm touch embraces her hands from behind, untying her restraints. She watches as a man walks past her with his pistol drawn and kicks Damian's knife away from his corpse. The man turns toward her, and she recognizes him immediately. Reuben Greyson holsters his weapon and goes to her.

"It's okay," he says. "You're safe now." Her restraints fall to the ground, and she leaps forward, wrapping her arms around him. Fresh tears flow from her face and soak into his shirt as she pours her relief into him.

"He won't hurt you anymore." As she lets go, Nea sees a woman digging through a backpack.

She must be the person who untied me.

Rueben must have noticed her focus as he says, "This is Sky. We're going to take care of your leg and shoulder, okay?"

Nea nods as Sky pulls out what appears to be two T-shirts, throwing one to Reuben.

"I'm sorry, we left our medical kit in the car," Sky says to her while wrapping one of the shirts around her leg. Nea can feel Reuben tying the other shirt around her shoulder.

"Thank you," Nea says, looking at Sky before turning to Reuben. "Thank you both so much. You saved me from that... from that..." She looks down at Damian and begins to cry again. Reuben and Sky finish securing the improvised tourniquets.

"That will hold for a bit, but you're going to need medical attention," Sky says.

Reuben stands and pauses for a moment. "I'll make the call," he says.

"What call?" Nea asks.

"I'm sorry, Nea. I know you're trying to lay low. But this house is in the middle of nowhere, and I can't let you bleed out. I'm calling Paul Peterson."

Her heart drops. The relief of being rescued is suddenly overwhelmed by the reality of being found.

20

THE UNSTOPPABLE FORCE AND THE IMMOVABLE OBJECT

Sky bites down on her chapped lip, watching as Reuben makes the call. A detached sense of nausea reaches from her stomach and constricts her throat. She can almost feel it incoming from the future—the rumbling of boots crashing their secret mission and Paul's contemptuous eyes looking down on them.

She paces with her hands clinging to her lower back, but it isn't the music they're about to face that fills her with anxiety. It's her, the girl, Nea. Sky looks at the poor soul, face still smothered in shock and dried tears. Everything happened so fast, yet she remembers each step and that awful split-second instance that nearly cost the girl her life.

It was the very instance she'd been training for, and she blew it.

The scar-nosed man with a knife.

Her pistol sights against his silhouette.

She took a breath, but her finger wouldn't squeeze the trigger. Muscle memory led her to that point, but she couldn't do it; she couldn't follow through.

Choke.

Frozen.

A gun went off, and the man collapsed to the ground. It wasn't Sky that fired the life-ending round that saved Nea from sure death. It was Reuben. He acted, and she froze. In all this time since Ray's passing, she's only made one promise to herself, and tonight she broke it.

Sky takes a breath and forces it down. This is not the time to break down. She looks up at Reuben and sees the subtle sense of fear in his eyes. His voice, however, remains calm, steady, and strong.

"Understood," Reuben says before hanging up the phone and turning to them. "They're on their way."

"How long?" Nea asks.

"Not long," he says. "Maybe ten minutes. They're going to an active emergency teleport in Snopes County. From there, it should only be a short helicopter ride to the house."

Sky lets out a sigh. "How'd he sound?"

Reuben shakes his head. "Even toned. Almost too professional."

"That bad, huh?"

"Yep." Reuben turns back to Nea. "Listen, I need to go look for something before they arrive. Sky will stay here with you and keep you company." He places his hand on the back of Nea's non-wounded arm before leaving the room.

Sky glances over at Nea. Her head remains drooped as she clenches the shirts covering her wound.

"Don't worry," Sky says. "The medics will be here before you know."

"I'm not worried about that," Nea says, wincing. "I know how much AIC loves to brag about their Quick Reaction Team."

Sky pulls a wet wipe from her backpack and kneels in front

of Nea. She flinches as Sky brings the wet wipe to her cheeks, and Sky pulls back a bit.

"Sorry, it's just..." Nea says, her voice shaking.

"I know. It's okay." Sky raises the wipe once more, her hand firm but gentle as it works to erase the dried blood from her skin.

"Thanks," she says. "That sick bastard..." Nea shakes her head and clenches her teeth as her eyes glaze over.

Sky looks over at the body. "Can't imagine." Thinking about what the man did, what Nea went through, turns her stomach. "I'm sorry," she says, coming to her feet. "Did you know him?"

Nea nods. "Damian. That's his name. We used to work together back in the old days of the project. His wife died in an accident, and he went... He was always a killer, but this. This was something else. There was no stopping him."

Why couldn't I take the shot?

Nea stretches her back and smiles. "I'm just glad you found this place in time. I guess it makes sense that it would be you that—" She suddenly stops herself. "It, ah..."

"Wait, what? 'Makes sense that it would be me' what?"

Nea's shifts in her seat and her lips twitch, but no words come out. "Navigator," she finally says. "You're the team's navigator, right? Makes sense that you would find this place."

"Yeah, I guess." Sky crosses her arms. "I helped us get here and all, but how would I know the location in the first place?"

"Well, how did you find it?"

"Reuben figured out the address."

"Huh." Nea licks her lips and tilts her head.

"What?"

Nea looks away, masking her eyes from Sky. "Nothing. Hey, listen, I'm not feeling so great," she says, shifting the subject. "It's like I'm...I'm..."

Sky, noticing Nea's parched lips, pulls out a small bottle of water and holds it up for Nea to drink. "Sorry, I know it's not much. The medics will have an IV."

As they wait there, Sky's mind returns to the moment Damian was in the crosshairs of her pistol. It's not that the shot was difficult. She could've easily given him a third nostril. It wasn't the idea of taking a life either. Damian was a sadist that was moments away from murdering an innocent person. There's no choice in that kind of situation, and she knows it. This was something else.

A part of her knows the reason, and it terrifies her to think of it. She believes in Chronos because it allows people to look back in history and learn from it. To her, history is something that happened to others, and her past is something that should be forgotten. But today, in the worst of moments, her past came back to taunt her, and no amount of firearm training prepared her for it. Ray's been gone for well over a year, but his ghost never left. And to Sky's distraught, it may never leave.

SHE HAS TWO RINGS. He gave her the diamond that day on the beach, pledging his affection and desire to be with her. A year later, she put on the band, a seal of her promise to be forever faithful to him. One of these rings is a lie, and for the life of her, Sky can't figure out which one it is.

SKY'S CHEST GROWS HEAVY, and her heart caves as she watches him, drunk and passed out on the couch. After hours of worry, Ray finally came home to her. The scene continues to play out in her mind: the endless voicemail prompts, calling everyone they knew, and the embarrassment of finally finding him stumbling around the lobby downstairs as her neighbors watched.

She struggled to make out his slurring words as he grabbed onto her, as his shameful eyes stared into hers. The only discernible sentence plays over and over in her mind.

'*I'm sorry,*' he kept saying.

What are you sorry about?

Sky ponders the question as she watches her husband's stomach rise and fall. Was it the drunkenness or something else? He's come home after a few beers before, but not like this.

Never like this.

He didn't even know who she was at first. But when he did recognize her, he began sobbing, crying uncontrollably.

What the hell happened?

She walks over to him with a blanket and pillow. A part of her wants to smother him for making her worry so much, but she could never do that.

Not to Ray.

Whatever he's done, he's been good to her, and she knows it. Drunken episodes can fade out of memory, but love lasts forever.

She takes off his pants and removes his wallet and phone from the pockets before setting them down on the counter. She yawns, and her eyes grow heavy. An evening of wine and worry has taken its toll. She turns off the lights and begins to walk toward the bedroom.

Then she hears it.

Soft, faint, yet unmistakable, she hears it. Sky turns as Ray's phone lights up from the counter, vibrating quietly as if whispering and pleading for her to take a peek.

It could be a buddy from work. Maybe the guy who got him drunk.

It's late, and it could be anyone. It's probably just someone that she called when she was looking for him. Whoever it is just wants to make sure he came home. Nothing to worry about. He's home, and everything is okay.

Sleepiness and trust make a good argument. She's tired, and her comfy pillow-top bed lies only a few feet away. But it's not quite persuasive enough. She's curious and looking would only take a second. Today he almost gave her a heart attack and came home obliterated. They share everything, and she deserves to know. It'll only take a second.

Eventually, Sky stops rationalizing and just walks over to the phone before picking it up. She taps the screen, and it illuminates though her heart dims.

An unmistakable message.

An intimate tone.

Another woman's name.

She drops the phone, and the world stops, the shock of it taking her breath. Her knees shake and buckle. She lets out an agonizing moan. Her chest tears open at the seams, and her heart falls to the floor.

Her husband. Her everything. The ground for which her entire life stands.

A lie, all of it.

His snoring continues, undeterred by the revelation. She steps toward the couch, and her ankles give way, collapsing to the ground as if she's somehow forgotten how to walk. Lying there, her lungs gasp in pain. Has she also forgotten how to breathe? It's as if the most fundamental truths of her life have all been a lie. He's not her husband, no. He's a stranger, a liar, a treacherous bastard who's violated her trust, her honor, and the very core of who she is. She's given him everything, and he's sold it all, pawned it like some junkie. And for what? A piece of ass? For some home-wrecking whore? Is that all she's worth to him? Is this all she is?

The tears burst from her eyes like a spring tapped into an endless well of despair. She continues to cry almost in silence as if a part of her hasn't fully registered and doesn't want to disturb his sleep. The man betrayed her in the worst way, and still, she instinctively cares for him. Her mind knows what he did, but her heart just cannot seem to accept it even as she lays there crying.

The time ticks endlessly, and her face droops from the weight of endlessly flowing tears. She keeps thinking about it, about what a fool she's been, never questioning or even suspecting any of it. As she sits there with her eyes rubbed raw by grief, all the signs emerge like darkness fading at dawn to reveal what was unseen but always there.

The late nights.

The vague excuses.

The growing distance and her unwitting blindness to all of it.

She looks up at him, and her blood begins to boil.

"You bastard," Sky mutters as she jumps to her feet with clenched fists. She storms toward him, an empty candlestick holder beside the couch capturing her eye. One swift blow is all it would take. He deserves worse, far worse, but one blow would do it. She reaches for the holder, and she sees it. She can see herself doing it, without hesitation, completely justified.

Then it happens.

Before she can raise her hand, the dimmest of lights strikes her ring...and pierces her heart. The glimmer is faint, but she sees it and can't for the life of her ignore it as if the diamond were shining into her soul. Everything in her wants to do it, to end it, to finish him. But she can't. The unstoppable force. The immovable object.

A promise and a commitment.

Two rings. Two lives. One choice.

A paradox.

She runs to the bathroom, slams the door, and turns on the lights. A chill runs down her spine as her eyes meet the mirror, as they meet themselves. A broken woman. A shattered soul. A victim. This is what she sees, and it turns her stomach into agonizing knots. She rips off both rings as if they were vermin crawling up her skin. They tumble to the floor like dice, rolling to determine her fate, but she doesn't care how they land.

Eventually, she picks the two rings up and stares at them. One of them, her wedding band, sits in her palm: plain, solid, sure. She thinks of the time it first slipped onto her finger. That day she had given herself to him before God and man. She meant the words then, and even now, can't fully break away from them. It's almost too much a part of her, a cancerous part perhaps, but with her regardless.

Then she looks at the other ring, the diamond ring, her engagement ring. It glistens and shines like a kaleidoscope of untamed beauty, but it's a false beauty. She shudders as the truth of it slices through her heart.

Sky opens the bathroom window and glares down the seemingly endless stories to the distant street below. She looks at the rings again before setting each of them on the window ledge. Knocking both off would feel good, and she knows it. But it's not about feeling good. How could it be now? How could things ever go back?

They can't. Not here, not in the real world. Not in time.

The first semblance of a blissful thought comes to her. The Agency. The AIC. Chronos. Ray took her from it and, for the first time since leaving that life, her heart yearns for it; to be where worlds and time could be made and remade, where the mysteries of past existences could be explored and known, and where the pain of today could be undone by yesterday.

She sighs and grabs her wedding band, tucking it into her pocket. The ring to her reflects who she is, for good or ill. It's her own words, and they mean something. No matter what happens or what comes next, it means something. She tries to take the diamond ring as well, but she can't. It's too much. More than a broken promise, it was a lie from the beginning. It can't go forward with her. Taking a deep breath, she flicks her hand

and watches as the ring flies down toward the earth. Like Lucifer falling from heaven, it shines and glimmers before disappearing into the abyss, taking with it all of its promises and beauty.

Sky weeps and the night with her.

21

LIFE AND LIVING

Reuben's fingers tingle as he reaches for his flashlight, the adrenaline lingering while he maneuvers through the darkened queer house. The foreign familiarity haunts the misplaced walls and furniture. He knows where to go but doesn't recognize the path. It's precisely how he dreamt it, the feeling, and yet looks little like it.

Devoid of natural light, electricity, and caring tenants, the house marinates in its own rot as if it were a decaying corpse. Eventually, Reuben reaches what appears to be a bathroom embedded into the hallway. With no doors or entrance, only a change in wallpaper separates the spaces.

"What in the hell," he mutters, staring at the strange space.

Reuben stands in the middle of the house but couldn't feel further from its heart, from that tangible thing that reveals what something is. To know is to understand, and when it comes to this bastardized labyrinth, he doesn't know a damn thing.

A grime-filled sink and cracked toilet stand side by side along one end of the pathway. Across from it lies a bathtub. Mildew and cobwebs intertwine along the tub, glistening in the beam of his flashlight. All the elements are there: tub, shower-head, spout, drain, and curtain. It would be an ordinary bath-room if it weren't sitting in the middle of a hallway...and something else.

The shower curtain.

Opaque and covered in mold, he can see it, but it hides nothing. The brackish water likely residing in the pipes would spray all over the bathroom without hindrance. The curtain is only for show, oddly lining the back wall.

Or where a back wall should be.

He parts the webbing and pulls the curtain back.

Nothing.

Darkness and nothing.

There's no wall or barrier, just an opening. A chill grips the back of his neck as the darkness stares back at him, as a stale, moldy stench emerges from black. He shines his light into the opening and jumps back in disbelief.

A staircase?

Without further hesitation, he steps over the tub and begins to ascend the stairs. Shining the light upward, he can see the oak wood steps leading to a set of double doors at the top. His hands run along the railing on the ascent, feeling the rough aged wood against his fingertips. This is absolutely happening, and none of it is a dream.

Reuben opens the set of double doors and crosses into the ample open space, his stomach fluttering as he recognizes the room. The library's many vivid details spark to life. Unlike much of the rest of the house, this open space is verbatim as he remembers it. Everything is precisely the same, from the finish of the mahogany trim lining the fireplace wall to the propor-tions of the desk at the center.

His jaw dangles, but no words emerge as his eyes check off each item from his dream. Then one final comparison comes to him. He darts his flashlight toward the other side of the library and sees it. Just a few feet from him lies the reason he and Sky traveled so far. The reason he's kept secrets and lied. The reason he's standing there with a smile, even after having shot a man dead. The tall lonesome safe along the wall glows against the light's reach. Entrenched within its hold lies the answer waiting for him.

He removes the key from his pocket, inserts it into the safe, and attempts to turn it, but it won't move. Using both hands, Rueben throws his weight behind the key.

Nothing.

He releases his grip and lets out a breath. Suddenly, a faint whooping noise echoes from outside, growing louder by the second.

It's the helicopter.

Paul Peterson will be walking into the house any minute now.

Reuben balls his hand and uses it to tap a few inches above the resting key before applying more pressure.

The key turns.

He grabs the latch, pulls it down, and opens the door. The flashlight reveals a single object on the center shelf. Reaching in and pulling it out for examination, his memory jogs back further than it's gone in a long time.

Why do you keep wearing that old thing?

His childhood voice dangles in his mind as he stares at his father's old wristwatch. Nolan's missing journal, the mysterious key left for him, a bizarre dream, Croatoan, Kirk's death; all these things remain unexplained, producing cruelty, sadness, and intrigue. Everything remains unknown to him except one thing. All of it drove him here: a dead sociopath, a saved girl, and his father's watch resting in his palm.

He grips the watch close to his chest, and tears fill his eyes. Holding it tight, he can almost hear his father's voice and feel his presence. In this world of science and reason, he can't justify or explain why he feels it, but he does. It's tangibly in his hands and truly in his heart. Time may have pushed Nolan Greyson further away from him, but it's clear that his father has fought to defy it to draw closer to him.

Reuben takes a breath and slips the watch into his pocket. Closing the safe, Rueben rushes downstairs. Even with the random meanderings of the spaces and hallways, it takes him less than a minute to reach the room.

Sky turns to him as he enters. "She's dehydrated from the blood loss. Can you stay with her while I run to get an electrolyte pouch from the car?"

"Yeah, of course. I heard the helicopter fly by a minute ago. I'm sure the medic will have something."

"I'm sure he will, but his focus will be the bleeding. It'll be one less thing. The least I can do, you know?"

Reuben nods.

Sky makes her way toward the exit. "Besides, I can meet Paul and the others as they land and make sure they find the room quick."

"Sounds good. I'll stay here with Nea."

"Did you find what you were looking for?" Nea gets out after Sky departs.

"Yeah, I think so." He kneels to lessen her strain of looking up. "Do you know what this place is?"

Nea shakes her head. "I'm sure he did." She nods toward the body.

"I didn't want to do that."

"I know. I had to look into his eyes before you came in here. He wasn't going to stop. I could see that. I'd be dead if you didn't do what you did."

"Did he tell you where Drazen is?"

"No. I was only conscious for a few minutes before you got here. He was looking for something. I lied to him, and he knew. And I... And I..." She begins to sob. "I almost gave it to him. I almost gave you up." Nea's mouth trembles, but only a sob comes out.

Reuben lays his hand on hers. "I never asked you to do that, Nea. I don't even know you. Why would you risk your life for me?"

She pauses and looks up at him. "It's not about you," she says. "I never said the words or anything at all when your father gave it to me, but I made a promise. When he saved my life, and I ran with it, I was making a promise."

"My dad." Reuben's heart clings to the words.

Pride. Sadness. Love.

The man gave everything, and what was it all for?

"What did he give you?"

Nea struggles to extend her arm. Several feet from them is a suitcase, its belongings scattered around it. He scoops the belongings back into the suitcase and brings it to her. Reuben guides her bloody hand onto the surface of her things. She feels around before pulling out a book and passing it to him.

Blood across the cover, he reads the title aloud. "Paradise Lost." Reuben turns to her. "This is what they were chasing you down for?"

"Inside."

He tilts the book down as gravity pulls its pages to the book-marked spot, and he sees it, the orange octagonal disk.

"For your meeting later," she says.

Reuben smiles. "You still haven't told me how you know about that."

She winks at him, mirroring their first interaction at Kirk's gravesite. Before the moment can linger, patters of rapid foot-steps race from the halls beyond the room. Reuben shuts the book and reaches out for his backpack. In a single motion, he slips the book into the outer pouch and zips it closed.

Familiar faces rush through the entrance. The two suited agents at the front of the pack sweep their guns at the high-ready across the room. Their gazes barely touch Reuben and Nea as they maneuver the room. Reuben quickly identifies the two professionals as the man and woman who brought him to the Agency months ago.

Scott and Quinn.

Paul Peterson strides in a few brisk paces behind them. Reuben's eyes meet his. Paul says nothing, only stares for a few seconds before turning to Nea. "Right there, in the chair," Paul calls out to the medic rushing past him to attend to Nea.

Paul walks past Reuben to Nea without a word, his eyes fixated on his prize. "You've been running a long time," he says to her. "There's no need for that anymore. We've come to bring you home."

"T-shirts?" the medic says, turning to Reuben.

"It slowed the bleeding down, didn't it?" Reuben quips in return.

"Am I going to die?" Nea asks the medic.

"You'll be fine," he responds. "We just can't hang out here for long. Your wounds will need to be redressed soon. Stitches will be in order, too. Do you know your blood type?"

"A Positive," Nea says as the man writes it on her forearm in black marker. Another medic reaches the room with a stretcher, and Reuben scurries to help him wheel it in. The first medic doesn't hesitate to inject an IV bag into her arm as Reuben, and the other quickly grab Nea and lift her onto the stretcher.

Sky runs in with the electrolyte pouch.

"I brought her this," Sky says as she tries to hand the pouch to the medic.

"The fluids are already going," the medic says, dismissing her.

"What..." Nea clears her throat with a raspy cough. "What flavor is it?"

"It's cherry splash," Sky says.

"My favorite." Nea smiles at her as Sky presses the pouch against the medic's chest. He reluctantly takes it.

"We'll save it for you," he says to Nea. The two medics wheel the stretcher out of the room, leaving Rueben, Sky, and Paul to stare at one another. Silence hovers as it binds the lingering seconds to the room's growing tension.

"Scott, Quinn," Paul says, breaking the silence. The two move toward him, but his eyes remain fixed on Reuben. "Please, take Ms. Fernandes and search the remainder of the site. It's much too menacing to leave to itself."

Sky hesitates, her eyes darting to Rueben. He lets the moment sink in, allowing Paul to see that he is not the only power at play before nodding. He notices Sky open her mouth, and then close it before trailing off after the agents, her head shaking.

The door closes behind her, leaving Paul and Rueben alone. The creaking floors sing outside the four walls, setting an eerie backdrop to their silent duel. Paul is the first to break eye contact, glancing around the room.

"Calling me was the right thing to do," he says as he turns back to face Rueben.

"We didn't have a choice."

"That's not entirely true."

"I wasn't going to let her bleed out."

"No, of course not."

"Listen—"

"You had many choices today," Paul interrupts, nodding toward the corpse. "Performing as you saw fit at that moment. An operator making split-second life-and-death decisions, knowing full well in the back of your mind that there will be consequences. It takes real courage."

"I just did—"

"What you had to. Yes. That much is evident." Paul leans over the body, and Rueben swears he sees recognition in the man's eyes. "You know what makes courage more unique than just 'doing the right thing?'"

"Paul, do we really have to do this right now? Nea's on her way to the hospital, and Drazen—"

"Adam Drazen is not here." Paul says, "*You* are here. Acts of courage can save lives, but they'll never absolve you of consequences. Do you understand that, Greyson?"

"No one is free of consequence." Reuben pauses. "That includes people in power."

"Haven't I warned you about veiled accusations?"

"You did. So, allow me to be clear. I know I have to face up to what I did, going behind the Agency's back to try and find Drazen on my own without authorization. Yeah, that's digging a hole for myself. I knew the risk. And I did it, just like you knew the risk of sending an inexperienced navigator to a war zone. To your benefit, you weren't the one who had to endure that consequence. It was the kid you sent. He's the one who took on your arrogance and stupidity with his dying breath. And, yeah, I know there's more I could've done to save him. I admit that, and I'll always carry it. But there's one thing you didn't have to do." Reuben's eyes blaze, the heat of his own blood flaming through his veins. "I had to look into his eyes and watch the life go out of 'em. So don't lecture me about consequences."

For the first time since meeting the man, Reuben can see his own words pierce the cold, calculating, and stoic Paul Peterson. Reuben watches as Paul's jaw clenches and his eyebrows flare. He says nothing for close to a minute, then finally takes a breath to swallow his rage.

"Prior to me being put in charge as the sole Director of AIC," Paul says, taking his own veiled breath. "Circumstances were very different. The Stewards, your father, they ran the show. It was their responsibility to govern and supervise the project. Twelve diverse experts of every creed, color, and background attempted to move in a single direction. On paper, it was brilliant, but it didn't play out that way. Each one of them believed devoutly that their vision for the project was the right one. It was perhaps the only commonality between them. The bickering and infighting eventually turned to murder until Chronos ran red with the blood of the Stewards. It was all well-intentioned but, in the end, only produced violence and chaos.

"And you know what, Greyson," Paul continues. "You dealt some powerful and potent truths today. Congratulations. Grandstanding suits you. But would you like to hear the most potent truth? It was that blood, your father's blood, which paved the way for me. When the Stewards fizzled away, the Agency saw the necessity of a single vision. And here I stand. Kirk's blood is just like any of them. A service to something greater."

Blood and rage converge on Reuben's core. His wrath-fueled hand grips the handle of his holstered pistol. He imagines himself doing it as the gun begins to rise from the holster with ease. It comes out only an inch as Paul's words replay in his mind.

It was that blood, your father's blood, which paved the way for me.

They taunt him to end his life.

...there will be consequences.

A fair warning to spare it.

Reuben closes his eyes, shoves the pistol back down, and releases his hand from the grip. Paul says nothing, his face as cold as ever.

Reuben breaks away before turning back to him. "That's why you want us to capture Drazen, isn't it? You don't give a damn about my father or catching a killer. It's all about eliminating your threats."

"It's not just my threats, boy. You haven't the slightest inclination the stake or scope of what we're facing."

"No. No, maybe I don't. But you know what? I don't think

you do either. You're probably just as much in the dark as the rest of us. None of us knew Drazen and Aperio could hack Chronos. No one at AIC knew about this place. And neither of us have been able to lock down anything that will bring us closer to catching that monster."

Paul edges toward the exit but veers back to Reuben before departing. "You know, despite your stupidity and renegade tactics, particularly today, I do believe sincerely that you are wrong. Damian Barker. That's who you killed. And now we know for sure he's the one who's been helping Drazen. And better yet, we've eliminated one of Drazen's most valuable resources.

"You uncovered their hiding place and saved an innocent girl from death by a sadist. I may cringe when I dwell on your defiance and, believe me when I say my blood boils at the sight of you, but I won't rob you of the progress you made here today. Because of you, we've made our most significant step yet against this enemy."

Paul exits for a moment before returning. "You're also wrong about my feelings. I know my approach is unabashed and harsh. And I won't apologize one iota about it. But I do care about what happened to your father and the rest of the Stewards. Chronos may be better without them, but the world isn't. When this finds its conclusion, I couldn't care less if you end up unemployed or in confinement. But I hope nothing short of Adam Drazen rotting in hell."

With that, Paul departs, leaving Rueben's mind drowning in thought. His gaze rests at the door before veering down at the empty bloody chair.

He's not wrong.

Nea is out of immediate danger, and Adam Drazen no longer has a reliable safehouse or henchman. Still, he knows the prospect of capturing Drazen seems to only grow with every step closer. Paul may hope the man rots in hell, but Reuben would settle on just finding him. He can't run forever.

Chem lights dangle along suspended string, lining the winding path through the house. Following them, it doesn't take long for Reuben to reach the entrance. He steps past the kicked-down door and onto the porch. The clear night sky greets him as the whooshing of a nearby helicopter cuts through the thick spring air. He watches as it takes off just outside of the estate.

"You'll be okay, Nea," he whispers to himself as the helicopter vanishes beyond the twilight horizon.

A creaking sound breaks beside him, and he turns to greet it. A shadowed outline strides toward him from the edges of the wrap-around porch. He recognizes her gait before he can make out the face. The dim reflection of her eyes cuts into him, and he smiles.

"Hey," he says as she approaches. "Did you guys find anything else in the house?"

"Not much, mostly trash, books, and some empty liquor bottles. Oh, and I guess a really expensive unopened bottle of scotch. Scott told me that they're bringing in an additional team to go through everything in the morning. It's impossible to be thorough without electricity or daylight."

"Will they be able to turn the power on?"

"That's just it. The house isn't even hooked up to any power source. There isn't even a generator on the property as far as we can tell."

"That's weird. The house is old, but it has light switches and outlets."

"Well, whatever powered it is now gone." They both look out across the landscape and into the night. "It does make the stars brighter, though."

"Thanks for coming out here with me," he says. "You didn't

have to help me. Paul gave me an earful earlier, and you'll probably be in some trouble too."

"I'm not worried about that. Paul's never yelled at me. He even thanked me for attending to Nea on his way out." She pauses. "Try not to let this weigh you down, but I think it's you who he doesn't like."

Reuben lets out a chuckle. "You get that impression, too?" They both laugh for a minute before reverting to silence once more.

"What was in the safe?" She asks.

Reuben digs in his pocket and places it in her hands. "It was my father's watch. Growing up, he would always have it on. He even forgot to take it off in the shower a couple times. I asked him once why he wouldn't just get a new one. It was out of date and always breaking. I'm sure he spent more money on repairing it than what it was worth. He told me there was no replacement for it. He knew its exact weight and feel, each imperfection and quirk."

Sky hands back the watch. "I think it's a beautiful piece."

"Thanks. Not exactly the way I'd describe it, but I'm glad I have it now."

"If this is where Drazen has been hiding out, do you think he's the one who left the key for you?"

"No. I mean, I can't say for sure, but I don't think so. He may have been staying here, but I don't think this house was his. In my dream, the man who brought me here, the faceless bearded guy, said the house used to belong to him. He also told me that someone else was staying here. In the dream that *someone else* came at me like a shadow trying to kill me."

"You think that *someone else* is Drazen?"

"I do, yeah. It looks like he's been squatting in this house for a while. I'm sure he even saw the safe but couldn't open it. Whoever sent me the key knew we'd show up when Drazen would be out. They knew we'd stop Damian from killing Nea."

Reuben sees it briefly, a subtle yet almost dreadful look on Sky's face as if bothered by what he said. He wants to ask about it, but the moment passes.

"Maybe," she says. "It could also be a coincidence."

"It could be, yeah. But this..." he holds up the antique watch, "this part isn't a coincidence. Whoever set the key in my room wanted me to have my father's watch."

"Well, however it happened, I'm glad you have it now. I'm sure he'd want you to have it."

* * *

SKY STEPS toward the porch railing. "Hey, so..." She pauses to collect her thoughts before continuing. She wants to tell him but isn't quite sure what there is to tell. "Did Nea say anything to you about the house or us finding it?"

"Ah no, not really. I mean, I asked her if she knew what it was."

"And?"

"Nothing. She didn't say anything. Just shook her head. Why?"

"I don't know. It was bizarre. She seemed to think that I was the one that found out about the address. And when I asked more about it, she tried to backtrack and pass off what she meant. Like it was because of my nav skills, which she somehow just knew about. Was just really odd."

"Huh," Reuben grunts.

"That's what she said."

Reuben raises his eyebrows.

"She said 'huh' at some point, too. Like she couldn't understand something. Like I can't understand something. We all just found our way mysteriously to some creepy mangled abandoned house in the middle of nothing, and no one knows a thing." Sky lets out a frustrated sigh.

Reuben scratches his beard. "Maybe, uh…"

Sky watches as the gears struggle to turn in his head. "It's whatever. Maybe we're not meant to know."

Reuben smiles at her as she says it.

"What?" she says.

"Ah, nothing," he says, looking up slightly as if recalling a memory. "That's just something my dad would always say. One of his Nolanisms as I called it, about how sometimes we're not meant to know all the answers."

Sky pulls back a subtle smile. She never knew Nolan Greyson well, but the more she learns, the more she wishes she had.

Reuben gazes back down at his father's watch. Sky watches as he opens the clasps and lays it over his left wrist, where his Chronos watch had been two months prior. He looks back up at her with a concerned look on his face.

"What?" she says.

"Nothing. I'm sure it's nothing. It's just earlier. I want to make sure you're okay."

"Okay with what?" She's mystified, but something about his tone unsettles her as if he'd just struck a deep unpleasant chord.

"Earlier, when I mentioned how we stopped Damian from killing Nea, you made this face…" Sky's heart skips as he continues. "And listen, Sky, I'm not trying to overanalyze or anything. I know we walked in on a pretty gruesome scene. I guess I'm just wondering if you're all right."

He knows.

She tries to mask the feeling, but it's too much.

Ray.

Damian.

The shot taken, and the shot missed. Her most dreadful memory reared its ugly head at the worst moment, and a girl nearly lost her life because of it. She can't bottle it up. Not this.

Months ago, she lied to Reuben about not having regrets because he hadn't earned the truth, then. And right now, it no longer matters if he's earned hearing it. Today they're a team, and he cares for her. She closes her eyes, breathes, and just tells him.

Sky tells him everything— her marriage to Ray, leaving the AIC, and finally the affair and the night where everything went wrong in the worst way.

"It was cold, and after I threw the ring out, I went to bed, leaving the window open. I didn't care if we froze." Sky can feel her eyes fill with tears. "A part of me really wanted us just to die."

"Sky," he says, looking earnestly into her eyes. "I'm so sorry. I had no id—"

"That's not even the worst of it," she interrupts.

"What happened?"

"I killed him." Sky watches the instant shock on his face as she says it. The pain, guilt, and hell of that night all flood back in. In all the countless hours of therapy and grief counseling and all the times she would tell herself that she's okay. It feels as if all that progress is suddenly eroded by the words and Reuben's reaction to it.

Reuben looks away for a moment before turning back toward her, grabbing her hand. He doesn't say anything, only looks at her as if patiently waiting for her to continue. It's not judgment or condemnation in his eyes.

It's concern.

It's heartbreak and empathy.

He's not here to know for himself or to pry. He's here for her. So, she continues.

"It was an accident. A man snuck into our apartment through the window. Our unit was so high up, I never expected anyone to be able to do it but, somehow, he got in." She pauses, the tears pouring from her now. "They were fighting in the dark. I never saw Ray fight so hard in his life. He almost knocked the guy out, but the man pulled out a knife. I ran to grab my handgun from the nightstand, and when I came back, the bastard had the knife to his throat. He was going to kill Ray. So, I— So I—" Sky fights with everything in her to say the words, to finish the story, but she can't. She sobs uncontrollably as the memory returns to her.

The weight of the gun.

The crosshairs against darkened shadows.

The muzzle flash and echo of the exploding round.

It all comes back to her, and she can't stop it. Ray never knew what happened. The bullet killed him instantly. It's the only semblance of solace Sky's ever had, that Ray died fighting for her and never had to bear the weight of what his wife knew about him.

Reuben embraces her as she continues to cry into his shoulder. An eternity passes before Sky wipes her eyes and looks up at him, ready to finish the story and to close this chapter of her life maybe once and for all.

"When you first came on board, do you remember what I told you about Chronos?" Sky asks.

"'You don't have to alter the past to change the future,'" Reuben says.

"That's right. Ray died, and I knew I couldn't bring him back. But it took me a while to realize I wasn't powerless. Once I did realize it, I decided to do the only thing I could, to make sure something like that never happened again. I trained day and night to be the best shot I could be. The range became my sanctuary, the place where I could make everything right with the world. There wasn't a single target I couldn't hit...until today."

"Damian?"

Sky nods. "I had him in my crosshairs when we got in the house. He was about to kill that girl, and I choked. In those few seconds, it felt like I was back in that apartment again with Ray, and I was the same incompetent, naïve—"

"Hey," Reuben interrupts, "that's not you. What happened was awful, but it was an accident. I know I didn't know you then, but I know you now. We've been through war zones together, and you risked everything to come with me today. I didn't ask you to come, but here you are. This is who you are."

Sky smiles. She wasn't looking for reassurance or affirmation. It's never meant much to her. But it strikes her heart nonetheless, not as flattery or a false sense of positive thinking, but as truth from someone who really cares.

"You're right, you know," Reuben says. "Yesterday might be gone, but tomorrow's still worth fighting for."

With no other light source around, they look to stars. Walking side by side, they veer their gazes to each other simultaneously for a euphoric moment before returning to the night sky. Each simmering twinkle of starlight radiates its own ancient story. Weary but enduring, the scattered lights travel spacetime to recount their tales and display their beauty. Independent and unique, their imprints congregate in the sky, creating a collage of worlds unknown, unifying as a single illuminant display of creation. In this moment, Sky and Reuben share in the mysteries of life and living.

22

NIGHTHAWKS

As Reuben waits, he thinks of her, and his insides recoil. Not because of her. It could never be her. But because of himself. His teeth chatter as he recalls the moment. She poured her heart out and told him everything. But he couldn't tell her this, at least not then, and not now. He cares for her more than she knows, but he couldn't tell her about this meeting.

He couldn't.

The bell on the door chimes, snatching his attention.

It's finally time.

He looks up and sees the person he's been waiting for.

The man spots him through the mostly empty diner and walks toward the booth. His neon raincoat wisps against lone spectating chairs and tables. Reuben takes a sip of the scalding hot coffee and cringes as it cooks his tongue and throat on its way down. Moments later, the man jumps into the booth across from Reuben. They look at one another in silence before Reuben finally speaks.

"So, this is what you meant by Nighthawks?"

"Clearly," Aperio says.

"You could've just given me an address and a time to meet. Most people would've done that."

"Do I strike you as most people?"

Reuben doesn't answer. He's not sure what to make of Aperio, an aging Steward with no known history or track record of trust. His father never mentioned the man, and no one in his circle really knew him; no one except Caleb, who has nothing but contempt for Aperio. But here Reuben sits, meeting secretly with a man whose whereabouts he's obligated to report. It's insubordination at best, treason at worst, and imprisonment at the most likely. It turns his stomach to think about it, but he can handle it.

He can survive it.

If it gives him answers, then it may be worth the cost. What he can't handle, what he can't think about right now, is how he's left her out. Sky put her career and life on the line for him.

All he can do is get through this. All he can do is learn something that will help end Adam Drazen. Otherwise, it's all for nothing, and nothing will cause him to lose everything. Nothing is not an option.

"If a Steward is to stay alive, he must be clever," Aperio says. "If I had just given you the address, you probably would have written it down. From there, it could be found by anyone looking for it. I assume you wrote out the word 'Nighthawks' somewhere and maybe even searched it in the Agency's systems. Thankfully, outside of the context for you individually, the term means nothing to anyone else. It's only a reference to a painting. I'm also a bit of an artist myself. Adding a pinch of theatricality to something as mundane as directions breathes life into an otherwise dull task."

"You're an artist?" Reuben asks. "I thought all of you physicists were supposed to be heavier on the left-brain stuff."

"I'm not a physicist. What on earth gave you such thought?"

"But you said that you were a—"

"A Steward, yes. I never mentioned physics. Did you think all of us were a bunch of scientists sitting around in our lab coats, scribbling random letters and numbers on a whiteboard?"

Reuben hesitates before responding. "Yeah, kind of."

"I'm assuming Paul doesn't say much about us. No wonder you don't know a damn thing. No offense, by the way. I realize that part isn't entirely your fault."

"That's one of the reasons we're meeting, right?"

"Absolutely. We have much to discuss and time as always is against us."

"So, let's begin."

"I could not agree more." Aperio reaches for the plastic-coated menu at the corner of the table.

Reuben shakes his head. "You're hungry?"

"I didn't ask to meet in a crummy old diner for the ambiance. When I came to this country, people talked about freedom and opportunity. It's adequate, but what really makes this country special is the endless possibility for late-night eating." Aperio waves the elderly waitress to the table.

"Welcome, hun," she says, placing a napkin in front of him. "Sorry, I didn't see you come in. Would you like a coffee, too? I was telling your frien—" She catches herself, looks to Reuben, then back at Aperio. "Or whoever you are to this gentleman..." She rolls her eyes and continues, "how we brew it fresh every hour, most hours."

"That sounds excellent," Aperio says.

"All righty, then. I'll be right out with it."

"Actually," Aperio says before she can finish turning toward the kitchen. "I believe I'm ready to order."

The waitress pulls out her order booklet and pen. "What'll it be, darlin'?"

His eyes shift downward at the menu. "I'll have the eggs,

three please, over easy. Umm, bacon and sausage. Does that come with a biscuit?"

"If you make it the combo, it does, yeah."

"Well, then a combo it is!"

"Okay." She tucks the booklet back into the pocket of her apron.

"Ah, I see here it says that you can add 'fluff' for an extra $2.99 to any meal."

"That's right," she says, pulling the booklet back out. "You can do French toast, waffles, or pancakes."

"All three sound terrific. Thank you."

The waitress lowers her order pad with a raised brow. She pulls her glasses down slightly, held up only by the tip of her nose as she stares at him. "You want all of that?"

"Yes, please."

"I'll go and let the kitchen know." She scribbles a few lines in the booklet and turns to leave.

"Oh, wait, sorry," he calls out. "Would you mind leaving the butter off? I'm trying to watch my cholesterol." She says nothing in response, only nods, and continues on her way.

"Don't you think that's a bit excessive?" Reuben asks.

"Of course, it is. But it should give us more time until the next interruption. Like I said, time is against us."

Reuben opens his mouth, but no words follow. He allows an audible inhale in preparation to speak but, again, nothing.

"So, you're an artist?" Reuben says finally.

"Of sorts, yes. Each Steward brought something unique to the project. Your father, as you know, was a physicist. There were a few other science-based disciplines but still diverse. We had an economist, a systems engineer, a policy advisor, and many other professions. Everything but a historian." He laughs to himself. "Joking, of course. We had one historian who, like many of us, didn't quite pan out. My specialty, however, was the ability to weave, tell, and dissect a narrative."

"I'm sorry. I hope this doesn't come across as rude, but how would that be relevant?"

"Life's a story, Reuben. When we go through time, we are interacting with a plot. There are characters, settings, themes, action. It may be real life, but it doesn't make the story any less significant. Life imitates art or something of the sort. And the project needed someone with an artistic eye, just as it also needed the pragmatist and the physicist."

"How did Adam Drazen fit in?" Reuben fidgets with the handle of his mug.

"Not well, I'm afraid. His task was useful to us but dangerous. Drazen specialized in psychological operations. He knew how to get in the minds of those we encountered during missions. He could always see what made a person tick: their ambitions, hopes, fears, and dreams. It was of great use. We learned much from him and the skillset he provided. Sadly, however, there came a time when he would use it against us, his own people. He never took to being called a Steward, you know? Saw the name as weak. Didn't like the idea of being submissive. I don't believe he ever really understood what it meant to be a Steward."

"What does it mean?"

"It means we are in service to something greater. In particular, it means that we are the guardians and overseers of Chronos."

"Are? As in present?"

"Why wouldn't we be? The Agency may have moved on, but they never officially dismantled us. You still recite the Traveler's Creed, don't you? Who do you think came up with that? Sure, Paul calls the shots as director, yes, but I still have my obligations. I swore an oath and allegiance to a brotherhood. Not even a bleeding-heart artist such as myself can pretend otherwise. I'm only operating outside the Agency's scope because that's what's required right now."

"So, you'll come back at some point?"

"When the time is right, sure. But it is not this day, I'm saddened to say."

Reuben runs everything Aperio just said through his mind as each point attempts to veer into its own tangent. One in particular leaps out to him as he recalls the crumpled paper Paul Peterson had given him after his training.

"The Traveler's Creed," he whispers.

"Yes, what of it?"

"You said we recite it."

"I did, yes. You do, right?"

Reuben shakes his head.

"Bloody bureaucracy. Takes the joy out of something as exciting as time travel." Aperio sighs before pulling back his droopy shoulders and smiling. "That creed is our history, our legacy, our future, and our duty. It represents our obligation and reminds us of the dangers we face to fulfill it. Reciting the Traveler's Creed grounds us in where we've been so that we can know where we're going."

"*From beginning to end,*" Reuben begins to recite it. "*I watch it—*"

"Not here," Aperio mutters. "I'm thrilled you know it, but now's neither the place nor time, of which we're so desperately short. Perhaps someday it'll return to the forefront of the organization, to be the basis and heart of our missions through Chronos. The AIC has lost its heart and its way. Only when it's recovered can the true meaning of that creed be lived."

The waitress returns to the table with a cloudy coffee pot and a stained mug. Without saying a word, she sets the coffee mug down and fills it to the rim. "Shouldn't be too long on your food," she says.

"No rush. Thank you," Aperio says as the waitress departs.

"How many of you are left?" Reuben asks once the waitress is out of hearing range.

"Not many."

"But there are others still alive?"

"There were some that survived Adam's initial attack. Of those few, even less were able to stay in hiding. He was always very good at finding people. Adam spent years working alongside us, getting to know each of us and how we think. It's difficult to hide from a man like that. I'm not entirely sure why I'm still alive. He's smarter than me and knows my weaknesses. I have to be careful. That means, for the most part, staying off the radar and not contacting many people. This includes other Stewards who may still be alive. I believe there are more in the shadows, but *who* and *how many*? Well, I'm just not sure."

Aperio lifts the mug from the table and presses the porcelain to his lips. Reuben watches as the man's face jerks and scrunches. Instantly, he releases the coffee, allowing it to flow down his chin and back into the mug.

"I probably should have warned you earlier,' Reuben says. "It's scalding hot."

"I suppose if the caffeine won't wake me, then the second-degree burn will." He sets the backwashed beverage to the corner of the table before pointing to Rueben's wrist. "I see you've managed to recover your father's watch. It's odd to see someone else wearing it. Where did you find it?"

"Didn't—" Reuben stops himself, realizing that Aperio likely wasn't the one who'd left it for him.

Or maybe it's a trick.

Rueben tries to read the man's expression, but the Steward gives him nothing more than a stalwart smile.

Maybe he's testing me. Why am I risking everything to trust him?

"You should know," he finally says.

"Well, if I should, then that means I would, right?" Aperio leans forward, reaches for his coffee, and lifts the mug from the corner of the table. He sets it back down in seconds, seeming to recall its hellish temperature. "I know that we don't know each other. I also know that you're taking a substantial risk meeting me here. Reuben, there is a reason you let me go that day, and it's the same reason we're at this diner. To be clear, I don't have all the answers. I can't even share everything I know, but I can tell you far more than the Agency. For that to work, you need to be able to open up about this. That watch was missing from your father's body the day he died, and it's essential that we figure out where it's been all this time."

"34 Canto Lane."

Aperio's eyes instantly widen before averting their gaze. Reuben has struck something, though it's not immediately clear what. Aperio leans back in the seat with a gulp. His eyes dart around the room as if expecting a murderous lunatic to jump from the shadows at the mere mention of the address. "You went there? How did you know where to find the house?"

"Don't you know?"

"Would I ask you if I knew?"

"I don't know, would you?"

"Yes, probably in most cases. But that address is known to no one, not even the Agency."

"Well, they know now. Damian was holding Nea there as a hostage, torturing her. He would have killed her if we didn't show up."

"Nea? Is she okay?" Reuben can hear the concern trembling out of his voice.

"Yeah, she's fine," Reuben says. "I mean, there was blood loss, but she should be able to recover okay." Reuben continues to explain what was found at the house. "I only knew about the address because of a dream I had." He spends the next few minutes describing the experiences of the dream, including the shadow figure, Clemens, and the bearded man.

"It was next to your bed, wasn't it?" Aperio smirks.

"What was?"

"You know what. That thing that if you were caught with you'd be confined for a very long time."

Reuben can feel the hard indentation of the manila envelope inside his breast pocket, and his heart flutters.

"Come on. I would be the last soul to rat you out to an Agency I never talk to. Besides, I have one, too. It's how Stewards get around. You shouldn't sleep next to it. Strange things happen that way."

"Anyway, the bearded man told me that it was a dream but that it was real too or something. I'm struggling to remember parts of it."

"Well," each of Aperio's fingers tap against the laminate tabletop in quick succession, "given where it draws its energy, it's not surprising you were able to get the address and a detailed look at parts of the house. Did you recognize any other environments in the dream?"

"No, not really. The house is the only thing I remember with the most detail."

"That's not surprising either."

"What is that place?"

"It's nothing. At least that's what it is now. It *was,* however, a very different place many years ago. There's a reason why Adam Drazen has been hiding out there. It used to serve as a secret space for Stewards. It's where we would practice manipulating time, space, and even architecture. It was very similar to your training room, 47A. As it so happens, 47A was modeled after the house, or the concept anyway. And like your training room, it was powered by the residual energy from Chronos. After Day Zero, when your father deleted the records to protect us, the power to the house was cut. Without the energy from Chronos, the rooms are stuck in place. Or out of place, depending on how you see it. Either way, it's now useless real estate that only Stewards know about. I guess I should say '*knew* about.' There are less and less places for us to hide and less of us to hide in them."

"If we can capture Drazen, then no one has to hide anymore," Reuben says. "And with some of the Stewards back, we can work to change things. I know you guys set up Chronos a certain way with the rules. Seems like much of that was because of Adam Drazen. With him gone, then we can go back and save the other Stewards. No one else will have to die, and those that did can have their life back. I know that's what my father would do." Reuben watches in complete surprise as Aperio's jaw clenches and his nostrils flare in anger.

"Is that what you think? Just a wave of a bloody wand and all is made right again? All we have to do is stop Adam Drazen, and all our problems are gone forever? I see now. You believe that this whole thing is because of one person. Do you even know why this one person did what he did? Drazen was like me. He was like you and Paul Peterson. All he ever wanted to do was change things. He didn't see the point of time travel outside of manipulating events and others."

Aperio pauses. His eyes close as he takes a deep, slow breath.

"I'm sorry for getting heated. I have to remind myself that you haven't been told about any of this. Do you know how Chronos began?" Aperio says, his eyes softening.

"Croatoan," Reuben says. "My dad wrote it in his journal. I still don't know what it means. We searched the Roanoke Colony and didn't find much."

"That's because we made sure to cover our tracks. At least as much as we could. I know you found Harriot's notebook. That was an oversight on our part. I wanted you to uncover the truth, but I couldn't risk your team taking it back to Paul."

Reuben's back turns to concrete as a grave realization strikes him. "That was you shooting the arrows? You attacked Governor White's men and almost killed Alex."

"It's true. I hacked Chronos the day of your first mission. Unlike Caltanissetta, I made sure that my watch's signature was untraceable. That was the first time I had been back to the Roanoke Colony since before Adam went rogue. Of course, it was the same place but about a year since the previous expedition because of the locks. White's men were inconsequential. I'm sure you know this, at least in theory. As for Alex, I made certain that he would not be harmed. I knew that you'd be able to tackle him in time. And if by chance you weren't, the arrow would have missed. I don't mean to boast, but I'm an excellent marksman."

Reuben's brain scrambles to process Aperio's words. From every conceivable line of thought, many questions surface, but only one captivates amongst the rest. Of all the strange things that happened that day, there's only been one true mystery. "What happened to the settlers?" Reuben asks.

"You spoke with White. Alex read parts of Harriot's notebook, right? The pieces are there."

"Governor White mentioned 'others.' I'm guessing that's you and the rest of the Stewards. Harriot's notebook seemed weird. It wasn't just writings. There was a sketch, too—"

"A sketch of what?" Aperio interrupts.

"It was some kind of circle, colored in black. I don't see how it's related."

"Fair enough. I only ask because I enjoy seeing stories from a non-linear perspective. Sometimes, if you give people enough pieces, they can begin to make out the narrative. You're right about us being the 'others' that Thomas Harriot encountered. He was helpful to us."

"Wait. If Harriot knew of you and wrote about you, how could it ever have lasted past the original trip? Nothing is supposed to take effect after departure. We can't change the past."

"We can't change the past *now*." Aperio lifts his mug a final time and gulps down the now lukewarm coffee. Reuben leans in, eagerly awaiting Aperio to clarify or backtrack as if he somehow misspoke, as if history-altering time travel wasn't possible, and that it never happened. But Aperio doesn't say any of that, and Reuben begins to cling to his every word.

"Day Zero was the day your father finished the years-long project of encoding Chronos with its locks. These locks, all seven of them, act as restraints and rules. Among these restraints is the ability to alter events in time. Prior to this, Chronos operated with savagery. We had personal rules for ourselves, but enforcement became difficult, even among the Stewards."

"What did you change?"

"The black circle in Harriot's notebook, it was what your father called a spontaneous micro wormhole. For a while, it connected our time with that of the settlers at Roanoke. It acted as a bridge between two worlds previously separated by time and space. This bridge would eventually be named Chronos. It was the beginning of the project. The Agency brought together twelve experts from various fields to explore this bridge. On our expeditions to the colony, we learned much about the people and what life was like at the time.

"I used to write short stories before coming to the project," Aperio continues. "I even had a few of them published. One of my favorite things I got to do as a writer was to jump around in my story. If I didn't like an ending, I could change it. If I wanted to alter the course of events, I could easily go back to the beginning. Chronos gave me the chance to live out that role in our world. At first, I could think of nothing better. Sure, I stuck by the rules for the most part. But day after day, I would fantasize about all the things I could do with it. Eventually, it began to eat me up inside. It was torture. I went from altering a meaningless story to being forced not to modify the ultimate tale: life. It didn't take long for my desire to grow into the contemplation to commit the act. It was even less time before the contemplation led me to do it.

"I envisioned a story in which the characters from the beginning would skip to the end." Aperio pauses to pick up his napkin, clasping it close to his chest as moisture begins to pool between his eyelids. He closes his eyes and tilts his head back. A deep breath passes into him before he looks back at Reuben and continues.

"So, I gained their trust. I waited one weekend when I knew the other Stewards would be gone, and I walked the bridge. The colonists were all there to meet me. I led them to the mouth of Chronos and had them follow me. I kept thinking the entire time how wonderful it would be to introduce them to our world. I arrived on the other side in our time. The bright light from the jump faded into a deep red.

"The settlers weren't in one place, but everywhere." Tears begin streaming from his eyes in mass, flowing down his cheeks and dripping onto the table. "Chronos tore them to pieces, and their remains scattered throughout the lab floor. I killed them. I never meant to, but it happened because of me. By the time I looked at the data records, I saw that it had changed. Forever, it entered the history books as the Lost Colony. I told the other Stewards what happened. They were as horrified as me. We found out later that organic material had difficulty moving to foreign destinations forward in time. I'll always remember your father as the one who hugged me and told me that we would make sure this kind of thing never happened again."

"I'm so sorry," Reuben says. "I didn't know."

He watches as Aperio attempts to rub his eyes dry and mop up his tears. It's as if the worst part of him had spilled out, revealing an ugly and terrifying nakedness. Reuben feels sorry and embarrassed for Aperio and, for the first time, he understands the man. He still doesn't know or trust him, but he understands him.

"The truth is, Reuben, we all wanted it. And we still do. Drazen was just the one who was bold enough to betray everything he knew to get it. I'm sure your father felt the pull, too, but you're wrong. It's not what he would do. Nolan Greyson was the first one among us to see all of our weaknesses and set up a barrier against them. Your father didn't give his life to stop Drazen. He did it to stop all of us from destroying ourselves."

Silence seizes them for what feels like an eternity. A part of Reuben wishes he hadn't heard it, but he did. So much of himself has been invested in a world that he cannot change, in a father that cannot be brought back, and in a bridge that was never meant to be built. It's not the truth he's been chasing. It's himself and his own wishful thinking. Aperio has now crushed that truth, and now Reuben has nothing to say and everything to take in.

Before either of them can speak, the waitress stops at the table with two large trays of food. From the trays, she sets five plates in front of Aperio. "Three eggs with bacon and sausage, combo." She points to the biscuits. "And each kind of fluff. Anything else I can get for ya, hun?"

"A few to-go containers," Aperio responds. "I'm not feeling particularly hungry right now."

The waitress rolls her eyes. "I'll get that right to you." She refills both their coffee mugs before waltzing away from the table.

"You know you're going to have to leave a pretty large tip," Reuben says.

"Without question. I can be difficult." Aperio shuffles through his jacket pocket. "I have something for you. It's evident from our conversation that there are many good things that you don't know about your father. The best way to bridge the gap is to read the words the man wrote." He pulls out a leather-bound book and sets it at the center of the table.

Reuben recognizes it immediately and can feel himself light up. "My father's journal," he says, picking it up. "You broke into the AIC building to take it?"

"Don't be ridiculous. I could've, yes, but that's a lot of effort for something I've had in my possession for a long time."

"How long have you had this?"

"It's been a while. This may not make much sense to you since I know you've had it in your possession before. But your father had me hold it for safekeeping before he passed. I promised him that I would personally place it into your hands."

Reuben clasps the journal tightly to his chest as if it were the Prodigal Son himself returning home. He holds it up to his nose and inhales the scent of the rustic pages. His gratitude to hold it once again exceeds his confusion. How it had been at AIC headquarters and in Aperio's keeping, seemingly at once, is a question for another day.

"I have something for you, too." Reuben pulls out a book of his own from the backpack beside him. He hands it to Aperio, who mouths the words of the title.

"Every writer enjoys classic literature, even copies stained with blood smears," Aperio says while turning the cover outward toward Reuben.

"What is it they say about books and their covers?"

"Ah yes, but practically speaking, a good cover doesn't hurt." Aperio raises his eyebrows. "Unlike clichés." He flips through the pages before stopping at the bookmark. "Is this...?"

"I don't know what it is, but Nea wanted me to give it to you. I am curious, though, if you'd want to shed some light?"

"I do, but I can't. Like I said earlier, there are some things I can't tell you. At least not at this juncture."

"Okay," Reuben says.

Each of them secures their respective swapped items. The

door chimes, and Reuben hears the faint voice of the waitress attending to the newly entered customer.

"We're about to close," she says in the distance.

"This won't take long, ma'am," a familiar voice responds.

Reuben freezes, his heart racing as his ears recognize the voice before his brain can process it. Finally, he looks up and sees the man just as he's gazing toward their table.

"I'm here to meet those gentlemen seated in the back," Caleb Jones says with a grin.

"Suit yourself if you want to waste time with those cryin' weirdos. Actually, could you take these to-go containers on your way over?" She hands him the boxes.

"It will be my pleasure."

Reuben looks up with a sharp intake of breath, struggling to keep calm and stay focused. He risked everything to get to the truth. It's a costly truth, and the time has come to pay for it.

23

UNTRUTHS OF OMISSION

S ky approaches the house, takes a breath, and knocks on the door. Of all the things to do today, this is probably the most dreadful. Time seems to stand still as she waits for an answer. Then everything comes back.

Kirk lying lifeless in a pool of his own blood.

Fighting to bring back his body in the chaos of combat.

Standing then where she stands now, dreading the moment his grandmother would open the door.

She had to tell her that Kirk wouldn't be coming back, that they would no longer be taking that vacation to Florida. Now here she is—back on that dreaded doorstep, waiting. It's not that Sky doesn't care, but that she cares so much that it hurts. She took Kirk under her wing. He was her protégé and partner, and now he is only a memory, a ghost summoning her to his grandmother's house once more.

The door opens, and a warm smile greets her. Kirk's grandmother, Loraine, gives her a tight hug and takes her inside as if Sky were her grandchild. It's been months since they've seen each other, but Loraine's face lights up as if it had been years.

She pours Sky a cup of tea, and they sit down at the small kitchen table.

"Thank you, Mrs. Fowler," Sky says as she takes the mug.

"Oh, please, I know I'm old, but you can call me Loraine."

"Okay, Loraine." Sky smiles, taking a sip of her tea. "How've you been? I'm sorry I haven't stayed in touch." A sadness fills Loraine's eyes.

"I've been fine," Loraine says. "What can you expect, you know? The Lord's taken too many good men from me. My late Charles. And now...and now..." She can barely say it. "My Kirky." The words come out, and she pauses as if she had uttered something in a foreign tongue for the first time. "But he's still good, you know, the Lord. I've lost my husband, most of my siblings, and now my grandson," She looks Sky stern in the eye as if reinforcing her resolve. "But I haven't lost faith. I can't lose that. You lose faith, then you have nothing."

Sky sits quietly sipping her tea, nodding from time to time as Loraine continues. It strikes her as she listens in silence—she has no one else to share this with. No one to talk to. No one to grieve alongside her.

Nobody.

"Has your son stopped by recently?" Sky asks.

"Who? Senator Important Pants?" Loraine chuckles to herself. "Oh, brother. Don't get me started on that son of mine. I love him, God knows it, but I can see why he and Kirky never got along. It's always about the bottom line for him. I mention the groceries, and he goes and hires some schmuck to get them for me. It's nice, sure, but it's not about the groceries. To be honest, it was never about the groceries. I'm old, but I can still get out and about. When my grandson would come here, he'd always stay and have a meal with me. I can't even get my son to give me a call." Loraine sighs and refills her tea. "You know, since everything happened, he's been really interested in that place you work."

Sky shakes her head. "It's just an off—"

"Just an office. I know, I know." Loraine says sarcastically. "You can't talk about it. I get it. Don't worry. Kirk never said a peep about whatever it was you G-men were up to. But you should know my son's coming after your boss, Peter-whatever."

"Paul Peterson?"

"That's him. I don't know what he's up to, but my son isn't one to let things go. I tell him this life's too short for that kind of obsession. Too short."

Sky never met the Senator, but she feels like she knows him too well. She remembers Kirk's burdened look whenever his name would be mentioned as if it were some albatross he'd been barring around his neck all those years. A disgusting taste fills her mouth and turns her stomach as she thinks of this man and what he's done, what he's continuing to do.

"Anyway," Loraine says. "I didn't call you out here just to chat about James. I have something for you." She gets up from the table and grabs a package from the kitchen counter before setting it in front of Sky.

Bewildered, Sky reads Kirk's sloppily written name on the box. "I don't understand," she says.

"Inside."

Sky pulls back the already opened flaps to find a folded manilla envelope stuffed inside like a protected crustacean in its shell. A feeling strikes her as she reaches to pull it out. Like the house on Canto Lane, Caltanissetta, and Roanoke before that, a vivid sense of unease grips her spine like an iron clamp. She feels the letters written on the envelope in an almost premonitory way, even before reading them. Then she sees it, and her heart drops.

Sky.

There's no sender, recipient, or address. It's only her name written in red ink staring back at her.

Her heart races as she looks back up at Loraine. "What is this?" Sky says as she jumps to her feet.

"I don't know, dear," Loraine says. "I got that package the day Kirky passed. He was going to take it, but then work called, and he ran out the door. It's just been sitting here all this time. I didn't want to open it because a part of me..." Her voice cracks, and she reaches for a handkerchief on the counter as tears begin to flow. "A part of me still thought that Kirky would come back for a meal or just a visit, and I'd give it to him then. I know it's stupid. It's stupid. But I didn't want to...I didn't want to open it."

Sky embraces Loraine as she cries into her shoulder. She can feel her heartbeat against her own chest and its yearning void, like withered grass thirsting for water in a drought. Sky has no words to take away her pain, no anecdote to distract her, and no answers to bring relief. All Sky has is her presence and her touch, and she doesn't hold back either.

Minutes later, they sit back down at the table, and Loraine continues. She tells Sky about the months that went by before she could bring herself to finally open the package and the shock of finding a strange envelope with Sky's name on it.

"And that's when I called you," Loraine says. "If it were some other hussy's name on it, I would've torn the envelope open and looked inside. But it was your name. Kirky always said good things about you, you know. He really liked you, trusted you. You were good to him, and I couldn't do that. So, I called you."

"And here we are," Sky says. "Do you know who left it?"

"Some strange man. He put it right on the doorstep. I told Kirky that it wasn't my mailman, Mr. Walters. I don't know who it was."

"Do you remember what he looked like?"

"More like what the back of his head looked like. He had darker hair, but most of it was covered by some hat. It's all I remember, honestly. Lord knows my memory isn't what it was, even though that son of mine would beg to differ."

After finishing her tea, Sky takes the envelope and says her goodbyes. She gives Loraine a final big hug before leaving and promises to visit again soon.

Alone, parked in her car, she stares at her name on the unopened envelope. Anxiety fills her chest like a slowly expanding balloon as her mind races to guess what's inside. She rips the seal and reaches in.

Nothing.

She finally tilts the envelope down, and something tumbles onto her palm. The feeling hits her before her eyes can process. Her heart stops as she stares at the tiny promise in her palm.

Her ring.

Its diamond shines as bright as that day on the beach, but that isn't the memory that comes to her. It's the blinding muzzle flash against a blackened silhouette, a shot in the darkness and Ray's lifeless body striking the ground. Her head becomes light, and her breath grows heavy as it comes back to her. It's always coming back to her, like the sand on that beach and the tide that pulled at it.

Never-ending.

Always returning.

Forever with her.

* * *

Paul picks up his pace to match the ticking of his watch. Time measures his every thought and action, dictates each decision, and drives him continually forward. He can feel his heart thumping against his chest, wanting to up the tempo, to throw him off rhythm, to consume him with the pressures of running the AIC and capturing Adam Drazen. He doesn't allow it to seize him. Control is everything, and submission is death.

So, he lets out a breath and continues forward.

It doesn't take long to reach the tiny room at the end of the hallway, the same room he had told Reuben about his father's murder and Chronos. His teeth clench and grind each time he ventures into this section of the facility. He can almost feel his blood boiling beneath his skin. It's not because of all the dust collecting or even the people who had worked there years ago. It's because it was Adam Drazen's sanctuary. It's where he worked, and it's where he began executing those who trusted him the most.

Every other area in the facility has been renovated and made new. But not here. Here is the place where the past lives forever and the future never comes.

Paul pauses after unballing his fists, his hand now resting on the door handle. He could've set the meeting up in any other room, but he didn't.

It has to be here. The same as with Reuben.

He opens the door to find her leaned back against her chair.

"Hello, Nea," Paul says as he pulls up a nearby seat across from her.

"Hey," she says, making eye contact.

"Recovering well? I trust all of the accommodations we've provided are adequate."

Nea rubs her bandaged thigh under the table. "It's been fine, I guess. I've never been stabbed before, so I'm not really sure how long it's supposed to take to heal."

"The medics didn't tell you?"

"They gave me a vague idea, yeah. You know how doctors can be."

"Yes. Professionals. The sort that saved your life."

"I'm grateful for that. But they wouldn't have had much to work with if it weren't for Reuben."

"Lucky us," Paul says without a trace of emotion.

"Where is he? Haven't seen him since—"

"We'll circle back to that."

"He saved my life. I'd just like to—"

"I'm sure you would," Paul interrupts again. "But now is not the time."

"Why do you hate him?"

"I don't."

"Well, you don't like him either."

He stares at her for several seconds. Something about her intrigues him, but he can't quite pin it down. It isn't anything she's done wrong or said. No—it's her subtle facial twitches and the way she responds. All of it is off somehow, and he doesn't know why.

"Your record," Paul says finally. "I believe it says your birthday is tomorrow. Thirty-six, is that right?"

Nea looks down for a moment before answering. "Yeah, that's right."

"You don't look a day over twenty-five."

"I'm flattered," Nea says, rolling her eyes.

"It's not meant as an insult."

"Well, when old people tell you that your entire life, it starts to get old. I've got good genes. What do you want from me?"

Paul smirks but says nothing.

"So, where is he?" Nea says. "Where's Reuben?"

"Reuben Greyson buries himself in isolation and paranoia. I understand these traits led him to you in your moment of need, but they've also jeopardized everything we're trying to do here."

"Isolation and paranoia?"

"Yes."

"Seems more like keeping others safe and staying alive."

"This is precisely why I wanted to meet with you, Nea. It's a misconception. You managed to evade Drazen and us for a long time, but it didn't last. Eventually, you were found. Eventually, you were hurt. And if you continue this dangerous behavior, eventually you will be killed."

"I don—"

"You want my honest assessment?" Paul leans in toward her. "With everything Reuben is and what he's done. Even what he's doing at this very second. I don't think he can be saved from himself. He's drowning in his rebellion like a drug he can't divorce himself from because it flows in his veins, and it doesn't stop." He leans in even closer and whispers, "You're not him. It's not too late for you."

Nea breaks eye contact and shoves her seat backward, away from Paul. The metal legs of the chair grind against the concrete floor, sending jolting shockwaves of pain into their ears.

"You don't get it," she says, looking back up at him. "Nolan Greyson died for me. If it weren't for him, I would've died, too. You know, I used to be complacent. Not anymore. Not after everything. Nolan was the one who snapped me awake to what was going on. Damian wasn't able to capture me because I was paranoid. He abducted me because I wasn't careful enough. I let my guard down when I thought it would be safe. I know now that he was waiting. Waiting for me to slip up, become complacent, and do something stupid." She shakes her head. "I'm not the one with the misconception."

Paul's thoughts race as something strikes him, as his mind struggles to recreate what she's told him. He tries to piece it together against what he knows, but something doesn't connect, like jigsaw pieces from a foreign puzzle set.

"Nolan Greyson," Paul finally says, watching as Nea's eyes widen before looking away. "You both disappeared over a decade ago. And, somehow, after nearly ten years, his dead body magically appears on the Chronos lab floor with a fresh gunshot wound. No one else was there. No footage of anyone coming in or going out. Just his body. You know, Nea, when I got that call from Reuben, I was shocked that you were still alive after all this time. I have many questions for you but, for right now, help me understand this. How is it exactly that Nolan died for you when you were nowhere to be found?"

He can see it in her eyes even as they refuse to look at him. She's trying to think of something, anything. A lie, a believable backpedal, something. She eventually looks up at him and still says nothing, as if yielding to his suspicions but clinging to the only defense she has left.

Her silence.

Paul stands up and tucks his seat into the space under the table. "Several months ago, Reuben Greyson sat in this room, in the exact chair you're sitting in now. I presented him with the facts and provided him with the option to join our unified endeavor. He then broke out of the room, assaulted a guard, and trespassed restricted areas on the property. At the time, he recently learned the nature of his father's passing and was told about time travel. I decided to show empathy and allowed his recklessness to go unchecked as an isolated incident. I should've viewed his initial actions as a precursor to patterns of insubordination. I will not allow myself to repeat that mistake. Today, I'm presenting you with an opportunity to tell me what happened. What you decide to do next will be consequential and permanent. Do you understand?"

Nea nods.

"We're getting close to finally capturing Drazen. Our intelligence and operational efforts, most notably the location of Drazen's safe house, have provided valuable insights and leads. However, as you know, our enemy is adaptive. Any temporal advantage we attain diminishes quickly. We need to fill in any possible missing gaps that could lead to his capture. I believe you can provide us information that will help put an end to this. So, I am asking you for your help." Paul opens the door to exit. "You have twenty minutes to think about how you want to proceed."

"Wait," Nea calls out. "What about Reuben?"

"What about him?"

"What will happen to him?"

"Reuben Greyson made his decision. It's time to make yours." Paul shuts the door hard, but he doesn't slam it, just enough to leave a heavy impression without scaring her.

He lets out a breath and continues toward the conference room on the other side of the facility. There's only one meeting left before everything falls into place. A guilt-driven hollowness pools in the pit of his stomach, but he knows he can't give in. Too much has happened to get to where he is. Too many have paid. Reuben, Sky, Alex, and even Caleb may all end up hating him for what he must do, for what he's already done, but it doesn't change anything. Paul stops mid-stride and glances down at his watch, staring as the second-hand glides along the clock, reminding himself of the reason, of the greater cause.

We all have our roles to play.

Paul recomposes himself and moves forward. When he reaches the conference room door, he pauses and lets it leave him.

The doubt.

The guilt.

All of it.

There's no place for it beyond the door, no reason to bring it in. But for some reason, he can feel it wanting to reach out, to tell them the entire truth instead of just the part they need to hear. If the truth will have its day, then he must first plunge into night.

He opens the door and sees their faces staring at him, like blank canvases ready to absorb the story he's about to paint.

We all have our roles to play.

* * *

Driving back to the teleport station, arriving at AIC, showering and changing—Sky remembers none of it. She knows it happened. How else could she be here in the conference room with a fresh set of clothes? Since being reunited with the ring, she can think of nothing else. It sits snug in her jean pocket, the worthless promise digging into her thigh. She can almost feel a strange energy in it, a tingling heat burning her leg as if the ring had just come out of the furnace freshly forged and cooling into its shape.

Sky can remember the day she tossed it out the window, and her life changed forever. A part of her has always imagined what became of it. Was it discovered by a passerby and pawned, or did it tumble into a storm drain, forever lost? Wherever it had gone and whoever brought it back may be forever unknown, but today, at this moment, nothing else seems to matter.

Alex mumbles something to her. She turns to him in a confused state and nods as if she were on stage in some play, mindlessly following the cue cards in front of her.

"Hey, did you hear what I said?" Alex says.

Sky shakes her head as the words finally register. "I'm sorry, what?"

"Where are you?"

"Here," Sky says as if trying to convince both of them. "I'm here."

"You know this isn't good, right? Our comms have been shut down. Reuben and Caleb are nowhere to be found. And, oh, yeah, Paul used all caps in his text as if the calm, collected stoic of a man was shouting the word 'URGENT.' I barely got here in time, you know. Had to bring the dad mobile. Now my wife is stuck with all three kids, stranded without our van."

Before Sky can respond, the door opens, and Paul enters.

They look up at him from their seats and say nothing, sitting in silence as they wait for him to speak. Suddenly, it dawns on her.

The basement. Reuben. Paul knows.

Her shoulders tense as she waits for his words to confirm her thoughts.

Paul taps a nearby tablet. A hologram fills the table, easing its way into sight. As the resolution clears, their eyes latch onto the object hovering over the table.

A pair of flex cuffs.

Alex leans forward, adjusting his glasses. "What is this?"

"We'll get to that in a moment," Paul says.

Sky swivels her seat slightly, squaring her shoulders toward Paul. "Does this have to do with Reuben?"

"Yes," Paul says, "but it's not only about Reuben. You both have been loyal companions to him. Perhaps too loyal. He will answer for his violations, as will anyone else who continues to enable his behavior. The two of you are valuable assets to us. I don't believe Reuben can help us stop Drazen, but you can."

"Why wouldn't he be able to help?" Alex asks.

"Moments ago, I met with Nea," Paul begins. "I described to her the reality of our situation. I provided her a choice to make, and I will soon return to collect. I didn't inform her of what was recovered from your mission to Caltanissetta. Revealing it to her would leave little sway in her decision making. However, it is imperative for both of you to know the truth. You're close to Reuben. I can't allow your proximity to him to cloud your greater judgment."

"Paul," Sky says, "if this is about the basement—"

"It's not," Paul interrupts. "I know about the inconsistencies between Reuben's debrief and what was recovered from the nav sweep. But that's not why I've called you here, and it's not what I'm here to show you. Do you recall the events of the operation? Particularly, when you entered the house?"

Sky's mind races as she struggles to recall each moment of

that day. So much of it has been fixated on Kirk that all the other details blur around it.

"Sky, I know I don't have to remind you of how painstaking it is to pull an environment from a nav sweep. However, when you know exactly where to look, you can discover the truth pretty quickly. All of your debriefs made it seem as if you entered the house only moments after Reuben encountered Aperio, the way he still had his rifle trained on him. I recruited outside contractors to work around the clock to recover the moments before the four of you busted through the door. It will still be months before we can interact with the scene in the training room, so I asked them to focus on the audio. Here's what we have so far." Paul taps the tablet screen. The recording plays:

"REALLY? You had... You...You made that seem important like—"

"It is important. Your friends will be here any minute, and they likely won't allow me to start smoking this once things get rolling. Otherwise, it might seem awkward or even rude."

"Uh..."

"Oh, yes, forgive me. You had asked who I am. My name is Aperio Talesworth. I'm a Steward of Time."

"Steward?"

"I know you've heard of us, Reuben. We're endangered, not extinct."

"What do you want?"

"Time, just like anybody. When Caleb Jones and the rest of your team march in here, we won't have much of it. You have questions. Questions that you would never get a straight answer to from the Agency. I can help with that."

"Or I can take you in with us and ask you anything I want when we get back."

"You think Paul Peterson would allow that?" *audible laughter*

"You don't trust me. That's understandable. But the fact that you're considering it tells me that you distrust the Agency even more. It's with good cause too."

"What makes you think I'm considering anything?"

"Your rifle is still lowered. It was pointed at me earlier, which reminds me. As soon as the door is breached, lift your gun back up at me. I'll raise my hands in submission. At some point, Caleb will toss you restraints to handcuff me. Tighten them so that they won't fall off but leave them loose enough for me to slip out."

"You really believe I'll do that?"

"With certainty. Don't concern yourself too much about it. You'll get a chance to question me alone. When that happens, you can decide whether or not to tighten the cuffs and bring me back to AIC headquarters or leave me on my way, and you have my word that we will meet again another time. From there, I can provide you more."

audible crashing noise

THE RECORDING ENDS, and the hologram of the flex cuffs continues to rotate. Sky can feel her blood wanting to boil through her veins, but it can't. She's too shocked, speechless inside and out. She looks up at the clock on the screen, feeling as if it should just pause so she can take it all in. But the time doesn't stop.

It never stops...

...*with Chronos, we can travel back in time.*

Reuben's words return to her from that evening on the rooftop.

We can slow things down or speed them up, but we can never stop it. The sun will always set just as it will always rise.

After a month with us, you've finally seen it, she had said then.

Seen what?

The irony.

It's always been the irony. She trusted Reuben like she trusted Ray before him. Men who've told her the greatest lies for her to see the most painful truth about herself. It is unwavering faith, as immovable as the past, and a relentless storm of deceit, as unstoppable as time itself.

Could this really be? Has she been so blind? Sky can feel a tighter knot in her stomach as all of it continues to run in her mind. If it's true and Reuben betrayed her trust, then everything seems to make sense in a twisted, tragic sense. But if there is something else, if there is a greater truth that she can't see, then absolutely nothing makes sense. Nothing makes sense but that single unprecedented feeling that distinguished Ray from Reuben. She realized it in Caltanissetta and remembers it now.

Hope.

It's all she has, and none of it makes sense.

"Did you examine them?" Sky finally speaks after a long silence, trying desperately to get to the truth.

"We did," Paul answers. "Caleb made the discovery and personally inspected the cuffs in the training room. They were loose."

"Maybe he forgot to tighten them," Alex says. "I mean, yeah. Initially, he put the flex cuffs on loose. But there was an explosion right before Drazen killed Kirk. I'm sure he would've gone back to tighten them if it weren't for all the chaos. Besides, Reuben knew we were doing a nav sweep. He's the one who asked for it. Anything that happened would be subject to discovery."

"Reuben also knew the recovery process would require ample time," Paul says. "Plenty of time for him to cover his tracks."

"Reuben risked everything to save Nea," Sky says.

"No," Paul says. "Reuben risked everything and *happened* to save her. He disregarded procedure, and you followed him. To think you'd give the man that much trust, someone you've only known for months. You grew up alongside this Agency. It's not a second home to you, Sky. It's your first. And let me tell you that it's far more important than treasonous adventures with Reuben Greyson."

"Treasonous?" Alex interjects. "We don't even know if he did it. Sure, all of this is compelling with the recording and the cuffs. But it's circumstantial. It proves nothing."

"I understand that what I'm telling you is difficult to hear. You both trust him, and it's hard to imagine that he'd intentionally do this. Worse, it's harder to believe he wouldn't tell you about it. You can't accept it because it betrays the deep truths you hold about him."

"Even if he did..." Sky begins but doesn't finish.

"There would be a good reason?" Paul's eyebrows rise. "Is it worth all that effort? Twisting yourself to justify his actions, his betrayal?"

"But what if there *is* a good reason?" Sky says.

"*If* he did it," Alex says.

Paul folds his hands and lets out a sigh. "He did do it. And if there was a good reason, then why are both of you in the dark? Let me ask you this: where is he now?"

Neither of them answers.

"Do you even know? Why would I come to Reuben's most loyal friends if I weren't confident you'd come to see what he's doing? Do you believe I'm wasting my breath? And I wouldn't approach you with only circumstantial evidence. I've had circumstantial evidence for months. I'll tell you where he is at this very moment." Paul's ticking watch cuts the brief silence. "He's about to walk into a diner, and so is Aperio Talesworth. They're going to meet, just like they discussed on the recording."

"How do you know that?" Sky says, knowing that she's only mere moments from making a decision from which there will be no return.

"Caleb worked closely with the analytical unit and figured it out. He's on his way there now with a tactical team to take both of them in. Reuben will likely be facing serious treason and conspiracy charges."

Alex sighs and peels his glasses off. "What do you want from us?"

"Your help."

You've finally seen it.

Sky's own words return to her a final time.

The irony.

She closes her eyes and breathes deep, knowing what must come next and what she must do.

You've finally seen it.

24

PAY THE TAB

"I bet this ain't the reunion you had in mind, is it?" Caleb says as he approaches the foot of the table.

Reuben tenses and feels for his hidden handgun.

"I wish I could tell you I'm offended that that is the first thing you'd reach for," Caleb continues. "Truth is, I'm starting to get numb to all of your bullshit."

"Jones," Reuben begins, "you don't know the whole story here."

"I know enough."

"If I may shed some light," Aperio chimes in.

"You already had your chance, old man," Caleb says. "Both of you did. We're all armed here—"

"I'm not," Aperio says. "Unless you count these meals. Heart disease is a real killer." Caleb and Reuben turn toward Aperio. "What? It does more damage than your bloody firearms."

"Of which we'll all keep holstered," Caleb says. "I didn't come in here for a fight. Although, it's taking everything in me to not throw down. There's an armed tactical team outside. They're prepared to go any direction with this. Believe it or not, I'm the one who's come as the facilitator of peace. You can have your last sip, take your final bite, and walk out with me. No one gets hurt."

"Can I pay the tab?" Aperio asks as Caleb rolls his eyes. "I may have gotten a deal on the biscuits, but the fluff costs extra. Don't want to add stealing to the charges."

Caleb nods, and Aperio pulls out his wallet.

Reuben's eyes dart in every direction of the diner, his mind yearning to find escape, but no plan jumps out to him. Off guard and outmaneuvered, he sits in restrained silence, one move from checkmate and two moves from flipping the board on its head. He pictures the tactical team outside near the entrance, eager to wave their barrels at him, prepared to lash out bullets of wrath. A SWAT officer or two may even be guarding the rear exit.

He looks up at Caleb, the first and final barrier between himself and any semblance of freedom. Reuben sees him as a good man, someone who lives faithfully by and for the book. It kills him inside to be on opposite ends, to contemplate moves against someone who, in their right, is doing precisely what they should. Caleb would die for him, and he knows it, but if they get captured, everything is over. The quest for Drazen. Justice for his father and Kirk. The mysteries of Chronos.

Everything.

Reuben's heart pounds against his chest as Caleb's eyes bounce between all the hands on the table. There isn't time for a cost-benefit analysis. His freedom and life are at stake, and he's not sure if he has the chips to call.

Finally, his eyes meet the recently refilled cup of coffee to his side, and he reaches for it. Slow and subtle.

Smooth is fast, and fast is smooth.

He grips the mug tight, its heat radiating through the thick porcelain. His gaze shifts to meet Caleb. Locking onto one another, their eyes do not dance in deception, nor do they barricade themselves in hiding. Reuben tells him what he's about to do without saying a word, and Caleb reciprocates.

There will be no surprise. His newfound desire for transparency has entirely and unapologetically screwed him.

His muscles tense.

Dammit.

Caleb's hand sweeps toward his holster while Reuben swings the mug at Caleb's face. Inertia launches the burning black liquid into the air. It collides against his face, burning his eyes and pores.

Before Reuben can inspect the damage, he jumps across his seat and into the aisle. "Aperio, now!" he calls out. Without looking back, they dart toward the back of the diner in a dead sprint.

"All units move in!" Caleb shouts.

Reuben and Aperio race through the kitchen, toppling dish racks and pans. His heart pounds violently against his chest as a stampede of boots vibrates from the entrance behind them.

He braces the rear door, and it gives, swinging open into the dark and ragged alleyway. Puddles of rainwater and garbage runoff collide against their shoes as they run. The stench overtakes everything, but he doesn't care.

Pleasantries are behind them.

Freedom is ahead.

His legs begin to cramp, but he keeps running, glancing back only to ensure Aperio is still close behind. He can see it, just within reach, an illuminated intersection less than a block away. He looks back once more and watches as the tactical team pours out from the diner like marbles rolling out of a jar.

The intersection is empty, and the alleyway is now filled with hired guns eager to take them in. Forward is the only option, so he sprints and Aperio with him.

They reach the intersection, and it happens.

Out of nowhere, it happens.

A speeding white van screeches to a stop blocking their path.

This is it. It's all over.

The side door slides open, and he sees her face.

Sky's face.

In the microseconds it takes for him to recognize her, he sees it in her eyes. She knows. Has she come with Caleb and the others to capture him? Is this how it ends? It's the payment for his deceit, a complete unraveling of the entire plan. Before Reuben can throw his hands up in defeat, she screams something at them.

"Come on, get in!" Sky yells. Neither Reuben nor Aperio hesitates to comply. Sky slams the door shut, and the van speeds off. Reuben settles into a seat and lets out a sigh, though his heart is still racing.

The van veers and accelerates as its passengers scramble to move aside toys and booster seats to get buckled in. Reuben gazes around the darkened space, orienting himself to the environment as the van levels out its speed.

Slivers of passing yellow beams cut in from the streetlights, slowly revealing the familiar faces around him. The passing light reveals Nea's face across from his own.

"Nea?" he says before turning to acknowledge the other person seated beside him. "Sky? What are you doing here? How did you know—"

"That an armed tactical team would chase you down at your secret meeting spot?" A voice calls out from the driver's seat. Reuben shifts his focus to the rearview mirror and recognizes the eyes peering back at him through thick-rimmed glasses.

"Alex. You, too?" Reuben says, struggling to process what his friends had done for him. "You all came for me. I'm not sure what to say."

"Well, I'll go ahead and say 'thank you,'" Aperio chimes in. "I certainly appreciate the lift."

"Yeah, thank you." Reuben looks up at Sky, almost afraid of speaking to her. He sees a brief look of disappointment through her mostly forced half-smile.

"We didn't have much of a choice," Sky says, nearly monotone. "Paul told us about your meeting and how Jones was on his way to grab you. We couldn't let that happen."

Reuben puts his hand on hers as he leans in. "I'm so sorry I didn't—"

"Another time," Sky says, pulling her hand away.

Sudden nausea takes Reuben's stomach. He's unsure if it's Alex's driving or having to watch Sky bear the burden of his reckless actions.

Reuben turns to the rest of the team as the sirens fade.

"I'm thankful, really. But we have a head start, at best. It won't be long before their trucks catch up to us."

"I took care of that," Nea says, holding a knife. "It's not high-tech, but it slashes tires just fine." She glances at Aperio, who nods in return.

"I'm glad you're okay," Aperio says to Nea. "Reuben told me what you went through. I'm sorry." He pulls only the corner of the book from his jacket pocket. "It's in good hands now."

"Wait," Reuben says, shifting his attention to Nea. "How were you able to escape? I thought Paul had you on lockdown."

Nea smiles. "He did, but Paul's definitely not as smart as he lets on. All the cameras were shot out in the section he had me in. By you, I believe."

Reuben snickers, recalling that first day at the facility.

Nea continues, "It made it almost too easy for Sky and Mister Sucks at Driving over here to bust me out."

"Hey!" Alex shouts from the driver's seat. "Let's not forget that it's my dad mobile making this whole adventure possible. And you know what else? My driving is actually top tier. Go ahead and ask my students from the neighborhood driving school." Alex wags his fingers behind the rearview mirror, perhaps not realizing the unconscious slip into dad-mode. "Also, to be clear, it's actually a very hurtful stereotyp— Whoa, hold on!" he yells before the van jolts them upward, forcing their butts to smack their seats. "Sorry, that pothole came up so quick." All the passengers in the van laugh as they regain their footing. "Ah, screw you guys," Alex says through his smile.

"Where are we going?" Reuben asks. Sky unbuckles herself to dig through a nearby backpack. She pulls out an object and extends it to Reuben. Before he can reach out to grab it, a sliver of passing light glistens against the shape. It's his triangle-shaped badge that Paul had given him. He takes it from her hand and rubs the inscription along the bottom, feeling the words through the darkness, speaking its truth into his touch.

Loyalty, Duty, Friendship, Bound by Time and Space.

"You left it in your room," Sky says.

"I..." Reuben struggles to hold back the pathetic look on his face. "I forgot it."

Sky inches closer to him, gazing dead into Reuben's eyes. She pulls back a smile for a moment and says only one word to him. "Don't."

Reuben nods and opens his mouth to say something, but he can't. The words will come, but he knows it won't be today.

"Oh sh—" Alex cries out as Reuben and the remaining occupants lunge forward. Glass shatters and sprays. Reuben's body whiplashes, and pain shoots through his collarbone.

Seatbelt.

In a millisecond, he sees her. His eyes widen, and panic fills him.

Sky. No seatbelt.

Her body floats in the air, weightless and unburdened. Then time returns to them.

Projectiles fly through the van from all directions. Gravity pulls them from every angle as the lights, street, and night sky tumble past.

Reuben watches helplessly as Sky bounces against the front seat then the roof, metal crumpling in around them. Blackness comes and goes, the world with it. Screams cut in and out as Reuben fights with everything to keep his eyes open, to stay conscious. He grips the seat, but the force doesn't stop. The world keeps spinning, and the van continues tumbling.

A blur flies past him, and he reaches for it. The weight rams against his chest, taking his breath. He pulls it even closer and squeezes tight. Hair flings into his face, and he can smell the sweetness.

It's her.

It's Sky.

He's caught her.

Reuben smiles, and the world goes black. A final shockwave of force hammers him, then nothing.

* * *

RINGING PROTRUDES INTO HIS EARS, and his eyes flutter open as time and space return to him. Everything hurts, but it's all numb somehow. He lets out a gasp, a sharpness piercing his head as it grows heavier with each passing second, his eyes filling and ready to pop. He can see the sky beneath him through squinted eyes.

Upside down.

Reuben glances at the ceiling, and his heart recoils. Sky lays there unconscious, his blood dripping onto her from above. He braces the battered-in roof with one hand, using the opposite to undo his seatbelt. His joints crack, and his head smacks the roof as he drops.

Without hesitation, he goes to her, taking her hand in his and laying his head beside her nose. Listening.

He hears it and sighs.

Breathing, she's breathing.

"Sitrep!" he yells, looking around. He can see the others stirring.

"Up," Alex calls from the driver's seat. A few feet away, Nea attends to Aperio, who's beginning to come to. Seeing that everyone is alive, Reuben crawls toward the back of the van. He knows he needs to get everyone out of the vehicle to assess for injuries. He reaches for the emergency trunk latch and pulls, watching as it pops open, revealing the side of the road.

Reuben drags his body through the exit before crawling over jagged rocks and gravel just outside. A gust of wind billows over the ditch, filling his eyes with dust. He reaches out to feel his way forward, and a calloused hand grips him, pulling him to his feet.

Reuben coughs and rubs his eyes, struggling to see the silhouette in front of him.

"My team," Reuben says. "In the van."

"I'm not here for them."

Reuben's jaw drops.

No.

He's never heard the voice but, somehow, can't imagine it sounding any other way—a deep, ragged baritone marred by pain.

Why does his voice have so much pain? Reuben's hands tremble as they hurry to get to his jacket pocket. There's no time, it must be now.

In moments, a pair of hands jerk his collar. Reuben tries to kick and swing, but it's too late. A gasp bellows from his throat as the ground beneath him leaves, as air rushes past his body. By the time he realizes what's happening, gravity summons him back down.

A rigid pain shoots up his back as it collides with the asphalt. He rolls to his side and wipes his eyes.

Finally free of obstruction, he sees it.

He sees him.

The boots march toward him, kicking aside large rocks and battered vehicle remnants from its path. Reuben looks up, and the man's face comes into focus. His stomach sinks and twists as it all comes back to him, as he recognizes the face he's not laid eyes on since it rested in the crosshairs of his rifle before vanishing. It's a face scarred by the terrors of its own making, a face quenched by neither death nor hell but given to both.

Reuben looks on from the shadows of the evening sky as Adam Drazen comes to destroy him.

25

WALL OF STONE

Adrenaline and oblivion surge through his blood and bones, thrashing his muscles into action. He jumps to his feet and sweeps his concealed handgun from the holster.

Drazen sprints toward him. Reuben raises the gun, and everything slows: his breathing, the wind, and time itself. Everything slows but him, the beast of Canto Lane, Adam Drazen. Reuben's eyes cling to the impending silhouette as the sights of his gun lag to align against it.

Too fast... Too late.

Adam Drazen's shadow suddenly floods Reuben's gun hand, locking onto his arm and driving a fist into Reuben's temple. The world blackens, and a deep groan echoes out from his belly as elbows, knees, and rage follow, battering his body to a pulp.

Reuben tries to strike back, but all he can feel is the pain.

The pain...and the gun.

Still in my hand.

He fires, and the blast batters his ear. In the flash of the muzzle, he swears he sees it, a deep red in the white of Drazen's eyes.

The flash fades, but Drazen remains.

Dammit. Missed.

Drazen rips the pistol from Reuben's hands like a pair of pliers tearing out a stubborn nail with ease. In seconds, Reuben's disoriented and bleeding head meets the barrel of his gun. Reuben has one more option if Drazen doesn't pull the trigger in the next few breaths.

He sighs as it hits him, as Drazen delays a swift execution. There will be no turning back.

"Finally." Reuben spits the word out as Drazen holds the handgun steady, inches from Reuben's head.

"Just like you pictured?"

"More or less." Reuben shifts his gaze just over Drazen's shoulder. Alex emerges from the van several feet behind him, moving toward them with his own gun pointed at Drazen.

"Set it down slow," Alex shouts as he approaches. Drazen releases the firearm, allowing it to drop to the ground. "So much for slow."

Reuben and Alex make eye contact and nod. Reuben knows the plan is far from perfect. It's a stupid, reckless, nuclear option, but it couldn't feel more right for some reason.

It couldn't be more right.

His shoulders relax as a brief sense of ease and control comes to his steady hands. He pulls out the manila envelope, tears it open, and smiles.

Now's the time.

The bulky object slides into his palm, and the screen illuminates. He unfastens the straps and attaches the traveler's watch to his wrist, side by side with his father's, uniting legacy and posterity.

"That's not an ordinary watch," Drazen says. "Neither of them are."

Reuben looks at him, the man who murdered his father and so many others. Disarmed and within reach, Adam Drazen's dead and unyielding gaze pierces him. Reuben refuses to look away, to give in, to submit. He can sense an emptiness in Drazen's hollow eyes, a void beyond knowing, whose gravity is untamable.

Were you ever a man?

Alex moves closer. A dismembered bumper from the wreck snags his boot, and he stumbles. Drazen breaks his gaze and veers back, sweeping to tackle Alex before Rueben can react.

Reuben knows the one move left, and it's now. He double-taps his traveler's watch and lunges toward Drazen. The night sky flips to bright white light as pulsating waves shoot like daggers into their ears. They collide and tumble to the ground before the light and sound fade.

Reuben leaps to his feet, encompassed by the new environment.

Stone walls, statues, and medieval weaponry surround them. Echoes of distant water drops slapping the cold floors fill the damp, chilled air. Only the fireplace along the furthermost wall provides any source of light in the windowless chamber.

Reuben's heart races as he sprints to the weapons rack nearest him and yanks a sword from it. Sparks simmer across his hands as the steel grinds against stone. Handle at his sternum and blade out, he edges toward his opponent. Drazen stands in place, unarmed, with a gaze as cold as the steel in Rueben's hands. Reuben lunges closer, but Drazen doesn't move.

"This place, there's a version of it in the training room," Drazen says. "I'd spend hours training Caleb and others in medieval combat with Damian. No one was ever good at it when they first picked up a sword. Even me. It's amazing if you think about it. Something that meant life and death for thousands of years now has no significance to us. Just point a gun and shoot. No swordsman has a prayer in hell."

"Pick up a sword." Reuben inches even closer.

"This isn't the training room, is it?"

Reuben shakes his head and steadies his hands.

Why does he seem much more dangerous unarmed?

"We're in the actual chamber," Drazen says. "I can always tell by the air. We could manipulate time, space, and even scent. But the feel of the air was always off in that place. Can you tell the difference?"

Reuben doesn't answer.

"It's subtleties like the air that determines what's real."

Reuben presses the tip of the blade against Drazen's neck, the grip so comfortable as if the sword were melded to his hands. "Turn around and go pick up a sword." He could end it now in a single swoop, but that would be too easy. Drazen deserves more. Nolan Greyson, Kirk Fowler, and all the countless others deserve more.

Drazen leans into the tip. The surface punctures and a thin stream of blood seeps down Drazen's neck and Reuben's sword.

"Is that how you think things are going to play out?" Drazen begins to pace the room. "You used a modified watch to lure me into your trap. Congratulations, I'm here. It's not a terrible plan. Before anyone learns where we've gone, it'll be too late for them to link in. No interruption, that's good. We also made the jump with your watch, meaning it's our only way out. So, if you decide to destroy it, we're stuck. You've thought this through. I'm impressed."

Reuben shifts his stance to break Drazen's pace. It's not Drazen's room or his plan. Reuben can't let him take it. Raising his sword, Rueben slashes Drazen's cheek.

"I said pick up a sword."

Drazen wipes the blood and smirks. "Ah, I think I understand the bigger picture. Now, I'm really impressed. The swords. Some kind of poetic justice for your friend. Is that it? You've spent too much time with that cigar-smoking idiot. Not everything is a story. Sometimes, things happen and, sometimes, things need to be fixed. That's it. No good guys. No bad guys. We're all just doing what we have to do. So, go ahead."

Reuben visualizes the blade of his sword slashing through Drazen's skull. But he holds his extended arm still. "You don't get to do this," he says after moments of silence.

"What? Force you to make your own damn decision? I did what I did. All those people, dead. I didn't like it, even hated it most times, but I did it."

"Shut up."

"No. You lied, manipulated, and broke all the rules to get me here. And now you don't have the stomach? Did you think this was going to be pleasant?"

"Just pick one up."

"I don't think you get it." Drazen chuckles to himself. "If I grab a sword, nothing on Earth will make me put it down. It's not just that I'll put up a fight. I'll end it. I'll end you. And everything you've done, everyone you've hurt, it'll all have been for nothing. Do you really want that? Tell me one more time, and I won't hesit—"

"Do it." Reuben swipes his sword in a warning. Air swishes past the blade. Reuben stares ahead and sees no one.

Suddenly, a blunt force strikes his lower back. His body lunges several feet before another force slams him into the ground from the opposite angle.

"You're not the only one with a modified watch," Drazen says as he lifts Reuben by the neck and slams him into a nearby table. His body cracks, and the table splinters. Reuben screams as pain shoots up from the small of his back to his shoulder blades. Before he can let out another sound, Drazen squeezes his throat. He begins to feel the life bleed out of him, vision shrinking to nothingness. He struggles to force away Drazen's crushing hands. His strength diminishes with each passing second of no oxygen.

He slips the fingers of his left hand between his own throat and Drazen's hands. Applying pressure upward, he uses his right hand to reach for his fallen sword. It's too far. He balls a fist and strikes Drazen on the open gash of his cheek. Drazen lifts Reuben several inches from the ground and slams his body back down, shifting them closer to the sword.

Reuben reaches again. His fingers graze the handle twice, but he can't grip it. Its hilt glistens in the light of the fire, teasing him as it dangles its unattainable salvation mere inches from his grasp. His vision, breath, and strength dwindle.

Fleeting.

Fleeting.

Nearly gone.

He leans right, attempting to roll onto his side, but it's useless. Drazen has him pinned. The firelight dims, and the room fades as feeling leaves his fingertips, as Reuben's body grows as cold as the stone floor.

Air. Need Air.

Reuben swings his hips but feels nothing, then pain. His back, rocks scraping against it.

Moved. I've Moved.

Reuben reaches for the sword once more. It isn't a graze of the fingertips. It's a grip of the palm, the handle in his grasp.

Salvation.

Reuben holds it tight and swings. The pressure against his throat suddenly ceases, life returning. The sword sweeps past air and over nothing, blade digging into the wooden table on his opposite side. Reuben jolts up, gasping for air as his vision and strength return to him, battered and dizzy. Coughs pour out uncontrollably in a sweet relief before the truth can dawn on him.

Suddenly, knots of every size pervade his stomach as he stares into the open chilled room.

Vanished again.

"You're good, but you can't keep up," Drazen's voice echoes from the darkened end of the chamber.

Reuben lifts his sword, stands, and turns to face the dark. "I'll—" His cough robs him of his thoughts before he can muster them. "I'll die here if it means you never leave." He removes the traveler's watch, tosses it to the ground, and crushes it.

Drazen's smiling teeth emerge from the shadow. "That just means *you* can't leave. As you can see..." Drazen vanishes. He reappears less than a second later, standing on a bench near the fireplace. "I can get around just fine. Your watch was the one that was limited. Mine can do..." he disappears again before forming only a few feet from Reuben, "so much more."

He picks up his watch from the ground as the thought sinks in. "No, no, no, no," he says to himself, attempting to turn it on. Reuben's hands tremble as the panic begins to set. A light shines through the cracked screen. He double-taps it.

Nothing.

He taps it again.

Still unresponsive.

"Dammit." Reuben looks up to see Drazen has vanished again. He brings up his sword and rotates his body, perusing for his enemy as fear grips his raging heartbeat.

Drazen emerges facing the fireplace, holding two swords of his own. He extends one into the fire, using it as a makeshift poker. The embers glow and crackle as the burning wood shifts. Flames rise and brighten as oxygen flows into them. "It wouldn't take much to end it, you know. And it won't take long for the flame to burn out. Things would be different if this towering stone structure didn't bind it. The fire would have its own will and its say. It could be what it was meant to be. But that's just the nature of a fireplace, trying to control something that it was never meant to contain." Drazen turns away from the fire to face Reuben. "Why do you think you're the only one justified? Aperio's actions led to more deaths than I caused. I only wanted to fix his mistake. Like you—"

"I'm not like you." Reuben steps slowly toward the fireplace, struggling to control his breathing.

"That stupid smug look of yours, where did it go?" Drazen smirks to himself. "And how are you so sure we're not alike? I saw travesties happen. Not just at Roanoke. Auschwitz, Rwanda, Rome. History is built on the bodies of genocide. We all knew it and had the power to go back and do something about it. They did nothing. Instead, your father and the rest of them decide to take that power away, building a wall of stone over something that had endless potential. Potential to do something good. I knew I couldn't just stand by passively. I had to act. So, I did what I had to. You experienced several personal tragedies. Because of this, you broke the rules, betrayed people, and now you are willing to kill to do what you feel is right. What is it that makes us so different?"

Reuben steps closer but says nothing. With a scowl on his face and swords in hand, Drazen scrapes the blades together in a clash of sparks. In the glimmer of it, Reuben can see it in his dark eyes, the same thing he'd heard in the man's voice. Cloaked by anger but rooted in pain. Drazen blinks, and the darkened eyes vanish, the man with them.

He time-jumps to another position across the room, leaping onto the table and scraping the blades. In a breath of time, he does it again, appearing now below the candle chandelier as the metal grinds in his grasp.

Rueben shudders and holds his blade close. Drazen materializes beside the weapons rack and scrapes the blades before time-jumping to each corner of the room, grinding the swords repeatedly.

The speed picks up, and Drazen's figure begins to blur. An artificial gust of wind billows out from the motion, displaced matter and entropy sweeping through the chamber. It quickly extinguishes the fire, and the room goes black.

Reuben spins around in every direction but sees nothing. He stumbles through the abyss of darkness as his enemy drapes himself in it. He pauses for a moment and listens, striving to block out everything else—the echoes of random droplets against the stone, the crackling of remnant embers in the fireplace, his own heart, and the fear that holds it. All of it and everything, Reuben knows he must block it out or surrender to a worse fate.

The blades of Drazen's swords collide, moving place to place. The collisions speed up. In seconds, the sound of rapidly grinding steel surrounds Reuben, taking him back to the basement in Caltanissetta. Déjà vu. It's happening again, but this time there is no Aperio in the shadows, no savior, no rescue. If history repeats itself in its telling, then this story may never be told.

Reuben lifts his blade in front of him, shielding his face from potential blows. He closes his eyes in the darkness, breathes out his fear, and concentrates on the directions of the sounds, attempting to pinpoint a pattern of movement.

Left, up, right, down, right, up.

A sudden jolt of pain slashes Reuben's thigh as Drazen's blades swipes past him. He lets out a scream as the exposed wound begins to bleed, his head growing light to the loss. Yet still, he doesn't lose track of it, the sounds roaring around him.

Up, right, down, right, up, left.

He raises his sword upward, blocking Drazen's attack.

I have you. Right, down, right, up, left, up.

He moves his sword to the right, this time in a swinging motion. It collides with the tip of one of Drazen's blades, causing a spark. Reuben follows through and feels his weapon scraping flesh. The noises cease. He swings his blade in multiple directions but hits nothing.

"I hit you," Reuben whispers.

"You did," Drazen's voice responds through the darkness. "Congratulations." The voice shifts to another location. "You know..." Drazen continues jumping from spot to spot. "There is an old cliché...about winning battles...and losing wars...I loathe clichés, but I can't deny...there is a reason they exist..."

Reuben feels a hand grip his shoulder. Before he can counter, a blade slips just above his Adam's apple.

Drazen whispers, "You spent months planning this moment. Locating the chamber. Practicing your melee. Modifying your watch to trap me. All of it. You even managed to adapt to my time jumps. After you smashed your ticket out of this place, a part of you still believed...still believed that maybe, just maybe, you still had the advantage or could somehow regain it. The truth is, you never had it. You're standing in this very spot because it's exactly where I want you. Vulnerable, bleeding out, and stranded. Even now, you believe that you were the one who brought me here. Open your damn eyes, Reuben. I brought you here."

Drazen's sweaty hand reaches behind Reuben's head and down the inside of his shirt collar. He grazes the metal chain before returning to it. His fingers latch onto it, clawing it from Reuben's shirt, exposing it.

"What are you doing with that? It's—"

"Your grandfather's dog tags," Drazen interrupts. "Only, it's so much more."

Reuben hears the controlled tapping of Drazen's fingers against a small flat surface.

His watch.

Reuben's heart drops, and the room bleeds its black, shedding the darkness and tearing them from the spacetime fabric of the medieval chamber.

Minutes and seconds turn into void nothingness.

One realm leaves them, and another arrives.

26

A DREAM OF STEWARDS

A sudden thrash, and everything goes black. Sky tries to lift herself from the wreckage, but she can't. There is nothing to move toward, no surrounding, and no sounds.

Nothing at all.

Thoughts run through her mind, but she can't discern them as if they were encrypted somehow. It feels like there is no space around her, and therefore no time, immediacy, and infinity reconciled in a fathomless paradox.

Then, almost without realizing it, everything comes back to her: defying Paul, breaking out Nea, rescuing Reuben, and the crash. It must've been a crash. Red and blue lights bleed into sight before disappearing. Sirens come and go. Voices muffle and fade.

Sky can feel it still in her pocket. The ring pierces her skin, burning a hole into her leg. She screams and rips it out. Then it hits her.

I can move.

Sky looks down and sees her own body for the first time since entering the void.

No blood, no bruises, no scars.

It's only the fresh clothes on her back and the diamond ring in her hand. The darkness remains, but her path illuminates before her.

A strange house forms in the distance. She moves toward it, unable to recognize the house at first. It's not Canto Lane or even her own childhood home. This is something else, familiar, yet foreign. As she moves up the steps, a sense of calm eases her mind and relaxes her shoulders. She looks down to find herself wearing the diamond ring, not on her left hand but her right.

Sky sees it on the doormat, and her heart races with excitement. She sees the name, his name.

Greyson.

It's Reuben's home where he grew up, looking just as it did in the training room. She rushes through the front door and into the living room, looking for any trace of him. Suddenly, the room darkens as if someone had turned off the light switch to its existence.

No.

Where is he? Where did he go? Where am I?

For a moment, all she can hear is her breathing before it begins to fade. Her thoughts become shorter and less conjoined, struggling to hold on and remember, encrypting once more.

Again?

Wait...has this happened before?

It's the last sentence she can hold onto until it, too, disappears.

Faces emerge above her, followed closely by bright lights flooding her pupils. They say something to her, but she can't respond. Then she slips back into the void, back into the darkness, back into nothing.

* * *

SKY LOOKS on as the bearded man approaches her. The moon's light creeps through the window and glistens against his full white beard, though his face remains hidden in shadow. She hears his voice but fails to see his lips move at all.

"I've been waiting for you," he says.

Sky looks past him, ignoring his words as her eyes dart around the darkened room, struggling to recall how she's arrived here.

She's been here before, and it all materializes in fragments. The bearded man, this conversation, and the dream—it's déjà vu.

In snippets, she relives it all. The man himself fades, but his words remain.

"What matters now is time. It's how we make sense of things. It binds everything. You cannot exist outside of it. But very soon, you will be pushed to the limits of what that means. You're not meant to know right now. But this I promise, you'll see soon, and you'll know. You've felt things. You'll continue to feel them. Don't be frightened of it. You're worried right now, but you shouldn't be. You won't remember it, but I need you to know it. It's already time..."

It's not a sense of peace that grips her to the core but a sense of duty. And only in her journey does she see it.

From Roanoke to Caltanissetta.

Reuben, Ray, and Kirk.

The diamond tossed from the window.

The promise at the beach.

Treachery and lies. Friendship and love.

In all of the pain, the fear, the overcoming, and fighting for the future, Sky sees its source and knows where she must go.

The heat withers, and the light fades.

Sky's eyes open as she awakes.

* * *

It's not the Traveler's Creed or the fate of the world that runs through Nolan's mind as he prepares the cards.

It's his son.

It's Reuben that he's thinking about. The cards are for him, not Chronos, Adam Drazen, or anyone else. Nolan knows he's dedicated much of his time and efforts to everyone and everything else necessary. But today is about his son.

Today is the day, and it belongs to Reuben.

It will be over a decade before his son, or anyone else, will learn the truth. Nolan knows what they'll think about him.

A man ran scared only to be found dead on the Chronos platform nearly ten years later.

He'll be seen as a coward to some and maybe something mythical to others. The truth is neither. The truth is complicated and simple. The physics, timing, and logistics are complex and intricate. If any of the calculations are off by even a single nanosecond, everything collapses. But the reason is simple. It's always been simple.

Nolan smiles as he spreads all ten cards across his desk in the study of his house. The sunlight from a nearby window pierces into the room, casting a shadow down the center of the cards.

Half in light and half in darkness...

He folds each card and places them in their respective envelopes, concealing their messages until it's time. With the flick of his pen, he scribes the name and reason for all of it on every envelope.

Reuben Greyson.

To do this, to go through with the plan, he must sacrifice his reputation and his life. Nolan wishes with everything in him that there could be something else he could trade, something else he could do, someone else he could be. But there is no one else, and there is nothing else.

Only him.

Past, present, and beyond.

The reason is simple, but the cost is immeasurable.

Nolan organizes the cards into an accordion-style briefcase, each one to its own labeled slot beginning with '*Year One*' and ending with '*Year Ten*.' Afterward, he takes a breath, hoping it will ease him, but it doesn't. If there is ease, comfort, or peace, it's not in today but tomorrow. This is what he's fighting for—tomorrow and the days after.

He leaves the office and walks through the kitchen to the stairs. Dirty dishes, stained appliances, and a dusty kitchen floor greet him, but he barely notices any of it. As he makes his way to the top of the stairs, he can see the door to Reuben's room cracked open. Pine oil and musk strike the tip of his nose as he enters it. An evenly tucked comforter hugs Reuben's full-sized bed, flaunting its puffed pillows and smoothed bedspread. Two green duffle bags lie beside it as they test the tensile strength of overburdened zippers.

It strikes him hard as he stands there, staring at an almost unrecognizable environment.

It's pride.

Not the kind that blinds a man, but the kind that makes him see. It's the type of pride that has little to do with himself and everything to do with his son. It's the sort of thing that drives a father to sacrifice his time and comfort so thoughtlessly: coaching ballgames, late-night tutoring, and summer camping trips filled with mosquitoes and rain. Nolan grins at the thought, remembering the precious moments that will never return.

But this, this is different. He's not dealing with an inadequate education system or a playground bully harassing his child. It's more than his time being asked for. It's his life. His smile fades slightly as he dwells on it, as he thinks of what must happen within the next few hours.

But his heart doesn't sink as before. The burden, the cost, the toll—it all remains, but the brunt of it dulls.

Nolan passes the bed and opens the closet door near the empty nightstand. He pulls out a tie rack, his fingers trailing over the pretied knots. Removing each tie, Nolan undoes the knots one at a time, smoothing out any wrinkles in the process and placing them back into the closet.

Minutes later, he circles back to the family room. A pair of reclining chairs, a blue linen couch, and a series of historical paintings fill the warm space. He sits in one of the chairs but doesn't recline. Instead, he peers over at the other empty seats, recalling the years prior. The ghosts of laughter, intimate conversation, and the blissful silence of reading a classic novel with his wife beside him linger in the cold seats of his mind. Reuben would run circles around the coffee table playing cops and robbers with his father as a child. Today, for Nolan, any conversation is an inner monologue, any moment of silence is lonesome, and any instance of play can only be a memory.

Mira's death and Reuben's upcoming departure remind him of time's inevitable march to alter everything and his powerlessness to stop it. As he sits in silence, a glare of light from his watch blinds him. Nolan squints and pulls it from the sunlight's path. The minute, hour, and secondhand rest in the same position. He knows the broken memento serves him no pragmatic purpose, but he checks it, nonetheless, grooming his mind to accept its true meaning.

Not today.

Door hinges creak in the distance, breaking his concentration.

"Dad," a voice calls out.

"In here," Nolan calls back.

Reuben enters the family room seconds later. "What are you doing up here?"

"It's my house, isn't it?" Nolan smiles at his son.

"Yeah, it's just. It's just you're never in here. Not since Mom passed, anyway."

Nolan looks down then back up at Reuben. "I see you have most of your belongings packed."

"Most of what I'm allowed to take with me. They're strict about the packing list. The recruiter said that they'll throw out anything that I'm not authorized to have."

"Times have changed."

"How?"

"When I was a kid, your grandfather would tell me stories of his boot camp days. The drill sergeants would toss out everything, even items they were issued. Then they blamed the soldier for not securing his belongings."

"Well, that seems like overkill."

"I thought the same thing when I was growing up. Excessive. The way they treated them. But I don't recall my father ever misplacing anything. As he said, it was all for a purpose." Nolan looks down at the coffee table. "Sit down, Son, please." Reuben obliges, seating himself in the other reclining chair across from Nolan. "I want you to know that I'm proud of you, of what you're doing. I know we've been distant. And it might seem like my actions and attitudes have opposed you. But the truth is—"

"Listen, Dad—"

"No, you listen. You may not believe it now, but I need you to remember my words. Everything I did and everything I'm doing is because I love you." Reuben remains silent. "I have something for you." Nolan gets up before crouching beside the library's safe on the far side of the room.

This is it.

He lets out a sigh and types in the code.

07-18-13

He reaches inside and removes a small, antique wooden box before handing it to Reuben.

Reuben opens it and pulls out the object by its chain. A curious smile comes to his face as one of the dangling metal pieces strikes his palm. He reads it aloud, "Greyson, Liam R." Reuben jumps up from the chair and looks solemnly into his father's eyes.

"These identification tags belonged to your grandfather." Nolan puts his hands on his son's shoulders. "He didn't survive the war, but his story did through these tags. His story is now entrusted to you."

Reuben places the dog tags back in the box, closes it, and hugs his father. "Thank you," he says before pulling away.

"There's something else," Nolan says.

"What is it?" As Reuben asks it, Nolan can see genuine curiosity in his son's eyes, and it pierces him to his core, knowing what he has to say, committing to what he must do.

"This breaks my heart, Son," Nolan begins. "But I won't be attending your basic training graduation. As it stands, you won't see me for a long time to come."

"What? Why?" The curiosity in Reuben's face transitions to hurt, like a blood-red sunset whose only fate is darkness.

"I..." Nolan chokes on his own words as his eyes glaze with moisture. He wants to tell his son the whole truth, but he can't. Revealing too much will jeopardize everything. If the truth sets people free, then he's never felt more like a slave. "I have to go away for some time," Nolan finally says.

"Is this another stupid work thing?"

"It's more than that. I'm sorry, Son, I have no choice."

"When do you leave?"

"Tomorrow morning."

"And you're telling me now? Dad, I leave for basic next week."

"I know. I know, Son. But in a number of years when you see me again—"

The box slips from Reuben's fingers, but he doesn't try to catch it. "Years?" Reuben says, almost whispering to himself as if the word and its meaning were foreign to him. The wooden frame of the box cracks as it smacks the floor.

Reuben stares at his father in silence before finally speaking. "You sat me down telling me all this bullshit about loving me and about grandpa, and now you're just going to leave?"

The glaze in Nolan's eyes begins to pool, a single blink away from flooding his cheeks. "Please, understand—"

"No! Go ahead and leave. You've never really been here anyway. Things have only gotten worse with you since Mom died." Reuben begins to hold back tears of his own. "You know..."

"Son—"

"This is the biggest thing that I've ever done with my life, and you can't be there. Dad, you know what this means to me. What is so important that you can't be there? Huh? And not just the graduation, but anything else, for what? Years? What could be so important?"

Nolan knows the answer in his heart of hearts. He's rehearsed it, and it's a part of him. It's the greatest truth he's ever known, and he'll never get to utter it, at least not here and not now when it could make all the difference. He looks at the pain in his son's eyes, struggling to remind himself of the reason. It makes sense. All of it. The reason is solid, and Nolan has never doubted it, even now. But there is no solid, sure, or pure reason in Heaven or Hell that can take this agony away from him.

Reuben shuts his eyes and sighs. Thin wet streams run down his face as if flowing from a loosened water pipe. He wipes them and looks up, but not at his father, as if he were averting his eyes from Medusa herself. "Okay," Reuben says quietly. He leaves the room, and Nolan's heart recoils within.

Nolan's tears pour over his cheeks. He collapses, body slamming to the ground. He grabs his face to stop the flow, but it's useless. The tears bleed through his hands and spill onto the floor. He weeps for the next hour.

Eventually, he manages to extend his hands away from his face long enough to grab onto the nearby couch and pull himself up. He stumbles across the house until reaching his study, perching himself onto the seat in front of the desk. The area split between light and dark earlier lies only in shadow now. Nolan regains enough composure to open the bottom drawer to his desk. He pulls out his leather-bound journal and begins to write:

To my only son, my most precious gift in life—May this guide you on your way as you surpass your most desired of dreams in pursuit of truth.

THE REASON. The written word. Today is the day, and it belongs to Reuben.

27

KEYS OF TIME

R euben wakes to the cold flat ground numbing his aching back through a thin layer of shirt. Confusion and disarray seize his thoughts as he parts his dry mouth in stunned silence. He jumps to his feet before his arms snag him back down, restraints clinging tightly around his wrists. The metal cuffs are secured to thick waist-high chains cemented to the concrete floor. He grips and yanks one of the chains, but it's useless. The chilled links dig into his palms and fingers, branding his futile attempt to escape.

The sense of panic dwindles as he remembers.

Drazen and the tags.

The tags?

Reuben crouches to feel for them around his neck, his heart racing as his fingers tear at his throat.

Nothing.

"The only thing worse than clichés is stating the obvious," a voice calls out.

Reuben peers upward into the shadowy space beyond his reach. A dim light hovers behind him, but it is not enough to pierce the darkness that surrounds him.

"But what the hell," the voice continues. "They aren't there anymore. Around your neck." A hand dangling a shiny silver object breaks the plane between dark and light as if it were emerging through the slit of an invisible curtain. Adam Drazen's face follows it, a sly grin announcing his victory. "These are far from ordinary." Drazen sways his hand back and forth as the dog tags clink and clatter. Reuben lunges toward him. His shoulder blades pull tight as he leans forward, unable to close the distance. Drazen parts the chain's opening and drapes the tags around his neck.

"I'll kill you," Reuben says, spitting and gnashing his teeth as the rage rushes through his veins.

"How?" Drazen says, eying Reuben's chains.

Reuben continues to pull against his restraints until the veins in his forehead feel like they are about to burst. Before they can, Drazen kicks him in the chest. Reuben's back slams into the ground as he gasps for air, pleading for his wind to return. Rapid breathing slowly transitions into slower, deeper breaths.

"You really thought you had me," Drazen says, circling his prey. "It took a lot of effort to hide what I was doing, but none of it was all that hard. Tedious and slow, sure. But not hard."

Still lying on the bare concrete, Reuben rolls himself over, watching as Drazen encircles him. Memories and small moments from the day flood his mind, and his heart races.

The diner. Aperio. Escaping.

Then other memories come to him.

His modified watch. Melee training. The plotting and planning. And this, his capture and imprisonment. It's disjointed somehow, but he doesn't see it. He can't see it, like plots and points on a map with no path, no lines, nothing to connect.

How? he thinks. *How?*

"I may not be able to read your mind, but I can see it in your eyes. You're struggling to recall exactly how you ended up in this place. You're trying to think of the point when everything shifted against you. Do you know why nothing comes to mind? Because..." Drazen pauses his pacing, "it didn't happen at a single point in time but multiple. They were all under your nose, even before you got involved with the project. The diner you conducted your private meeting, how did you come to be there?"

"Did...Aperio, he—"

"Didn't betray you. Believe me. I loathe that fat, cigar-smoking clown. But the truth is, he was loyal to Nolan. He'd never betray you. But it didn't mean that I couldn't use him. Every good game of chess needs unwitting pawns."

"How?"

"I worked with Aperio and the others for years. It took only months to see what made each of them tick. It didn't take much longer to learn what ideas they absorbed and how they absorbed them. I would periodically test this. For an entire week once, I walked around with a pack of spearmint gum, pulling it out and chewing a piece everywhere I went. I noticed before that spearmint was the flavor Aperio would constantly chew. I'd offer him a piece, day after day but, every time, he rejected it. I knew then that he didn't take to overt suggestions. It wasn't in him. The man's an artist. Why would he? So, then I thought of it.

"I was browsing through a local thrift shop until I found something I could use. It was a painting, or at least a framed poster of one. I purchased it and hung it up in our shared work-space. I made sure not to choose a spot directly in front of Aperio's desk. It would be too obvious. Instead, I placed it off to the side. To see it from his desk, he would need to make an effort to twist his neck. But when he got up from his desk to leave, it would be the first thing he'd see before leaving the room. From there, I only needed to say the name of the painting once. Nighthawks."

"The diner." Reuben shoots up as it hits him.

"That's right. It was the very diner you drove by leaving your father's funeral. I made sure of that."

"How's that possible?"

"Do you remember the number of brochures you received for funeral homes after your father died? It was one, the one you chose."

"You sick son of bitch," Reuben mutters before looking down in disbelief. "You wanted me to drive past that diner. How could you even know that—"

"It would take? I didn't. That's why everything I did I had to reinforce and constantly restructure. There were dozens of failed attempts before a successful one. I did it to the point where, eventually, you would have no other choice. I waited for Aperio to go to Caltanissetta. I knew he was desperate to meet you. Still, I could see you were on the fence about trusting a stranger. So, I needed to do something terrible. I had to push you over the edge. That's when I killed Kirk, knowing what it would do to you. Your anger and distrust for the Agency could only grow from there. Bringing you and Aperio to the diner was just the beginning, though. You needed opposition, someone who would work against you, pushing you in my direction at just the right time. Caleb Jones was the perfect candidate."

"You used him to come after me."

"I didn't have to do much. It only cost me less than thirty dollars. I subscribed Caleb to a tactical gear magazine, knowing this month's issue would feature a pair of handcuffs on the cover. The suspicion was already there. I just fed it, stepped back, and allowed it to turn against you. From there, the course of events took care of itself and eventually brought you to me."

"All of these little things, these details—the painting, the brochures, all of it. You've been planning them for what, years?"

Drazen looks up as if contemplating for a moment. "No, that's just it. There isn't always a plan, not specifically anyway.

There is only a trajectory, a line that can cut through any path. The fire is always raging. The key to it all is to always have irons in them, even if you don't know just yet when or how you'll pull them out."

"Why are you telling me all of this if you're only going to kill me?"

Drazen pauses, and Reuben sees it. A moment of life, a solemn look in his cold hollow eyes. "I'm only telling you this *because* I'm going to kill you. I've caused you nothing but grief. I know that. It's only fair that you know why."

"No wonder my dad did everything to try and stop people like you."

"Oh, the locks?" Drazen smirks. "Your father's legacy was those locks. I hated him for that. Finding all these different ways to tie our hands behind our backs as history cries in agony. But as your father knew, there had to be a key with every lock he set up. And every key needs a guardian."

"You mean a steward?"

"If you must call it that. Years ago, Nolan entrusted you with something, didn't he?" Drazen lifts the dog tags.

Reuben's bones shrivel up as he glares at the tags, finally understanding what they must be.

"Shit," Reuben mutters to himself.

"This, Reuben, is the beginning," Drazen says. "It's the first of six other keys waiting to be recovered. Do you know what this one does? Take a look around."

Reuben complies. "What is this place?"

"Come on. I know you recognize it."

Reuben spins his head around the room once more.

"It's where we first met," Drazen says.

"The basement," Reuben says with a breath.

"Yes, the one in Caltanissetta. I'm sure you were puzzled when you found out that it didn't exist in the schematics. Do you know why that is?"

"It wasn't there. You must have brought me somewhere else."

"I didn't bring you anywhere. The basement is a part of the house. We're beneath it right now. You're probably asking yourself how that's possible."

Rueben struggles to piece it all together, to find the truth mixed within the labyrinth that Drazen has created.

"The basement didn't exist during World War II," Drazen continues. "It was built much later. We're not in the year 1943. You may think it's because we aren't allowed to travel to the same destination twice. That's partially true. The locks also prevent us from doing other things, such as altering events. To understand how the locks work, you need to understand why they're so specific. Do you know why we can't go to the future? Or even recent history?"

"Maybe we're not meant to."

"But we are, Reuben. You see, the lock prevents traveling after the year 2007. That's the year it happened. That's when the bridge was formed to go back into the past. You know about Roanoke and what we did there. You know what happened to those who went forward. This specific lock keeps the bridge going in a single direction, always back and never forward. And more than that, it keeps that date—2007—locked so that it could never continue its drift into present time."

"What does this have to do with the basement?"

"When you walked down into it, you didn't just walk into a later time. You walked into the future. I wasn't waiting in the shadows to ambush you. I followed you in. You're the one who opened the door." Drazen looks down at the dog tags now around his neck, rubbing the two metal pieces together. "That's when I knew for certain that you had it, the first key. Right now, the date is July 18, 2013. It's exactly seventy years since the invasion. Most importantly, though, we're in a time that we should not be allowed to be in. Yet here we are, all because of your grandfather's dog tags."

Reuben feels his heart fall from his chest to his stomach. "What are you going to do with it?"

"Out of courtesy, I've explained to you what I did and how I did it. You're better off not knowing what happens after."

"You're a coward," Reuben says.

"Is that how you see me?"

"That's how you are. I'm not just talking about how you fought me in the dark or used cheap tricks to trap me here. You stole, cheated, and manipulated your way to where you are now."

"Like you?"

"No. You murdered your friends, my father, people who trusted you." Reuben watches as a subtle, puzzled look comes to Drazen's face before continuing. "You stabbed a brave young man in the back. And, right now, you don't have guts to look me in the eye and tell what you're going to do."

Drazen crouches next to Reuben, grabs his face, and squeezes. "You already know what's going to happen to you. Why do you care so much about what happens after?"

Reuben stares into his eyes and says nothing.

"I'm going after it." Drazen releases his grip.

"The other keys?"

"No. The key of keys. Chártis is what we called it. It's the map to them all."

"Map?"

"That's right. And like these dog tags, they've been guarded for a long time."

"But why—"

"Just stop. You think you want to know, but you don't. I've told you about the keys because it's the right thing to do. Hopefully, that'll give you some closure or catharsis, knowing your father trusted you enough to carry something so priceless. But that's all I want to share right now. You see, I'm trying to make this as painless as possible for you. So, please, just...don't ask and accept what's about to happen here. Believe me, we'll both be better off."

"I just need to know—"

"Dammit, Reuben! You can't just move on, can you?" Drazen stands and closes his eyes. Reuben can hear the dread exhale from his lips. His eyes part as truth and horror bleed from them. "Where do you think it is? How do you think I'm going to get it?"

"I don't understand."

"Yes, you do. Deep down, you know, but your mind is suppressing it. And for good reason. So just let it go."

"Where is it?"

Drazen sighs. "I hated that place and never wanted to go back. But I have to."

Reuben's face widens as it hits him. "AIC."

Drazen nods.

"That's where everyone is, probably waiting for me to come back," Reuben says. "Sky, Alex, Nea, Caleb—"

"Aperio, Jefferson, Paul. Yes, they're all there. They'll want to stop me. But we both know that won't happen. And you know I can't let them continue chasing me."

"No!" Reuben shouts, stands, and grunts.

"I warned you not to ask."

"You...you can't."

"I wish there was another way. I've always wished that. But you don't see it, just like your father and the others. History won't just let you change it. Doesn't work that way. I'd give anything to trade for it, but only blood pays for blood."

Drazen turns and walks back into the shadows. Reuben collapses to his knees as they lament in anguish and plead for mercy. His chest caves inward as he begins to dry heave. Then it comes to him, almost randomly yet perfectly fitting somehow.

The only thought that can truly encapsulate the dread. His hands shake as the scene plays in his head. It's the final conversation with his father and his actions all those years ago, flooding his memory and tormenting his conscience—Nolan Greyson, lying in a pool of his own agony.

'*You may not believe it now*', Nolan had said before continuing, '*but I need you to remember my words.*'

This is what I get.

This is it.

His eyes close for a moment. Adam Drazen's swords grind against each other. Reuben opens his eyes as Drazen steps forward from the shadow.

"I'll only need one," Drazen says as he tosses one of his swords to the ground. He grips the remaining blade, handle firmly in both hands, Reuben's jaw quivering as his executioner approaches. The tip of the sword greets Reuben's shoulder with a chill, extending forward before pulling away.

Reuben closes his eyes a final time as the blade swings away before coming back down like a pendulum, gravity propelling it toward him as the world speeds and nothing stops. The blade sweeps down and strikes his neck. The sharp slit softens the tremor as it cuts into him. Shock dulls any sense of pain. It's over before his bodiless face can hit the ground before his eyes can reopen.

Yet, his eyes do open.

Reuben looks down and sees his body still very much intact.

"I'll only need one," Drazen says. Reuben raises his gaze as Adam Drazen tosses one of his swords, realizing the occurrence before the blade hits the ground.

"No," he says aloud.

It's déjà vu.

Why does it have to be this one of all moments to relive? Please. Why?

Drazen approaches him, repeating the actions of Rueben's vision. He lifts the sword from Reuben's shoulder in preparation to swing it back.

I said 'no' out loud just now. I don't remember saying that.

He looks up and meets Drazen's gaze.

"No," he says again.

'You may not believe it now, but I need you to remember my words.' Nolan's voice comes back to him again, but it continues this time. In snippets of a single instant, he hears everything his father told him that day, the last day they would ever see each other. *'Everything I did and everything I'm doing is because I love you... As it stands, you won't see me for a long time to come... I have to go away for some time... I need you to remember my words...need you to remember my words...need you to remember...I love you.'*

The blade sweeps down, and Reuben ducks. Drazen swings again, this time in a vertical motion, as Reuben crosses his arms. The sword strikes the crisscrossed chains and absorbs the blow. Wrapping the chains around the edge, Reuben pulls his cuffs tight as he snaps the blade in two.

He sweeps his legs across the floor, tripping Drazen onto him. Reuben absorbs the weight of his toppling body and delivers his elbow into Drazen's temple. Before Drazen can counter, he strikes again, grabs Drazen's arm, and double taps his watch. In seconds, they're overwhelmed by the pulsating jump.

The light fades to reveal seven tall pillars surrounding them, taming the fires of its fury, restraining its wrath in the presence of lesser creatures, guarding them against the terrors of worlds kept unknown. The god of time weeps in its chains as Reuben finds himself free from his own, lying in the center of Chronos's platform.

A tactical team of at least a dozen SWAT officers rushes the debris-covered platform. Reuben rips the watch off Drazen's wrist, preventing him from jumping his way out. Drazen leaps to his feet as the tactical team charges him. Reuben knows what comes next—it's the end of the chase, the end of Adam Drazen. Since learning of his father's death, he exhales in a true and deep sigh of relief for the first time.

It all began with Croatoan but will end here, at the foot of spacetime's passage and the locks that hold it.

Reuben phases out the sounds of squeaking tactical boots, shouting commands, and Adam Drazen's stubborn grunting. Everything fades from his mind until only silence remains. Then it hits him.

Gentle yet firm. Soft yet sure. Meek yet commanding.

He looks down at his wrist, at his father's watch, and the secondhand ticks to life. Reuben and his father's love become one.

*   *   *

SKY'S EYES FLUTTER, and the world returns to her. She can still see it, however—everything and nothing. The dream, déjà vu, the bearded man, and Chronos. It's all there in her mind's eye, then without warning or cause, everything vanishes.

Everything but him.

"Reuben!" Sky shouts as she sits up from the infirmary bed.

He's not here.

No one is here.

She knows there's no time but doesn't understand how she knows it. It's a sense, a deep feeling within her, pleading with her to run to him. This isn't Roanoke or Caltanissetta. This isn't something happening to her, but rather something she's doing. She's going to get to him. She must get to him.

Her hospital gown slips, and she nearly trips over it, knees locking up as she leaps from the bed. She eyes her torn bloody clothes on the nearby stand, but there isn't time to change. Reuben will be returning any minute.

He must. And it will be in the only place that it could happen, the epicenter of everything. Chronos.

I have to get to him.

Sky reaches for her holstered pistol atop her clothes and nearly knocks it over—not the gun, no. Something else. Her legs shake, and she nearly collapses to the ground. She can't tell if it's the accident or a spell cast by the haunting glimmer. Dimly shining atop the barrel of her Sig 9mm pistol is the 1.5-carat callback to her most dreaded moment. Always with her, enduring like an albatross around the neck of her entire existence—past, future, and forever.

It's her ring, and the fires of her hell have failed to destroy it.

She grabs the diamond, and her legs fumble even more. A part of her wants to toss it again, to get rid of it, to stop letting it define her. But she doesn't. There's no time for self-reflection or catharsis. She has to get to Chronos, to Reuben, she must. Without hesitation, she leaves the ring on top of her clothes, grips the pistol tight, and sprints out of the infirmary.

Her gown wisps around her as she darts down the hallway, sending a cool stream of air against her naked backside. There's no time for blushing and embarrassment. She turns a corner, then another. Suddenly the facility quakes as if it were having a seizure. Nearby carts and shelving collapse as ceiling tiles drop like hail from above. Sky trips and falls to the ground as debris flings at her from every direction. The lights flicker and die, bringing the entire facility into an eerie silence.

Emergency lighting stutters to life as Sky emerges from the debris. She doesn't let it slow her down, using the flashing trail to deliver her to her destination.

"What are you doing here?" a familiar voice calls to her as she bursts through the entrance. Sky turns to see Paul Peterson's dust-covered face.

"Where's Reuben?" Sky says.

Paul turns toward the Chronos platform, pointing. The

tactical team is swarming toward two figures in its center. Sky inches closer to get a better look. Then she recognizes them, both of them. Adam Drazen faces the SWAT team head-on as they rush him while Reuben lies several feet away, his outstretched hand gripped tightly. He smiles to himself, and it warms her. Her leg shifts to run to him before a queer pang strikes her square in the gut. It isn't relief or excitement. It isn't good at all.

No.

Then it happens.

Sky watches Adam Drazen drop to the floor as the first tactical officer reaches him. His hands grab something from the rubble and rolls with it. Before anyone can react, Drazen emerges from the dust with a fractured sword, swinging it at the first officer. The man's jaw drops as the blade whooshes through the air and cuts right through him. Before his body can strike the ground, Drazen seizes it and pulls it to himself. Bullets erupt as Drazen's human shield takes the brunt of the force.

Sky watches in horror as Reuben snaps to and struggles to come to his feet. The rest of the tactical team moves on Drazen, but it's too late. He grabs hold of the dead man's side pistol and reigns headshots on the survivors. The members of the SWAT team drop like dominos.

In seconds, they're gone.

Drazen veers toward Reuben before raising the barrel to his head. Sky freezes, and her insides scream, but her arms won't move—nothing moves. Drazen's muffled voice barely carries to her. She can't make out the words, but the raspy sense of pain couldn't be more precise.

Is this how it ends?

Ray, Nea, and now Reuben, lives that lie in the hands of killers. Killers she could stop, killers who need to be stopped.

But she can't.

It's not her.

It's never been her.

Drazen pulls the trigger, and she screams. It's too much. Her heart, body, and soul recoil, and she nearly vomits as she collapses to the ground. She screams again, the agony and regret coursing through her like a burning fire desperate to destroy anything in its path. The grime and dust along the ground cling to her fingers. She can see its filth while staring down at it. She wants to look away and face the truth above, but she can't. Her heart convulses at the thought.

Another *click* follows, like the first, a cold pull of the trigger. A sound she's heard a million times from her own hand echoes the story of its beholder. Firm and smooth is control. Quick and jerked is chaos and a missed shot. Drazen's first shot was the former, and this one now is certainly the latter—full of panic.

Sky feels a smile coming to her face and her breath returning. It's life and living, and it's here. In the midst of death and earthly hell, life is somehow here.

And I can hear it—the click.

Amid the blast, no ear could ever pick it up, could ever really know. Yet, she knows. She can feel Adam Drazen's angst as he pulls the trigger a third time. Finally, Sky's eyes confirm it as they break from the ground, gazing ahead at the stunned pair. Then she hears it again, just like the last trigger pull, alike in every way. Drazen grunts and pulls it again.

A trigger pull. It was only ever a trigger pull. No blast. No recoil.

Misfire.

Sky leaps to her feet and draws her pistol from the holster. She watches as Drazen uses the blunt end of the gun to knock Reuben to the ground before redrawing his fractured sword. Her crosshairs align against his head.

"I've been waiting for you," she muffles to herself, not realizing what she's saying until after the hammer strikes the pin. Her voice, calm and gentle, her hands fierce and strong.

This is who she is.

The bullet strikes him. There is only one blast from a single shot, and it echoes against near stillness as it pierces Drazen's skull. They all see it—Sky, Reuben, Paul, and anyone still left alive. The fugitive, the seemingly mythic god-like killer, flopping to the ground, brought down by a single small piece of metal and a pair of steady hands.

Blood seeps from the wound and onto the Chronos platform.

Like Nolan Greyson before him, the god of time has come to collect Adam Drazen.

"I've been waiting for you." Sky repeats the first words the bearded man ever spoke to her. She couldn't see his lips in the shadows, but she had felt the words in the dreamworld beyond. And, for the first time, as she utters it aloud, Sky understands that it wasn't him that was waiting. It was her.

This is who she is.

28

THE CHRONOS PROJECT 2032

"I've been here long enough to know there are bigger rooms, even some with windows," Reuben says, sitting across from Paul in the tiny box-like space where he had first learned of Chronos, his father's murder, and Adam Drazen. "Why did you bring me back here?"

"Typically, we bring subjects in here as an intimidation tactic. Today, it returns to its previous function as a storage room."

Reuben pauses, a smile cutting into the edge of his face as he finally sees it. It's Paul Peterson's tell written all over his face —a twitch of the eyebrow just slight enough that it has escaped Rueben until now. Reuben can't help but feel at ease for the first time speaking with the man.

"It's more than that," Reuben says, his mind at work. "When I first got here... The single guard, the unlocked door. It was almost too easy." Reuben stops himself, catching his tongue before it can sell him out and reveal the journal's existence.

Does he know?

Did he set the whole thing up?

"Too easy to what?" Paul says after an extended pause.

"To almost breakout," Reuben says without missing a beat.

"Ah. Well, I suppose we'll have to make it more difficult for you next time. Anyway, I also figured this would be an appropriate time and setting to conduct your final debrief." Paul stands his tablet onto the table, facing away from Reuben. He swipes the screen multiple times in silence before closing its cover and setting it down.

"I think I've seen enough," Paul says as he looks back up at him. "As you are aware, and I'm obliged to remind you, all actions have consequences. This is not a set of rules or principles that stem from my desire to see you punished. This is natural law. If a person overindulges themselves in sweets, drinks, and other vices, their body absorbs the toll. If I shoot a gun, the kinetic energy from explosive gun powder must be directed somewhere. Adam Drazen has been neutralized, facing the consequences of his decisions."

Reuben looks down, sighs, then glances back up at Paul. "And I'm ready to face mine. I disregarded procedure and lied. I put myself and others in danger. I was reckless and insubordinate."

"You certainly were. You were also warned repeatedly." Paul pulls out Reuben's belongings: his ID card, handgun, and badge. He then pulls out a sheet of paper, signs it with a pen, and slides it to Reuben. "This is a chain of custody form officially releasing these items back to the Agency. Please, sign at the bottom." Reuben complies and hands it back to him. "You'll receive these back in three months."

"Three months?"

"Yes, that's how long your suspension is. It's paid, so I hope you can find a sufficient hobby in the meantime."

Reuben can barely find the words to say. "What I did...it could constitute treason."

"Could. Yes."

"You're not arresting me?"

"Are you wearing cuffs?"

Reuben peers down at his bandaged wrists. "Well, no—"

"Have I read you your rights?"

"Would you?"

Paul raises an eyebrow and smirks. "Look at yourself. You have more bandages than skin showing. You also helped bring down a dangerous killer, the greatest threat to our entire operation. Good consequences exist, too. Don't think you're immune to those either."

"You're saying I don't deserve to go to prison?"

"Far from it. You may end up there in the future, but it won't be today. Besides, with Drazen gone, operational missions will likely resume. It would be a greater headache to try and refill your position. The team needs their leader."

"What about Alex and Sky?"

"Minor disciplinary action. It hasn't been solidified yet but will likely be a combination of tedious administrative tasks and a temporary Section 7 suspension. They'll both be here when you return."

"How's Jones?" Reuben asks.

"You'll be able to ask him yourself. He's just outside the door and will be escorting you after this meeting. You'll need to be escorted for the remainder of today until you can get your belongings packed. When you come back in the fall, your credentials will be returned to you."

Throughout the remainder of the debrief session, Reuben recounts the events that led him to the diner and later fighting Drazen in the chamber. He explains how Drazen manipulated him, Aperio, and even Caleb into a trap. Paul doesn't ask about locks or keys, and Reuben doesn't volunteer it. Reuben stands and limps around the table toward the exit when the questioning ends.

"Last time we were in this room," Reuben says, "I was short with you."

"You'd just come from your father's funeral. A man attempted to kill you, and two government agents brought you to this place with no explanation. I never took it personally. Apologies are humiliating. Save them for people who care." Before Reuben can respond, Paul turns, pulls out an envelope, and hands it to him. "This wasn't officially issued by us, so we can't legally keep it from you."

Holding it, Reuben's heart flutters as the envelope weighs down his hands. He knows what's inside before his eyes can see it. A rip, a tear, and peer inside confirm his thoughts in all its metallic glory. It's the thing he's always had but never known.

His grandfather's dog tags.

A literal key to the future.

Reuben smiles, seals the envelope, and opens the door to exit.

"Just remember," Paul says before Reuben can leave the room, "I hear and see everything, from overt mischief to the subtle tick of that watch."

Reuben glances down at his wrist. The minute, hour, and second hands, true to themselves, seemingly forsake their autonomies and unite to strike *twelve*. Independent and conditionally bound. A paradox of spacetime seared in a tangible memento of his father's love and duty.

"You ready or what?" a voice says behind him. Rueben turns to find Caleb standing beside the door with a solemn smirk.

"Uh yeah," Reuben says, forgetting that he'd be there waiting to escort him. They proceed down the hallway in silence.

Caleb slows his pace to match Reuben's limping strides. "I'm taking you to the conference room to say your goodbyes to Alex and Sky. From there, one of them will take you to your room to pack up your things. Those two places, some of the corridors, and the teleport will be the only authorized places you can go. And even those will require escorts at all times."

"What about the bathroom?" Reuben jokes, trying to lighten the mood, but Caleb doesn't respond or even look at him. They continue past the first corridor. "Hey, listen, man. I'm sorry for throwing coffee in your face and for everything else that happened. You're an asset to the team and one of the most badass people I know."

Caleb stops mid-stride and faces him. "Wish I could say it's all good. But people get killed for doing much less stupid."

"I know. And I understand if you'd want to transfer out when I get back."

"Who the hell do you think I am?" Caleb raises his voice. "You go around doing dumb reckless shit like some fool. Every cut you have on you right now was because of what you did. I'm this team's security officer. It's my job—no, it's my *duty*—to keep you and the rest of the team safe. It's my responsibility to equip you and everyone else with the weapons and training to stay alive. You might not be my favorite person right now, but don't think for a second I'm going to neglect what I'm here to do on account of our differences. I followed you when you first got here, and I'll follow you when you get back."

"I just figured after everything that you wouldn't want to."

"You figured wrong, Staff Sergeant. And, please, remember that next time you're considering who to keep in the loop."

"I will." They shake hands and continue toward the conference room.

Caleb swipes his ID and opens the door for Reuben. "I'll see you in a few months." They nod at one another, and Reuben enters the room.

He sees Sky first, sitting at the table talking to Alex. His heart dances as her eyes meet his with a smile. There is no need for conversation. Words would just muddle everything that their eyes are already saying. His feet remain planted, but his heart goes back somehow, back to the stars and Canto Lane, to the rooftop and the training room. From the chaos of war and the grief in loss to the thrill of adventure and the undeniable bond that intertwines their stories. This is where his mind goes back to. It isn't nostalgia or blissful sentiment. It's her.

Sky leaps from her seat and runs to embrace him. Reuben flinches before falling into her, his arms gliding over her back as he holds her in his battered hands.

"Hey, man, can I get in on that?" Alex interrupts.

Rueben turns to him and smiles. "Eh, sure. Why not. Get in here."

Alex pulls back after a few semi-awkward seconds. "I think that's long enough."

They all share a laugh.

"I'm glad you guys are okay," Reuben says, repositioning himself onto his good leg.

"Us?" Sky says. "I only got this one scratch." She points to a small bandage across her eyebrow. "That and a few bruises. Alex apparently cut his thumb at the crash site."

"It's still sore," Alex says. "I'm surprised it didn't need stitches."

"We're fine," Sky says, punching Alex on the arm.

"Hey, what was that—" Alex says before falling silent as Sky raises another fist with a laugh.

Her eyes grow heavy as her attention shifts to Rueben, however. "You're the one who gave me—who gave *us*—a good scare."

"Yeah," Reuben says before pausing. "I'm okay and, in a few months, we'll be back to traveling missions. I wanna say, though, you both put your careers, safety, and lives on the line for me. Not many people would do that."

"What choice did we have?" Alex smiles. "Were you able to bring it back?"

"I smashed it," Reuben says, picturing himself destroying the watch. "I thought that it would stop him by trapping us in the chamber. Or, at the very least, slow him down. But it didn't work. He had a modified watch of his own, a lot more powerful than what we could muster up. The things he could do with it were scary. What he was planning..."

"But you stopped him," Sky says.

Reuben smiles. "I brought him here. You're the one who stopped him. And for good, too." He can see it in her face: the ease, comfort, and pride. It's not a morbid look, the type that a psychotic murderer might display when they relive the killing in their mind.

No, this is different.

It's confidence and peace. Her husband may have died by her hands, and Nea's life almost lost at Sky's hesitation. But, at that instant, when everything was on the line, when Reuben's life was at stake, she did it. Sky saved him and became who he's always known her to be. Not a weak, helpless victim, but a fierce warrior.

A damn hero.

Rueben has known it since they first met and, for the first time, he sees that she believes it, too.

"You would've done the same," Sky says.

Reuben chuckles. "Ah, yeah, maybe. But I would've missed the shot. That distance, with all the debris, and how quickly Drazen was moving..." Reuben shakes his head, recalling when it all happened. "There's no way I would've made that shot. No way."

Sky pulls back an even bigger smile. "Well, I'm just glad that we're all okay and that he's gone. He can't hurt anyone ever again."

Reuben feels a weight in his chest as her words linger. He immediately recalls his conversation with Aperio in the diner.

Drazen was like me. He was like you. All he ever wanted to do was change things.

"It's true," Reuben says. "He can't. But that's just it. This world is full of Adam Drazens...and I'm one of them."

"You're nothing like that sick monster."

"I used to think that. And sure, I wouldn't go around killing innocent people but, in a lot of ways, I'm not much better. He wanted control, to be able to change things, and so did I."

"We all want that sometimes, but it's not who you are," Sky says. "If it were, you wouldn't have smashed that watch. You gave up your control to protect others."

"Wait," Alex chimes in. "If you broke the watch, how did you get back to the platform?"

"I used this." Reuben pulls out a traveler's watch from his pocket. "Drazen was wearing it when I tackled him. I knew he preprogrammed it for here, so all I had to do was push the button."

"If he was the one wearing the watch, you shouldn't have been able to make the jump. This isn't the training room. Any organic matter that Drazen was holding would have been shredded on its way back here. You'd be dead... Excuse my language, but that's one hell of a modified watch."

Reuben drops it to the ground and crushes it with the heel of his boot. "Was."

Alex's eyes widen. "Why would you do that? That was probably the most advanced watch out there!"

"Would you want to be caught with that?"

"Well, no...but...I'm sure it did all kinds of cool things." Alex sighs before Reuben continues telling them how he defied déjà vu and death.

"I'm not sure how—"

"How?" Alex interrupts, pulling at his thinning black hair. "There is no 'how,' man. It's not possible. I'm not just talking anecdotally, either. Listen, I've sat through enough boring scrum meetings to be very familiar with how the technical units run their tests and let me tell you. Categorically, there has been no simulation within Chronos or the training room that's defied déjà vu. It's as inescapable as gravity.

"You being able to survive a time jump without a watch of your own can be explained away by Drazen's tech," Alex continues, "but no amount of tech could save you from déjà vu. Whatever it is, however it works, the phenomenon is written in the very fabrics of spacetime. So, unless you have a magical device that allows you to escape the laws of Chronos, you should be dead."

Reuben lets out a breath, clinging to Alex's words and attempting to reconcile them to his experience. He glares down at Drazen's shattered watch, then back up at Alex. "I guess I should be, yeah."

"You're either astronomically lucky, or you may have just broken the spacetime continuum, and we're all doomed." Alex pulls back a playful grin. "But either way, man, it sure is good to see you alive on this side of things."

"I second that," Sky chimes in.

"Shoot." Alex looks down at his watch. "I told Jefferson I'd go over the new comm relays with him. After that, I've got to find a way to take my wife to our anniversary dinner without our minivan."

"Uber?" Reuben says.

"Dude, we've got three kids and rarely ever any privacy. That van is more than transportation, you feel me?" Alex winks before blushing.

"Oh!"

"Yeah...anyway, I really should go."

"Go ahead," Sky says, eyebrows raised with a grin. "I can escort Reuben."

"Thanks," Alex says, rushing off with a wave.

Alone with Reuben, Sky holds her smile and runs a strand of her hair behind her ear. "Cheating death, huh?"

"Yeah, it's crazy." Reuben clears his throat. "I don't know how it happened, only that it did. I saw it. I was dead. And there was something about it. Something...eerie. Something I couldn't escape, like I was being marked for it, like I was meant to. I don't know. It was like..." He struggles to come up with a metaphor. "I guess...I was drowning out at sea somewhere, with the waves pounding the life out of me. But, for some reason, a rope was thrown to me. I grabbed on, and it pulled me from it. You know, death. It wasn't a choice either, but all I could do. And when everything was happening, I kept hearing it. I kept hearing my dad's voice. I'm not sure if I'll ever understand what happened or if it'll always be this mysterious thing. But what I know for sure, what I'll never forget is that I was dead, as dead as it gets. And now...now I have this. Life."

Sky extends her palms and brushes Reuben's face. "Very poetic," she says, smiling, half-sarcastically.

Reuben chuckles to himself. "Yeah, yeah, I know. It sounds cheesy as hell. But, honestly, I don't know how else to describe it. That's what happened.

"It's the strangest thing," Reuben continues. "Throughout all of it, I made my choices and Drazen his. I planned, he planned. I moved, he moved. But despite everything, it didn't end the way either of us thought. We used each other to try and get what we wanted. And us plotting and moving against one another accomplished something else entirely. I keep thinking about what Aperio said to me at the diner. 'Life's a story.' Stories are written and not by the characters. But they still move and interact and decide things that can go in a million different directions. In the end, though, things only move toward a single end on one trajectory, and we only ever see it in hindsight." Reuben sighs. "A Nolanism my father would always say is, 'A paradox is always true but rarely right,' or something like that."

Sky grins, and Reuben chuckles.

"What? Was that too cheesy, too?"

"Maybe." Sky tilts her head. "But, honestly, however you

want to tell the story, I'm just glad that you lived to tell it." She pulls away. "I was...was, ah—"

"Worried?" Reuben interjects.

Sky shakes her head. "No...I mean, I was hoping you'd make it back to us, to the facility. But that's the thing. I knew you would."

"Now *that* sounds cheesy." Reuben pulls back a wide grin, and Sky slaps his arm. "Seriously, though, how'd you know I'd make it back? Because I sure as hell didn't think that I would."

"Remember those weird feelings I was telling you about? That I kept having at each place we went to and even that house?"

Reuben nods.

"Well," she continues, "it was different each time. Every place would have its own unique vibe to it. And it was almost always uncomfortable. After the van crashed, I was unconscious for a while. Didn't wake up until we were already back here at HQ." Sky breaks eye contact and rubs her neck. "When I was out, I had a dream. It was so real, but I can barely remember it." Her eyes look up as if trying to summon a memory. "I tried so hard to get it back, but it was gone. The only thing left was the impression it left on me. I woke up, and I just knew that you were coming back, that I had to get to you. There was no doubt. When I was running to get to the lab, Chronos roared to life, the power went out, things started falling all around, then it all stopped, and you were back."

They sit in silence, struggling to make sense of it. Looking into each other's eyes, they acknowledge the only fact they can decern from the entire experience. That the dreams, both hers and his own, are somehow connected to Chronos and perhaps one another. How it all works and the greater question of 'why' lingers, but the fact of the occurrence remains. They don't say any of this aloud; they don't need to.

"I guess it's like that other thing your dad said," Sky finally says.

"What?"

"You know, about not always understanding things."

Reuben smiles. "Ah, yes. Sometimes, we're not meant to...at least not yet."

His heart eases as he looks into her eyes again, seeing that she understands him, and he her. Then something changes in his heartbeat—it picks up tempo as he thinks about what he really wants to say to her. He doesn't know the time nor place to say it, if ever. "Time's too fleeting to not take advantage of." His external words finally settle the internal debate.

"What are you talking about?" She smiles even as her cheeks redden.

"I'm talking about us."

"Us?"

Reuben can see the gleeful unease on her face. "You and I have been doing this dance. And as oblivious as I can sometimes be, I'm not imagining this, you and me."

"No, you're not imagining it." She breaks eye contact and fidgets with her hair. Reuben cusps her hands, holding them in his bandaged palms as she looks back at him.

"I just want to let you know. We can take this as slow as we need to go, especially with everything that's happened. I should've told you about Aperio and the plan to stop Drazen. I should've been honest with you then, and I wasn't. But let me be honest with you now. This is, without a doubt, the direction I'd like for us to go."

The glee in Sky's face subsides, eyes falling as she pulls her hands back.

"And if it's weird, because of our professional—"

"It's not," she interjects. "You don't have to ask me to know how I feel about you, about us. But it isn't about how I feel..." Sky clears her throat, and a solemn weight fills her voice. "I understand why you acted the way you did. I'm sure a part of you was just shielding me from a dangerous, reckless plan. I get it. And, honestly, it's what a good team leader would do. Protect his people at all costs.

"And it does have a cost," she continues. "I hate that it does, but that's how it is. Reuben, I forgive you a thousand times over as a friend, and I don't even hold it against you as a team lead. But this? What you're asking."

"Yeah," Reuben says, listening, heart sinking low.

"You know what happened to Ray. Not just the accident, but about what he did, what he was hiding. I saw it in his eyes and only recognized it later. It was shame and regret...I see it in your eyes now. You hate that you lied to me, but you still did it. And it's true that remorse goes a long way on the road to healing and learning. Believe me, I've faced down worse demons. But remorse doesn't make things right, doesn't justify things. And for us to go down that path, we'll need more than just remorse. We'll need trust."

"I understand," Reuben says.

"I'm not saying 'no' forever. I don't even know if I'm saying it now. But I just want you to know what it is that I'm looking for. Does that make sense?"

Reuben nods and allows the words to sink in more before responding.

"I hear you. And I know I can't change what I did. It killed me inside—not telling you—it still does." Reuben sighs before continuing, "You know, I understand Drazen in a way. The things he saw, wanting to change what was done wrong...but he was wrong even about that. If there's one thing I've learned from all of this, from Chronos, it's that it isn't about being able to change the past. It's about how we use that past to make a better future. I see what I've done, who I've been. The good, the bad, and the asshole." Reuben grabs Sky's hands again and brings them close. "I know who I want to be...to myself, to this team, and to you."

Her greenish-blue eyes light up as he says the words, though her demeanor remains solemn. Then she smiles. "I guess time will tell."

Reuben smirks. "Time travel puns? Haven't we moved beyond that?"

Sky touches his face, her fingers playfully ruffling his beard. "I don't know, Reuben. I mean, it would be weird...and inappropriate if we didn't report it."

"Oh, yeah, of course." Reuben nods. "So, what do you say? HR disclosure and the whole nine yards?"

She inches closer to him. "What do you think?"

He lifts her chin with his fingers, drawing her in. They lean in toward one another, easing their eyes shut. Reuben kisses her gently, and she reciprocates.

* * *

FINALLY BACK IN HIS ROOM, Reuben limps to his bed and collapses onto his covers. Exhaustion and soreness wrap him like a blanket, enticing him to fade into sleep. As he rolls onto his back and closes his eyes, he can see it—his father's face smiling down on him.

Reuben jumps up to greet him, but the face is gone when he opens his eyes. In its place is his jacket across the room, draped over his dresser. His muscles ache in revenge as he defies them to stand up, reach for the jacket and pull his father's journal from the inside pocket.

The leather grooves feel as they did the first time he held the journal months ago. Tears pool, and his lip quivers as he rereads the personal note inside, reminding him of his father's desire for Reuben to surpass his *most desired of dreams*. He tilts the journal, and a small envelope slips through the loosened pages. He thumbs over the handwriting as his eyes widen, seeing it, his name across the envelope, '*Reuben Greyson.*'

His heart skips a beat as he breaks the seal, pulls out the card, and begins to read:

SON,

BY NOW, your 28th birthday, you should know of my fate. If events play out as I have fought for them to be, my killer will be stopped. I sought to have you brought onboard so that you may learn the evil plots of men and serve to protect others from an inner nature that haunts us all. We determined the best way to fight these evils was to guard against them. Locking away the paths that led to destruction was the most pragmatic solution we could come to, but it's not final. As long as the paths exist, there will always be gravitation toward them. It may be difficult to come to terms with our decision. History, after all, is not short of atrocities. But those who caused devastation cannot be the ones to repair it. The past can't change, but the future is determined by how we choose to remember history.

This is my tenth and final letter to you. I leave you this journal, raw and unedited, so that you may see my thoughts, know my intentions, and feel my heart. I'm with you in these words. It pains me, writing this, knowing that I must leave you. I'm not going away to wedge the distance between us but rather to bridge it together. It may be hard to accept that my love for you has caused me to depart. But, in time, you'll come to understand. For now, just know that I never stopped loving you. Know that I will plunge into the deepest depths, face the greatest evils, and endure the most painful agony to bring you where you are today, reading this letter.

I may not be physically with you right now, but you haven't been left alone. You have friends. They will become your family. You have a purpose and, soon, there will be tasks to complete. Pursue truth, fight for the cause of good, and share love.

HAPPY BIRTHDAY. I love you always.

YOUR FATHER,
Nolan

* * *

"SENATOR FOWLER'S OFFICE CALLED AGAIN," Jefferson says as he enters Paul's office.

"And?" Paul says.

"I gave the usual spiel. He's going to keep calling, you know?"

"I know. I'm working on that." Paul nudges toward the door. "Close that." Jefferson complies and takes a seat. "Did the results come back from the lab?"

"Oh, yeah, that." Jefferson flips through his tablet before swiveling it toward Paul. "I was able to go through the forensic evidence collected ten years ago when Nea disappeared from the lab. They had found one of her hairs on the floor and bagged it. We were able to compare against a recent sample."

"And?"

"You were right. Relatively the same age, meaning... I mean, I can't believe it, but—"

"She's not from here, not our time."

"She jumped ten years into the future," Jefferson says. "That shouldn't be possible. Chronos doesn't allow forward travel like that."

"No."

"Anyway, we've installed trackers so we can monitor all her communications and every—"

"Disable them," Paul says.

"But, sir, if she's—"

"I said disable them. Not that it isn't important, but we have greater concerns right now. Besides, that girl has been through enough. What's the latest on the body?"

"Comatose, likely permanent. There's very little brain activity, which isn't surprising given the bullet in his head, but he's still alive. It's a damn miracle." Jefferson shakes his head and shivers. "Sir, I, ah....I get it. Why we're doing it, but it doesn't seem right. I mean, don't you think Reuben should know?"

Paul feels it again, the temptation, the hesitation, the guilt. "No," he says with a deep sigh. "Not today."

"When, then?"

Paul can feel the conviction and concern in Jefferson's voice. "Jefferson," Paul says before clearing his throat.

"Sir."

"When this is all over, when everything is right with this project, or maybe when we find ourselves on our deathbed, we'll ask if any of this was right or wrong. We'll ask if it was worth the cost, if we did some good in this world, and if people will remember that good. Or we'll ask if we were the instigator, the monster, the very thing we sold our souls to get rid of. I know what I'm asking of you. It's not fair. None of this is. But we've already done it. I've already done it and far worse. As I see it, there are only two real options. We can either rot away in second-guessing and self-pity, or we can make this mean a damn. For Reuben. For the Stewards. For the project."

Jefferson nods but says nothing else.

* * *

REUBEN STROLLS through the AIC halls and, for the first time since he's first walked them, he feels at home.

A black flat-brimmed Stetson hat strikes the side of his head. It ricochets and glides to the ground. "You were supposed to catch that," Alex's voice calls to him.

Reuben crouches to pick up the hat from the training room floor before turning to acknowledge the thrower. "Most people yell 'heads up' when something might hit someone. Especially if they're the one doing the throwing."

Alex nods. "Touché. Regardless, the hat is yours. You should try it on and get used to the feel a little before we go out."

"You know hats really aren't my thing, right?"

"It's been a few months since you've been around, so let me remind you. It's mandatory. This won't be like Roanoke, where we can sweet talk our way through. The Wild West is called 'wild' for a reason. You have to play the part. You know, man, toughen up a bit."

"That's why you have me," Caleb interjects as he approaches, handing each of them a revolver. "You both know how to fire it, but remember its favorite position is in the holster. If you pull it out, everyone around is going to think that you mean business, and they will act accordingly."

"You're lecturing us about being trigger happy?" Alex says.

"Hey, I may be a jarhead, but we don't stay alive by being dumb. Sometimes, you 'gotta know when to hold em...' or some shit like that."

"Oh, yeah, Kenny Rogers."

"Sure. Just don't fire from the hip like in some cowboy movie. You won't hit anything, and you'll just look stupid. Now, if you'll excuse me, I have to go and sign for our ammo." Caleb departs, leaving Reuben and Alex at the base of the room.

Reuben tosses his hat upward. Its brim spirals and hovers through the air, up and up until it smacks into the Observer's box and drops to the ground.

"Huh," Reuben says. "I completely forgot that was there."

"Yeah, it's weird how that happens," Alex says. "Whenever someone new walks in here, it's the first thing they're fixated on. Doesn't take long for it to be invisible, though, does it?"

Reuben picks up his hat once more, this time setting it on his head.

"That's not a bad look. Which reminds me, I should hand out the rest of these." Alex walks over to a box nearby.

Reuben tips his hat down and proceeds with the preparations, verifying each team member has their equipment and uniform. Later, he stops by Sky's prep station as she updates the watches with geographical markers.

"How are things coming along?" he asks her.

"Good," she says, looking up at him. "We have sweeps from thirty years prior and ten years after. Granted, there was a ton of expansion at the time, but it should be enough to piece a good map. It'll make calibration easy, which will make my job easier."

"How are you?" Reuben extends his hand to meet hers. She clasps it.

"I'm okay." Sky looks away but continues to hold his hand close to her. "This is our first mission back." She veers her head back toward him. "Last time—"

"I know. The truth is, what we do isn't safe for any of us. But thanks to you, my father, Aperio, and everyone else, I know that what we're doing has meaning. We have a solid team, and we're more prepared this time. It's no guarantee that things will go well, but at least we know we're moving toward something good. Besides, we have each other."

He kisses her forehead, and they embrace. The time passes quickly, but the moment lingers. It's not the touch that warms him. It's the hearts behind the touch and the hope that lies before them. It's life, death, and everything in between. It's a story, their story, and now it's time to live it.

Several minutes later, Reuben gathers the team to deliver their briefs before leading them to the Chronos lab floor. A fresh coat of beige paint hugs the walls as they enter the lab, blotting out the stale white of old and filling the space with warmth. Updated monitors and hardware rests along the rows of the workstations, amplifying the newfangled lab as it paves the path to the platform. One of the project's returning lab techs, Nea, sits at the desk nearest the platform. She shares a smile with Reuben and the team as they pass.

"I love a good western," a voice calls, approaching them from behind. Reuben turns to see Aperio walking toward them with a cigar in hand.

"I'm pretty sure Paul would have you escorted from the building if you lit that in here," Reuben says.

"Well, you know what they say about a story without conflict. It's useless. Paul may still be director but, as the deputy, it's my duty to counterbalance."

"Where is Paul? I thought he'd be here for the launch."

"As the deputy director, I also have a duty to step in now and again in his stead. I do wish you all well on this mission."

"Thanks," Reuben says as the rest of the team begins to board the platform. "You know, since coming back, I've only had more questions. The Stewards, the dreaming, Chronos. I learned so much but still feel like I don't know anything."

"*C'est la vie.*" Aperio chuckles to himself. "Besides, this is not the end of the story. There will be plenty of time to revisit all that." He pauses and winks. "We're just beginning, you know."

Reuben nods. "Yeah, I guess." He glances around the room before looking back at Aperio. "So, aren't you going to ask me if we're ready to go?"

"Why would you be here if you weren't?" Aperio whips out a match, strikes it, and lights his cigar. "C'mon, let's get on with the bloody jump."

Reuben joins his team on the platform. Aperio picks up a

nearby tablet and reads the destination date aloud before continuing, "Objective. To gather any information leading to the identity resolution of the bandit who calls himself 'The Highwayman.'

The columns spin as Chronos roars to life. Reuben looks past the spinning lights toward the rear of the lab. He thinks back to his first walkthrough during reception, with Sky by his side nearly a year ago. The walls in the lab were bare and stale, but her voice was warm as she told him about the Chronos his father, Nolan Greyson, fought for.

You'll see, she had said then.

And now he sees it.

He reads the freshly painted words on the wall and recites them in his mind, knowing that the day is today, and he finally sees it.

From beginning to end, I watch it all
Through the perils of venture since the Fall
Yesterday I explored the night
For tomorrow's protection, I bring my fight.

ACKNOWLEDGMENTS

I may not watch a lot of sports (okay, none really), but I've always admired how so many winning athletes begin their thanksgiving. Not to the moon and stars to which they point, but to the Creator who has set their place. Without God, this story would not exist, and neither would the one He's telling, in which we all have our roles. I may not always desire Him or like it when He points out my follies, but even I, the king of a great and sinful domain, cannot deny His power and place. My words will wrinkle and fade, but His are forever. "Remember me," said the thief on the cross. "Remember me, still," says I.

This story first found life inside my head and just a few scribblings struggling to be an outline. Without my wife, Erica, that's where it would still be. Thank you, my love. Not just for giving me the much-needed nudge. But, well, for everything. This hasn't been just a season or a sprint in time. It's been a marathon, and you've been running beside me for its entirety. In its infancy, you read this book despite all its flaws, purple prose, and missing commas. I know that you never imagined it would take this long to write, rewrite, rewrite, rewrite (x4), and edit. And yet, you never stopped encouraging me. And I'll never stop loving you.

Acquaintances tell us the things we want to hear. Friends, true friends, tell us what we need to hear. Allen, you are a true friend. I've been harping to you about this for over a decade, and here it is, my man. You encouraged me when this thing was nothing more than a messy outline on a dated Windows XP PC.

You were honest, even when the truth was less than flattering. And all in all, it has served the story well. Thank you.

In his memoir *On Writing*, Stephen King equates writing a novel to excavating a fossil from the ground. It was always there; it just takes a writer to uncover it. I'm not sure exactly how I got these bones out of the earth, but they'd still be a jumbled mess without my editor, Tyler Sherman. Thank you for helping to restore, polish, and reassemble these literary bones. Because of you, they've been given a newfound life, beautifully displayed to tell their story.

If someone tells a story, and no one is around to hear it, does it exist? I don't know the answer to that, but I can answer in confidence that this story would not exist without my wonderful beta readers. And if it did, it wouldn't be very good. You all rock, and because of your honesty, encouragement, and feedback, *A Dream of Stewards* exists the way it does.

Beta readers: Allen, Amanda, Cait, Elizabeth, Erica, Ian, Jen, Jessica, Lauren, Rachel, and Tyler.

A huge thank you to my cover designer, Jeff Brown. Your art is beautiful, and you knocked this one out of the park.

Thank you to Tim Marquitz at Dominion Editorial for your wonderfully thorough proofreading services.

To the countless friends and family members who have provided words of encouragement throughout the years. Thank you. I've been promising you this novel for a while and am happy it's finally in your hands.

ABOUT THE AUTHOR

Yohann Martin is the author of the *Keys of Time* series and its debut entry, *A Dream of Stewards*. He lives in Virginia with his wife and two children. When not writing and consuming stories, he enjoys bike rides with the family, weightlifting, and the occasional lightsaber battle with his two-year-old son.

Join his mailing list for the latest updates at https://www.yohannmartin.com/email-signup

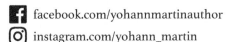

facebook.com/yohannmartinauthor

instagram.com/yohann_martin

Made in the USA
Coppell, TX
15 February 2022

73607184R00260